To John White
and
Stuart Blue Harary

Contents

Acknowledgments

"Consciousness Localized in Space Outside the Body" originally appeared in the April 1974 issue of the *Osteopathic Physician.* Reprinted by permission of the *Osteopathic Physician.*

"Experiential Aspects of Out-of-Body Experiences" is an expanded and revised version of "Aspects of Out-of-Body Experiences," which appeared in the *Journal of the Society for Psychical Research,* Vol. 48, No. 768, 1976. Reprinted by permission of the Society for Psychical Research.

"Some Varieties of Out-of-Body Experience" originally appeared in the *Journal of the American Society for Psychical Research,* Vol. 70, No. 2, 1976. Reprinted by permission of the author and the American Society for Psychical Research.

"A Psychophysiological Study of Out-of-the-Body Experiences in a Selected Subject" originally appeared in the *Journal of the American Society for Psychical Research,* Vol. 62, No. 1, 1968. Reprinted by permission of the author and the American Society for Psychical Research.

"A Second Psychophysiological Study of Out-of-the-Body Experiences in a Gifted Subject" originally appeared in the *International Journal of Parapsychology,* Vol. 9, No. 3, 1967. Reprinted by permission of the author and the Parapsychology Foundation, Inc.

"Out-of-the-Body Vision" originally appeared in the April 1973 issue of *Psychic* magazine. Reprinted by permission of *Psychic* magazine, 680 Beach Street, San Francisco, California 94109.

"Out-of-Body Research at the American Society for Psychical Research" originally appeared in the *Newsletter* of the American Society for Psychical Research, No. 22, Summer 1974. Reprinted by permission of the author and the American Society for Psychical Research.

"Experiments with Blue Harary" is adapted from a chapter of the same title which originally appeared as Chapter 2 of *In Search of the Unknown* (Taplinger Publishing Company, 1976). Copyright © D. Scott Rogo, 1976. Reprinted by permission of Taplinger Publishing Co.

Preface

In many respects, editing an anthology is more challenging than writing an original book. Three years ago I decided that a really analytical book on the out-of-body experience (OBE) needed to be written, so I began outlining the cases and research that I felt should be covered in such a volume. However, it soon became clear to me that it would be much better to reprint this material in full than to summarize it. This plan had its pitfalls, though. In order to keep an anthology to a reasonable length, an editor cannot include everything in his book that he might wish. An author can decide exactly how much to write about his subjects, but an editor doesn't have even that prerogative! So I have collected only those papers that I feel offer the best experimental approaches to the OBE or that constitute insightful or provocative analyses of the OBE or theories about it.

In order to help make this research meaningful to the reader, I have added introductory essays to each part of the volume, which explain the rationale behind this work, summarize related research that could not be reprinted, and analyze just what these data indicate about the OBE. I hope these essays will serve as an integral part of the book. Unlike most anthologists, I have not written a time- and space-consuming opening statement, since the OB phenomenon is far too complex to be evaluated or even introduced in a few pages. Instead I have written a concluding essay in order to sum up what I feel this research is telling us about the OBE. This concluding chapter complements the four introductory essays. Thus, in many respects this volume is not only a Reader on the OBE, but also a personal statement of my views and evaluations of the phenomenon. However, I have tried to include papers that represent many opposing ways of approaching the OBE and that reflect many different schools of thought about it. I have not in any way tried to chose only research or theoretical papers that share my own opinions about the experience. In fact, I have tried to do exactly the opposite.

There are four ways by which one can approach the study of the OBE. Until relatively recently, parapsychologists merely collected firsthand accounts of the experience and analyzed them. Then, beginning in the 1960s, parapsychologists began experimenting in their laboratories with people who could induce the OBE at will. The experimental approach to the OBE became a minor "fad" in the early 1970s and a symposium entitled "Research on Out-of-the-Body Experiences: Where Do We Go from Here?" was programmed as part of the Sixteenth Annual Convention of the Parapsychological Association, which was held on the campus of the University of Virginia from September 6 to 8, 1973. Another approach to the OBE is to study what the people who have had many of these experiences say and report about them. A person who has had several OBEs may be in a better position to evaluate the experience than someone who has had only one or two. Finally, many people might be more interested in the theoretical puzzle the OBE poses. Is it a hallucination, a dream, a mind-body separation—or what?

I don't believe that any one approach to the OBE is necessarily better than any other. To me there is only *good* research or *bad* research, no matter what approach one takes to the OBE. So this volume is comprised of four sections, each devoted to a different aspect of the OBE. By far the longest section, though, is devoted to experimental research into the OBE question. Parapsychology is, after all, an experimental science today, so I have given some priority to these reports. Furthermore, many of the experiments conducted to study the OBE have not been designed merely to prove the reality of the OBE, but to discover just what is happening to the subject during the experience. This research, and the implications that can be drawn from it, must be considered the most pertinent data parapsychology has to offer about the experience to date. While other approaches might prove just as fruitful, this experimental data will probably be especially appealing to the psychology- or science-oriented reader.

Repetition is another problem the anthologist faces. When drawing together several papers dealing with the same topic, one is bound to find some material repeated by different authors. On rare occasions I have edited these papers in order to delete needless reiteration. (These deletions were made with the permissions of the authors.) I have also, in some cases, formalized the references for the sake of general uniformity. Finally, some authors use the abbreviation OOBE for the out-of-body experience, while others use the initials OBE. For the sake of conformity, I have used only the latter abbreviation in these papers.

D. Scott Rogo

I. ON BEING
OUT-OF-BODY

Introduction: Analyzing
the Phenomenon

D. SCOTT ROGO

During the summer of 1965 I was a student attending classes every day. It was extremely hot that August and, after classes ended at 1:00 in the afternoon, I could hardly wait to get home, flop on my bed, and take a nap. This was a ritual to which I adhered almost every day. One day, however, turned out to be different. I came home as usual, kicked off my shoes, turned on the radio, and lay down on my back patiently waiting for sleep to overcome me. Then it happened. I began to feel oddly chilly and started to tremble. I flipped over onto my side, realizing at the same moment that my whole body was pulsating and that I was almost paralyzed. I concentrated on these sensations and soon afterward blacked out for a moment. An instant later I found myself floating in the air and, in another instant, I was standing at the foot of the bed staring at myself. I made an abrupt about-face (I didn't walk around, I merely willed myself to turn) and tried to walk toward the door to my room, which led to a hallway. I felt as though I were gliding through jelly as I moved, and I lost balance for a moment and almost fell over. Everything was blurred by a cloudy hue that enveloped a whitish form, which I perceived as my body. A moment later I found myself awakening on my bed. But I also realized that I had never really been asleep!

I was not in the least frightened by my experience. I had been studying parapsychology for a few years and knew that I had undergone an out-of-body experience. The OBE (as we call it for short) is an experience during which the percipient feels as if his "mind" or "consciousness" has left his physical body and is functioning independent of it.

The OBE seems to be a rather common phenomenon and several books have been written over the years presenting firsthand accounts from people who have experienced it. Some people report that their OBEs occurred as they began to doze off. Others have apparently had them when ill or near death. And a few gifted individuals are able to induce this peculiar experience at will.

Is this experience a dream, a delusion, or what? While it is hard to rule out the possibility that some OBEs may be dreams, we know that the experience is not a delusion. Many times the person having the OBE is able to "see" events he could not possibly have known about unless some element of his mind were somehow momentarily functioning apart from his body. For example, a British Army colonel related the following experience to the Society for Psychical Research, a London-based organization that collects and investigates cases of psychic phenomena. This account was published in their *Journal* in 1948 (pp. 206–11). The colonel was suffering from pneumonia and pleurisy. Even his doctor had told him that his prospects for recovery were practically nil, but the colonel fought with all his might to live. Suddenly:

I felt quite certain that I left my body. I felt it getting heavier and heavier and sinking into the bed. I was sitting on top of a high wardrobe near the door looking down on my bed at myself, and the nurse sitting by me. I was disgusted at my unshaven appearance. I saw everything in the room—the mirror on the dressing-table and all small details. Fear was absent entirely. The next thing I remember was my nurse holding my hand and shortly afterwards heard her say, "The crisis has passed."

Some time after all this, I told the nurse what had happened to me, described what she was doing at the time and the details of the room. She said I was given up and that it was because I was delirious.

"No, I was dead for that time, but made myself come back."

People who have undergone the OBE have had varying reactions to the experience. Most people find the encounter peaceful, or even blissful. Just as the colonel in the preceding example responded to the sight of his physical body, many individuals look upon their own material bodies with disgust or lack of concern. Yet, other experiencers find the OBE frightening, although this reaction is apparently rare. During the summer of 1973 I was working at the Psychical Research Foundation (PRF) in Durham, North Carolina, helping to test a young man who could induce the OBE at will. I was also engaged in studying cases of spontaneous OBEs that were being reported to and collected by the Foundation. Only one person who contacted us reported a panic reaction to the OBE, and this case especially caught my attention. Part of her lengthy narrative reads:

. . . In 1966 and prior to the arrival of our first child (March 1967) I began to have very vivid experiences and could only describe them to my husband as "my nightmare thing," except that it was not a dream. I would be lying in bed, just before going to sleep and a strange feeling would come over me, my eyes would go to tunnel vision and I would feel like some huge suction was pulling in me. Then suddenly I would be plastered against the ceiling and could see my body lying in bed. I wanted back in that body more than anything else, but something pulled on me and would take me into the hallway. I would struggle with every ounce of energy I could muster against this. Then when fear would reach its peak, I would be "lowered" back into my body.

But can *we* be as sure as this correspondent obviously was that the OBE was not a dream? I think so. For several reasons we can at least be sure that the OBE is no ordinary dream: (1) People who have had the experience remain subjectively convinced that the encounter was not a dream and that the experience was qualitatively different from any dream they have ever had before or since. (2) Many people report entering the OB state from *waking* consciousness. (3) They often correctly perceive events taking place miles away or in neighboring areas after journeying there while out-of-the-body. For example, an OB percipient might wander into an adjacent room and see a relative engaged in some unusual activity, such as cleaning the ceiling. Later, having regained normal consciousness, he then might go into the next room and verify everything he had seen moments earlier. (4) A person undergoing an OBE is sometimes seen as an apparition by other people. In other words, the OB subject might "project" to a friend and later that person will report that he saw an apparition of the percipient at that very time. As I will explain in my report on Stuart Blue Harary (see chapter 8), with whom I worked in Durham, one night a weird red light cascaded through my bedroom. Later I learned that Blue had tried to OB to me at roughly the same time. Many of the P.R.F. team who were working with Harary reported similar encounters during the course of the investigations.

So, if the OBE is not a dream and not a delusion, what is it? This is the crucial issue that has prompted me to compile the reports comprising this anthology. It is hoped that clues about the nature of the OBE will become apparent as we study, analyze, and speculate about these reports and experiments.

Conventional psychology certainly does not offer us any answers about the nature of the OBE. It has preferred either to ignore the subject altogether, or to classify it as an aberrant psychological phenomenon. Dr. Graham Reed of York University, Canada, has labeled the experience "ego splitting." He suggests in his book *The Psychology of Anomalous Experience* (1974) that these experiences "are common defensive reactions to the loss of a loved one." That is about the only explanation he gives for the OBE! Yet we know from case collections of OB accounts that Dr. Reed's remark is fallacious. OBEs occur under a great variety of dissimilar conditions. Other psychologists have come up with equally fanciful theories about the OBE. Otto Rank believed that the experience occurred when the percipient wished to escape from feelings of guilt. Freud, on the other hand, thought it occurred when the individual was overcome by infantile complexes. However, none of these psychology-oriented theories is capable of explaining the vast range of OBE phenomena.

Parapsychologists have made by far the most fruitful investigations into the nature of the OBE. Parapsychology (meaning "beyond psychology") is the study of ESP, psychokinesis, and other psychic events, and the OBE seems inherently related to these phenomena. As I mentioned earlier, many OB accounts indicate that the percipient used ESP during the experience. For example, Celia Green, an English parapsychologist, collected several OBE-ESP cases when she began amassing OBE accounts in the 1960s (Green, 1968). As one percipient wrote to her:

I was in hospital having had an operation for peritonitis; I developed pneumonia and was very ill. The ward was L-shaped; so that anyone in bed at one part of the ward could not see round the corner.

One morning I felt myself floating upwards and found I was looking down on the rest of the patients. I could see myself: propped up against pillows, very white and ill. I saw the sister and nurse rush to my bed with oxygen. Then everything went blank. The next I remember was opening my eyes to see the sister bending over me. I told her what had happened; but at first she thought I was rambling. Then I said, "There is a big woman sitting up in bed with her head wrapped in bandages; and she is knitting something with blue wool. She has a very red face." This certainly shook her; as apparently the lady concerned had a mastoid operation and was just as I described.

She was not allowed out of bed; and of course I hadn't been up at all. After several other details, such as the time by the clock on the wall (which had broken down) I convinced her that at least something strange had happened to me.

Rarely, but just as importantly, a few OB experiencers seem to possess the ability to manipulate household objects or otherwise affect the physical world. One correspondent wrote to Green that one day as she began to fall asleep she found herself leaving her body and floating about in an apparitional form. She proceeded to float downstairs where she was overcome by the desire to prove objectively the reality of the experience to herself. So,

seeing a vase of *anemones* on a side-board, which was higher than the table, and therefore easier to reach, I was able to stretch my foot as I "flew" past and grasp a *blue anemone* between my toes, but as I moved away it fell onto the floor, and I could not reach it. I memorized the colour of the flower, and also noticed a green light coming from a mirror on the wall, for which I could not account. . . ."

Seconds later the percipient "snapped-back," as she described it, to her body and awoke. She rushed downstairs and immediately saw the same odd green light that she had seen while out-of-the-body. On walking into an adjoining room, she saw a blue anemone on the floor, which had somehow been lifted from a vase full of them that was resting on a sideboard in the kitchen. No one else in the house remembered seeing or dropping the flower.

These two accounts illustrate the fact that the OBE is a psychic as well as a psychological phenomenon. Nonetheless, there are two different ways to interpret these experiences. One group of parapsychologists (including myself) believes that the OBE actually represents a physical separation of the mind from the body. Another group of parapsychologists believes that the OBE is really a vivid dream or hallucination, but that the percipient uses ESP and psychokinesis (PK) to reinforce it. For example, Green's percipient only dreamed that she was floating out-of-the-body, but used ESP to perceive the green light and then used PK to move the flower. She was not, though, really out of her body. This is the grand debate that researchers investigating the OBE are trying to resolve. The fruits of this research will be presented in Part II, so I will not discuss the issue here. Each reader must make up his or her own mind how good the evidence in support of either theory really is.

Parapsychology today is an experimental science. We analyze data, figure out testable theories about ESP and psychokinesis, and then run experiments to see whether the results will support our views. Parapsychologists are now approaching the OBE in the very same way, and several parapsychology laboratories are or have been experimentally exploring the OBE. This research has been approached from two different angles. Most parapsychologists have tried to work with individuals who feel that they can voluntarily produce OBEs. On the other hand, at least one researcher has tried to induce OBEs in unselected subjects. But parapsychology is also a descriptive science in that it studies, investigates, and evaluates spontaneous cases of ESP as it occurs in everyday life. Analyzing large bodies of ESP reports was at one time the main work of parapsychologists. This aspect of psychical research has, though, been overshadowed by the trend toward experimentalism that has overtaken the field in the last thirty years or so. Nonetheless, a few researchers have tried to study the OBE by collecting and analyzing firsthand accounts of spontaneous experiences. So before proceeding to the essays which comprise Part I of this volume, I would like to comment on what these researchers have learned about the OBE.

Dr. Hornell Hart, a Duke University sociologist, attempted to make a scientific and meaningful analysis of OBE reports in the early 1950s. In fact, he was one of the first parapsychologists to realize the importance of examining the OBE. His work was followed by that of Dr. Robert Crookall, a British geologist, who first appeared in print on the subject in 1961. Crookall has spent close to two decades analyzing OB accounts. Both of these analysts, using rather different approaches to the study of spontaneous OB narratives, have uncovered a wealth of knowledge about both the evidential and the experimental aspects of the phenomenon.

Hornell Hart was intrigued by the fact that many people who have OBEs also demonstrate ESP during the experience. As I mentioned earlier, this is one of the most provocative aspects of the OBE. The first account I drew from Celia Green's case collection is a typical example of a "veridical" (or verifiable) OBE. This phenomenon was called "traveling clairvoyance" in older parapsychological literature, but Hart suggested that a more embracing term should be coined to account for these veridical experiences. He proposed "ESP projection." This new classification encompassed all OBEs in which the percipient had either *(a)* correctly reported what had occurred at some distant location after visiting there while out-of-the-body, or *(b)* had been seen as an apparition by an independent onlooker.

Eventually Hart drew together a large body of well-attested cases of ESP projection and presented an analysis of ninety-nine of them in his pioneering paper, "ESP Projection:

Spontaneous Cases and the Experimental Method," which was published in the *Journal of the American Society for Psychical Research* in 1954 (Hart, 1954). He broke down his cases into five groupings:*

1. *ESP Projections Induced by Hypnotic Suggestion.* Hart uncovered twenty well-verified cases on record. In most of these instances, the experimenter merely suggested to a hypnotized subject that he should travel to some distant location and report back what he saw there. Some of these cases are extremely impressive. The following is a typical case originally published in the *Proceedings of the Society for Psychical Research* in 1891–1892 (vol. 8, pp. 49–53):

On April 22, 1850, John Park was mesmerized by William Reid, who instructed his subject to visit two whaling vessels, the *Hamilton Ross* and the *Eclipse,* which had been at sea for several weeks. Park reported back that he had somehow traveled to the *Hamilton Ross* and described how the captain and surgeon aboard the vessel were dressing the second mate's hand. Apparently part of his fingers had been sheared off. Reid hypnotized Park again the next night, and during this session Park again traveled to the *Hamilton Ross* and reported that the ship would return to port before the *Eclipse* with some one hundred tons of oil. After the ships returned home, Reid verified the accuracy of most of his subject's statements. The mate actually had shot off part of his fingers while fishing. An outside witness, William Boyd, had heard Park's statements before the ship arrived, so he was able to verify Reid's report.

It is hard to label this experience as a true OBE. Simple ESP could explain this incident just as easily. But the report does suggest that the mind has the ability to perceive scenes taking place miles away.

2. *Apparitions of the Living Projected by Mere Concentration.* Over the years, several people have claimed that by merely concentrating on a distant location they have been able to make an apparition of themselves appear there. Hart

*The following headings are adapted from Hart's.

included fifteen of his reports under this heading. One of the best-attested cases was collected originally by Dr. Gardner Murphy, the eminent American psychologist, who received it from someone who had attended a lecture he had given on parapsychology:

On November 13, 1938, in New York City, Mr. Lawrence S. Apsey resolved that he would try to appear psychically to his mother without any previous warning to her or expectation on her part. After focusing his mind on her for five or ten minutes at 11:15 P.M. he resolved that he would manifest to her at 12:30 A.M. He reports that at that hour while his physical body was still lying in his bed: "I then saw my mother in a flesh-colored nightdress sitting on the edge of her bed. A peculiar fact which I particularly noticed was that the night-dress was either torn or cut so exceptionally low in the back that my mother's skin showed almost down to her waist." He then roused himself and wrote a memorandum of his impressions.

Next morning at breakfast he told all this to his wife, and showed her the notes he had made during the night. He went to work without having seen his mother. During that forenoon his mother told his wife (without having had the subject mentioned to her) that she had been awakened by an apparition at 12:30 the night before. That evening his mother came to his apartment and immediately told him about the apparition. She said that she had been wearing a flesh-colored nightgown which had been a gift and did not fit her very well, being cut low in the back, so that it hung down and revealed her skin even to the waist. She was awakened, she said, by some person bending over her and putting his face close to hers. She said it looked like a blond young man who did not resemble her son (whose hair is dark). She screamed and opened her eyes, after which the figure persisted for several moments and then faded away.

This case is more OB-like since the experiencer seemed to have the feeling of being out of his body. OBE or some sort of reciprocal telepathy?

3. *Self-Projection by More Complex Means.* Hart placed thirteen cases in this category. In most of them the experiencer found himself in an OB state and traveled to a distant locale but was not seen as an apparition by anyone he

visited. Nonetheless, he still was able to report accurately about what had occurred there during the time of his visit.

4. *Spontaneous Apparitions of the Living Corresponding to Corroborative Experiences of the Projectionists.* Some of these thirty reports represent Hart's most impressive cases. Among them are instances of people who *(a)* underwent an OBE; *(b)* were aware that they were appearing as apparitions; *(c)* were seen as apparitions by witnesses; *(d)* remembered that they had been so seen after returning to the body; and *(e)* correctly reported what had transpired at the scenes of their appearances.

Probably the most impressive case of this class of phenomena ever recorded is the famous "Wilmot case," which was reported in Volume 12 of the *Proceedings of the Society for Psychical Research.* Mrs. Wilmot was seen while out-of-the-body not only by one witness, but by two independent onlookers. As you will read, Mrs. Wilmot had typical sensations of leaving her body during her adventure. Mrs. Wilmot's husband reports as follows:

On October 3rd, 1863, I sailed from Liverpool for New York. . . . On the evening of the second day out . . . a severe storm began, which lasted for nine days. . . . Upon the night following the eighth day of the storm . . . I dreamed that I saw my wife, whom I had left in the United States, come to the door of my state-room, clad in her night-dress. At the door, she seemed to discover that I was not the only occupant of the room, hesitated a little, then advanced to my side, stooped down and kissed me, and after gently caressing me for a few moments, quietly withdrew. Upon waking I was surprised to see my fellow-passenger, whose berth was above mine, but not directly over it—owing to the fact that our room was at the stern of the vessel—leaning upon his elbow, and looking fixedly at me. "You're a pretty fellow," said he at length, "to have a lady come and visit you in this way." I pressed him for an explanation, which he, at first, declined to give, but at length related what he had seen while wide awake, lying in his berth. It exactly corresponded with my dream. . . . The day after landing . . . almost [my wife's] first question when we were alone together was "Did you receive a visit from me a week ago

Tuesday?" . . . On the . . . same night when . . . the storm had just begun to abate, she had lain awake for a long time thinking of me, and about four o'clock in the morning it seemed to her that she went out to seek me. Crossing the wide and stormy sea, she came at length to a low, black steamship, whose side she went up, and then descending into the cabin, passed through it to the stern until she came to my state-room. "Tell me," she said, "do they ever have state-rooms like the one I saw, where the upper berth extends further back than the under one? A man was in the upper berth, looking right at me, and for a moment I was afraid to go in, but soon I went up to the side of your berth, bent down and kissed you, and embraced you, and then went away. . . .

5. *Other Cases of ESP Projection.* Under this heading, Hart placed twenty-two assorted cases, such as visions of distant events, drug-induced OBEs, spontaneous OBEs, and so forth.

Hart also gave a numerical "evidentiality rating" to each of his cases based on the strength of the documentation supporting it.

After studying these ninety-nine cases, Hart came to some definite conclusions about the OBE. He suggested that deep hypnosis was the means most frequently and systematically employed to induce the experience. He also adduced that the psychological traits, receptiveness to hypnotism, and level of emotional tension aroused in the subject were key factors in bringing about a successful ESP projection. Further, he broke down the experiential aspect of the OBE and found that, by and large, eight factors seemed to be commonly reported in the accounts. Hart felt that these characteristics were typical of ESP projection cases in general: (1) The subject can make correct ESP observations about distant places and persons. (2) His apparition is often seen at the same time. (3) The experiencer is usually aware of having been an apparition. (4) The subject is able to see his own body from a point outside the body at some time during the experience. (5) He usually perceives himself in an apparitional body. (6) This body can float or otherwise defy gravity. (7) It can pass through physical matter. (8) It can travel quickly through the air. Because of these characteristics, Hart believed that the OBE was not merely a particularly dramatic form of ESP, but something much more complex.

At about the time Hart was finishing his analysis of OBE reports, Dr. Robert Crookall was starting work on his monumental case collection in Great Britain. To date, Crookall has amassed over one thousand accounts, which he has published in such books as *The Study and Practice of Astral Projection* (1961), *More Astral Projections* (1964), and *Casebook of Astral Projection* (1972). (Astral projection is the older occult term for the OBE.) Crookall's work differs from Hart's in one important respect. Remember, Hart was primarily interested in appraising only those OB accounts that contained an ESP or veridical factor. Crookall, on the other hand, did not limit his collection in any way. He was interested in analyzing *any* case in which the experiencer found himself out-of-the-body. His plan was to collect as many cases as possible, analyze them, and map out the characteristics of the OBE. Crookall's line of reasoning developed along these lines: If people reporting the OBE all seem to agree on the basic characteristics of the experience, then we are probably dealing with a genuine phenomenon. Furthermore, these characteristics will help us determine just what the OBE really is. If, on the other hand, OB accounts are the product of lying, cribbing, or delusion, then the accounts should not follow any set patterns.

Crookall did find that people undergoing the OBE do report almost identical experiences. He also determined that there are specific characteristics of the OBE. Interestingly enough, these characteristics closely match those Hart had uncovered during his analysis of ninety-nine selected cases. In fact, Crookall uncovered five aspects of the OBE which *exactly* match Hart's findings: (1) The percipient is able to see his own body from a new and spatially independent vantage point. (2) He finds himself in some sort of bodily or apparitional form. (3) This body is immune to gravity. (4) This body may be seen as an apparition by an onlooker. (5) The OB percipient sometimes demonstrates ESP during the experience. Crookall also found three other attributes of the "typical OBE": (1) The percipient usually first floats over his physical body before carrying out any other OB manoeuvre. (2) His form and his physical body are often connected by some sort of link or cord. (3) The OB percipient may see other apparitions during the experience. Crookall also discovered that OB percipients often undergo a momentary "blackout" at the point of leaving and/or reentering their bodies.

The "cord" connection, which some OBers have seen linking the physical and apparitional bodies together, is one of the most peculiar aspects of the OBE mystery. Crookall found that over fifty of the first 250 people whose cases he collected reported seeing this link. When Dr. Louisa Rhine of the Institute for Parapsychology (of the Foundation for Research on the Nature of Man, in Durham, North Carolina) turned over twenty-three new and unpublished cases to me, I discovered that roughly 25 percent of her reporters had seen this connecting cord or something like it during their OBEs. Yet Celia Green, who collected a large number of cases in England in 1966, found that practically *none* of her correspondents reported seeing this link! (These cases were subsequently analyzed by Miss Green in her book, *Out-of-the-Body Experiences*, which was issued by the Oxford-based Institute of Psychophysical Research in 1968.) This connecting-cord link cannot be dismissed as merely an illusion, since many independent OB percipients have made note of it. Several of these reporters have even testified that they had never heard or read anything about the OBE before they had their own experiences. The following is a typical description of this phenomenon and is drawn from Crookall's *The Study and Practice of Astral Projection* (1961):

One night I went to sleep. My next recollection is of standing in my room; the furniture and other details were quite clear. Although the room must have been pitch dark, there was a soft, evenly distributed, pale, yet clear light. . . . [Later, on leaving the house] . . . on turning around I saw a white cord, two or three inches wide, composed of four or five loosely woven strands, stretching from my body, as far as I could see back to the house. The next thing I knew, I was standing at the side of my bed and saw my Physical Body. The cord was attached to the head of my Psychical Body and to the center of my Physical Body. I thought, "I must get in," and slipped back into bed and awoke. I had not been aware of leaving the body, but reentering it felt like slipping the hand into an easy fitting glove.

Crookall's next major discovery about the OBE came when he broke down his cases into two separate categories (Crookall, 1964). For the sake of analysis he pooled those OBEs that occurred naturally (i.e., when the subject was asleep, due to illness, when close to death, and spontaneously from a waking state) and then compared this body of cases to OBEs that were enforced (i.e., due to suffocation, drowning, deliberate OBE attempts, hypnotic suggestion, etc.) The British geologist found that, while all OBEs share common characteristics, these two groups of experiences adhered to separate patterns. Natural OBEs were more vivid, ESP was reported more often, and the experiencers had more definite feelings of leaving and reentering their bodies. Natural OBE percipients often found themselves contacting a world of intense and radiant beauty. (This might indicate that these OBE percipients were undergoing an extreme expansion of consciousness.) People undergoing enforced OBEs usually found themselves spontaneously standing by their bodies, traveling to earthly places, or often enveloped by mist. (During my own first OBE I found myself engulfed by a pinkish fog.) Enforced OBE percipients did not see cord connections nearly as often as people undergoing natural OBEs. Crookall felt that the differences between these two groups of OBEs were statistically significant. (That is, the differences were not the result of coincidence but represented a genuine distinction between the two groups of experiences.)

Hornell Hart was greatly impressed by Crookall's data and set out to verify his colleague's findings independently. Eventually he wrote two papers firmly supporting Crookall's discoveries (Hart, 1966, 1967). Hart, though, did have one criticism of his British colleague's data. He felt that the differences between natural and enforced OBEs might be due simply to the fact that the former cases are usually reported in more detail than the latter ones. Thus, Hart suggested, the differences between the two groups of cases might be indicating a difference in how people *report* their experiences, and so might not represent an intrinsic distinction between the cases themselves. In 1967 Hart reanalyzed Crookall's data, taking into account this factor, and still found a statistically significant difference between the characteristics of natural and enforced OBEs.* He also believed that the OBE represented the actual release of a "soul body" that would ultimately survive the death of the physical body. Crookall's data all but proved this interpretation to his mind.

Hornell Hart died in 1967 and Robert Crookall was eighty-seven in 1977. No one today has really followed up on their work, nor has anyone tried to map out the patterns of the OBE so systematically. In fact, the work of Hart and Crookall has been sadly neglected by contemporary parapsychologists. Hart (1966) once wrote a paper blasting parapsychologists for ignoring Crookall's work. Little did he suspect that his own studies on the OBE would be ignored in time as well.

However, a recent analysis of spontaneous OB accounts was made in 1967 by Dr. John Poynton, a biology professor at the University of Natal, South Africa. Poynton published a questionnaire about the OBE in the South African press and requested that anyone who had undergone the experience write to him. He received 122 analyzable accounts in return. He found that most of his correspondents underwent the OBE while either asleep, relaxing, or dozing. Over 50 percent of the reporters claimed that they had been in a normal mental state when the phenomenon occurred, and four corre-

---

*Dr. John Palmer, of the University of Virginia and later an associate research psychologist at the University of California, Davis, did an independent check on Crookall's data and concluded that they were not statistically significant. His opinion stands in striking contrast to Hart's. However, it is hard to resolve the issue, since neither Hart nor Palmer ever published detailed reports on what statistical measurements they used when making their analyses. Whatever the case, any reader of Crookall's book will see that there is, indeed, a strong *qualitative* difference between these two groups of cases.

spondents claimed that they had been seen as apparitions while out-of-the-body. Some 74.5 percent of the percipients perceived themselves projecting in an apparitional body, but only 9 percent reported seeing a connecting "cord" linking the apparitional body to the physical body. (Crookall found over double that percentage in his cases.) Similar to Crookall's findings, 24.5 percent of Poynton's correspondents had definite sensations of leaving and reentering the body.

Celia Green, whose work I mentioned earlier, began her case collection at about this same time. She obtained 577 cases by advertising for OB accounts over the British media (Green, 1968). Unfortunately, Green's evaluations are qualitatively oriented and she does not offer the types of statistical breakdowns that Crookall and Poynton made from their data. However, her findings are similar to Poynton's and Crookall's, with one major difference. A great number of her correspondents reported that they had *not* seen themselves traveling in apparitional forms during the OBE, nor did they see any "cord" connections. However, she did discover that her correspondents described typical sensations of leaving and reentering the physical body. These sensations were virtually the same ones that Crookall isolated in his studies. Green, like Poynton, also discovered that most of her subjects were relaxed when the OBE occurred. Green's OBE reporters often found themselves floating over their physical bodies at the initiation of the experience. This is reminiscent of Crookall's findings.

So, despite occasional discrepancies, analyzers of case collections have come up with roughly similar findings about the OBE.

Part I of this volume is devoted to three papers that throw added light on the experiential content of the OBE. The first is by Dr. John Palmer who, while working at the University of Virginia's division of parapsychology, conducted a lengthy research project on experimentally inducing OBEs and judging their relationship to ESP. Dr. Palmer suspended his OBE research when he took a position at the University of California, at Davis, in 1975. His paper "Consciousness Localized in Space Outside the Body" offers a brief discussion of what we have learned about the OBE, when it seems to occur, why it is of interest to parapsychologists, and what types of research strategies have been devised to explore it. His essay sets the tone for the rest of this volume.

The two papers that follow discuss the range and types of OBEs that people have reported. The first is by Dr. Michael Grosso, a philosophy instructor at Jersey City State College. The second, written by myself, is an analysis of several hitherto unpublished cases I collected while working under a grant and fellowship at the Psychical Research Foundation in Durham, North Carolina, in 1973. Both papers address themselves to the same problem: Are there phenomenologically distinct types of OBEs? My own answer is Yes. As I will explain, there seem to be four specific and different types of OBEs. Dr. Grosso comes to a diametrically opposite conclusion. He rejects the idea of discrete forms of OBEs and suggests that there are no truly definable characteristics typifying the experience. Instead, he posits the existence of an OB continuum, comprising many different types of experiences. In a way, these two papers are typical of the great divergence of opinion parapsychologists harbor about the OBE. They illustrate how two investigators can analyze similar data yet come to opposite opinions about what those data indicate.

REFERENCES

Crookall, Robert. *Casebook of Astral Projection.* Secaucus, N.J.: University Books, 1972.

_____. *More Astral Projections.* London: Aquarian Press, 1964.

_____. *The Study and Practice of Astral Projection.* London: Aquarian Press, 1961.

Green, Celia. *Out-of-the-Body Experiences.* Oxford: Institute for Psychophysical Research, 1968.

Hart, Hornell. "A Chasm Needs to Be Bridged." *Journal*

of the American Society for Psychical Research 60, (1966): 380–89.

_____. "ESP Projection: Spontaneous Cases and the Experimental Method." *Journal of the American Society for Psychical Research* 47 (1954): 121–46.

_____. "Scientific Survival Research." *International Journal of Parapsychology* 9 (1956): 43–52.

Poynton, John. "Results of an Out-of-the-Body Survey." In John Poynton (ed.), *Parapsychology in South Africa.* Johannesburg: South African Society for Psychical Research, 1975.

Reed, Graham. *The Psychology of Anomalous Experience.* Boston: Houghton-Mifflin, 1974.

1 | Consciousness Localized in Space Outside the Body

JOHN PALMER

It is an axiom of human nature that man identifies his consciousness with his physical body. However, a number of people have had experiences where such identification appears to break down. One such experience is the mystical experience, where the person realized an expansion of consciousness beyond the boundaries of self, culminating in an identification with all of nature or with God. Another such experience differs from the mystical in that consciousness seems to be localized at a specific point in space outside of the physical body. This experience is called the "out-of-body experience" (OBE) and has been of particular interest to parapsychologists.

Parapsychologists have not agreed on a single definition of the OBE or on the criteria that must be met for an experience to be placed in this category. Having adopted the principle "when in doubt, make as few assumptions as possible," I prefer at this stage of the game to include in the OBE category any experience where the person believes that his consciousness is localized in space outside his physical body. While I see this definition as stressing what might be called (for lack of a better term) the "proprioceptive" aspect of the experience, the great majority of OBEs reported in the literature contain a visual component as well. In many OBEs, the person first realizes that he is "out" by "seeing" his physical body from a point in space outside of that body, usually above it. He may perceive his consciousness to be enveloped in some kind of vehicle or "astral body," but this is not always the case. In more advanced OBEs the person may "travel" to distant places. Sometimes he just suddenly will find himself at this distant place, while in other cases he will experience the trip itself, often discovering that he can move through walls and otherwise transcend the barriers that impede the in-the-body traveler. He may interact with other people while he is "out" and he may perceive them interacting with him. Finally, the person may have visions that do not conform to ordinary reality. These experiences can range from a distorted view of the normal physical world to experiences of color patterns, abstract designs, or archetypal material which persons having OBEs often interpret literally as visits to other worlds, planes, or levels of reality. Such experiences customarily occur in the latter stages of the OBE, following the more mundane experiences.

Survey data suggest that a surprising number of people have had an OBE at least once in their lives. Celia Green (1967) asked two samples of undergraduates from two British universities whether they had ever had an "experience in which you felt you were 'out of your body'?" She received 19 percent positive responses out of 115 in the first sample and 34 percent positive responses out of 380 in the second. Hornell Hart (1954) received 27 percent positive replies from 155 Duke University sociology students, while Charles Tart (1971) received 44 percent positive responses from 150 experienced marijuana users.

Neither Green nor Hart reported any sex differences in the incidence of OBEs. Tart, however, reported that among his marijuana users a greater proportion of females than males experienced OBEs, but that multiple experiences (i.e., more than one OBE) were more common among males.

Under what might be labeled normal states of being, OBEs tend to occur most frequently when a person is in the light stage of sleep, what dream researchers call the hypnagogic period. The light stage of sleep is when normal dreaming occurs, and dreaming-like imagery is also noted sometimes during the hypnagogic period. Such imagery may develop into an OBE, and some persons who have reported the ability to induce OBEs voluntarily in themselves suggest techniques whereby one becomes aware during a dream that he is dreaming (i.e., a "lucid" dream) and then turns this into an OBE.

Indeed, OBEs are often difficult to distinguish from lucid dreams.

A disproportionate number of OBEs also seem to occur under conditions of physical stress such as severe illness, accident, or surgery. In the case of surgery, general anesthesia likely contributes to the experience. Several years ago there was a report in the *Canadian Medical Association Journal* (Macmillan and Brown, 1971) that illustrates an OBE occurring during severe illness, in this case a cardiac arrest in an intensive care unit. The patient described his experience as follows:

. . . Then I am looking at my own body from the waist up, face to face. . . . Almost immediately I saw myself leave my body, coming out through my head and shoulders. . . . The "body" leaving me was not exactly in vapour form, yet it seemed to expand very slightly once it was clear of me. It was somewhat transparent, for I could see my other "body" through it. Watching this I thought "So this is what happens when you die" (although no thought of being dead presented itself to me).

Suddenly I am sitting on a very small object travelling at great speed, out and up into a dull blue-grey sky, at a 45-degree angle. . . .

Down below to my left I saw a pure white cloud-like substance also moving up on a line that would intersect with my course. Somehow I was able to go down and take a look at it. . . .

My next sensation was of floating in a bright, pale yellow light—a very delightful feeling. Although I was not conscious of having any lower limbs, I felt something being torn off the scars of my right leg, as if a large piece of adhesive tape had been taken off. . . . I continued to float, enjoying the most beautiful tranquil sensation. . . .

Then there were sledge-hammer blows to my left side. . . . After a number of these blows, I began to count them and when I got to six I said (aloud I think), "What the —— are you doing to me?" and opened my eyes. . . .

Parapsychologists are interested in the OBE primarily for two reasons. First, the OBE might be a state particularly conducive to ESP. Second, the OBE might be literally what its name implies: some aspect of the person, including his consciousness or that of which consciousness is a property, actually might be capable of functioning outside of the physical body. Such a discovery in turn would have implications for the question of survival after death, in that what can function outside the body before death might be able to function independently of the body after death.

We have no data systematically comparing the incidence or quality of ESP during OBEs as compared to other psychological states. However, there are scattered reports in the literature of rather impressive ESP occurrences during OBEs which, to say the least, are titillating. For example, Tart (1968) conducted a series of experiments with a "Miss Z" who claimed the ability to induce OBEs in herself during sleep.* One night, while her brain waves and other physiological measures were being recorded by polygraph, she was able during an OBE to correctly identify a five-digit number placed on a shelf above her bed. The possibility of such a correct identification occurring by chance is one in 100,000, and the polygraph would have revealed it had she gotten up during the night to take a peek.

The question of whether some aspect of a person literally leaves his body during an OBE ultimately involves complex philosophical issues that are beyond the scope of this article. Suffice it to say that most parapsychologists seem to believe that the best way to approach this problem scientifically is to look for evidence of observable or measurable effects occurring at the place to which an out-of-the-body traveler claims to have traveled at the time he claims to have been there. Again, there are scattered reports of such phenomena in the literature. Hart (1954), for example, has reviewed a number of cases where an out-of-the-body traveler was "perceived" as an apparition by a person or persons at the place to which he independently claimed to have traveled. The evidence we have so far can be considered no more than suggestive that

*Dr. Tart's complete report on this experiment can be found in Part II.—ED.

the OBE is a literal separation from the body, and empirical methods may never be able to settle the matter conclusively, but continued research might at least make such a hypothesis scientifically respectable and credible, and that would be no small achievement.

Most of the experimental work completed so far on this topic involves attempts to discover the psychophysiological concomitants of the OBE in persons who claim the ability to have the experience voluntarily. It would be desirable to discover a pattern of psychophysiological indices associated with the OBE, because this would allow us to supplement the verbal reports of the OBE with an independent and nonvoluntary measure, much as can be done with dreams. Unfortunately, no truly distinctive psychophysiological correlates have yet been discovered. The only consistent finding emerging from these studies is a reduction in eye-movement activity during OBEs.

Three parapsychological research centers are currently engaged in long-term research projects on the OBE. At the American Society for Psychical Research in New York City, Dr. Karlis Osis is using methods borrowed from perceptual psychology to try to differentiate "OBE perception" from the kind of perception characteristic of "ordinary" ESP (1972, 1973). By the use of optical devices such as prisms and mirrors, Dr. Osis is able to make the spatial relationships among a set of target objects placed in a box appear distorted from the point of view of a person looking directly into the box. He predicts that a person traveling outside his body and looking directly into the box will see the objects in the distorted arrangement. On the other hand, such distortion should not characterize ordinary ESP, where the person persumably is perceiving the target from the location of his physical body.

Osis has tested about one hundred persons who claim the ability to leave their bodies voluntarily, but only a small percentage have shown any evidence of paranormal ability in this state. More positive results have been obtained with one particular subject, an artist named Ingo Swann, and we are awaiting a detailed report of these findings.

The research of Dr. Robert L. Morris at the Psychical Research Foundation in Durham, North Carolina, has emphasized means of detecting the out-of-body traveler at the location to which he claims to have traveled. Dr. Morris has worked almost exclusively with a male Duke undergraduate named Stuart Blue Harary. Various devices used to detect changes in electrical fields at the target location (a room in the building next door to where Blue's physical body is located) have not yielded positive results, nor have "human detectors" been able reliably to identify Blue's "presence." However, some very intriguing results were found with Blue's pet cat. The researchers discovered that during eight randomly preselected periods when Blue had "traveled" to the target room, the cat was unusually quiet and did not meow once. In contrast, during eight randomly preselected control periods when Blue was not having an OBE, the cat was significantly more active than during the OBE periods and meowed a total of thirty-seven times (Morris, 1973). This finding has been repeated several times.

No one in the target room knew the specific times Blue was to "visit" them, so it is unlikely that they influenced the cat themselves. It is also noteworthy that these results could not be duplicated when Blue only pretended to leave his body by imagining himself traveling to the target room. This finding suggests that the cat's behavior could not be accounted for simply by Blue's influencing the cat telepathically, although this interpretation cannot be completely ruled out.*

Much more research will be needed before we can expect to understand fully the OBE either psychologically or parapsychologically. This will include both experimental work and study of spontaneous OBEs. The medical setting is an

---

*The third laboratory where OBE research was being carried out, when this article was written, was the division of parapsychology at the University of Virginia. The research was conducted by Dr. Palmer himself. However, I have deleted this section of Dr. Palmer's article, since he will offer a detailed report on his work in Part II. There too the reader will find full reports on the Blue Harary and Ingo Swann experiments.—ED.

ideal source for spontaneous OBEs because so many OBEs seem to occur in conjunction with surgery or during severe illness. I would be most interested to learn from physicians reading this article of any OBEs reported to them by their patients. Such reports would be particularly valuable if records are available providing accurate information about the nature of the illness, medications, or particular anesthetics used, et cetera.

Although I am mainly interested in the OBE because of its theoretical implications, the experience some day may have practical applications as well. Many persons who have had striking OBEs report that the experience convinced them of survival after death and eliminated their fear of death. Whether or not this conclusion can be considered objectively valid, it does suggest some therapeutic possibilities for the OBE.

For example, the experience may help persons in occupations where there is a genuine risk of death and where fear of this danger may adversely affect their performance. A convincing OBE also might provide comfort to patients in certain stages of a terminal illness. Finally, the experience might be useful in treating an irrational fear of death in certain psychiatric patients. Whether or not the OBE can be sufficiently harnessed to fulfill these goals is just one of many challenging questions facing the investigator of this fascinating aspect of man's experience.

REFERENCES

Green, C. E. "Ecsomatic Experiences and Related Phenomena." *Journal of the Society for Psychical Research* 44 (1967): 111–31.

Hart, H. "ESP Projection: Spontaneous Cases and the Experimental Method." *Journal of the American Society for Psychical Research,* 48 (1954): 121–46.

Macmillan, R. L., and K. W. G. Brown (correspondence). "Cardiac Arrest Remembered." *Canadian Medical Association Journal* 104 (1971): 889–90.

Morris, R. G. "The Use of Detectors for Out-of-Body Experiences." In W. G. Roll; R. L. Morris; and J. D. Morris (eds.), *Research in Parapsychology 1973.* Metuchen, N. J.: Scarecrow Press, 1974.

Osis, K. "Perspective for Out-of-Body Research." In W. G. Roll; R. L. Morris; and J. D. Morris (eds.), *Research in Parapsychology 1973.* Metuchen, N. J.: Scarecrow Press, 1974.

————. "Toward a Methodology for Experiments on Out-of-the-Body Experiences." In W. G. Roll; R. L. Morris; and J. D. Morris (eds.), *Research in Parapsychology 1972.* Metuchen, N. J.: Scarecrow Press, 1973, pp. 78–79.

Tart, C. T. *On Being Stoned: A Psychological Study of Marijuana Intoxication.* Palo Alto, Calif.: Science and Behavior Books, 1971.

————. "A Psychophysiological Study of Out-of-the-Body Experiences in a Selected Subject." *Journal of the American Society for Psychical Research* 62 (1968): 3–27.

2 | Experiential Aspects of Out-of-Body Experiences

D. SCOTT ROGO*

In the past, qualitative analyses of out-of-body experience (OBE) narratives have been approached from two different perspectives. Hornell Hart limited his analysis of OBE reports to only those cases containing a veridical element. After examining the literature of psychical research, he assessed ninety-nine cases of ESP-projection (OBEs in which the percipient was able to correctly "see" or report some person or scene at a distance) and attempted to find set characteristics of the experience (Hart, 1954). After categorizing these cases, Hart discovered that, by and large, ESP-projection cases do share eight common characteristics: (1) the subject reports observations of distant places or persons apparently paranormally; (2) an apparition is seen by a percipient during the experience; (3) the subject is usually aware of having been seen as an apparition; (4) the subject sees his own physical body during the experience from a point of space outside his body; (5) the subject sees himself in an apparitional body; (6) this body can defy gravity, (7) this body can pass through solid matter; (8) this body can move quickly through the air.

A second approach to the study of OBEs has been offered by Robert Crookall (1961, 1964), who has also analyzed a large quantity of spontaneous cases. However, he, unlike Hart, did not limit himself solely to veridical OBEs but included any anecdotal account that could be classified as an

*The research for this paper was carried out in part under a fellowship at the Psychical Research Foundation, Durham, North Carolina, under a grant from the Parapsychology Foundation. The author would like to extend his appreciation to both these organizations for their support. The author would also like to thank Dr. Louisa Rhine, who supplied several of the out-of-body accounts upon which this study was based.

out-of-body experience. By analyzing over 250 such accounts, Crookall also found eight general characteristics of the experience. Five of these corresponded to Hart's findings: (1) the subject sees his own body from a spacially distinct vantage point; (2) the subject finds himself in an apparitional body; (3) this body is immune to gravity; (4) its perception might include ESP; (5) this body may be seen as an apparition by a percipient. Crookall also found three other general aspects: (1) the subject hovers above his physical body; (2) the physical and apparitional bodies are seen connected by a cord; (3) the percipient often sees forms representing discarnates during the experience.

Two general conclusions can be drawn from these attempts at general content analysis: (1) since the OBE may or may not employ ESP, the total experience seems to be something more than merely a form of conventional ESP; (2) since the characteristics of both veridical and nonveridical OBEs share almost identical patterns, the close similarity between them would indicate that both types of cases may be equally suitable for analysis, since they seem to be of the same intrinsic nature.

It is unfortunate that, since the work of Hart and Crookall, little has been done by way of analyzing spontaneous OBE case material. This study is offered as a similar type of phenomenological study of twenty-eight new cases.*

It is my belief that Hart and Crookall fell into a similar trap when analyzing their cases. Both researchers assumed that *all* reported OBEs represent only one type of phenomenon. Furthermore, both based this view on the hypothesis that, judging from the anecdotal literature, in all cases the OBE represents a release of an ultraphysical "soul body."† Both these hypotheses may be in error. In looking over Hart's cases, I find it clear that what he termed ESP projection

---

*These cases were collected by the Psychical Research Foundation, Dr. Louisa Rhine, and the present writer.

†This is implied in no uncertain terms in Hart's last contribution to parapsychology, "Scientific Survival Research," *International Journal of Parapsychology* 9 (1967): 43–51.

consists of various types of experiences. For example, he includes cases of traveling clairvoyance (an ESP experience in which a person feels that he is merely "seeing" a distant event as though he were there even though no ultraphysical body is reported or even suggested); astral projection (OBEs in which the subject reports the projection of an apparitional body); and apparitions of the living (cases in which the agent is seen as an apparition by another individual but has no memory of ever leaving the body.)* I am tempted to ask: Does the OBE represent a group of different types of phenomena which, because of some' similarity in their phenomenology, have been grouped together?

Breaking down the twenty-eight cases collected for this study, there seem to be three distinct forms in which the subject may perceive himself. These are: OBEs that report the freeing of a parasomatic body;† those cases that report that the consciousness was enveloped by mist or a ball of light but no body; and those cases where the consciousness is released from the physical body and is not accompanied by any form whatsoever. There is also a special class of OBEs representing combinations of the three.

A large number of out-of-body experiencers do report seeing an parasomatic form (twelve out of the twenty-eight reports mention such a body, while several more *imply* such a form.) The following two cases are representative of this type of OBE:

*For example, compare the following types of cases Hart classified together as ESP projections: (1) the case of S. H. Beard, who concentrated his attention on his fiancée; she saw his apparition, although Beard himself had no knowledge of being "out of his body" (p. 128); (2) the case of Rev. Mr. Bertrand, who felt himself leaving his physical body in an ultraphysical vehicle when he nearly froze to death (p. 134); and (3) the case of Lt. Morales, who "saw" what was occurring at a neighboring village as though he were actually there during a drug experiment, but had no sensations of actually leaving his physical body (p. 130).

†The term "ecsomatic" was suggested by Celia Green (1968) and is meant to be synonymous with "out-of-body." Green employs the term "parasomatic" to describe the apparitional body often seen by out-of-body percipients.

. . . I was awakened by the sun shining through the door across my face and eyes. I got up to close the door, placed one hand on the knob, the other on the door itself in order to close it quietly, then changed my mind and walked across the room to the dresser. Up to this time I didn't notice anything strange or different. I felt perfectly normal too, but when I looked in the mirror I saw the strangest thing there. It looked like me but it was just a white vapor-like image of myself. I wasn't frightened, just puzzled. I thought I must be ill and should go back to bed at once. A quick glance around the room showed both my sisters sleeping with their heads covered up. Perhaps the light was bothering them also. When I reached my bed there was I in bed and sound asleep. There were two of me.

The following case was induced by the subject experimenting with self-relaxation techniques:

. . . I began to get a little dizzy, as I could not draw a breath. All of a sudden I felt my body begin to rise off the bed. I felt myself "floating" in the air over my bed. I reached down with my hands to grip the bed, and I felt my own body there in bed. I turned my head to look at the bed and saw myself there in bed. I was never so scared in all my life. I started to wave my arms and legs about and I was back upon the bed, sitting up.

These two experiences represent the "popular" conception of the OBE. Nevertheless, several cases have been reported in which the subject emphatically denied that any form or body was liberated during the experience. Such cases prompt us to ask certain questions. Is the seeing of the "double" an illusion? If, in fact, we do possess a "double," does it need always be projected during an OBE? Or, are we talking about two phenomenologically distinct experiences? These questions will be discussed later. The following experience is typical of this form of OBE:

. . . I was near the ceiling by the north window that opened in the rear garden. The colors of everything were vivid and flowing. I did not see myself as having any form. . . . Time was suspended; suddenly I was on the bed again feeling my body as heavy.

If OBEs neatly fell into these two groupings we would be entitled to say that there are indeed two different types of phenomena that have been categorized together. However, this distinction is complicated by the fact that some OBEs report a midway point between the release of a parasomatic body and merely a "liberated" consciousness:

... One night while lying in bed I became gradually aware that a roll of what I will call "mist" was gathering against the ceiling and wall directly above my bed. It was stirring, very gently, in a somewhat rocking motion. It also moved very slowly in a sideways direction. I could feel its presence and its motion as though I, Helen, *was* the mist and the knowledge came with the words, "Oh, I am up on the ceiling." I was not asleep. I was not dreaming. I could see it there, though not with my bodily eyes. I was detached from it and there was no sentiment of any kind in regard to it. There was no fear, no questioning—simply a quiet acceptance of the fact that I was outside my body, hovering over it. There was a sensation of pushing against the ceiling, lightly, and of being stopped by it, as a toy balloon which has got away would be stopped. This caused a sensation of uneasiness in the center—what I call the "thought center"—of the mist, a light frustration but no vexation. I could see the wall, the mist spreading away from its center, my bed, my body, other parts of the room—but none of this with my bodily eyes. . . . It ended when I was aware of being back in my body.

Notice in this case that the subject specifically keeps from describing herself in a "body." This midway point is also illustrated by the following description of an OBE by Blue Harary, who has the ability to control his OBEs consciously and is taking part in a lengthy research project at the Psychical Research Foundation. The experimental aspects of Harary's OBEs have been reported elsewhere (Janis, et al., 1973; Morris, et al., 1973). He frequently has OBEs in which he sees himself as a glowing ball of light and not as having a body (although he has had this experience also). The following account is taken from an experimental out-of-body session run at the Psychical Research Foundation on July 5, 1973. The object of the experiment was for Blue to project to a target area some distance away and try to affect a target animal (a cat) and people at the target area:

. . . I left my body quickly and traveled to the detection area. . . . Although some of my awareness remained with my physical body, most consciousness was centered in my OOB self which seemed to be a large, glowing ball of greenish tinted light which appeared to be the size of a standard beach ball. . . .

After traveling to the detection area and carrying out the experimental task, Blue returned to his physical body:

. . . I returned slowly to my physical body and, still experiencing myself as a glowing ball of light, hovered above the chair where I could see my body reclining below me in the psychophysiological lab. I floated down and into my physical body and signaled the monitor a few moments later.

An analogous case from our collection reports a similar phenomenon:

. . . Twenty-five years ago I was seriously sick and was rushed to the hospital in a very serious condition from loss of blood caused by a hemorrhage. In this weak condition the doctor decided on an exploratory operation. As he gave me ether and I drifted into a deep sleep, I felt as though I were going to die. The sensation was not painful, but as though I felt a tugging and pulling as in a game of "tug-o'war." Finally a little light hovered over my still form and all my senses were transformed into this small light. . . . I, or rather this little light, flew around the operating room watching everything that was taking place. I soon tired of this and flew right through the window and not feeling any pain but rather a glorious free sensation.

These experiences reveal three distinct forms that the OBE may take. In retrospect, other case studies (Crookall, 1961, 1964) also show such a distinction. If the OBE can be classified based on the criterion of the "form" that the experiencer takes, then it seems clear that spontaneous cases do in fact break down into three distinct categories. Unfortunately, previous case analysts were either unaware of this distinction or gave it no consideration. A continuum of experiences might also exist, but spontaneous cases do seem to group around three distinct forms of the experience with little intergroup variation. I think that it is justifiable to believe that these types of OBE reports are not only descriptively distinct, but phenomenologically distinct, though related as well. In other words, they represent different forms of the OBE just as clairvoyance, telepathy, and precognition represent experientially distinct forms of ESP.

My position is further supported by the fact that, in a few cases, there seems to be a double-release during the OBE. The consciousness is released from *both* the physical body *and* the ecsomatic body, each of which is seen from a spacially separate vantage point. Such reports are rare in out-of-body literature and our log included only one such report. Cases in which such a distinct double division is reported cannot easily be explained away as due to incorrect observation, expectancy, or errors of reporting. Double-release OBEs are so extraordinary that one wonders if they can be so readily explained on any grounds except that some sort of physical separation is really taking place between the mind, the body, and some sort of ultraphysical body. The following is a case of double-release OBE that occurred during an illness:

. . . Sometime during the night, although I was unconscious, I saw the hospital room with doctors surrounding Dr. G. who was at my bedside, bending over me, listening to my heartbeats with a stethescope, her fingers on my wrist taking my pulse. At the same time I saw, over my body, lying on the bed, another body of me suspended in mid-air in the exact position, hanging from the ceiling by what seemed to be a cord attached to my navel. I seemed to be an observer, but from where, I cannot say. All I know is that I saw two bodies of myself. I watched this sight for some time.

Two similar cases will be cited from out-of-body literature. The first is from Robert Crookall's *More Astral Projections* (1964):

. . . I was in bed running a temperature of 104°. Suddenly I found that I could see my physical body lying in the bed and another body outside the bed, also in a recumbent position about a foot higher than the physical body. The second body was a very scintillating blue, pulsating with light. But it seemed to me that "I" was still in another body looking at these other two, although I was completely unconscious of any form for the third body. It seemed that that which was the "I" saw both the physical body and the bright body.

The final case of double-release is from the writer's own experience (Rogo, 1973):

. . . I had been asleep but awoke with a rapid feeling of linear movement. I felt myself in both the physical and astral [bodies]. All of a sudden I felt that I had been catapulted from the physical body and had a glimpse of it. However, as odd as this may seem, I realized that my consciousness and sight stemmed from a point not within either body. I was viewing both bodies from another side of the room. I did not feel I had any body at all, but could feel the movement of my "double." I began to lose consciousness and found myself in the body again.

If, indeed, all the preceding cases represent four different types of OBEs, they seem inherently related for two reasons: (1) they form a natural continuum, and (2) various forms of the OBE may manifest conjointly.

No discussion of the implications of these data will be set forth at this time. These cases are presented only to verify the opinion held by some that what we term the OBE may actually represent a hierarchy of phenomena. It also indicates that the simple "objective-body" theory about the OBE (that the body contains an ultraphysical duplicate that is necessarily projected during the OBE) must be revised. It does not follow, however, that the conception of an ultraphysical body is negated, but that the projection of this presumed body may represent only one type of OBE.

In conclusion, I do not believe that the OBE represents a gradual continuum of experiences, but that it represents three distinctly different types of effects: (1) the separation of an ultraphysical body from the human organism, (2) the separation of mind from the body, and (3) the projection of the mind along with some ultraphysical vehicle other than a body. Sometimes two of these types may be combined during the same experience.

REFERENCES

Crookall, Robert. *More Astral Projections.* London: Aquarian Press, 1964.

_____. *The Study and Practice of Astral Projection.* London: Aquarian Press, 1964.

Green, Celia. *Out-of-the-Body Experiences.* London: Institute for Psychophysical Research, 1968.

Hart, Hornell. "ESP Projection: Spontaneous Cases and the Experimental Method." *Journal of the American Society for Psychical Research,* 48 (1954): 121–46.

Janis, J., et al. "A Description of the Physiological Variables Connected with an Out-of-Body Study." Research brief presented at the 1973 Convention of the Parapsychological Association.

Morris, Robert, et al. "The Use of Detection Devices in Studies of Out-of-the-Body Experiences." Research brief presented at the 1973 Convention of the Parapsychological Association.

Rogo, D. Scott. *The Welcoming Silence.* Secaucus, N. J.: University Books, 1973.

3 | Some Varieties of Out-of-Body Experience

MICHAEL GROSSO

INTRODUCTION

The theorizing that parapsychology is in need of can take two forms. The first is highly ambitious and aims to construct a conceptual scheme which will comprehend all the data. Endeavors of this type usually bite off more than they can chew. A second sort of theorizing operates on a lower plateau of comprehensiveness, and attempts to clarify smaller areas of the baffling terrain. In this article I shall descend even lower in the attempt to shed light on the nature of the out-of-body phenomenon itself.

Prima facie, it looks as though the parapsychologist is here studying a phenomenon in which a human subject, normally in some sense "in" his body, appears in some paranormal fashion to get "out." There is no reason to dispute the correctness of this view at a certain level of observation. In my opinion, however, when we look more closely, we arrive at a very different picture of what is happening. At least one advantage of this revised picture is that it renders the phenomenon of OBE simpler and consequently more intelligible. The difference is this: the subject, instead of paranormally getting "out" of the body, is already, in substance, "out." If so, it is not a matter of being in or out, or of two mutually exclusive and discrete states, but rather, of varying degrees of being "out," where at one end of the continuum we observe the dramatic phenomenon parapsychologists call the OBE; at the opposite end we observe something quite different, the subject wholly enmeshed and entangled in his bodily existence to such a degree that he *experiences himself* as *identified* with the events and vicissitudes of his bodily organism.

I will begin by making a few observations on the relationship between mind and body a propos the OB phenomenon. Then, in support of the notion of an OB continuum, I will attempt to show that there are a variety of states, or behavioral modes, which, while they favor the occurrence of what we can call the OBE proper, *already* display some of the marks of the latter.

OBSERVATIONS ON THE MIND-BODY PROBLEM
WITH RESPECT TO THE OBE

OB phenomena raise fundamental questions about the perennial puzzle of metaphysics: the relationship between mind and body. However, before we can begin to address ourselves to this puzzle, we need to clarify our understanding of the OB phenomenon itself. What happens when a subject has the experience of being out-of-the-body? We might begin by asking what being "in" the body means. Now "in" cannot be taken to mean anything comparable to "identity," where being *in* one's body means being identical with it, as some philosophical materialists hold, since this would *logically* exclude the possibility of "getting out." A second possibility would be to construe "in" literally as describing a spatial relationship, interpenetration, enclosure, or the like, in which case we would think of the OB experient as a spatially extended entity, occupying and then slipping out of the body, like a handkerchief plucked from a vest pocket. A certain amount of evidence seems to support this conceptualization; furthermore, it easily accommodates itself to the imagination which, to a large extent, is weaned on spatio-visual experience. This second view might only involve us in a subtle refinement and extension of materialism. In this article I am not concerned to argue for or against such a view, which, incidentally, does not seem to be incompatible with a third possibility I wish to consider. The third possible conceptualization (I don't mean this to be an exhaustive list) entails that the subject *always was out-of-the-body* and that the paranormal OBE represents one type of empirically dramatic and self-certifying instance of becoming fully conscious of the fact.

In a weak sense, that is, implying nothing paranormal, the assertion that the subject is already out of the body would be an acceptable way of talking except to an identity theorist for whom mind and brain are empirically identical. Thus, even to the epiphenomenalist, consciousness is already "out" of the body (logically distinct *and* ontologically separate), however causally inefficacious this condition of being "out" may be. The model I am proposing goes far beyond epiphenomenalism. It would be closer to *hypophenomenalism*. Ducasse (1961) introduced this term, though not the conception it is intended to express. "Thus, the soul is not in the body, but the body is in, and dependent upon, the soul, which both precedes and survives it, and whose force gives form and organization to the matter of which the body is composed" (p. 81). So, instead of thinking of consciousness as in some sense located "in" the body and sometimes managing in some paranormal fashion to get "out," it may be more in accord with the truth to think of the body as located "in" the field of consciousness. Needless to say, this is still talk at the level of metaphor, keeping in mind that the right metaphor often proves to be crucial in the nascent stage of theoretical revolutions.

"In," in this context, could be interpreted to mean "epistemologically derivative" in the sense that Descartes understood knowledge of the thinking subject to be logically prior to knowledge of the thinking subject's body. For Descartes this was part of the proof that consciousness survived bodily death. This, however, would seem to be of little help to the parapsychologist. Another, somewhat related, philosophical consideration is this: if we place ourselves in the attitude of the phenomenologist—whose method is to catch and display phenomena prior to their getting caught in the net of explanations and interpretations—then the body appears to consciousness as one, albeit curiously privileged, image or object of experience among an all-encompassing host of other images and objects of experience. It is only one of the objects in a subject's field of consciousness. The idea that consciousness is a (relatively insignificant) by-product of the brain is the result of a certain set of mental calculations. It never occurs on the level of primordial perception, the wellspring of all theoretical constructions. At that level my body is an image I experience, not the cause or explanation of it.

More in accord with the findings of parapsychology, however, there are at least two ways we can take this which make empirical sense. My body is *in* my consciousness in the sense that, as the data of parapsychology indicate, the field of consciousness extends in time and space beyond the field of my bodily organism's functioning. From this it would follow that it would not make sense to speak of my consciousness getting out of my body. Viewed in this manner, it makes perfectly good sense to construe the meaning of "in" spatially, though the relationship of inclusion we are attempting to clarify probably entails a great deal more than spatial parameters—temporal, for example, and in the case of psychokinetic effects, apparently some form of energy.

A second way of taking the relationship of inclusion is this: my body is *in* my field of consciousness in the sense that my normal bodily functions tend to obstruct the fuller and wider potential of consciousness. The meaning I wish to attach to the above assertion is again to be grasped in relationship to certain data of parapsychology. Evidence indicates that altered states of consciousness (ASCs) activate the extended psi-field of functioning (Honorton, 1974; Honorton and Krippner, 1969; Ullman and Krippner with Vaughan, 1973; White, 1964). What does this mean in terms of bodily functions obstructing the field of consciousness? Normal bodily functions enable the organism to maintain a homeostatic relationship to the immediate plane of life. The normal relationship of the organism to the plane of life and practical survival, mediated by the brain, I shall designate by the expression "sensori-motor reflex." Now, it looks as though ASCs involve an inhibition or disruption of the sensori-motor reflexes of the organism, thereby liberating consciousness from being fixated upon the immediate plane of life. As an obvious example one has only to think of the yogi in meditation, immobilized in the appropriate posture while attention is systematically withdrawn from external stimuli. Similarly, the dreamer's sensory intake and motility are drastically reduced. The reduction of sensory intake and the restriction of motility are important parts of hypnotic induction procedures (Gill and Brenman, 1959). My body inserts itself in the field of consciousness like a shield which, while it serves for protection, also constricts the range of my possible awareness. ASCs are so many ways of dropping the shield. So, on this view, it is not a matter of getting out of the body but of the body—its normally incessant sensori-motor mechanisms—getting out of the way of my consciousness. Nothing is added; certain obstacles are merely dismantled.

So much only to make sense of the notion that the body is "in" consciousness, even though this way of describing the matter is contrary to ordinary English usage, common sense, and current scientific dogma. (Fortunately, it *is* compatible with much of the thought in Oriental psychology and philosophy.) Once we assume that consciousness is already "out" of the body, and that the preponderating impression that we are "in" our bodies is the effect of certain average biological automatisms impinging themselves on the field of consciousness, then it is reasonable to assert that there are degrees of being "out"; that, in fact, there is a continuum of states which deviate markedly from the normal—and ultimately deceptive —experience of solidarity with the body.

At this point the reader may object: the notion of an OB continuum is inconsistent with the premise that consciousness is already categorically "out of" the body. For in that case one is either "in" or "out"; and there would seem to be no room for degrees of being "in" or "out." The inconsistency, however, seems to me to be more apparent than real. The sentence "X is either red or not red" does not exclude that "red" can refer to one of an indefinite number of shades of red. Even so, it might be more correct to say that the OB continuum refers to a continuum of appearances or experiences the subject has of being more or less out of the body, more or less identified with the body. However, this does not quite do justice to the facts; for, while the conscious subject may ultimately be "out" of his body, he normally *behaves* as if he were very much "in" it. It does not merely *appear* to him that he is "in" his body.

The notion of a continuum I propose to sketch in this article is based primarily on phenomenological data. And yet the importance of such a notion lies, I believe, in the fact that there are *also* logical and empirical grounds for asserting that the conscious subject both *is* and sometimes *behaves* as if out of the body. All this lends some credence to the paradoxical view that under normal conditions the average human subject *mistakenly* identifies himself with his body. In the words of Shankara (1947): "Man is in bondage because he mistakes what is non-Atman for his real Self. This is caused by ignorance.... Through ignorance man identifies the Atman (pure consciousness) with the body, taking the perishable for the real" (p. 53).

ON THE NOTION OF AN OB CONTINUUM

If there is truth to the hypothesis that the OB condition actually constitutes a continuum of states, then we should not be surprised if we found individuals reporting and behaving in such a way that disclosed a series of states which cluster around and blend by degrees into a more spectacular type of OBE which is the subject of paranormal research. In discussing what appears to me to be a *small sampling* of these states, there is no intention to obliterate the uniqueness of the type of OBE parapsychology has recently been focusing upon. One hopes that a study of the neighboring states will provide clues to a wider understanding of the basic OB phenomenon.

Traveling Clairvoyance and Hypnosis

The phenomenon of traveling clairvoyance supports the continuum hypothesis I am advancing. It seems to me to illustrate rather nicely the continuity between ESP and OBE. This phenomenon shows a kind of stretching out more consciously and explicitly into the public space of the extrasensory target. The subject will report feeling as if he were right on the scene of the events being clairvoyantly experienced; even sometimes the sense of having flown at high but finite velocities over great areas of landscape. The scene is "described as if seen from a particular point in space, and gives the impression that the clairvoyant is standing in the room and looking round exactly as a person materially present in the room would do" (Tyrrell, 1963, p. 132). The elusiveness and inconsistency of the experient's sense of location in this type of clairvoyant excursion is manifest in a remark of Harold Sherman's (1974): "I'm not conscious of being out of the body, but I *am* conscious of being at whatever point I am focusing my attention on. I'm just suddenly there." Is this an example of clairvoyance, of out-of-body experience, or of a distinct and third type of phenomenon? It seems simpler to assume that the three terms "clairvoyance," "traveling clairvoyance," and "out-of-body experience" denote three aspects, in varying degrees, of the same process.

Certain physical phenomena associated with the hypnotic condition suggest an overlap with OBE from a different point of view. Let us consider just two examples. Salter (1963) was able to induce deafness to gunshot occurring within five feet of a number of subjects, objectively indicated by a complete absence of rise in blood pressure. Barber (1970, pp. 140–44) in his review of the relevant studies, found that "suggestions of blindness given under a hypnotic experimental treatment are at times effective in eliminating an involuntary physiological response which normally follows visual stimulation, namely, alpha blocking on the EEG" (p. 142). These examples suggest that it makes sense to speak of a subject being out of the body, that is to say, *behaving* as if not present in the physical organism, at least with regard to the particular sense modalities in question. If, in fact, one were seeking objective criteria for defining the OB state—in addition, let's say, to demonstrations of ESP and indications of a distinctive OB spatial orientation—these examples provide an excellent type of objective or operational criterion.

Schizophrenic States

There are strong indications that schizophrenics often experience alterations in their body image.* They tend to disidentify themselves from their bodies, often to the degree that the outside observer encounters as body that seems inanimate, inaccessible, an entity of "flattened affect" (Lowen, 1967). This may very well represent a strategy of escape from a "reality" that has become intolerable (Laing, 1965). Or it might be, as some theorists hold, that the state of disidentification from the body is the consequence of a pathology of cognition, traceable perhaps to some malfunctioning in the reticular system (Chapman and McGhie, 1969). The schizophrenic, whose brain, according to this theory, is not doing its job of keeping consciousness focused on personal survival, is ovewhelmed by an unmanageable sea of impressions and accordingly struggles to shut off the machine, the mass of sensori-motor reflexes which keep the subject hooked on the offending stream of consciousness. Mediation of consciousness through the body gets to be too much for the schizophrenic; hence he does his best to quit and vacate the troublesome organism.

OBEs, especially when they occur spontaneously, can be read as a response to violent and intrusive assaults on the organism, accidents or operations, or extreme emotional stress; in short, a method of retreat, as with the overloaded or oppressed schizophrenic, from an intolerable reality. From this angle the OBE shows itself as a strategy of transcendence, the organism's spontaneous adaptation to disaster. The schizophrenic's distorted body image may be an expression of a peculiar aspect, phase, or stage of arrest in the adaptive OB process.

*Dr. Grosso's point is debatable. Two independent surveys have shown that distortion of body image is not a common feature of schizophrenia. (See A. Argyle's report "The Experience of Body-self Is Schizophrenia" in the *Arch. Neurol. Psychiat.* 35 [1936]: 1029–53, and S. Fisher's "Body Image and Psychopathology" in the *Arch. Gen. Psychiat.* 10 [1964]: 519–29.—ED.

If there is anything to this, medical science might profit by further investigation of the matter. The schizophrenic may turn out to be a person possessing mechanisms which permit a labile relationship between consciousness and the body. Symptom might be a source of healing. The schizophrenic may need to soar out of his body and explore, aided and encouraged by science, the vaster hinterlands of consciousness. The cured schizophrenic might be the soul aviator, the shaman (Silverman, 1967).

In some cases what the schizophrenic reports seems to be an OBE proper. "When I am ill I lose the sense of where I am. I feel 'I' can sit in a chair, and yet my body is hurtling out and somersaulting about three feet in front of me" (Pfeiffer, 1970, p. 55). This is an example of what in the literature is called autoscopy. The following is excerpted from a description of an experience of a patient's five days *in extremis;* the OBE signals the start of the consummation of and release from a period of concentrated torture. "It was not imagination—but something stronger. Mere imagination, however vivid, cannot transport a person tied down hand and foot in an insane asylum to set them free in some far place. I found I was standing somewhere on a pebbly beach at dawn . . ." (Wapnick, 1969, p. 61). In this case, the OBE was clearly functioning as part of the schizophrenic's healing process, and was instrumental in "setting [her] free."

Drug States

The linguistic phenomenology of psychedelic experience reflects alterations in body image—a theoretically unbiased way of describing OBE. "Getting high," "going on a trip," getting "spaced out," having one's "mind blown," etc., are expressions I would interpret along these lines. Even the more academic expression "transcendence," whose root meaning is "climb across or beyond," reflects an essentially *spatial* modification of experience.

The Varieties of Psychedelic Experience (Masters and Houston, 1966) contains a chapter, "Experiencing the Body and Body Image," in which the authors describe a number of effects which variously express modifications of normal sensori-motor identification with the body. Subjects report feeling their bodies shrink to minute or expand to cosmic dimensions, become ponderous or weightless, change into nonhuman animals or inanimate substances. In some cases, experients describe their bodies as dissolving into pure light or energy, even into a sense of being bodiless. In the literature of OBEs there are frequent reports of similar light and energy effects.

In primitive cultures, drugs (along with a number of other techniques) are utilized deliberately to induce the out-of-body state. The shaman is the specialist in the OBE. "Healer and psychopomp, the shaman is these because he commands the techniques of ecstasy—that is, because his soul can safely abandon his body and roam at vast distances . . . " (Eliade, 1964, p. 182). It is notable in this context that anthropologists who have experimented with *ayahuasca,* a drug used by South American shamans, report having OBEs (Harner, 1973). This suggests that the action of the drug in inducing the OBE is effective independently of cultural set and expectations.

The drug-influenced modifications of the subject's body image shade off imperceptibly into clearly experienced out-of-body states. There does not seem to be a sudden phenomenological leap between experiencing one's bodily self as glass, some rubbery substance, a tiger, a bird and, for example, a more explicitly out-of-body state such as Wasson (1961) describes, having participated in a Mazatec mushroom ceremony: ". . . as your body lies in the darkness, heavy as lead, your spirit seems to soar and leave the hut, and with the speed of thought to travel where it listeth, in time and space . . ." (pp. 156–57).

Drug-related alterations of body image which range from experiencing oneself as taller all the way to being bodiless illustrate the continuum thesis pretty nicely, and, I suspect, offer the most promising field for the experimental induction of the OB effect.

Meditative States

My point in citing what I have termed OBE-facilitative states is not to set out evidence for causal relations, which, of course, is a matter for empirical investigation. Rather, I am concerned with the concept of out-of-body experience and wish to show that states, or modes of behavior, which sometimes favor the occurrence of OBEs *already* involve conditions in which the experient begins to get loose from his physical organism. The variety of changes in body image experienced by users of psychedelics is a case in point. The assumption is that it makes sense to speak of there being degrees of out-of-body experience. I have also hypothesized a causal mechanism whereby changes happen in the OB continuum: namely, the disruption, voluntary or involuntary, of the normal functioning of the sensori-motor reflex by which consciousness remains focused upon the plane of life.

Let the meditative state serve as a further example. The meditator radically alters his mode of attending to the world, deautomatizes his consciousness (Deikman, 1966); the quantity of sensory input is reduced and concentrated. The disruption of the normal sensory input results in a disruption of the normal motor output. The meditator just sits, or gets into a posture which is maintained, a kind of voluntary catatonia. An essential feature of the meditative process is duration. One does not meditate for a few seconds. According to Bergson (1960), it is this duration, or qualitative intensification of consciousness, through which the self reflects upon itself and thus enters into the "depths" of the mind. What this spatial metaphor would signify for Bergson is detachment from the plane of life, from immediate sensation which reflects the spatial properties of the extended world. The meditator, by withdrawing into himself—that is, into the duration of mind—*ipso facto* is withdrawing from the world of physically extended objects of which his own body is one of the most intimate and peculiar. On this view, consciousness is perpetually poised between an outward spatial orientation and duration; any increase in the orientation toward duration, or internal states, entails an orientation out of the body.

The following is an example of the meditative process leading to an OBE. The account is from my own collection of accounts of OBEs. The subjects are a young woman who meditates regularly and her husband, a student of psychology who is highly critical and skeptical with regard to his wife's psychic capers. The description is of the first in a series of three OBEs. Mrs. C. writes:

My husband and I were sitting in the living room. I was meditating on the floor, sitting in a modified yoga posture. Jack, my husband, was lying on the couch, watching. The room was dark except for a light on in the foyer, which was streaming in. The object used in the meditation was a gold ring. I had been contemplating it for some time, just feeling in my mind's eye its color, texture, and great personal value.

It was then that I began to feel a sort of discomfort in my feet and ankles. I wanted to move them, but for some reason couldn't. I then proceeded to experience a sense of complete mental uplift. I could no longer feel my body; it was as if it was not there. The sensation was that I had no body and was completely enveloped in my mind.

Then suddenly I was above my body looking down. I saw myself sitting there on the floor. I saw my knees, then my thighs, then my chest and shoulders. I was so comfortable at the time that I was beyond wondering what was happening to me. I began to hear some grunting in the room, at which time my experience was interrupted.

Mr. C. writes the following account:

I saw my wife's face begin to elongate, and then a vapor-like substance began to rise above her, taking on the resemblance of the shape of her face and shoulders. I was unable to speak, only to make noises [the grunting which eventually interrupted Mrs. C.'s experience]. I wanted to stop her but was too stunned to move. Then as this substance rose higher, very slowly, I saw a cord-like shiny or luminous substance that was connected between the vapor and the back of her neck. It was at this time that I started to try verbally to stop it, or her, but I could only make nonsense noises. It then stopped almost as spontaneously as it began. The whole occurrence took only about fifteen or twenty seconds, but it was enough time to scare the hell out of me.

I have quoted these reports at length because they both seem highly graphic and reasonably objective, but more importantly because they apparently corroborate each other. In addition, Mrs. C.'s description of the process of her OBE seems to illustrate the thesis of degrees or stages of the experience I am arguing for. There are a number of identifiable stages in her OBE. First, there is the stage of "contemplating," "just feeling." Then there is the first noticeable physiological effect, a discomfort in the feet and ankles. This is followed by a sense of "mental uplift," then a sense of having no body and being enveloped in the mind. Finally, Mrs. C. notes her unique OB spatial orientation.

Reflective States

Similar to meditation, but more characteristic of Western philosophic method, is a reflective process that entails a voluntary effort, a peculiar mental gesture whose purpose it would seem is to inhibit the sensori-motor reflex. What lies behind this gesture is the intent to achieve a certain attitude, perspective, or mode of awareness which is free from habit, attachment to immediate sensation, and compulsion. Psychosynthesis and the school of Gurdjieff call it "disidentification." Plato spoke of "loosing and separating" the soul from the body; Patanjali, in the Yoga Sutras, of separating the seer from the seen; Husserl and the phenomenologists of the *epoche,* reduction, or suspension of the natural standpoint. The esthetic attitude has a name for this inner gesture, "psychical distance," or becoming "disinterested." All these have as their effect the severence of consciousness from absorption and entanglement in the "world" viewed as a biologically useful construction of reality. In the process of reflection, consciousness "bends back" upon itself, away from the body and its immediate concerns. While in the classic OBE the conscious self appears to be functioning outside the organism, in the reflective process the self lets go from within the organism, rehearsing as it were for the departure. It is probable that many spontaneous OBEs are disorienting and frightening for lack of reflective preparation. Exercises in this type of reflection should, I believe, be incorporated into procedures for the experimental induction of OBE.

According to Green (1973, p. 13), there is a class of OBE which appears to be induced by reflections of a philosophic nature, particularly on the problem of personal identity. An experience of mine will serve as an illustration. An oddity is that I was dreaming while reflecting on my personal identity; at that time I was a graduate student in philosophy, without any awareness of or interest in OBEs or psychic phenomena. In retrospect it looks like a case of incipient "whirlwind projection," to use the apt expression of Yram (1965). My immediate response of panic terminated the experience rather abruptly.

March 3, 1966

In my dream it seems I am talking to myself, musing on the problem of my personal identity, forming phrases, expressing thoughts to myself of the order "*I* am, *I* etc. . . ." I reflect to myself that the *I* might very well be superfluous, a false way of describing the facts of consciousness—as, for example, Sartre would say: not *I* plus the predicate but an impersonal grammatical construction more accurately describes conscious phenomena. At any rate, while musing so in my dream I decide to cut out the *I*; I suppress it from the stream of consciousness. Then I heard a noise, a sucking sound, like water swirling down a drain, and a powerful force like an icy wind took hold of me round the neck and began to draw me into itself. Feeling quite helpless I resisted this force and woke up in a panic, my heart pounding.

Dream States

Let us assume for a moment that people dreamed and reported their dreams to others only about as frequently as people have OBEs. There would probably be no single word to describe the experience of dreaming due to its rarity. One might describe what we call dreaming as being out of the body. After all, what would the experient report but that he was lying in bed, enjoying a bit of refreshing oblivion, when suddenly he experienced himself quite other than where he knew his body was; flying through the sky, battling with monsters, dallying with strange lovers. These could accurately be described as out-of-body experiences. Yet all of us in fact have these "out-of-body" experiences whenever we sleep. The habitual nature of the phenomenon has veiled its inexplicable strangeness. We call it "dreaming" and banish it to metaphysical nullity. It was, we say, "only" a dream.

But how do dreams differ from OBEs? One distinguishing feature would seem to be the degree of self-awareness and autonomy the OBEer claims to possess. Second, some, though by no means all, OBEs seem to occur in the normal, public space-time world; and this seems to be confirmed occasionally by displays of paranormally acquired information. These differences, however, begin to break down under closer scrutiny. With regard to the first point, it sometimes happens that dreams are experienced with a peculiar lucidity, a quality of self-awareness, which provides the dreamer with an enlarged capacity for autonomy over his dream environment—certainly not much less than the autonomy the average OBEer reports being able to enjoy.* Further, the condition of lucidity in dreams is said by some (e.g., Green, 1968) to be an important factor in producing the classic OB effect. At the phenomenological level this supports the notion of a continuum between dream states and OBEs—with lucidity, or the quality of self-awareness, emerging as the factor linking the two states.

As for the second point, dreams are indeed generally oriented toward the private world-space of the dreamer. But the contrast with OBEs is by no means so rigid or absolute. OBEs, for example, often reveal a spatial orientation which is a curious mixture of private and public characteristics.

*Dr. Grosso is a little obscure here. A "lucid dream" is simply defined as any one in which the subject realizes that he is dreaming. —ED.

Furthermore, just as the OBE *sometimes* shows veridical contact with public space, the dreamer, perhaps in a more distorted and symbolic fashion, on occasion demonstrates an ability to contact public space and events by means of telepathy or precognition. In fact, Stevenson (1970) found that in the 125 precognitive dreams he analyzed only 13.5 percent involved symbols; as for the rest, the manifest content of the dream came true. In the same study Stevenson found that 45 percent of the precognitive dreams were experienced as unusually vivid. What this shows is that the quality of reality is characteristic of some dreams—which renders them somewhat closer on the spectrum to the OB experience, which is often described as qualitatively indistinguishable from "reality." My aim is not to equate the average dream with the more striking type of OBE. I do think, however, that we are dealing with a group of interrelated phenomena which crisscross and overlap, and which derive from a fundamentally similar mechanism: the suspension of the sensori-motor reflex. The manner or state in which this suspension takes place—sleep, accident, illness, drugs, meditation—would account for the great variety of conditions in which the OBE articulates and manifests itself.

CONCLUDING THOUGHTS

The foregoing was intended to give some examples of states or conditions of consciousness which of themselves *already* and in *various ways* show characteristics which can be construed as "out of body." I tried to confine myself to examples of conditions which are known to be sometimes related to the sort of OBE studied by parapsychologists. (Other types of experience could be used to carry out the analysis—for example, relaxed and ecstatic states.) The picture that begins to emerge is that the ostensibly paranormal OB condition is an extreme manifestation of a process which is evinced in a variety of conditions of human experience, normal and abnormal as well as paranormal. An exercise of deliberate disidentification with regard to the body is very different from a hypnotized subject who (in measurable objective terms) does not hear a gun fired next to his head. Yet each example in its own way illustrates a profound alteration of the conscious subject's relationship to his bodily organism. Unless I am wrong, the utter normality of out-of-body experience is established in the above cursory analysis of dreams. Or, if in fact dreams were not such a common experience, we would be obliged to consider them as no less paranormal than OBEs. Dreams thus demonstrate the continuity between the paranormal OBE and normal waking life. In a similar vein, the phenomenon of traveling clairvoyance demonstrates the continuity between OBE and ESP.

If there is substance to the notion of a continuum of OB states, evidence in support of it should continue to show itself on that band of the continuum constituted by the OBE proper. Do we in fact observe *degrees* of being out of the body in case of the ostensibly paranormal OBE? The evidence is clearly inconsistent. The inconsistency, however, argues in favor of the hypothesis I am advancing. Some subjects report finding themselves in a duplicate body, exact even to the touch; at the other end of the spectrum the experience is one of complete disembodied being. Then there is a great variety of intermediary states in which one experiences a bevy of odd forms of embodiment, from some that resemble the human corporeal shape to increasingly abstract modes of self-representation, points of light, et cetera. The "material" form might best be described as an ideoplastic appendage of the conscious subject engaged in an OB excursion. The descriptions of the varieties of embodiment are reminiscent of the alterations of body image suffered by schizophrenics and users of psychedelics. These parallels suggest that we are dealing with varieties of a single *type* of phenomenon.

Having an OBE then does not imply a single identifiable characteristic; rather, that the customary constraints of certain properties of normal bodily existence are noticeably attenuated. First to go is the normal sense of mass; the subject is, again in varying degrees, released from the shackles of gravity. From this it follows that there are varying degrees in the sense of expanded motility experienced by the subject. Examples range from lumbering about within a few feet of the physical organism to what seems like instantaneous transport over large distances. Clearly, some subjects experience themselves as *more* out of their bodies, that is, *freer* from the causal properties and limits of their customary earthbound frame. There is another example of this variability in the ideoplastic appendage. Some subjects are able to experience passage through what would normally be a physical barrier, ceilings, windows, etc. Others experience blockage in comparable situations. As far as the phenomenology of OBE is concerned, the latter are clearly *less* out of their bodies than the former: that is to say, in their experience the ability to defy the usual laws of physical existence is rather less extensive than that of the OB travelers more free from the body.

Finally, there is the fact that there seem to be degrees of voluntary control over what happens during an OBE. It is as though there is a sort of biomagnetic field surrounding the physical organism which automatically tends to attract the temporary escapee from the body back into the orbit of biological existence. For the most part the attracting force seems to operate via the subconscious of the subject. In some cases, however, the subject, thanks to his voluntary efforts, is able to prolong and explore the experience. Some habitual OB experients speak as though a type of OB motor control can be learned. And degrees of such voluntary control imply degrees of being out of and free from the body.

REFERENCES

Barber, T.X. *LSD, Marihuana, Yoga and Hypnosis.* Chicago: Aldine, 1970.

Bergson, H. *Time and Free Will.* New York: Harper Torchbooks, 1960.

Chapman, J., and A. McGhie, "Disorders of Attention

and Perception in Early Schizophrenia." In A. H. Buss and E. H. Buss (eds.), *Theories of Schizophrenia.* New York: Atherton, 1969, pp. 47–74.

Deikman, A. J. "Deautomatization and the Mystic Experience." *Psychiatry,* 29 (1966): 324–38.

Ducasse, C. J. *A Critical Examination of the Belief in a Life after Death.* Springfield, Ill.: Thomas, 1961.

Eliade, M. *Shamanism: Archaic Techniques of Ecstasy.* Princeton: Princeton University Press, 1964.

Gill, M. M., and Brenman, M. *Hypnosis and Related States.* New York: International Universities Press, 1959.

Green, C. E. *Lucid Dreams.* London: Hamish Hamilton, 1968.

————. *Out-of-the-Body Experiences.* New York: Ballantine Books, 1973.

Harner, M. *Hallucinogens and Shamanism.* New York: Oxford University Press, 1973.

Honorton, C. "State of Awareness Factors in Psi Activation." *Journal of the American Society for Psychical Research.* 68 (1974): 246–56.

Honorton, C., and Krippner, S. Hypnosis and ESP performance: A Review of the Experimental Literature." *Journal of the American Society for Psychical Research,* 63 (1969): 214–52.

Laing, R. D. *The Divided Self.* Baltimore: Pelican Books, 1965.

Lowen, A. *The Betrayal of the Body.* New York: Collier Books, 1967.

Masters, R. E. L., and Houston, J. *The Varieties of Psychedelic Experience.* New York: Delta, 1966.

Pfeiffer, C. C. *The Schizophrenias: Yours and Mine.* New York: Pyramid Books, 1970.

Salter, A. *What Is Hypnosis?* New York: Citadel Press, 1963.

Shankara. *Crest-Jewel of Discrimination.* Trans. by Swami Prabhavananda and C. Isherwood. New York: Mentor Books, 1947.

Sherman, H. "Interview: Harold Sherman," by J. G. Bolen. *Psychic,* February, 1974.

Silverman, J. "Shamans and Acute Schizophrenia." *American Anthropologist,* 69 (1967): 21–31.

Stevenson, I. "Precognition of Disasters." *Journal of the American Society for Psychical Research,* 64 (1970): 187–210.

Tyrrell, G. N. M. *Apparitions.* New York: Collier Books, 1963.

Ullman, M., and Krippner, S., with Vaughan, A. *Dream Telepathy.* New York: Macmillan, 1973.

Wapnick, K. "Mysticism and Schizophrenia." *Journal of Transpersonal Psychology,* 1 (1969): 49–67.

Wasson, G. "The Hallucinogenic Fungi of Mexico: An Inquiry into the Religious Ideas among Primitive Peoples." *Botanical Museum Leaflet.* Cambridge: Harvard University Press, 19 (1961): 156–57.

White, R. A. "A Comparison of Old and New Methods of Response to Targets in ESP Experiments." *Journal of the American Society for Psychical Research,* 58 (1964): 21–56.

Yram (pseudonym). *Practical Astral Projection.* New York: Samuel Weiser, 1965.

II. LABORATORY INVESTIGATIONS

Introduction:
Experimental Studies

D. SCOTT ROGO

J. B. Rhine stirred up one of the most heated controversies in contemporary psychology when his book *Extra-sensory Perception* was published in 1934. Since 1927 Rhine and his wife, Louisa, had been relentlessly studying ESP and testing subjects for this elusive faculty at the Psychology Department of Duke University, where Rhine taught. By 1934 Rhine felt that he had solid evidence substantiating the existence of an extrasensory faculty in man, and he published his findings in a 240-page book complete with test results, charts, graphs, arguments, and theories. A year later the Duke University Parapsychology Laboratory became an autonomous institute at the university. Psychology would never be the same again.

The 1930s not only brought about a revolution in psychology, which was laboring in the throes of Watsonian behaviorism at the time, but in parapsychology as well. After Rhine's breakthrough proved that the psychological establishment could be forced to confront the ESP issue, psychical researchers all but gave up their interest in collecting anecdotal reports of ESP, chasing mediums, and sleeping in haunted houses. "Experimentalism" was now the magic word and parapsychologists, as well as many psychologists, became absorbed in the hope that they could experimentally demonstrate ESP to the satisfaction of the scientific community. To be sure, ESP testing dated back to the 1880s, but now experimentalism became *the* most pursued aspect of parapsychology. And as a matter of fact, it still is.

A phenomenon so provocative as the OBE could not escape the critical eyes of the experimentalists for long. As far back as the 1860s, scholars and scientists had been actively attempting to demonstrate the reality of an OBE-like phenomenon. Their rough attempts to critically evaluate these phenomena are very similar to the experiments contemporary parapsychologists have designed in recent years.

The mesmerists were the first investigators to take the OBE seriously. In the 1770s, a Swiss physician named Franz Anton Mesmer discovered that he could entrance his patients by passing his hands or magnets over them. It was not until the 1840s that James Braid, an English doctor, discovered that the trance was caused purely by suggestion. Mesmerism became the rage—and the scourge—of Europe. Mesmerists who claimed that they could heal and cure disease abounded, even though a French commission condemned the practice as worthless in 1784. Nonetheless, the art spread and flourished in every country of Europe.

The mesmerists scandalized the scientific establishment of its day by making several further sensational claims. Chief among these were that the entranced subject "may perceive the past and the future through an inner sense of his" (Mesmer, 1770). They also claimed, among other things, that their subjects could read minds, diagnose the illnesses of people brought to them, predict the future, and report accurately about activities taking place miles away. It was as though the mesmeric subject could literally "see" scenes taking place hundreds of miles distant. This phenomenon was called "traveling clairvoyance": the ability of the subject to "send" his mind to a distant location and report back what he saw there. The mesmeric concept of traveling clairvoyance is very similar to what was eventually called the out-of-body experience and, in fact, in later literature the terms were often used interchangeably. Traveling clairvoyance was such a commonly demonstrated feat during the nineteenth century that Sir William Barrett, one of the first parapsychologists and a founder of the Society for Psychical Research, reported on the phenomenon in 1879 when he delivered a paper on ESP before the British Association for the Advancement of Science. (Barrett's paper nearly caused a scandal, though, and the Association refused to publish it.)

The reports of traveling clairvoyance that have come down to us from the nineteenth century consist of an assorted lot of tales, anecdotal cases, and experimental reports. Yet we can see in these reports the beginnings of scientific interest in the OBE. For example, the following dates back to the mid-1800s (Smith, 1973), and was reported by a Scottish savant, Professor William Gregory. Gregory, while visiting a friend who lived outside Edinburgh, met a lady there who, when mesmerized, seemed endowed with extraordinary ESP abilities. A demonstration was immediately scheduled for the visiting professor. Gregory, eager to test the subject's ability, asked her to "visit" his son, who lived in a town about twenty miles away, and tell what he was doing. As Gregory reported:

She soon found him, and described him accurately, being much interested in a boy she saw playing in a field outside a small garden in which the cottage stood. It was some distance from town, on a rising ground. The boy was playing with a dog. I knew there was a dog, but had no idea of what kind, so I asked her. She said it was a large but young Newfoundland, black with one or two white spots. It was very fond of the boy and played with him.

"Oh," she cried suddenly, "it has jumped up and knocked off his cap." She saw in the garden a gentleman reading a book and looking on [everything she said about him was correct]. . . . Being asked to enter the cottage, she did so and described the sitting room. In the kitchen she saw a young maidservant preparing dinner, for which meal a leg of mutton was roasting at the fire, yet not quite ready. . . . On looking again for the boy, she saw him playing with the dog in front of the door, while the gentleman stood on the porch and looked on. Then she saw the boy run upstairs to the kitchen, which she observed with surprise was on the upper floor of the cottage, and receive something to eat from the servant, she thought a potato.

Professor Gregory made detailed notes recording everything the subject had told him and was later able to verify the accuracy of her remarks by contacting his son's household. The psychic had made only one slight error. The boy had been given a biscuit, not a potato.

Now, you might ask, did Professor Gregory's subject undergo an OBE or did she simply use ESP? (From here on I shall use the term "simple ESP" to denote any form of ESP perception in which the subject has no sensation of leaving the body or projecting the mind.) It is hard to tell. However, there are some indications in Gregory's report that the subject was demonstrating something more than ESP. Those of us who have studied ESP and have tested subjects for the ability have often seen how really imprecise ESP impressions are. ESP is rarely exact or even accurate. Errors and distortion of the ESP message are commonplace; the message is often fragmented, symbolized, or obscured; and usually the subject perceives only part of the total scene or idea we are sending to him. Yet none of these problems hampered this lady's extraordinary performance. She seemed to "see" the scene—exactly and unmistakably—as though she were actually physically present and witnessing what was taking place. In other words, she seemed to be employing a faculty akin to physical sight, and did not seem to be relying on purely mental impressions. Now, we have to ask ourselves, does clairvoyance vision follow the same principles that physical sight does? This is a problem I shall revert to when I discuss the OBE research of Dr. Karlis Osis of the American Society for Psychical Research. But for now, let me say only that, at face value, some cases of traveling clairvoyance indicate a psychic process at work that is much more concise and accurate than ESP has ever been shown to be.

However, we should keep in mind that clairvoyance and the OBE might be two aspects of the same phenomenon. The existence of one might very well imply the existence of the other. J. B. Rhine devoted a lengthy section of his *Extrasensory Perception* to theories about ESP and suggested that when a person is using clairvoyance some element of his mind actually *leaves the body,* latches on to the information it is looking for, and then draws it back into the body and brain (Rhine, 1934). This theory posits a process very similar to the concept of an OBE. Rhine's theory suggests that an element of the mind can function independently of the body, while the OBE suggests that the mind, as an entity, can separate from the body. Rhine's theory is crucial to understanding the relationship between ESP and the OBE, and a critical examination of it has been made by K. Ramakrishna Rao (1966).

According to Rao, Rhine's theory "rests on two assumptions: (1) that some agency of mind which can function to some extent independently of the physical world is operative in ESP, and (2) that this agency has the capacity to 'go out' to meet the object which is outside the organism it occupies." Rao continues:

According to Rhine, psi phenomena suggest the existence of mind that under certain circumstances and to some extent can function independently of the physical limitations of the material body. Relation to space has been considered an invariable characteristic of physical operations. All our perceptual experiences, as far as they relate to the material world, are organized into the framework of space. But with regard to ESP, space apparently has no influence, and the inverse square laws, etc., are inapplicable to it, for no reliable relation has been found between the distance of the percipient from the target or agent and the success or failure of the percipient's calls in ESP tests. In view of this strange phenomenon and of the evidence of precognition, unknown to the physical world, Rhine goes on to suggest, there might well be some other energy, one peculiar to mind, which is radically different from material energies. He considers that the source of these distinctive results must be sought in the nature of the mind capable of such effects. . . .

Rhine goes on to make another important suggestion. He says it appears that the mind "goes out" to perceive extrasensorially. It is not that the mind receives the different patterns of energy emanating from the objects in order to interpret them, but that the mind of the percipient takes the initiative in ESP. Thus the mind's relative independence of the material universe consists in this appearance of mental causality, which is supported by the observation that space and time have shown no limiting effect on psi ability.

I see little difference between Rhine's concept and that of an OBE. In fact, Rhine seems to be saying that clairvoyance is a limited sort of OBE. (Rhine himself, though, would never draw this conclusion from his theory. He has long argued that OBE research is not a fruitful area of parapsychology to explore and that, at this time, we are in no position to discover experimentally the nature of the phenomenon [Rhine, 1974].) Indeed, a few parapsychologists have even tested to see whether the OBE could be used as a royal road to ESP. For instance, Dr. John Palmer carried out just such a project while working at the division of parapsychology at the University of Virginia. Dr. Palmer was not interested in proving whether or not the OBE represented the actual separation of the mind from the body; instead he wanted to determine what relationship the OBE had to ESP. He therefore set about to induce the feeling of being out-of-the-body in several unselected subjects and then tested them for ESP while they were in this state. Although his results were equivocable, Palmer's approach to the OBE is interesting. He approached it not as an objective phenomenon in itself, but to see if it were a psi-conducive *state of mind.* * It made little difference to Palmer whether the OBE was objectively real or only subjectively convincing to the subject.

The evidence for the existence of traveling clairvoyance does not rest solely on anecdotal accounts. Even the first parapsychologists attempted to demonstrate experimentally the existence of the phenomenon. The pioneering French psychiatrist Pierre Janet became fascinated with the phenomenon when he discovered a young psychic, whom he called Leonie in his reports. On several occasions he put her into a trance and then "sent" her to distant locations to test the accuracy of her clairvoyant faculties. As the Nobel prize-winning physiologist Charles Richet reports (1905):

One day Pierre Janet set her "travelling." In her hypnotic sleep she went to Paris to see me and M. Gibert who had left for Paris. On a sudden [*sic*] she said, "It is burning." P. Janet tried to calm her, she returned to sleep, but soon awoke again saying, "But M. Janet, I assure you that it is burning."

*A psi-conducive state is any state of mind in which ESP will occur more readily than when the subject is in a normal state of awareness. A few psi-conducive states that have been tentatively identified are hypnosis, sensory isolation, dreaming, and muscular relaxation (Braud, 1975).

In fact, my laboratory in the Rue Vauquelin caught fire at six that morning . . . and was burnt out.

On rare occasions not only could mesmerized subjects correctly report on distant scenes, but sometimes the people whom they visited either saw their apparitions or somehow sensed that something peculiar was going on. For example, Dr. Backmann, a Swedish doctor, discovered a subject named Alma L. with whom he carried out several experiments in the 1890s, sometimes supervised by officials from the S.P.R. As he reported in the *Annals of Psychical Science* in 1892, on one occasion he sent his subject to Stockholm to spy upon a friend of his. Alma L. was able to describe the man and his room precisely. Backmann then ordered his subject first to try and move some keys that she had seen on a table in his friend's room and then proceed to touch the man on the shoulder. Sometime later Backmann's friend, still unaware that he had been surreptitiously subjected to the psychic experiment, independently reported to Backmann about a strange experience he had recently undergone. He told the doctor that a few days earlier he had been overcome by a strange feeling. His mind, he said, kept focusing on some keys that he had placed on a table next to him. Shortly after, he had seen an apparition in his room. The time and date of these experiences precisely matched the time that Backmann had sent his subject to spy upon him (Richet, 1905).

There are two ways we can explain this case. Either Backmann's mesmerized subject physically projected some element of her mind to his friend, who was able to perceive her presence; or a perfect reciprocal ESP rapport formed between Backmann, his friend, and Alma L. at the exact time of the experiment.

Proving the existence of the OBE by requiring experimental subjects to exhibit ESP while in the state has been the basic approach parapsychologists have used to substantiate the reality of the phenomenon. However, there were some attempts *physically* to detect and demonstrate the existence of the OBE during these early years of psychical research. In France, researchers tried to see if out-of-body travelers could move physical objects, and they claimed considerable success. They also attempted to photograph the out-of-body apparition and apparently succeeded with one subject. It should also be noted that attempts to photograph the apparitions of OBE travelers were also carried out by at least one enterprising researcher in Great Britain. W. T. Stead, one of England's most esteemed journalists, devoted considerable time to psychical research and Spiritualism. Stead wanted to see if he could photograph the apparition of a friend who claimed that she could OB to his home at will. This friend made several prescheduled attempts to OB to the journalist's home, during which times Stead photographed the target room. He hoped to obtain at least some evidence that his friend was physically present. All attempts, sad to say, failed (Stead, 1891–1892).

Despite these few efforts to detect the OBE physically, parapsychologists have preferred to demonstrate the authenticity of the experience by giving their subjects ESP tasks to perform while out-of-the-body. Old-fashioned traveling clairvoyance-type experiments have been run fairly recently by parapsychologists. One of the most celebrated of these projects utilized the talents of Eileen Garrett, a noted psychic who later founded and administered the Parapsychology Foundation. (The Foundation was started in 1953 as an educational institute and to this day is one of the principal grant-giving agencies in the field.)

The experiment was conducted from San Diego, California, by Dr. Anita Muhl. Mrs. Garrett's task was to OB herself to the home of Dr. D. Svensen, chief of the Division of Mental Health in Reykjavik, Iceland.* Svensen had been advised of the time and date of the experiment in advance.

At the time the experiment was scheduled to begin, Mrs. Garrett sat back in a chair in Dr. Muhl's apartments and verbally described her visions and sensations as she traveled to Iceland. Her comments were recorded verbatim by Dr.

*In the original reports, the locations of the experiment were disguised and it was reported that the test was run between New York and Newfoundland.

Muhl and a secretary. At first the psychic described how she entered Svensen's home, viewed his garden and the nearby sea, and then focused in on Dr. Svensen. (Later Dr. Svenson claimed that he had "sensed" Mrs. Garrett's presence at this moment.) She described the objects Svensen had set up on a table and noticed that he was wearing a bandage around his head. After making these casual observations, she described how Svensen went to a bookshelf, took down a book about Einstein and relativity, and began reading a paragraph from it.

The entire experiment lasted a mere fifteen minutes. The transcript of the session was sent to Dr. Svensen, who immediately cabled Dr. Muhl advising her that he had indeed sustained a head injury that had required bandaging. The San Diego psychologist also received a letter from her Icelandic colleague a few days later verifying the accuracy of Mrs. Garrett's out-of-body vision and report (Angoff, 1974).

Again, one might ask, OBE or ESP? It is difficult to tell simply from Dr. Muhl's report. Mrs. Garrett could have obtained all her information through clairvoyance and there is little evidence that she actually "traveled" to Iceland. Since Dr. Svensen knew that the experiment was planned for that day, the fact that he sensed Mrs. Garrett's presence means very little. On the other hand, Mrs. Garrett's experience seems much more OBE-like when we take a look at the psychic's own introspective account of her inner feelings as she mentally traveled to Reykjavik. As she explained about the Muhl-Svensen experiment in her *My Life as a Search for the Meaning of Mediumship* (1939):

What is not generally accepted by science, but which I nevertheless know to be true, is that everyone has a double of finer substance than the physical body; it is referred to either as the astral or as the etheric body by most scientists. This is not to be confused with the *surround* which remains in position enveloping the human body, while the double can be projected. It is by means of this *double* that either accidental or conscious projection is accomplished; now in these experiments I was doing conscious projection, and I know from my own experience that when I project this *double* I do so from the center of my chest above the breasts. From the moment I begin to project, I am aware at this point of a pull, accompanied by a fluttering, which causes the heart to palpitate, and the breathing to speed up, accompanied also, if the projection is a long one, by a slight choking in the larynx and a heady sensation. As long as the projection continues, I remain aware of these sensations taking place in my physical body. While I am in a state of projection, the *double* is apparently able to use the normal activity of all five senses which work in my physical body. For example, I may be sitting in a drawing room on a snowy day and yet be able in projection to reach a place where the summer is at that moment full blown; in that instant, I can register with all my five physical senses the sight of the flowers, and the seas, I can smell the scent of blossoms and the tang of ocean spray, and hear the birds sing and the waves beat against the shore. Strange to say, I never forget the smallest detail of any such experience which has come to me through conscious projection, though in ordinary daily living I can be quite forgetful and memories may grow dim.

The process Mrs. Garrett described does not seem to be akin to ESP as we know it, but indicates a physical or physiological process. Mrs. Garrett's introspective report is doubly intriguing, since she was also gifted with ESP. She might therefore have been in a perfect position to judge the difference between simple ESP and ESP-projection.

Today in the 1970s, the old concept of traveling clairvoyance is once again being studied. Two physicists at the Stanford Research Institute (S.R.I.) in Menlo Park, California—Russell Targ and Harold Puthoff—are now experimenting with a procedure they call "remote viewing." This is almost identical to the older practice of traveling clairvoyance. The experimental subject is seated in an S.R.I. room and is instructed to "home in" on a distant location to which a second experimenter has driven. The subject is asked to envision the locale and report his impressions to the experimenter. Several sessions are run, and then the participant's visions (mentation reports) along with descriptions and/or photographs of the target sites are given to independent judges. They, in turn, try to guess which mentation report is supposedly describing which locale description.

The results of the S.R.I. work have been extremely promising. At first Targ and Puthoff worked with two psychics, Ingo Swann and Pat Price, who were both proficient OBE subjects. Both men reported the experience of traveling mentally to the distant sites during the remote viewing sessions. This suggests a process akin to the OBE. Both subjects were able to see the distant locales succinctly and oftentimes with amazing accuracy. Swann, for instance, often sketched out highly accurate diagrams of the target locations. Targ and Puthoff also noted that, on some occasions, remote viewing subjects actually described aspects of the physical terrain that the second experimenter, stationed at the site, could not see from where he was positioned. If, for example, the experimenter were standing in front of a house, he might not see a tree *behind* the house, which was blocked from his view. But the experimental subject might well report it. So telepathy between the experimenter and the subject cannot account for the S.R.I. results (Puthoff and Targ, 1976).

The next stage in the remote viewing work was even more enlightening. Targ and Puthoff discovered that unselected subjects, such as casual visitors to the lab, also did extremely well on remote viewing trials. In other words, they discovered that remote viewing was not a talent possessed by only a few gifted psychics. It seemed to be a faculty possessed in varying degrees by a large segment of the normal population. One subject, Helga Hammid, was even tested for "precognitive remote viewing." For these trials she would be asked to describe locales that experimenters would later select and drive to *after* the experimental session. Her performance was consistently accurate (Puthoff and Targ, 1975). Of course, precognitive remote viewing is even further afield from the concept of a discrete OBE than is clairvoyant remote viewing. But perhaps we should keep in mind what Dr. Grosso said in his paper on the possible existence of an OBE continuum (see chapter 3). As he suggests:

The phenomenon of traveling clairvoyance supports the continuum hypothesis I am advancing. It seems to illustrate rather nicely the continuity between ESP and OBE. This phenomenon shows a kind of stretching out more consciously and explicitly into the public space of the extrasensory target. . . . It seems simpler to assume that the three terms "clairvoyance," "traveling clairvoyance," and "out-of-body experience" denote three aspects, in varying degrees, of the same process.

Although Targ and Puthoff are recording phenomenal success with their remote viewing techniques, replication attempts by independent investigators have not fared so well. E. A. Rauscher of the Lawrence Berkeley Laboratory, along with J. Sarfatti of the Physics Consciousness Research Group and S. P. Sirag of the Institute for the Study of Consciousness, attempted to replicate the S.R.I. work and achieved only chance results. A few subjects did, however, give striking descriptions of the target locales, but the collective performance of the entire group of subjects tested was not statistically significant (Rauscher, et al., 1975). Another replication was essayed by a group of parapsychology students at the University of California, Santa Barbara. Again, the results were insignificant (Allen, Green, et al., 1975). On the other hand, at least one replication attempt using precognitive remote viewing procedures has been extremely successful (Bisaha, 1976).

Since remote viewing research is one of parapsychology's most recent trends, many more replication studies are in progress at the present time. Only time will tell how successful they may be. But so far, few researchers have been able to procure the consistent level of success that Targ and Puthoff have been reporting.

Laboratory research into more classical OBE-type experiences did not become a part of experimental parapsychology until the 1960s when Dr. Charles Tart, first working at the University of Virginia and later at the University of California at Davis, turned his attention to the phenomenon. Tart's experiments constituted a breakthrough in OBE research, although his general approach was not novel. He merely wanted to see if an OBE subject could float up above his or her body, look onto a shelf placed high on the wall, and read off a series of numbers laid out on it. This is, of course, a typical ESP task. But Tart was the first parapsychologist to monitor the OBE psychophysiologically. Why was this breakthrough so long in coming, you might ask?

It was only in the 1950s that researchers at the University of Chicago discovered that dreaming has consistent physiological correlates. For example, Dr. Nathaniel Kleitman discovered that the eyes dart back and forth rapidly when we begin to dream. Furthermore, heightened electrical activity in the brain accompanies these rapid eye movements (Aserinsky and Kleitman, 1953). Because of this research, the study of sleep, dreaming, and consciousness took a giant step forward. Psychologists had now discovered that different states of mental awareness could be studied objectively. Of course, the study of psychophysiology stretches back further than the Chicago research. But the 1950s heralded a major breakthrough in the study of psychophysiological states.

An experimenter can adduce the brain state of his subject by monitoring him with an electroencephalograph, which keeps continual track of the electrical output of the brain. Sleep, dreaming, and waking all produce semiconsistent brain-wave patterns. For his OBE research, Tart monitored his subjects in the same way one would monitor a sleeping subject. Electrodes, which led to the EEG and other apparatus, were attached to their scalps. Tart was able to work with two subjects who claimed control over their OBEs, and both of his reports are included in this book. As you will see, one subject, whom Tart calls Miss Z., unmistakably succeeded at the ESP task. But even more interestingly, her electroencephalogram traced an extremely puzzling pattern during the precise time of her OBE. Tart's other subject, Mr. X., did not fare so well. (Mr. X. was actually Robert Monroe, who has since written his own autobiographical account of his OBE experiences [Monroe, 1971].)

However, even Tart's work does not constitute iron-clad

evidence that the OBE is a psychic process distinct from simple ESP. So beginning in 1972 two further investigations were made into the OBE mystery. One project was spearheaded by Dr. Karlis Osis at the American Society for Psychical Research in New York, while the other was designed by Dr. Robert Morris of the Durham-based Psychical Research Foundation.

Why did parapsychologists turn such an eager eye toward OBE research at this time? This is a curious story in itself.

In 1949 a recluse Arizona miner named James Kidd disappeared, leaving behind a healthy bankroll and a most curious will. It stated that his estate, estimated at about a quarter of a million dollars, should go for "research or some scientific proof of a human soul in the human body which leaves at death." When Kidd was declared legally dead years later, the Arizona court invited any applicants who felt they had a right to the money to apply for it. Court hearing were initiated in 1967.

As you can well imagine, dozens of applicants staked their claims. Mediums who claimed that they were in touch with the dead were at the forefront. Philosophers who felt that they could best explore the mystery of death followed in close pursuit. One neurological institute was on hand as well. Two parapsychology institutes also petitioned for the money; namely, the American Society for Psychical Research and the Psychical Research Foundation. (The P.R.F. is, in fact, specifically endowed to study the survival-of-death question.) Both of these organizations were still in the running after the presiding judge, Robert L. Myers, whittled down the list of serious applicants. Both the A.S.P.R. and the P.R.F. offered expert testimony during the proceedings to the effect that the science of parapsychology was eminently qualified to meet the provisions of the Kidd will. The transcripts of the court hearing make fascinating reading (Fuller, 1969).

Dr. Gardner Murphy was the chief witness for the A.S.P.R. He argued before the court that parapsychology has, in fact, long been researching the very question Kidd raised in his will. He pointed out how the study of mediumship, apparitions, and deathbed visions indeed constituted "research or some scientific proof of a human soul . . . which leaves at death." Murphy also stated his belief that investigating the nature of the OBE with the Kidd funds would be a fruitful way of satisfying the conditions of the will. (Murphy's position was an abrupt about-face from his previous attitute toward the OBE. He even stated in his book, *Challenge of Psychical Research* (1961), that OBEs "are types of phenomena on which we have not succeeded in finding the kinds of data which we could offer to readers of a book like this with the assurance that it would be worth their time to study them." Murphy also suggested in his book that OBEs were probably not even psychic phenomena at all. He gave no explanation to the Arizona court for his sudden change of attitude.)

Dr. J. G. Pratt, one of Rhine's first co-workers at Duke University, was the key witness for the P.R.F. He too argued that parapsychology was the only science that had the requisite basis, traditions, and tools to tackle the survival-of-death question.

After the long hearings were concluded, Judge Myers awarded the Kidd money to the Barrow Neurological Institute in Phoenix, Arizona, which planned to use the funds to support main-line neurological research. Several of the applicants were annoyed by the ruling. After all, the Institute had no plans or strategies to investigate life after death and had even said so during the court proceedings! An appeal was lodged and the Arizona Supreme Court reversed the decision on the basis that "At least two of the appellants, the American Society for Psychical Research and the Psychical Research Foundation Inc. are qualified to carry out the specific purpose expressed in the will."

Judge Myers re-ruled his Kidd decision in July 1971 and awarded the money to the A.S.P.R., which in turn granted a sizable portion of it to the P.R.F. Both organizations turned to the study of the OBE to meet the requirements of the court.

The A.S.P.R. project was organized by Dr. Karlis Osis, a Latvian-born psychologist and director of research for the

New York-based organization. Osis's plan was to experiment with OBE vision. He realized that ESP impressions (and visions) are rarely detailed, precise, or accurate. So he theorized that OBE perception might follow optical principles similar to those which physical sight adheres to, and set about to explore this possibility.

Osis and his co-worker scheduled a "fly-in" as one of their initial phases of research. Osis decked out his A.S.P.R. office with a table divided by a partition and placed target objects on both sides of it. Anyone who wished to try could fly-in from his home and report back to the A.S.P.R. what he saw there. Over one hundred people from all over the country tried.

As Osis explains in "Out-of-Body Research at the American Society for Psychical Research" (see chapter 7): "The overall results were not significant; that is, only some of the OBers seemed to 'see' things clearly enough for definite identification." However, some of the descriptions of the A.S.P.R. layout related by the fly-in subjects were startlingly accurate. You might think that this is more like a typical ESP test, but Osis especially designed the fly-in in such a way as to judge whether the subject's visions were similar to physical sight or were more general ESP-type impressions.

As I said, Osis's table was divided by a partition. If an OBE-er flew into the room, positioned himself there, and then stared at the target table, he would see only *part* of the total layout. Osis was hoping to discover if (1) the OBE-ers would see only those objects they would normally be expected to see from their position in the office and (2) if they saw these objects in proper relation to each other. If the OBE-er situated himself to the left of the table, Osis thought that he might only see those objects placed on the left side of the barrier, and so forth. ESP impressions of the target objects and layout would not, Osis believed, be so restricted or precise.

To date there has been no formal report on the fly-in experiments. The overall results, as Osis states, were not significant. If anything, Osis and his co-workers discovered that they were up against an infinitely more complex phenomenon than they had expected. Nonetheless, there were a few striking successes during these pilot studies which deserve to be mentioned here. (For a full anecdotal account of the fly-in results, see Greenhouse, 1975.)

One of Osis's prize subjects was Maine psychic Alex Tanous. For one experiment, Tanous reported to Osis that he had flown to the New York office, hovered over the target table, and made note of the objects positioned there as well as described the partition. On one occasion he sketched the partition as he saw it from the ceiling where he had stationed himself. After receiving the sketch, Vera Feldman, an Osis assistant, climbed a ladder by the table to ascertain how the barrier actually looked from the ceiling. What she saw looked identical to Tanous's sketch.

A psychic, Christine Whiting, was stationed at the A.S.P.R. office during another experiment with Tanous. Her job was to see if she could "detect" Tanous's out-of-body presence at the time he made his fly-in from Maine. During the session Whiting described seeing Tanous's apparition, correctly described his physical appearance, and noted that he was wearing brown corduroy-like pants and a white cotton shirt. This was the apparel Tanous was actually wearing at the time he made his OB attempt from Maine.

Probably the strangest fly-in result was recorded on January 11, 1973. Once again Whiting was stationed at the A.S.P.R. The potential OBer was a Massachusettes psychic named Claudette Kiely. As Osis reported to the 1973 convention of the Parapsychological Association, Whiting saw Kiely's apparition at the scheduled time and accurately described her physical appearance. But, as Osis also admitted, "Then the psychic proceeded to describe a boy on roller skates. No boy was scheduled at the time. On checking with the writer [Kiely] we found she had a ten-year-old son who fit very well the description given by the psychic. At the time of the experiment the boy had fallen asleep while watching a TV movie showing waitresses on roller skates. It seems to me the psychic not only scanned the projection area but also the

Boston home far away from our New York laboratory . . ." (Osis, 1973).

What can we make of this odd report? Did Kiely really fly-in out-of-the-body or was the apparition only an ESP impression that Miss Whiting conjured forth from her own mind?* Or did Whiting actually detect Kiely's OB presence and then use ESP to latch on to her son's thoughts? Or did the boy have an OBE while he slept? There is simply no way to resolve these questions. As Osis himself sadly admitted to the Parapsychological Association, "Apparently such a single-variable approach as seeing an OB apparition will not separate the OB hypothesis from others."

The problem of ESP vs. OBE became even touchier as the fly-in experiments proceeded. Some OBE subjects described objects which were put onto the target table several days later! Other projectors seemed to "get lost," but accurately described what was going on in other rooms at the A.S.P.R. or in neighboring buildings.

Work with selected subjects fared better. One series of OBE trials was conducted with New York psychic Ingo Swann. For the experiments, Swann was asked to sit in a chair in an especially prepared A.S.P.R. room and "float-up" out of his body to a box-like platform suspended from the ceiling and report what he saw there. (Like Garrett, Swann does not enter sleep or trance while producing his OBEs. Instead he apparently projects one element of his mind in order to perceive the target locations while retaining enough conscious awareness of his surroundings to report what he is seeing to his experimenters.) The results of these target studies were striking and are contained in Janet Mitchell's report, "Out of Body Vision" (see chapter 6). It does seem as though

---

*Several parapsychologists have suggested that apparitions are telepathic hallucinations. The percipient subconsciously receives an ESP message that a person is trying to contact him; then the subconscious projects a hallucination (the apparition) in order to bring this information into consciousness. The apparition, according to this theory, is only a mental image and does not indicate that the person represented in the apparition is spatially or mentally present.

Swann could actually "see" the targets (which consisted of several objects) while out-of-body and could describe them in proper proportion and perspective.

A later experiment designed by Osis also employed the services of Ingo Swann along with Alex Tanous. For these trials, the psychics were asked to look into special optical boxes during their OBEs and report what figures or optical illusions they saw there. Osis believed that success at the task would indicate that his subjects were using a perceptual modality akin to sight and were not relying on mere ESP. The results of these experiments are included in a brief report by Osis (see chapter 7).

The implications that can be drawn from Osis's results are equivocal. The fly-in experiments did not substantiate that OBEs are a discrete phenomenon, unconnected with ESP. The vagueness of the results, the elements of precognition that complicated the tests, and the total failure of other subjects indicate that it is nearly impossible to differentiate between OBE and ESP perception. Osis's work might also have been based on a misconception about ESP, for he predicated his entire project on the premise that there is a distinct difference between OB vision and ESP perception: namely, that OB vision would follow optical principles similar to physical sight, while ESP would not. Seeing objects in proper perspective and perceiving their precise color and shape are all attributes of physical sight and Osis expected OB vision to conform to similar principles.

While this approach might be theoretically valid, there does exist some evidence to indicate that ESP perception may mimic, to a limited degree, the process we use to assemble visual sensory input into a meaningful whole. This research casts dark shadows over the assumptions that have guided Osis's work.

In 1933 Professor Hans Bender began work with a young psychic, whom he called Fräulein D. in his report, at the University of Bonn (cited in Rhine, 1947). For one series of tests, Bender prepared special cards by imprinting each one with a letter of the alphabet, wrapped them individually in cellophane, and then placed them in opaque envelopes. Later an assistant shuffled them. Fräulein D. was handed an envelope, which she placed under a cloth, removed the card, handled it, and then guessed which letter was imprinted on it. On other occasions she was not allowed to remove the cards from their envelopes or had to guess the letters on cards placed in sealed boxes. Fräulein D. made thirty-seven correct guesses out of 134 trials. By chance she should have achieved only five.

However, Fräulein D.'s successes were not Bender's sole interest. He was also intrigued by her method of processing her extrasensorily gained information before she made her guesses. Fräulein D. described how she would first get a vague image of the letter. This image would gradually take on a more specific shape and, finally, she would mentally "see" the letter imprinted on the card. Bender encouraged the psychic to make pencil sketches of all the images she perceived that led to her final vision of the letter. Later he tested her with a special apparatus that cast an illumination on the target cards. The lighting made the imprint invisible; however, by manipulating the light source Bender could cause the letter to emerge gradually from invisibility to clear visibility. Fräulein D. made a series of sketches of the imprinted letters as they became visible to her. The two sets of diagrams, one based on her ESP images and one representing her visual perception of the targets as they attained visibility, were remarkably similar. This would indicate that Fräulein D. processed information gained through clairvoyant perception in the same manner in which she processed and assembled visual information.

While no one has ever replicated Bender's work, his findings bear significantly on Osis's research and, for that matter, on all traveling clairvoyance research as well. Osis worked from the premise that physical sight and ESP perception function along different principles. Hans Bender has shown that this is not necessarily so. (I do not mean to imply that physical sight and clairvoyant perception utilize the same physiological process. I am only suggesting that the mind may use physical sight as a model to follow as it processes ESP information.) So Osis's work, like so much OBE research, still does not substantiate that the OBE is more than a form of oddly dramatized ESP.

Nevertheless, remember that Osis only required his subjects to look at simple objects and pictures while out-of-the-body. Bender required that his subject also report on extremely simple figures. Can we conclude that all traveling clairvoyance phenomena are just simple ESP impressions transmutated by the mind into visual representations? I still think not. Many times traveling clairvoyants have reported unbelievably accurate accounts and descriptions of far-off places as well as what was happening there. ESP is rarely so accurate, especially over any extended period of time. Garrett, for instance, was even able to quote Svensen's very words as he spoke to her when he sensed her out-of-body presence (see pages 82–83). No parapsychologist, to my knowledge, has ever reported on any experimental ESP subject whose ESP was so exact. So there does seem to be a qualitative difference between ESP perception and traveling clairvoyance perception. There was nothing wrong a priori with Osis's approaches. But he was too limited in what he required his subjects to do while out-of-the-body. Had he set more complex perceptual tasks for his subjects, his research might have offered us more conclusive evidence that OBE vision is something distinct from ESP perception.

A different approach to the problem of OBE perception has been made by Stuart Blue Harary, who is himself a talented OBE subject, and Gerald Solfvin of the Psychical Research Foundation (Harary and Solfvin, 1976). During his own OBEs, Harary discovered that his "hearing" was often a more reliable perceptual modality than his vision seemed to be. So he set about designing an experiment that would judge the accuracy of OBE hearing. He prepared twenty cassette tapes, each consisting of different sounds. These tapes were then broken down into five sets of four tapes. For each experiment only one cassette was used, drawn from any one of the sets. The tape was played at a P.R.F. building and the subject, stationed in another building, tried to OB to the target room and listen to the sounds being played there. After the session, the subject reported to the experimenters any auditory experiences he had perceived while out-of-the-body, listened to all four tapes in the target pool, and tried to identify which one was actually being played while he was making his OB attempt. The subject also had to guess or "see" whether or not an experimenter had remained in the target area as well. Harary's and Solfvin's first test utilized the services of six students from the University of North Carolina, none of whom had ever recalled having an OBE. The second series of tests was run with two gifted subjects who reported conscious control over their OBEs, Ingo Swann and George Kokoris. Although the results of the study were disappointing, Ingo Swann was accurate on all experiments conducted with him.

This experimental approach to the OBE does have some promise. As Harary and Solfvin conclude:

The use of nonvisual target materials may provide clues as to the sensory scope of OBEs. If it is indicated that psi may operate in multiple sensory modalities simultaneously during OBEs, and that the veridical quality of target responses in one modality is positively correlated with the accuracy of responses in other modalities, this would provide a testable hypothesis. If verified, it would lead to a definition of the OBE as a multisensory psi-conducive state instead of the present subjective or experiential definition.

However, even Harary's and Solfvin's interesting experiment does little to prove the objective existence of the OBE. ESP impressions often mimic normal sense perception. Many parapsychologists who have studied spontaneous ESP cases have noted that people will report how they "saw visions," "heard voices," or "smelled phantom odors." In other words, ESP can work through or hallucinate any sense modality. In fact, Dr. Louisa Rhine found that 435 cases of spontaneous ESP out of the 825 anecdotal accounts she analyzed were auditory experiences (Rhine, 1956). Her correspondents claimed that they had heard voices calling to them, heard cries for help at the same time a friend or relative had under-

gone an accident, were given warnings of future events by "inner voices," etc. So Swann's success at the Harary-Solfvin test still cannot be considered proof that the OBE is an actual mind-body separation.

Only one large-scale attempt has been made to bypass the ESP problem in OBE research. In 1972 Stuart Blue Harary stepped into the offices of the Psychical Research Foundation and announced that he could induce OBEs at will. The P.R.F. staff was intrigued by his claim, since they had recently been granted part of the Kidd money and wanted to study the OBE in order to meet the requirements of the will. Dr. Robert Morris, director of research for the P.R.F., took over the job of testing Blue, as he is known to his friends. Morris was well aware of the problems he faced and which Tart and Osis had failed to surmount. He wanted to test Harary in such a way that simple ESP could not account for any positive results he might obtain. Morris objected to Osis's designs, since he felt that they did not clearly differentiate between the OBE and ESP. As he states in his report on Harary (Morris, et al., 1976):

Two lines of thought have suggested that OBE's may be even more than a special, psi-conducive state; that they may in fact be evidence of an aspect of self which is capable of extension beyond the physiological body (externalization) and which might also be capable of survival of bodily death.

First, many have noted that OBE's most often are experiences that seem organized from a specific visual location in space and time, perceiving the world in a visually highly discrete way. Osis has argued that such a discreteness to the experience would legislate against a general ESP interpretation of such discrete experiences; since ESP in general seems to have an extremely capricious nature, often providing information in very indirect, symbolic ways. Recently Osis has attempted to test this notion by asking OBE'ers to view targets from a specific vantage point, to see whether they report the target as it actually is or as it would appear from the assigned vantage point. His results indicate a tendency in this direction. The interpretation of these results is unclear, however, as the OBE'ers may have simply been using general psi to respond to the specific instructions and intents of the experimenter. The Osis approach would also seem to ignore OBE's which are not visually discrete.

Second, the detection of OBE's may be viewed as evidence of externalization. If in fact this aspect of self is capable of tangible, discrete projection outside the physiological body, then it may well be detectable at its new location. Such studies can be done at two levels: the OBE'er can be asked to "visit" a variety of potential physical and biological detectors, including humans. Should any such detectors produce consistent responses, then such parameters as distance can be varied systematically, to see if the detector behaves as a true detector—always gives positive responses during actual OBE's that incorporate it; responds in a spatially discrete way to spatially discrete OBE's; and gives distance-dependent responses to OBE's that involve target locations increasingly distant from the detector.

Morris wanted to see if Blue could make people or animals react to his OB presence. The results of his research were provocative, and are contained and analyzed in a lengthy report "Experiments with Blue Harary" (see chapter 8).

Have researchers investigating the OBE proved its existence? This question raises two quite different issues. Have we proved that the OBE exists as a psychically "real" phenomenon? And have we proved that the OBE represents the physical projection of the mind away from the confines of the body? I think that we can answer the first question affirmatively. We do know that the OBE is at least a *subjectively* real experience, since the OBE subject can make observations about distant places and scenes consistent with the theory that his mind is functioning independently from his body. But that does not necessarily mean that the OBE actually represents the functioning of the consciousness apart from the body or that the mind is somehow spatially present at the site where the subject finds himself. All we can say for sure is that the OBE is a genuine genre of psychical phenomenon.

The second question is still unresolved in parapsychology. Certainly there are a number of aspects to the OBE that are not consistent with ESP. For example, OBE perception often seems more precise and, on rare occasions, the subject can move physical objects while in the OB state. (This could be due to long-distance PK, but the experimental evidence for such a phenomenon is not very strong.) Many OBE-ers go through a physical process, often unpleasant, as they project from the body. This is not in the least characteristic of ESP. On the other hand, some aspects of the OBE seem to merge with those indicative of ESP. OBE subjects, even gifted ones, are very inconsistent when the accuracy of their "vision" is tested over long periods of time. This is typical of ESP. (One might expect OBE vision to be more consistent.)

The problem seems to be that our conception of the OBE as a simple separation of the mind from the body is too naïve. Obviously the OBE is a more complex process than first meets the eye. I don't believe that it is just dramatized ESP. I think that it represents some sort of physical projection of "mind" beyond the confines of the body. This represents, of course, just my own thinking about the OBE. Few parapsychologists, even those who have studied the OBE, are prepared to share my own convictions about the nature of the OBE. For now, let me say that there is no general agreement within parapsychology about just what the OBE actually is. I will present my own ideas in the Conclusion of this book.

The following reports represent some of the best experimental explorations of the OBE that have been made to date. The importance of these papers are twofold. First, you will be able to read about and evaluate the exact procedures followed and the results obtained by these experimenters. Second, you will find what the experimenters thought about their own results. Parapsychologists do not uniformly agree on what constitutes a discrete OBE. Thus the experimental designs employed by different investigators researching the phenomenon have been based on different conceptualizations about the OBE and what a subject might be expected to accomplish while out-of-the-body. This is perhaps the most fascinating aspect of OBE research.

I have included here both of Dr. Charles T. Tart's psycho-physiological studies. Note that the data collected on each subject differ from those on the other. Although both of Tart's subjects reported classical OB experiences, to all appearances they were functioning in different psychophysiological states when they had them. Tart's data suggest that while the OBE might be a discrete *mental* state, there is no consistent psychophysiological state that accompanies it. This supports the idea that there might be not one type of OBE, but many types or a continuum of experiences, as Dr. Grosso and I contended in Part I.

The two papers that follow Dr. Tart's are based on the A.S.P.R.'s research. Both papers, one by Dr. Karlis Osis and one by his assistant, Janet Mitchell, describe their attempts to explore the accuracy and parameters of OBE vision and its relation to the principles governing visual perception.

The detection experiments with Blue Harary form the next report, which differs from the others included in this section in one respect. It is not a formal paper originally published in a scientific journal, because the reports thus far published on Harary are sketchy and incomplete. For this book I have prepared a behind-the-scenes account of the Harary project —the successes, the failures, and the reactions of the P.R.F. staff to it. The chapter is adapted from one of my previous books, and is more journalistic in style than the other chapters in Part II. I have taken pains to explain the precise methodology used for each of the experiments, however.

The two papers comprising chapters 9 and 10 present attempts to explore the relationship between ESP and the OBE. Chapter 9, written by Dr. John Palmer expressly for this book, recounts his attempts at experimentally inducing the OBE and gauging its relationship to ESP success. Chapter 10 is a summary-review of the S.R.I. remote viewing research.

REFERENCES

Allen, Steve, Green, Philip, et al. "A Remote Viewing Study Using a Modified Version of the S.R.I. Procedures." In J.

D. Morris, et al. (eds.), *Research in Parapsychology–1975*. Metuchen, N.J.: Scarecrow Press, 1976.

Angoff, A. *Eileen Garrett and the World Beyond the Senses*. New York: Morrow, 1974.

Aserinsky, E., and Kleitman, N. "Regularly Occurring Periods of Eye Mobility and Concomitant Phenomena during Sleep." *Science* 118 (1953): 273–74.

Bisaha, J. "Precognitive Remote Viewing in the Chicago Area: A Replication of the Stanford Experiment." In J. D. Morris, et al. (eds.), *Research in Parapsychology–1976*. Metuchen, N.J.: Scarecrow Press, 1977.

Braud, W. G. "Psi-Conducive States." *Journal of Communications* 25 (1975): 142–52.

Fuller, J. *The Great Soul Trial*. New York: Macmillan, 1969.

Garrett, E. *My Life as a Search for the Meaning of Mediumship*. London: Rider, 1939.

Greenhouse, H. *The Astral Journey*. Garden City, N.Y.: Doubleday, 1975.

Harary, S. G. and Solfvin, G. "A Study of Out-of-Body Experiences Using Auditory Targets." In J. D. Morris, et al. (eds.), *Research in Parapsychology–1976*. Metuchen, N.J.: Scarecrow Press, 1977.

Mesmer, F. A. *Mémoire sur la Découverte du Magnétisme*. Paris: Didot le jeune, 1770.

Monroe, R. *Journeys Out of the Body*. Garden City, N.Y.: Doubleday, 1971.

Morris, R., et al. "Studies of Communication during Out of Body Experiences." Unpublished manuscript, 1976.

Murphy, G. *Challenge of Psychical Research*. New York: Harper & Row, 1961.

Osis, K. "Perspectives for Out-of-Body Research." In W. G. Roll, et al. (eds.), *Research in Parapsychology–1973*. Metuchen, N.J.: Scarecrow Press, 1974.

———. "Precognitive Remote Viewing." In J. D. Morris, et al. (eds.), *Research in Parapsychology–1975*. Metuchen, N.J.: Scarecrow Press, 1976.

Puthoff, H., and Targ, R. "A Perceptual Channel for Information Transfer over Kilometer Distances: Historical

Perspectives and Recent Research." *Proceedings of the I.E.E.E.* 64 (1976): 329–54.

Rao, K. M. *Experimental Parapsychology.* Springfield, Ill.: Charles C. Thomas, 1966.

Rausche, E. A., Weismann, G., Sarfatti, J. "Remote Perception of Natural Scenes, Shielded against Ordinary Perception." In J. D. Morris, et al. (eds.), *Research in Parapsychology–1975.* Metuchen, N.J.: Scarecrow Press, 1976.

Rhine, J. B. *Extra-sensory Perception.* Boston: Boston Society for Psychic Research, 1934.

———. *New Frontiers of the Mind.* New York: Farrar & Rinehart, 1937.

———. "Telepathy and Other Untestable Hypotheses." *Journal of Parapsychology* 38 (1974): 137–53.

Richet, Charles. *30 Years of Psychical Research.* New York: Macmillan, 1905.

Smith, S. *ESP and Hypnosis.* New York: Macmillan, 1973.

Stead, S. T. *Real Ghost Stories* and *More Ghost Stories.* Special issue of *Review of Reviews,* 1891–1892.

4 | A Psychophysiological Study of Out-of-the-Body Experiences in a Selected Subject

CHARLES T. TART

INTRODUCTION

Out-of-the-body experiences (OBEs) have always been a peripheral problem in psychical research in spite of the fact that their important implications for the question of survival, as well as their inherent interest, have long been recognized. This neglect has been due to the fact that an experimental approach to the study of OB experiences is extremely difficult. In the vast majority of reported cases, the experience occurred only once in the lifetime of an otherwise "ungifted" person. The occasional persons who have claimed to produce such experiences at will (Fox, 1962; Muldoon and Carrington, 1956; Yram, 1965) have, by and large, not been investigated by psychical researchers, although the reason for this lack of investigation is not clear. The few "experimental" attempts to produce such experiences have almost exclusively been older attempts involving the use of hypnosis (Carrington, 1919; Durville, 1909).

Thus we have a phenomenon whose occurrence is quite rare, which we do not know how to produce experimentally, and whose "spontaneous" occurrence cannot be predicted. We cannot study a phenomenon very thoroughly which does not occur when we are prepared to study it. Aside from Hornell Hart's excellent beginning work (Hart, 1953, 1955, 1956) and some recent work by Robert Crookall (1961, 1964a, 1964b) on the *experiential content* of reported OB experiences and some of their reported antecedents, we know virtually nothing about the nature of such experiences and their possible causes.

I have been interested in OB experiences for several years

and have often talked about this phenomenon with acquaintances. During a conversation with a friend (whom we shall call Miss Z) a couple of years ago, she reported that she had spontaneous OB experiences approximately two to four times a week and that she would be interested in being studied in the laboratory. As this afforded an unusual opportunity for research, I studied her for four nights in a sleep laboratory in order to determine what, if any, psychophysiological correlates of her OB experiences occurred. This paper will describe Miss Z and her spontaneous experiences, and report on the psychophysiological studies which were carried out.

DESCRIPTION OF MISS Z

Miss Z is a young, unmarried woman in her early twenties, with two years of college education. Her education was temporarily interrupted at the time of this study because of her need to work in order to earn money to continue at college. She is a warm and highly intelligent person, and had great interest in what the study would show.

Psychologically, it is extremely difficult to describe Miss Z. My informal observations of her over a period of several months (undoubtedly distorted by the fact that one can never describe one's friends objectively) resulted in a picture of a person who in some ways was quite mature and insightful, and in other ways so extremely disturbed psychologically that at times, when she lost control, she could possibly be diagnosed as schizophrenic. Miss Z came from a broken home. She recounted a number of instances of apparent parapsychological interaction between her and her parents as well as between her and her foster parents. She had been hospitalized for several weeks for psychiatric treatment about a year prior to the present study. Despite numerous psychological difficulties in her personal life during the several months over which the experiment was carried out, however, Miss Z did not interject her personal difficulties into the experimentation.

Miss Z's OB experiences were almost all of one kind. She would wake once or twice during a night's sleep. Each time she would find herself floating near the ceiling, but otherwise seemingly wide awake. This condition would last for a few seconds to half a minute. She frequently observed her physical body lying on the bed. Then she would fall asleep again and that was all there was to the experience. As far as she could recall, these experiences had been occurring several times weekly all of her life. As a child, she had not realized that there was anything unusual about them. She assumed that everyone had such experiences during sleep, and never thought to mention them to anyone. After speaking about them to friends several times as a teenager, however, she realized that they were looked upon as "queer" experiences, and she stopped discussing them.

At the time of the experiment, she had never read anything about such experiences. After initially hearing about her experiences, I asked her to refrain from reading anything about them until our experiments were completed, and she complied with this request.

Note that Miss Z had never made any attempts to control her OB experiences, nor did she attach any great significance to them. She definitely felt that they were *not* dreams, but she was otherwise puzzled as to what they were.

On a few occasions Miss Z's OB experiences had seemed to transport her to distant locations, rather than just floating above her body. One experience she reported is particularly relevant here. It is not certain whether it was a nightmare with elements of ESP in it, or a genuine OB experience. At about the age of fourteen, she had a vivid "nightmare" in which she found herself walking down a dark street in a deserted part of her own home town. She noticed the clothes she was wearing, including a checked skirt; she realized that she did not own any clothes like this, and felt that she was in someone else's body. Someone was following her, and she was terrified. This person caught up with her, raped her, and then stabbed her to death. Miss Z's memory of what happened near the end of this sequence is very poor, but she awoke quite disturbed and horrified because this "nightmare" had seemed so terribly real. She reported that the next day there was a story in the newspaper about a girl who had been wearing a checked skirt having been raped and stabbed to death the previous evening in the part of town corresponding to her "nightmare" locale. This experience made a considerable impression on Miss Z and will be relevant to one of the events which happened in the laboratory, described below.

PRELIMINARY EXPERIMENT

My interest in OB experiences has two separate facets. On one level, I am interested in such experiences as a unique, psychological *experience*, possibly related to nocturnal dreaming. On another level, I am interested in the extrasensory aspects of the experience: in some OB experiences the person reports accurate information about the distant localities he seemed to be at, and such information would apparently have to have been acquired by some form of extrasensory perception. Thus we have a unique psychological experience, worthy of study in its own right, as well as an experience that often seems to have parapsychological aspects.

In my initial talks with Miss Z, I explained to her that I was interested in her OB experiences from both of these points of view. I suggested that she carry out some observations on herself at home, before we began all-night laboratory studies, in order that she might distinguish for herself whether this was a vivid type of dream experience only, or whether it also possessed parapsychological aspects. At my suggestion, then, Miss Z carried out the following procedure.

She prepared ten slips of paper with the numbers one to ten on them and placed them in a large cardboard box. Each night, after getting into bed at home, she shook the cardboard box to randomize the slips of paper, and then, without looking into the box, drew out one slip of paper and put it on her bedside table. She could not see the number on the piece of paper from her position in bed, but anyone with a vantage point of several feet above the bed would be able to read the number clearly. If she awoke while experiencing floating near the ceiling that evening, she was to memorize the number, and then check on awakening in the morning to see whether she had perceived it correctly.

When I saw her two weeks later, she reported that she had tried this for seven nights and found she had been correct each time on checking in the morning. While this cannot be cited as evidence for some form of extrasensory perception, as it depends entirely on the subject's word, it did suggest that the possible parapsychological aspects of Miss Z's OB experiences could be studied as well as the psychological experience per se.

LABORATORY PROCEDURE

I was able to observe Miss Z in my sleep laboratory for four nonconsecutive nights, over a period of approximately two months. The procedure was essentially the same on all nights, and will be described here.

Miss Z's electroencephalogram (EEG) was recorded each night as follows. Grass silver disk electrodes were applied to the vertex, the right occipital area, and the right frontal area (high on the forehead just below the hairline). Recording of the EEG was bi-polar, frontal-to-vertex, and vertex-to-occipital. Recording was continuous through the night on a Grass model VII polygraph, running at a speed of ten millimeters per second.

Rapid eye movements (REMs) were recorded by means of a miniature strain gauge, taped over the right eyelid. This technique for recording REMs is described in detail elsewhere (Baldridge, et al., 1963; Tart, 1963). Movement of the eye under the closed eyelid distorts the strain gauge and a corresponding electrical output is recorded on the Grass polygraph. This combination of two EEG channels and a REM channel is typical in sleep studies and allows one to discriminate the various stages of sleep, including dreaming sleep.

Basal skin resistance (BSR) was also recorded on the Grass polygraph. Silver-silver chloride electrodes were used, one on the thenar eminence of the palm of the right hand, the other on the right forearm. These electrodes, described elsewhere (O'Connell and Tunsky, 1960), have negligible polarization characteristics and provide an accurate record of BSR. Galvanic skin responses (GSRs) were recorded from the same electrodes at a higher sensitivity than BSR by capacitively coupling the output of the BSR channel into a high gain channel on a Sanborn polygraph. This latter polygraph ran continuously through the night at a paper speed of one millimeter per second.

On two of the four nights, heart rate and digital blood volume were measured by means of a Grass model PTT1 finger photoplethysmograph. This device transmits a beam of light through a finger, and measures the amount of light transmitted by means of a photo cell (Brown, et al., 1965). The output of this photo cell reproduces the pulse wave, allowing heart rate to be measured, and the amplitude of this tracing varies with variations in the blood volume in the finger. Technical difficulties with this device prevented its use on two of the four nights.

The sleep laboratory consisted of two rooms, each lined with acoustic tile for sound attenuation. A large window was between the rooms for viewing, but in this experiment it was covered with a venetian blind in order that the subject's room could be reasonably dark for sleeping. This blind allowed enough light to come through so that the subject's room was dimly illuminated, but not enough to disturb sleep. The polygraphs were located in the second room, and the door was kept closed. An intercom system allowed hearing anything the subject said. I monitored the recording equipment throughout the night while the subject slept and kept notes of anything she said or did. Occasionally I dozed during the night, beside the equipment, so possible instances of sleep talking might have been missed.

The subject slept on a comfortable bed just below the observation window. The leads from all electrodes were bound into a common cable running off the top of her head, and terminating in an electrode box on the head of the bed. This arrangement allowed her enough slack wire so that she could turn over in bed and otherwise be comfortable, but did not allow her to sit up more than two feet without disconnecting the wires from the box, an event which would show up on the recording equipment as a tremendous amount of sixty cycle artifact. Thus her movements were well controlled. Immediately above the observation window (about five and a half feet above the level of the subject's head) was a small shelf (about ten inches by five inches). Immediately above this shelf was a large clock, mounted on the wall. Each laboratory night, after the subject was lying in bed, the physiological recordings were running satisfactorily, and she was ready to go to sleep, I went into my office down the hall, opened a table of random numbers at random, threw a coin onto the table as a means of random entry into the page, and copied off the first five digits immediately above where the coin landed. These were copied with a black marking pen, in figures approximately two inches high, onto a small piece of paper. Thus they were quite discrete visually. This five-digit random number constituted the parapsychological target for the evening. I then slipped it into an opaque folder, entered the subject's room, and slipped the piece of paper onto the shelf without at any time exposing it to the subject. This now provided a target which would be clearly visible to anyone whose eyes were located approximately six and a half feet off the floor or higher, but was otherwise not visible to the subject.

The subject was instructed to sleep well, to try and have an OB experience, and if she did so to try to wake up immediately afterward and tell me about it, so I could note on the polygraph records when it had occurred. She was also told that if she floated high enough to read the five-digit number she should memorize it and wake up immediately afterward to tell me what it was. My conversation with Miss Z after I had prepared the target was, of course, minimal and could not have given her any clue as to the target number. In future experiments, however, it would be preferable for a second experimenter, who had had no contact at all with the subject, to prepare the targets.

THE NATURE OF SLEEP

As some readers may not be familiar with recent psycho-physiological findings on the nature of sleep, a brief review of these will be presented here. More detailed reviews and evaluations of the more than one hundred studies of the past decade which have so changed our view of sleep and dream activity may be found elsewhere (Foulkes, 1962; Kamiya, 1961; Kleitman, 1963; Oswald, 1962, 1964; Sneider, 1963, 1965).

Sleep may be defined in this paper as a stage of the organism indicated (in human subjects) by one of four EEG stages (Dement and Kleitman, 1957 a, b). The Stage 1 pattern consists of an irregular mixture of theta waves (4–8 cps), random low voltage activity, occasional isolated alphoid activity (waves of 1 to 2 cps slower than the subject's waking alpha), and occasional alpha waves (8–13 cps). Stage 2 contains spindle activity (14 cps) in addition to the above, and Stages 3 and 4 contain an increasingly larger proportion (up to 100 percent) of delta waves, 1–3 cps, high amplitude, in addition to spindle activity. The exact divisions between Stages 2, 3, and 4 are arbitrary, based on the percentages of delta waves in given epochs. The Stage 1 pattern is readily distinguishable from the other stages by its total lack of spindles and delta waves.

Stages 1 through 4 were initially conceived of as comprising a continuum from "light" to "deep" sleep (Aserinsky and Kleitman, 1953, 1955; Dement, 1955), but as other measures of the "depth" of sleep contradict this conception (Berger, 1961; Hawkins, et al., 1962; Kamiya, 1961; Snyder, 1963; Williams, et al., 1962), this paper will treat sleep as being of two qualitatively distinct types, namely, Stage 1 as one type and Stages 2, 3, and 4 as the other type. Distinctions between Stages 2, 3, and 4 will not be made, and they will be collectively referred to as Nonstage 1 sleep.

If subjects are awakened from the two types of sleep and asked to report on what they have been experiencing, the reports may be classified into two rather distinct types. One type, awakening from Stage 1 sleep or shortly (within, roughly, ten to fifteen minutes) after Stage 1 sleep has changed to Nonstage 1 sleep, possesses the characteristics traditionally associated with the experience of dreaming (Foulkes, 1962; Rechtschaffer, et al., 1963). Reports from Nonstage 1 sleep seem more like "thinking," and are generally called thinking by the subjects—these same subjects generally refer to their Stage 1 experiences as dreams. The psychological differences reported so far are quantitative rather than being completely dichotomous, but they generally give the impression of being distinct types of experiences.

Stage 1 sleep is almost always accompanied by binocularly synchronous rapid eye movements (REMs), and the evidence is very convincing that these are closely associated with the content of the dream, if not actual scanning movements of the dream imagery (Berger and Oswald, 1962; Dement and Wolpert, 1958; Roffwarg, 1962). Such REMs have not been reported in Nonstage 1 sleep, although there are some slow, rolling movements (Kamiya, 1961).

In view of these findings, the theoretical position taken in this paper is that an experientially distinct type of phenomenon occurs concurrently with the presence of Stage 1 sleep, which phenomenon will be called Stage 1 dreaming, or just dreaming. The mental phenomena of Nonstage 1 sleep will not be considered in this paper. Further, it is assumed that the experience of Stage 1 dreaming is essentially continuous* during the presence of Stage 1 EEG, whether or not the subject can always recall this experience on waking. This position is, in my opinion, supported by all the studies using the EEG and REM technique, and directly refuted by none.

For normal subjects, Stage 1 dreaming and Nonstage 1

---

*Within a continuous period of Stage 1 EEG, the content of the experienced dream may be divided into several distinct episodes so that, in a sense, there are several distinct "dreams" within a continuous period of dreaming. Dement and Wolpert (1958) present some evidence that such changes of topic may be accompanied by a gross body movement on the part of the subject.

sleep alternate in a regular cyclic fashion referred to as the sleep-dream cycle. As the subject falls asleep there is generally a brief (a few seconds to a minute or two) period of Stage 1, without REMs, but subjects' reports indicate that this is apparently a period of hypnagogic imagery rather than typical dreaming (Dement and Kleitman, 1957b; Oswald, 1962). At approximately ninety-minute intervals through the night there are periods of Stage 1 dreaming, each dream period generally being longer than the preceding one. The first Stage 1 period may last for ten minutes; the fourth or fifth one may last as long as fifty minutes. Altogether, Stage 1 dreaming occupies between 20 and 30 percent of the total sleep time of most young adults, spread over three to six Stage 1 periods. While the exact percentage of dream time and the number of cycles varies from subject to subject, for a given subject the sleep-dream cycle is generally quite stable from night to night (Dement, 1960; Dement and Kleitman, 1957a; Kleitman, 1960; Wood, 1962).

RESULTS

Night I

The first night in a dream laboratory is usually considered an adaptation night, with the data from it not being used in physiological studies. This is because of the so-called "first-night effect" in which a subject is liable to skip his first Stage 1 dream period, and the content of his dreams is often obviously concerned with the fact that he is being experimented upon (Agnew, 1966; Domhoff and Kamiya, 1964; Rechtschaffen, et al. 1963; Tart, 1964; Whitman, et al., 1962).

On her first night in the laboratory, Miss Z fell asleep rather rapidly, reached Stage 4 sleep within the first half hour after falling asleep, and then showed three Stage 1 dream periods during the course of the night. After the first dream period, there were scattered instances of prominent alphoid activity, that is, a Stage 1 pattern mixed with slowed alpha waves, and rather poorly developed sleep spindles. The only unusual feature of this night was that the subject showed REMs during Stage 1 drowsiness at the *beginning* of sleep, a very unusual finding. Rapid eye movements almost never occur in normal subjects during drowsiness, although they have been found to occur frequently in narcoleptics (Dement et al., 1966; Hishikawa and Kaneko, 1965; Pierce, et al., 1965; Rechtschaffen, et al., 1963). There is no evidence that Miss Z suffers from narcolepsy, however, and these REMs during drowsiness seem to be related to the unusually vivid hypnagogic imagery that she reportedly experiences on falling asleep.

Miss Z did not feel that she had had any OB experiences that night.

Night II

A number of interesting incidents occurred during Miss Z's second night in the laboratory.

As Miss Z went to sleep, she showed a drowsy pattern alternating with a waking pattern for approximately the first ten minutes. Then there was a minute of a drowsy EEG pattern consisting of occasional theta waves, some alphoid waves (alpha waves of one to one-and-a-half cycles per second slower than her usual waking alpha), and a good deal of flattening of the record, ending in thirteen seconds of waking alpha rhythm, nearly continuous, and then a large body movement. With this body movement, Miss Z called out that she was awake and that she had just had a sensation of starting to float up toward the ceiling immediately prior to her moving and calling out. The finger photoplethysmograph was being used on this night, and her heart rate during this time was a steady seventy-one beats per minute, not in the least unusual. Her BSR was steady throughout this time, no GSRs were seen at all, nor was there any body movement. Also, there were no REMs during this period.

Miss Z then went to sleep, quickly going into Stage 2 sleep, which lasted for about half an hour, and then a half hour of Stage 3 and Stage 4 sleep. This was followed by a short Stage 1 dream. Her Stage 1 dream period showed a classical Stage

1 pattern with REMs. This dream was followed by about an hour and a half of Stage 2 sleep, then twenty minutes of Stage 1 sleep, and then another period of unusual EEG. For approximately one minute Miss Z showed a pattern of alphoid waves mixed with poorly developed, low voltage sleep spindles. Then there was a two-minute period of alphoid waves superimposed on a generally low voltage pattern with no spindles and no clearly developed theta waves. This was followed by a minute of predominantly low voltage theta activity, with very poorly developed sleep spindles present. This terminated in a large movement and Miss Z awoke. There were no REMs during this four-minute period, heart rate was steady at seventy-four beats per minute, and BSR steady, with no GSRs. There were two small body movement artifacts during the terminal period of slowed alpha without spindles and one small body movement in the period of slowed alpha and poor spindling which began this unusual EEG sequence. The sequence occurred at approximately 3:15 A.M.

Upon awakening from this sequence, Miss Z called out, "Write down 3:13 A.M. I don't see the number, but I just remember that." Although she did not say anything more, the implication, confirmed by conversation later on that morning, was that she had floated somewhat above her body, high enough to see the clock, but not high enough to see the target number. Some further comments on this episode will now be made.

When going back to sleep, Miss Z showed a Stage 2 pattern for an hour, had a dream of twenty-five minutes' duration following that, then showed some Stage 2 and Stage 3 for the next hour. About fifteen minutes of record was then lost because of a paper jam. When recording was resumed, she was showing Stage 1 dreaming. This lasted for about ten minutes, and then the record became rather difficult to classify. For a period of approximately ten minutes the EEG consisted of a great deal of slowed alpha rhythm, no theta rhythm, and a fair amount of flattening. It could not be classified clearly as either a sleep or a waking pattern. There were some occasional body movements, a fair amount of REM activity scattered through, and some GSR activity. Miss Z then awakened by herself and reported that in the last five minutes she thought she had floated in and out of her body four or five times. Nothing else of interest occurred that night.

One day later, Miss Z told me that she had had a very frightening nightmare during her previous night in the laboratory, which she had not reported at the time because of its terrifying nature. She had wanted to forget it, but had not been successful. This nightmare had apparently occurred just before she woke, called out the time, and reported that she had not been able to see the target number. I cannot be sure of this, of course, as she did not report it at the time. The stimulus for now reporting it was that she had seen a television news program the night following her night in the laboratory which made her decide to write down an account of her nightmare immediately because it seemed to coincide with an item in the newscast.

Because Miss Z did not report this material to me before seeing the newscast, it cannot be considered evidential of extrasensory perception. As it is quite interesting psychologically, however, and fits in with the earlier traumatic incident of her childhood (described above) in which she had a nightmare or OB experience coinciding with the murder of a young girl, the material will be reproduced here. Her account, written *after* she saw the newscast, is as follows:

Sunday night—vague nightmare—recalled previous experience?—blocking on much of memory—young girl (13 to 16?)—outdoors—stabbing, but not knife, more slender—head hurt (slapped?)—not stabbed, surely—expanse of white, car white?—knew fellow (*she* knew, not I!) who also youngish—horrible experience but no support in papers this morning—so far so good.

Miss Z told me that the television newscast said that a young girl had been stabbed to death in Marin County. Whether additional information was given in the newscast is not known.

I did not check the newspapers at the time; I wanted the incident to die down as Miss Z was obviously rather disturbed about it. Several months later I checked the newspaper files in the library. Nothing had appeared in the papers until April 20, 1965. Miss Z's second night in the laboratory had been the night of April 18th. Thus, as she had said, there had been nothing in the morning paper after she had seen the TV newscast. I do not know if she saw anything which appeared in the paper after that. The following material has been taken from the April 20, 1965, edition of the *San Francisco Chronicle*. (I have left out details such as names and the like which are not relevant to Miss Z's nightmare.) The headline is "Girl Found Murdered in Marin." Marin is the county immediately above San Francisco, about forty miles north of the laboratory.

A pretty Daly City high school girl was found murdered on a flower covered slope in Muir Woods in Marin County yesterday afternoon.

She had been stabbed savagely in the head at least six times and her skull was crushed, Coroner Frank Keaton said. There was no indication that she had been raped. . . . The young victim was identified as Nonita—, sixteen. Nonita's boyfriend is also missing and is sought for questioning. . . . He was identified as Virgilio—, nineteen, a resident of a San Francisco hotel. He is driving a white 1960 Thunderbird, police said. . . . The victim was fully clad—though her underclothing was in some disarray—in a black sweater, red blouse, plaid skirt, tennis shoes, and white socks.

Keaton estimated that she had been dead three or four days. . . .

In the *Chronicle* for April 21, the information is given that the police are still looking for the boyfriend, and that the car has been found. ". . . the murder weapon—a sharp, thin instrument, a little thicker than an ice pick— was not found. . . . An autopsy showed that death came from six stabs of this weapon into her head, one of them penetrating the brain. . . ."

The *Chronicle* of April 22 reports that the girl was murdered in the car, according to bloodstains and signs of a struggle found in the car. The Thunderbird was parked in a

San Francisco parking garage late Friday night, and the body was apparently in it for attendants noticed a little pool of blood in the parking place after the car was checked out.

After a small notice on April 24 in the *Chronicle* that the FBI had entered the case, I could find no more information about the murder, though I searched the paper for the next several weeks.

With respect to the parallels between Miss Z's nightmare and the murder case, we note the following: (1) the victim was a young girl of sixteen, as estimated in the dream; (2) the setting of the nightmare was outdoors and the body was apparently outdoors, where it was found, at the time of the dream, although the murder took place in the car; (3) death was caused by stabbing with an instrument like an ice pick, not a knife; (4) Miss Z said her head hurt, that it was slapped, not stabbed; the girl was stabbed in the head and her skull was crushed; (5) Miss Z saw an expanse of white in her dream and thought it was a white car; the suspected murderer was driving a large white car; and (6) Miss Z said the murderer, a "youngish man," knew the girl; the suspected murderer was a young man who was a boyfriend of the girl.

The parallels between this nightmare, the actual killing, and the incident Miss Z reported from her early teens is striking. In the earlier nightmare incident, the girl Miss Z identified with was also wearing a checked or plaid skirt. In one sense, this entire recent incident may be a reactivation of the earlier trauma. (As mentioned above, the nightmare can only constitute suggestive evidence for extrasensory perception because it was not reported to me before Miss Z saw the television newscast.) An alternative hypothesis is that no nightmare took place in the laboratory, but that the TV news bulletin triggered the earlier trauma in Miss Z's mind and she fabricated (unknowingly) the incidents of the nightmare.

Night III

On her third night in the laboratory, Miss Z went to sleep quickly and showed an ordinary sleep pattern for the first half of the night, that is, Stages 2, 3, and 4 alternating with a couple of Stage 1 dream periods at approximately ninety-minute intervals. At 3:35 A.M. an unusual EEG pattern sequence started which will be described here. It began from Stage 3 sleep, which was clearly defined by frequent, well-developed sleep spindles and clear, high voltage delta activity. Then there was a minute of large body movements, followed by five minutes of alphoid activity with no spindles, some flattening of the record, and no REMs. Then there was another minute of massive body movements, followed by a half minute of rather poorly developed Stage 1 EEG, that is, a flattened low voltage slow pattern, but with the theta almost absent and no REMs. Again there was a half minute of body movements, and then five minutes of alphoid activity as before. There were several bursts of twenty-four cycle per second rhythmic activity in the frontal channel during this five-minute period, but it is not clear whether these were actually EEG patterns or some sort of external electrical artifact which happened to occur at this time. Then for two and a half minutes the alphoid activity was less prominent, there was some theta activity, but still no spindle activity. Then there were five minutes of record that could not be classified because body movements obscured almost all of it except for occasional slowed alpha. Then there was a minute in which the EEG record was clear and showed alphoid activity predominantly, but the strain gauge REM channel showed all sorts of artifact, such as one might get from tremors of the eyelids. This was followed by seven minutes of alphoid activity, with some flattening, and continual interference and possibly tremor on the strain gauge REM channel. Then, after some more body movement, there were three minutes of waking alpha rhythm with high amplitude REMs. The subject may very well have been awake during this brief period. Then followed a minute and a half of Stage 1 pattern with REMs (dreaming), although the theta was rather poorly developed. There were some occasional bursts of twenty-four-cycles-per-second activity in both EEG channels again. This gave way to seventeen minutes of alphoid activity with no REMs and only a couple of small movements of the body scattered through this period. There were occasional GSRs during this long period of EEG disturbance. Then there were a couple of minutes of Stage 1 EEG pattern, with occasional REMs (dreaming), and Miss Z awoke. She reported on OB experience. After her final awakening later in the morning, she wrote a full account of this experience, as follows:

I seemed to be flying, although too high and seemingly fast to recognize where I was; neither did I have any sense of where I was going. The flying disturbed me as I knew I was supposed to stand up in the room and read the number above my head. Therefore, I would rouse or questionably awaken and realize that I was still lying on the bed. Every time I drifted off to sleep I would resume flying, however. This was not preceded by any other activity—that is, there seemed to be no intermediate experience between falling asleep on the cot and flying. Finally, the third or fourth time I flew I decided to relax and let the experience come to completion.

Very shortly (that is, in far less time than was objectively possible —I would say less than two minutes) I realized I was on my way home; that somehow my sister was involved in the experience. Essentially simultaneously with this realization I found myself in my home in Southern California, in the living room. Seated in the rocker was my sister, dressed in her pajamas. She seemed upset, somewhat frightened; however, she recognized me immediately and did not seem particularly surprised to see me.

We did not talk, but we seemed to communicate (i.e., I knew she had had a nightmare, she welcomed me, etc.). After standing with her (she had arisen when I appeared) for a brief period of time, we walked back to her bedroom where I observed her body asleep on the bed—she was lying on her right side and seemingly tranquil. The sister with whom I had been communicating observed that it was probably time for me to go and I agreed. Almost simultaneously with this understanding I began to rouse and to realize I was back in the lab.

I was unable to contact the sister before Miss Z went home for a visit a few weeks later, so this experience cannot be considered as to possible parapsychological aspects. On this visit home, Miss Z discussed the incident with her sister, and reported that the latter vaguely recalled having a dream about Miss Z visiting her at about the proper time, but unfortunately no written records were made. As for the experience per se, this sort of OB experience in which she seemed to travel a great distance was unusual for Miss Z.

After reporting the experience described above, Miss Z went back to sleep, had a couple more Stage 1 dreams during the night, and was awakened by me at 6.50 A.M. so that she could get to work.

Night IV

On reporting to the laboratory on the fourth night, Miss Z seemed to be determined to have the right kind of OB experience. Although I had indicated complete satisfaction with her performance so far, she was angry at herself because she had not been able to float up and read the target number.

Miss Z went quickly to sleep, entering Stages 3 and 4 less than fifteen minutes after going to bed. The night was uneventful for the most part—there were several Stage 1 dream periods in the first two-thirds of the night, as would be expected for any normal subject. After four and a half hours of sleep, she had a Stage 1 dream period with REMs which lasted for half an hour. The EEG was technically rather poor on this night, being obscured with a great deal of sixty cycle artifact and requiring rather heavy high frequency filtering to make it clear, so the EEG findings should be taken with the realization that they are subject to more error than usual. Miss Z's Stage 1 dream terminated with several minutes of intermittent body movements and EEG artifact. Then (at 5:50 A.M.) the occipital channel showed an enlarged, slow wave artifact, the REM channel showed no REMs, and the record looked like a Stage 1 tracing; however, I could not be sure due to the considerations mentioned above. At 5:57 A.M. the slow wave artifact was lessened and the record looked somewhat like Stage 1 with REMs, but I could not be sure whether this was a waking or a Stage 1 record. This lasted until 6:04 A.M., at which time Miss Z awoke and called out that the target number was 25132. This was correct (with the digits in correct order), but I did not say anything to her at this point; I merely indicated that I had written the number down on the record. I then told her she could go back to sleep, but twenty minutes later I awakened her so that she could get ready to go to work. At this time, she described her experience as follows:

I woke up; it was stifling in the room. Awake for about five minutes. I kept waking up and drifting off, having floating feelings over and over. I needed to go higher because the number was lying down. Between 5:50 and 6:00 A.M. that did it. . . . I wanted to go read the number in the next room, but I couldn't leave the room, open the door, or float through the door. . . . I couldn't turn off the air conditioner!

It should be mentioned that Miss Z had expected me to prop the target number up against the wall on the shelf; actually, I had laid it flat on the shelf, which she correctly perceived. Also, I had put a second number on a shelf in the equipment room, but she reported she could not get into this room to see the number. Neither could she turn off the air conditioner, and she complained that although it had been stifling, it was too cold in the room by that time.

Since Miss Z's correctly calling a five-digit number (P = 10^5) was the first strong evidence that her OB experiences contained a parapsychological element, I inspected the laboratory carefully* the next day to see if there was any way in which this number could have been read by nonparapsychological means. As a first alternative to an explanation involving extrasensory perception, we decided that "sophisticated" cheating by Miss Z was not impossible. She might have concealed mirrors and reaching rods in her pajamas and used these during the period when the EEG was difficult to classify (due to movement artifacts) to read the number. While this is possible, I personally doubt that it occurred. The second alternative is that she might have seen the number reflected

*I was assisted in this by Dr. Arthur Hastings, whom I wish to thank.

in the surface of the case of the clock which was mounted on the wall above it. This was the only reflecting surface in the room placed in such a way that this might have been possible. Both Dr. Hastings and I spent some time in the dimly lit room to dark-adapt our eyes, and tried to read a number from the subject's position on the bed, as reflected on the surface of the clock. As the room was dimly lit and the surface of the clock was black plastic, we could not see anything of the number. However, when we shone a flashlight *directly* on the number (increasing its brightness by a factor somewhere between several hundred and several thousand) we could just make out what the number was in the much brighter reflection. Thus, although it seems unlikely, one could argue that the number constituted a "subliminal" stimulus in its reflection off the clock surface. Therefore, Miss Z's reading of the target number cannot be considered as providing conclusive evidence for a parapsychological effect.*

After calling out the number, Miss Z again returned to sleep and spent approximately twenty minutes in a stage where the EEG was again quite difficult to classify. It was a generally low voltage, flattened record which looked rather like a poorly developed Stage 1 record. However, there were no REMs to speak of, and there was only a small amount of alphoid activity. Upon awaking, she reported that she had had a number of floating sensations during this time.

DISCUSSION

In the course of four nights in the laboratory, Miss Z reported three clear-cut incidents of "floating" and two instances of feeling completely out of her body. The floating incidents, according to her accounts, were all characterized

*The set-up of the room was changed slightly in preparation for a fifth laboratory night, and the shelf was extended so that no reflection could be seen off the clock from the subject's position in bed. However, personal difficulties forced Miss Z to return to her family's home in Southern California before a fifth laboratory night could be scheduled.

by the feeling that she was starting to rise up above her body, but only slightly, and then being back in her body, usually waking in the process. The "nightmare" during her second laboratory night is not clearly classifiable as an OB experience.

Only the final night in the laboratory produced a report of an OB experience giving fair evidence of parapsychological concomitants (her reading of the target number), but as this evidence is not conclusive, the remainder of this discussion will focus on the *subjective experience* of being out of the body, and on the concomitant psychophysiological states.

It is difficult to state conclusively what kind of EEG pattern accompanied the floating experiences and full OB experience because we must depend on Miss Z's retrospective report for the approximate times when they occurred. In connection with most of these experiences, she reported waking up briefly several times during their course; thus, one would expect whatever pattern accompanied them to be mixed with transitory waking patterns, as well as with the body movement artifacts which generally accompany waking from sleep. My general impression of the EEG correlates of Miss Z's floating and OB experiences is that they occurred during a rather poorly developed Stage 1 pattern which was dominated by alphoid activity and often mixed with transitory periods of wakefulness. This alphoid activity was always one to one and a half cycles per second slower than her normal alpha rhythm. No REMs seemed to accompany these experiences and, judging from the one night when the plethysmograph was working satisfactorily and the two nights when the skin resistance channel was working satisfactorily, there are no marked autonomic alterations concomitant with the experiences; that is, heart rate stays at a normal, steady rate, and there is no pronounced change in either BSR or spontaneous GSR activity.

Further, it can be stated with some certainty that Miss Z's OB experiences do not occur in a normal state of Stage 1 dreaming. She showed normal, well-developed Stage 1 EEG and REM patterns, but she did not report OB experiences in conjunction with these patterns unless they changed into the alphoid pattern, without accompanying REMs.

Figure 1 shows a typical example of Miss Z's waking EEG pattern and an example of Stage 1 dreaming with REMs. Figure 2 shows a sample of Stage 2 sleep with an example of the prominent alphoid pattern she showed in conjunction with her OB experiences; this particular example is taken from her second laboratory night when she reported seeing the time.

Considering, then, that we have a fairly good correlation between Miss Z's reported OB experiences and a relatively distinct neurophysiological pattern, how would we describe her physiological state? Here we run into considerable difficulty. The mixture of Stage 1 and pronounced alphoid activity, along with no REMs or cardiovascular or skin resistance changes, has not been described before, to my knowledge, in the sleep literature.* The particular pattern cannot be unequivocally classified as a waking pattern, nor can it be unequivocally classified as any of the known stages of sleep. Nor is it a typical Stage 1 drowsy pattern by any means, because of the pronounced alphoid activity. Dr. William Dement, one of the world's leading authorities on sleep research, kindly looked at these patterns, and agreed with me that they could not very well be classified into any of the known sleep stages, nor could they even be classified unambiguously as waking or drowsy patterns.

From some points of view, we could say that Miss Z was in a hypnagogic state at the time of her OB experiences, or in a transitional state between sleeping and waking; but simply putting a familiar label on the state tells us nothing about its nature. Furthermore, the presence of so much alphoid activity is not typical of hypnagogic states. However, some

---

*Alphoid activity is usually mentioned as a component of Stage 1 sleep, but there are no quantitative standards available as to how much alphoid activity is typical. Thus I am depending upon personal experience with dozens of sleep records in forming my impression that Miss Z's alphoid activity was exceptionally prominent during her OB experiences.

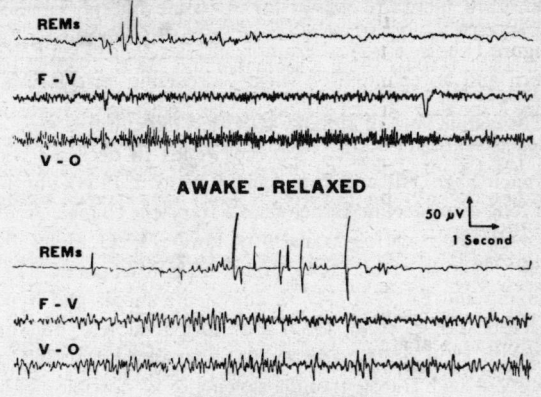

FIG. 1. A typical example of Miss Z's waking EEG pattern and an example of Stage 1 dreaming with REMs.

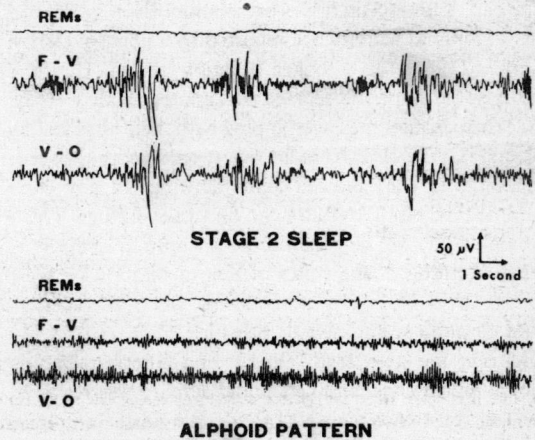

FIG. 2. A sample of Miss Z's Stage 2 sleep and an example of the alphoid pattern she showed in conjunction with her OB experiences.

interesting literature is starting to come out of Japanese laboratories on the slowing of the alpha rhythm during Zen meditation (Hirai, 1960; Kasamatsu and Hirai, 1963; Kasamatsu, et al., n.d.).

The significance of alphoid activity is difficult to assess. In ordinary subjects, alpha frequency tends to decrease with advancing age (Hill and Parr, 1963; Kleitman, 1963), but this is a long-term decline rather than a transient change. Acute alcoholic intoxication transiently lowers EEG alpha frequency (Davis, et al., 1941; Engel and Rosenbaum, 1945; Romano and Engel, 1944), as does acute anoxia and hypoglycemia (Engel, et al., 1945). For normal subjects not subjected to such drastic treatments, however, I can find no reports of such transient alpha slowing or its possible significance.

One other unusual experimental treatment has been reported to result in slowed alpha activity, namely, sensory isolation. Heron (1957) presents graphs which show a shift from alpha activity predominating at 10 cps for three normal subjects to 9 cps for two of them and 8 cps for one of them at the end of ninety-six hours of isolation. Even more drastic shifts to alphoid activity are reported by Zubek, Welch, and Saunders (1963) for a longer isolation period. Heron also mentions that some subjects felt as if another body were lying beside them, sometimes overlapping with their physical body, although it is not clear from his report whether these were the same subjects who showed alpha slowing. In any case, it would be interesting to follow up on these findings. This is a transient alpha slowing in otherwise normal subjects, but further equating of the states of Zen meditation or sensory isolation with Miss Z's state during her OB experiences would be quite speculative at this time.

There is one sleep study (Lester and Guerrero-Figueroa, 1966) in which considerable alphoid activity was reported in the sleep records as a result of chlorpromazine administration. Chlorpromazine is a fairly commonly used tranquilizer known under the trade name of Thorazine. A friend indicated that Miss Z might have been taking trifluoperazine (Stelazine) at the time of the study. Neither Miss Z herself, her roommate, nor her boyfriend recall that she was taking this at the time of the study, but it remains a possibility. There have been no studies of the effect of this drug on the sleep EEG, but the possibility should be borne in mind that Miss Z might have been taking this medication, and that it might have contributed to the alphoid activity in her patterns. But even if this were true, it would not account for the findings, as the fact remains that her OB experiences were associated with this unique pattern, which was quite distinguishable from the normal sleep stage patterns. Indeed, one might speculate that drugs which tend to slow alpha frequency might promote OB experiences, and this could be a possibly fruitful line of experimental inquiry.

It is important to note that Miss Z's psychophysiological state during the OB experiences was not at all what one would predict from reading various occult works on OB experiences or "astral projections" (Dunville, 1909; Fox, 1962; Muldoon and Carrington, 1956; Ophiel, 1961), or from accounts of OB experiences reported in conjunction with serious illnesses or accidents (Crookall, 1961, 1964a, 1964b; Muldoon and Carrington, 1953). These works lead one to expect that a "death-like trance" accompanies OB experiences, in which respiration and heart beat would be markedly slowed, temperature might fall considerably, and in which one would probably see the sort of brain waves (high voltage slow waves) characteristic of coma (Silverman, 1963). Miss Z did not seem to be in a "death-like trance." When it was measured, her heart rate was normal and steady, there was no unusual autonomic activity, and the Stage 1 and alphoid activity in the EEG was not what one associates with coma.

Closer reading of some of the techniques described in the occult literature for producing OB experiences (e.g., Carrington, 1958; Fox, 1902; Hall, 1916, 1918; Muldoon and Carrington, 1956; Ophiel, 1960), however, suggests that there may be several distinct sorts of experiences produced by the variety of techniques presented. Some of these techniques are dream-control techniques, in which the dreamer must recognize that he is dreaming and then convert the dream into an OB experience. Others are what we might call hypnagogic experiences, for they involve fixedly holding the idea of having an OB experience in mind while allowing oneself to drift into a hypnagogic or sleep state. Still other techniques seem to involve the creation of a "trance" state, but nothing further will be said about this third possibility here because writers use the term "trance" in very ambiguous ways, as will be discussed elsewhere (Zubek, et al., 1963). Miss Z's experiences may have been cases of hypnagogic phenomena following brief awakenings during the night, or of a Stage 1 dream being converted into an OB experience. Which alternative is true is not clear from the exploratory work of this study.

The tentativeness of the correlations reported here between OB experiences and brain-wave states should be noted. The EEG is a complex phenomenon that varies in terms of frequency, regularity, waveshape, spatial distribution over the brain, and interareal phase relationships. The analyses reported in this paper were confined to visual inspection: adequate investigation of the possible EEG correlates of OB experiences will have to use the most sophisticated recording and electronic analysis techniques, as well as running the selected subjects through control conditions to see which EEG correlates are unique to the OB experience and which appear under other circumstances as well.

In summary, this brief study found a fairly clear-cut correlation between several of Miss Z's reported OB experiences and a physiological pattern characterized by a flattened EEG with prominent alphoid activity, no REM or skin resistance activity, and normal heart rate. Much more work remains to be done before we can begin to understand the psychophysiological and parapsychological aspects of OB experiences, and it is hoped that the present study, insofar as it has shown that these experiences can be studied by the techniques of modern science, will encourage other investigators to carry out further experiments.

REFERENCES

Agnew, H., Webb, W., and Williams, R. "The First Night Effect: An EEG Study of Sleep." *Psychophysiology* 2 (1966): 263–66.

Aserinsky, E., and Kleitman, N. "Regularly Occurring Periods of Eye Motility and Concomitant Phenomena during Sleep." *Science* 118 (1953): 273–74.

_____. "Two Types of Ocular Motility Occurring in Sleep." *Journal of Applied Physiology* 8 (1955): 1–10.

Baldridge, B., Whitman, R., and Kramer, M. "A Simplified Method for Detecting Eye Movements during Dreaming." *Psychosomatic Medicine* 25 (1963): 78–82.

Berger, R. "Tonus of Extrinsic Laryngeal Muscles during Sleep and Dreaming." *Science* 134 (1961): 840.

Berger, R., and Oswald, I. "Eye Movement during Active and Passive Dreams." *Science,* Vol. 137 (1962): 601.

Brown, C., Giddon, D., and Dean, E. "Techniques of Plethysmography." *Psychophysiology* 1 (1965): 253–66.

Carrington, H. *Modern Psychical Phenomena.* New York: Dodd, Mead and Co., 1919.

_____. *Your Psychic Powers and How to Develop Them.* New York: Templestar Publishers, 1958.

Crookall, R. *The Study and Practice of Astral Projection.* London: Aquarian Press, 1961.

_____. *More Astral Projections: Analyses of Case Histories.* London: Aquarian Press, 1964a.

_____. *The Techniques of Astral Projection.* London: Aquarian Press, 1964b.

Davis, P., Gibbs, F., Davis, H., Jetter, W., and Trowbridge, L. "The Effects of Alcohol upon the Electroencephalogram (Brain Waves)." *Quarterly Journal for the Study of Alcohol* 1 (1941): 626–37.

Dement, W. "Dream Recall and Eye Movements during Sleep in Schizophrenics and Normals." *Journal of Nervous and Mental Disease* 122 (1955): 263–69.

————. "The Effect of Dream Deprivation." *Science* 131 (1960): 1705–7.

Dement, W., and Kleitman, N. "Cyclic Variations in EEG during Sleep and Their Relation to Eye Movements, Body Motility, and Dreaming." *Electroencephalography and Clinical Neurophysiology* 9 (1957a): 673–90.

————. "The Relation of Eye Movements during Sleep to Dream Activity: An Objective Method for the Study of Dreaming." *Journal of Experimental Psychology* 53 (1957b): 339–46.

Dement, W., Rechtschaffen, A., and Gulevich, G. "The Nature of the Narcoleptic Sleep Attack." *Neurology* 16 (1966): 18–33.

Dement, W., and Wolpert, E. "The Relation of Eye Movements, Body Motility, and External Stimuli to Dream Content." *Journal of Experimental Psychology* 55 (1958): 543–53.

Domhoff, B., and Kamiya, J. "Problems in Dream Content Study with Objective Indicators: II. Appearance of Experimental Situation in Laboratory Dream Narratives." *Archives of General Psychiatry* 11 (1964): 525–28.

Durville, H. *Le Fantôme des Vivants.* Paris: Librairie du Magnétisme, 1909.

Engel, G., and Rosenbaum, M. "Delirium III. EEG Changes Associated with Acute Alcoholic Intoxication." *Archives of Neurology and Psychiatry* 53 (1945): 44–50.

Engel, G., Webb, J., and Ferris, E. "Quantitative EEG Studies of Anoxia in Humans: Comparison with Acute Alcoholic Intoxication and Hypoglycemia." *Journal of Clinical Investigation* 24 (1945): 691–97.

Foulkes, D. "Dream Reports from Different Stages of Sleep." *Journal of Abnormal and Social Psychology* 65 (1962): 14–25.

————. *The Psychology of Sleep.* New York: Scribner's, 1966.

Fox, O. *Astral Projection: A Record of Out-of-the-Body Experiences.* New Hyde Park, N.Y.: University Books, 1962.

Hall, P. "Digest of Spirit Teachings Received through Mrs. Minnie E. Keeler." *Journal A.S.P.R.* 10 (November and December 1916): 632–60; 679–708.

———. "Experiments in Astral Projection." *Journal A.S.P.R.* 12 (January 1918): 39–60.

Hart, H. "Hypnosis as an Aid in Experimental ESP Projection." Paper read at First International Conference of Parapsychological Studies, Utrecht, 1953.

———. "Six Theories about Apparitions." *Proceedings S.P.R.* 50 (1956): 153–239.

———. "Traveling ESP." *Proceedings* of the First International Conference of Parapsychological Studies. New York: Parapsychology Foundation, Inc., 1955.

Hawkins, D., Puryear, H., Wallace, C., Deal, W., and Thomas, E. "Basal Skin Resistance during Sleep and 'Dreaming.' " *Science* 136 (1962): 321–22.

Heron, W. "The Pathology of Boredom." *Scientific American* 196 (1957): 52–56.

Hill, D., and Parr, G. (eds.). *Electroencephalography: A Symposium on its Various Aspects.* New York: Macmillan, 1963.

Hirai, T. "An Electroencephalographic Study of Zen Meditation (Zazen): EEG Changes during Concentrated Relaxation." *Psychiatria et Neurologia Japonica* 5 (1960): 5.

Hishikawa, Y., and Kaneko, Z. "Electroencephalographic Study on Narcolepsy." *Electroencephalography and Clinical Neurophysiology* 18 (1965): 249–59.

Kamiya, J. "Behavioral, Subjective, and Physiological Aspects of Drowsiness and Sleep." In D. Fiske and S. Maddi (eds.), *Functions of Varied Experience.* Homewood, Ill.: Dorsey Press, 1961.

Kasamatsu, A., and Hirai, T. "Science of Zazen." *Psychologia* 6 (1963): 86–91.

Kasamatsu, A., Hirai, T., and Ando, N. "EEG Responses to Click Stimulation in Zen Meditation." (Reprint; no other details available.)

Kleitman, N. "Patterns of Dreaming." *Scientific American* 203 (1960): 81–88.

_____. *Sleep and Wakefulness.* Chicago: University of Chicago Press, 1963 (2nd ed.).

Lester, B., and Guerrero-Figueroa, R. "Effects of Some Drugs on Electroencephalographic Fast Activity and Dream Time." *Psychophysiology* 2 (1966): 224–36.

Muldoon, S., and Carrington, H. *The Phenomena of Astral Projection.* London: Rider and Co., 1953.

_____. *The Projection of the Astral Body.* London: Rider and Co., 1956.

O'Connell, D., and Tursky, B. "Silver-silver Chloride Sponge Electrodes for Skin Potential Recording." *American Journal of Psychology* 73 (1960): 302–4.

Ophiel (pseudonym). *The Art and Practice of Astral Projection.* San Francisco: Peach Publishing Co., 1961.

Oswald, I. *Sleeping and Waking: Physiology and Psychology.* New York: Elsevier, 1962.

_____. "Physiology of Sleep Accompanying Dreaming." In *Scientific Basis of Medicine: Annual Review,* 1964.

Pierce, C., Mathis, J., and Jabbour, J. "Dream Patterns in Narcoleptic and Hydrancephalic Patients." *American Journal of Psychiatry* 122 (1965): 402–4.

Rechtschaffen, A., and P. Verdone. "Amount of Dreaming: Effect of Incentive, Adaptation to Laboratory, and Individual Differences." *Perceptual and Motor Skills* 19 (1964): 947–58.

Rechtschaffen, A., Verdone, P., and Wheaton, J. "Reports of Mental Activity during Sleep." *Canadian Journal of Psychiatry* 8 (1963): 409–14.

Rechtschaffen, A., Wolpert, E., Dement, W., Mitchell, S., and Fisher, C. "Nocturnal Sleep of Narcoleptics." *Electroencephalography and Clinical Neurophysiology* 15 (1963): 599–609.

Roffwarg, H., Dement, W., Muzio, J., and Fisher, C. "Dream Imagery: Relationship to Rapid Eye Movements of Sleep." *Archives of General Psychiatry* 7 (1962): 235–58.

Romano, J., and Engel, G. "Delirium: Electroencephalographic Data." *Archives of Neurology and Psychiatry* 51 (1944): 356–77.

Silverman, D. "Retrospective Study of the EEG in Coma." *Electroencephalography and Clinical Neurophysiology* 15 (1963): 486–503.

Snyder, F. "The New Biology of Dreaming." *Archives of General Psychiatry* 8 (1963): 381–91.

————. "Progress in the New Biology of Dreaming." *American Journal of Psychiatry* 122 (1965): 377–91.

Tart, C. "The Influence of the Experimental Situation in Hypnosis and Dream Research: A Case Report." *American Journal of Clinical Hypnosis* 7 (1964): 163–70.

————. "The Concept of Trance." Manuscript in preparation.

————. "Technical Note: Use of Strain Gauges to Measure Rapid Eye Movements." Paper, Association for the Psychophysiological Study of Sleep, New York, 1963.

Whitman, R., Pierce, C., Maas, J., and Baldridge, B. "The Dreams of the Experimental Subject." *Journal of Nervous and Mental Disease* 134 (1962): 431–39.

Williams, H., Tepas, D., and Morlock, H. "Evoked Responses to Clicks and Electroencephalographic Stages of Sleep in Man." *Science* 138 (1962): 685–86.

Wood, P. "Dreaming and Social Isolation." Unpublished doctoral dissertation, University of North Carolina, 1962.

Yram (pseudonym). *Practical Astral Projection.* New York, Samuel Weiser, 1965.

Zubek, J., Welch, G., and Saunders, M. "Electroencephalographic Changes during and after 14 Days of Perceptual Deprivation." *Science* 139 (1963): 490–92.

5 | A Second Psychophysiological Study of Out-of-the-Body Experiences in a Gifted Subject

CHARLES T. TART

INTRODUCTION

Reports of people finding themselves "outside" their physical body have come down to us from the most ancient recorded history and from a multitude of different cultures. The typical experience usually contains some combination of the following elements: (1) floating; (2) seeing one's physical body from the outside; (3) thinking of a distant place while "outside" and suddenly finding oneself there; (4) possessing a nonphysical body; and (5) being absolutely convinced that the experience was *not* a dream. For the vast majority of people who report this, it was a once-in-a-lifetime experience, and, although it was frequently reported as pleasurable, they had no idea what caused it or how to make it reoccur. It was also puzzling to many of the reporters, as they had never heard of such experiences and did not know what to make of them.

Because of its apparently universal distribution across cultures and throughout history, the out-of-the-body experience (OBE) constitutes what Carl Jung termed an archetypal experience—an experience potentially available to many members of the human race simply by virtue of being human. In the last fifty years, a very small number of scholars have taken an interest in the OBE, but this interest has been almost wholly a matter of collecting case reports, documenting them, and doing some analysis on the content of these spontaneously occurring cases (Crookall, 1961, 1964a, 1964b; Hart, 1956; Muldoon and Carrington, 1953). The main exception has been the use of hypnosis in an attempt to produce the OBE experimentally, but this is old work (Durville, 1909;

Hart, 1953) that has not been repeated under decent conditions in many years.

Most of the interest in OBEs has resulted from the fact that the content of the OBE sometimes provides information about real-world events occurring at distant places, thus indicating the operation of some form of extrasensory perception (ESP). This latter fact is of considerable importance in attempting to understand the nature of OBEs. Without it, one can regard them as interesting and unique forms of "subjective" experience, quite worthy of study in their own right. With the ESP component, the OBE takes on the characteristics of an "objective" event, the ultimate understanding of which has important implications for our view of the nature of man.

The difficulty in advancing beyond these two conclusions about OBEs is their once-in-a-lifetime characteristic. There are so many questions about the nature of OBEs that can only be answered by observing them while they are occurring. I had an exceptional stroke of luck two years ago in finding a young woman who was apparently able to produce OBEs while undergoing physiological measurements (Tart, 1968). Laboratory studies of the physiological state of a person during a "naturally" occurring OBE can not only give us information about the state of their nervous system per se, but may give us hints on how to produce that state by other means and thus possibly learn how to produce OBEs in *many* people. If we could produce OBEs at will in the laboratory, we could very rapidly solve many problems about the nature of the experience and the ESP component of the experience, in the same way that the 1953 discovery (Aserinsky and Kleitman, 1953) of the correlation between dreaming and a particular psychophysiological state, Stage 1 electroencephelographic (EEG) pattern, and presence of rapid eye movements (REMs) brought about a massive increase in research on all types of dreaming and has immensely increased our knowledge in the last decade.

During the fall of 1965, I was again blessed with luck in making the acquaintance and friendship of a man (hereinafter referred to as Mr. X) who reported that he had experienced hundreds of OBEs and was willing to try to produce them under laboratory conditions. Mr. X plans to describe his experiences in detail elsewhere (Monroe, 1971), and this paper will be concerned only with the psychophysiological studies I was able to carry out with him.

METHOD

Mr. X was monitored for nine sessions* at various times between December 1965 and August 1966. Eight of the sessions were in the evening, generally from about 9 P.M. to midnight or later; one was an all-night study of sleep patterns. I ran the equipment for the first four sessions; a technician, Mrs. Beverly Hudgins, for the later sessions.† In addition, a full-scale clinical EEG report on Mr. X was obtained from Dr. Lever Stewart, of the University of Virginia Hospital, in order to check for any EEG abnormalities.

In the experimental session, Mr. X had electrodes attached to his head for recording EEG (generally right and left frontal-to-vertex and vertex-to-occipital leads), REMS (standard electro-oculographic method), and heart rate (a chest-to-ear electrocardiogram lead). These potentials were recorded on a Grass EEG machine, at a paper speed of 15mm/sec. The subject reclined on a cot in one room; the technician and equipment were in a second room. A window between the rooms allowed the technician to observe the subject.

Data from two of the earlier experimental sessions had to be discarded, as the notes on equipment settings had been lost in the course of moving the data across country; this made the EEG tracings very difficult to interpret.

Because Mr. X believed many of his OBEs contained ESP elements, the following test situation was set up during each

*The monitoring was done in the Electroencephalography Laboratory of the University of Virginia Hospital. I wish to thank Dr. Lever Stewart for making these facilities available to me.

†This study was supported by a grant from the Parapsychology Foundation of New York City; Eileen J. Garrett, President.

laboratory session: A shelf was attached to the wall in the equipment room (*not* the subject's room), about six feet above the floor, above eye level. After Mr. X was in bed, the technician removed a cardboard strip from a sealed envelope and placed it face up, without looking at it, on the shelf. A five-digit random number, different for each session, had been drawn in large figures on the face of the strip. This number, the target, was prepared by me and given directly to the technician, so that Mr. X would have no ordinary way of knowing what it was. He was instructed to try to float near the ceiling of the equipment room, observe the face-up target, and memorize the number if he had an OBE. In the first four sessions, I knew what the number was but did not tell Mr. X; in the remainder I knew but was not present; the technician placed the target on the shelf without looking at it and so did not know what it was until the conclusion of the evening's experiment.

Before presenting the results of the experimental sessions, the following section will describe the EEG and its nature during sleep and dreaming, for those readers not acquainted with this area of knowledge.

BRAIN WAVES, SLEEP, AND DREAMING

If small electrodes are glued to the scalp and connected to very sensitive amplifiers, fluctuating electrical potentials will be found. These potentials arise from the electrical activity of the brain. Since what is detected on the scalp is a composite mixture of the activities of billions of brain cells, no particular kind of electrical activity can be associated, *in detail,* with the functioning of a particular area of the brain. However, various patterns of electrical activity recorded from the scalp— the EEG—have been associated with different states of consciousness (Hill and Parr, 1963). The primary states that can be distinguished are waking and sleeping. Within the waking state, one may distinguish various degrees of activation or alertness, ranging from rather frantic hyperalertness (emotional excitement or hard mental work) through relaxed attentiveness to drowsiness. Extreme alertness is associated with a low-voltage, generally fast and irregular pattern of 10 to 20 microvolts amplitude and frequencies ranging from 10 to 40 cycles per second (cps). Relaxed alertness is accompanied in many people by the alpha rhythm, a rather regular, sinusoidal rhythm whose frequency varies from about 8 to 13 cps, although in a single person the frequency is relatively constant. As a person becomes drowsy, this alpha rhythm breaks up, clusters of it becoming less and less frequent as they are replaced by a Stage 1 drowsy pattern. Consciousness waxes and wanes with the alpha rhythm, although it is impossible to say clearly at exactly what point consciousness is lost. The transitional state between waking and sleeping is called the hypnagogic state. Many people experience fairly vivid imagery as they pass through this state into sleep, but little else is known about its psychological characteristics.

The Stage 1 EEG pattern consists of an irregular mixture of theta waves (between 4 and 8 cps, low in amplitude), occasional alpha waves, and alphoid waves appearing irregularly (waves like the alpha rhythm but 1 or 2 cps slower than the subject's waking alpha rhythm).

Sleep is definitely present when a Stage 2 EEG pattern shows. This pattern is like the Stage 1 drowsy pattern except that a new kind of wave pattern, the sleep spindle, appears. These are short bursts of waves, at about 14 cps frequency, which start at a very low amplitude, build up to about 30–40 microvolts within a few cycles, and then taper off, giving the overall wave train a spindle shape.

Sleep is further divided into Stages 3 and 4. These stages are characterized by the appearance of delta waves, which are high-voltage (100 microvolts or more), slow (one cps or slower) waves. A few of these define Stage 3; a preponderance of them define Stage 4. Spindles and irregular theta waves continue in Stages 3 and 4.

Stages 1 through 4 were initially conceived of as comprising a continuum from "light" to "deep" sleep, but many other measures of the depth of sleep contradict this ordering. Stage 1 sleep occurring later in the night seems to have very distinct characteristics which make it a distinct *kind* of sleep, while Stages 2, 3, and 4 do seem to comprise a depth continuum in a second *kind* of sleep.

Stage-1 EEG sleep periods later in the night are accompanied by binocularly synchronous rapid eye movements (REMs), highly variable heart rate and breathing, and an inhibition of nerve transmission to the muscles.

If subjects are awakened from the two types of sleep and asked to report what they have been experiencing, the reports may be classified into two rather distinct types. One type—awakenings from Stage 1 sleep or shortly (within, roughly, ten to fifteen minutes) after Stage 1 sleep has changed to Nonstage 1 sleep—possesses the characteristics traditionally associated with the experience of dreaming. Reports from Nonstage 1 sleep seem more like "thinking" and are generally called thinking by the subjects (these same subjects generally refer to their Stage 1 experiences as dreams). The psychological differences reported so far are quantitative, rather than being completely dichotomous, but generally give the impression of distinct types of experiences.

Stage 1 sleep is almost always accompanied by REMs, and the evidence is very convincing that these are closely associated with the content of the dream, if not actual scanning movements of the dream imagery. Such REMs have not been reported in Nonstage 1 sleep, although there are some slow, rolling movements of the eyes.

For normal subjects, Stage 1 dreaming and Nonstage 1 sleep alternate in a regular, cyclic fashion, the sleep-dream cycle. As a subject falls asleep, there is generally a brief period (a few seconds to a minute or two) of Stage 1, without REMs, but subjects' reports indicate that this is a period of hypnagogic imagery rather than typical dreaming. At approximately ninety-minute intervals throughout the night there are periods of Stage 1 dreaming, each dream period generally being longer than the preceding one. The first Stage 1 period may last for ten minutes; the fourth or fifth may last as long as fifty minutes. Altogether, Stage 1 dreaming occupies between 20 percent and 30 percent of the total sleep time of most young adults, spread over three to six Stage 1 periods. While the exact percentage of dream time and the number of cycles vary from subject to subject, for a given subject the sleep-dream cycle is generally quite stable from night to night. Extensive and detailed reviews of the new sleep and EEG literature may be found elsewhere (Dement, 1965; Foulkes, 1966; Kleitman, 1960, 1963; Oswald, 1962; Snyder, 1963, 1965).

Thus, a laboratory study of a subject producing OBEs should be able to indicate (if the approximate time of the OBE can be judged from the subject's report) the EEG pattern accompanying the OBE. This pattern can be inspected to see whether the OBE occurs in conjunction with a known stage of sleep or in an entirely unknown state. Intensive analysis of EEG patterns (not possible without expensive equipment) might even reveal which areas of the brain seem to be involved in the production of OBEs.

RESULTS

The report of the full-scale clinical EEG on Mr. X describes his waking brain-wave activity as a quite well-developed, well-regulated, symmetrical, rather generalized 10 cps alpha rhythm which predominated posteriorly and altered appropriately on eye opening. Once, Mr. X tried to produce "spikes" in his EEG activity, and at another time he tried to produce a "vortex in the brain's electrical activity"; but neither of these subjective experiences was accompanied by any clear EEG change. The EEG pattern at these times was almost continuous alpha rhythm, indicating relaxed alertness. Intermittent runs of rather fast 13 cps alpha activity appeared in the frontal portions of Mr. X's EEG recording at times, but the significance of such rhythms is unknown (Hill and Parr, 1963). The examining physician felt that the waking EEG was within normal limits.

In the experimental sessions, Mr. X reported considerable difficulty in adjusting to the EEG electrodes, primarily because of a clip-type electrode on the ear which made it mildly painful for him to lie on his side on the cot. This was a technical oversight. He did not feel that he was successful in producing an OBE until the next to the last session, at which he was apparently successful. This will be described in detail below.

A general characteristic of all the experimental sessions was the finding that Mr. X's EEG showed such a variety of changes that it was quite difficult or impossible to classify it in the conventional waking and sleeping patterns on many occasions. His EEG was highly variable in both frequency and voltage. For example, he showed alpha rhythm frequencies ranging from 8 to 13 cps—an unusually large range—with voltages ranging from 40 to 100 microvolts. His sleep spindles ranged in frequency from 14 to 17 cps,* 30 to 100 microvolts; almost every other subject I have seen in the laboratory has shown sleep spindles that were at 14 cps, and 14 cps only. Frequently, the theta waves in his sleep patterns showed bursts of three to eight theta waves which had amplitudes of 150 to 200 microvolts; I have never seen theta activity in other subjects exceed about 50 microvolts. Finally, although Mr. X frequently fell asleep, I found no instances of clearly developed delta waves in any of his EEG patterns, whereas one generally sees delta waves within half an hour of falling asleep in all subjects. Thus, almost all of the subject's sleep patterns were classified as Stage 1 or Stage 2— never as Stage 3 or 4, because of the lack of delta waves. Whether the very high voltage theta waves constituted "speeded up" delta waves is unclear. There is some sparse indication in the sleep literature that delta waves may normally be rare in men in the fifty-year-old range. By and large, however, the empirical data have not been published that would indicate how atypical Mr. X's sleep patterns are, much less what this atypicality "means." On the basis of my personal sleep laboratory experience (primarily with adult males in the twenty- to thirty-year age range), Mr. X's sleep EEG

---

*The 13-cps frontal alpha reported in the clinical examination may have been confused with some of the spindling.

patterns look very atypical; and the classification into Stages 1 and 2 was often quite tentative, due to the lability of his EEG.

All but one of the experimental sessions were attempts by Mr. X to produce OBEs. When the EEG pattern indicated that he had been asleep for a long period of time, he was usually awakened by the technician and reminded of the experimental task of having an OBE. Stage 1 dreaming was seldom noticed in any of the other records, although I would have expected some from ordinary subjects.

There were a number of instances in which the subject reported that he had not been asleep—i.e., that he had remained conscious—between interruptions by the technician. However, the EEG record showed Stage 1 drowsy states and/or Stage 2 sleep states during these times. To know how to interpret this is difficult, as a number of recent studies indicate that sleep is not a period of total unconsciousness punctuated by the strange consciousness of dreaming. Rather, there seems to be a rudimentary sort of conscious awareness during nondreaming, Nonstage 1 sleep for many subjects, although memory of it is quite poor and its content is usually sparse and nonhallucinatory (Baldridge, Whitman, and Kramer, 1965; Fiss, Klein, and Bokert, 1966; Foulkes, 1962, 1964; Goodenough, Lewis, Shapiro, Jaret, and Sleser, 1965; Monroe, Rechtschaffen, Foulkes, and Jensen, 1965; Rechtschaffen, Verdone, and Wheaton, 1963). Descriptively, it seems as if normal thought processes went on at a very slow rate. Mr. X may have a particularly good recall of Nonstage 1 sleep, or he may be conscious to an unusual degree in this state.

There was a good deal of slowed alpha activity (so-called alphoid activity) scattered throughout Mr. X's records. Much time was spent in borderline states between sleep and full waking, i.e., in Stage 1 EEG pattern without REMs.

Heart rate was quite steady in all the sessions, ranging between sixty-five and seventy-five beats per minute across sessions and seldom varying more than a few beats per minute within any individual session.

For the final session, Mr. X slept in the laboratory throughout the night without attempting to produce any OBEs; we were interested in what his normal sleep cycle looked like. The timing and length of the Stage 1 dream periods seemed normal and, except for the EEG peculiarities mentioned earlier (no delta, varying frequency of spindles, etc.), there was nothing remarkable about this night.

During the eighth session, Mr. X reported two OBEs. He had spent an hour trying to get comfortable, with little success because of the discomfort of the electrodes. Then he took a ten-minute break for a cigarette (without leaving his cot). I quote now from his report, written by him the following day, of succeeding events:

After some time spent in attempting to ease ear-electrode discomfort, concentrated on ear to "numb" it, with partial success. Then went into fractional relaxation technique again. Halfway through the second time around in the pattern the sense of warmth appeared, with full consciousness (or so it seemed) remaining. I decided to try the "roll-out" method* (i.e., start to turn over gently, just as if you were turning over in bed using the physical body). I started to feel as if I were turning, and at first thought I truly was moving the physical body. I felt myself roll off the edge of the cot, and braced for the fall to the floor. When I didn't hit immediately, I knew that I had disassociated. I moved away from the physical and through a darkened area, then came upon two men and a woman. The "seeing" wasn't too good, but better as I came closer. The woman, tall, dark-haired, in her forties (?) was sitting on a loveseat or couch. Seated to the right of her was one man. In front of her, and to her left slightly was the second man. They all were strangers to me, and were in conversation which I could not hear. I tried to get their attention, but could not. Finally, I reached over, and pinched (very gently!) the woman on her left side just below the rib cage. It seemed to get a reaction, but still no communication. I decided to return to the physical for orientation and start again.

Back into the physical was achieved simply, by thought of return.

*Mr. X has developed a number of techniques for producing OBEs, which are described in his book (Monroe, 1971).

Opened physical eyes, all was fine, swallowed to wet my dry throat, closed my eyes, let the warmth surge up, then used the same roll-out technique. This time, I let myself float to the floor beside the cot. I fell slowly, and could feel myself passing through the various EEG wires on the way down. I touched the floor lightly, then could "see" the light coming through the open doorway to the outer EEG rooms. Careful to keep "local," I went under the cot, keeping in slight touch with the floor, and floating in a horizontal position, fingertips touching the floor to keep in position, I went slowly through the doorway. I was looking for the technician, but could not find her. She was not in the room to the right (control console room), and I went out into the brightly lighted outer room. I looked in all directions, and suddenly, there she was. However, she was not alone. A man was with her, standing to her left as she faced me.

I tried to attract her attention, and was almost immediately rewarded with a burst of warm joy and happiness that I had finally achieved the thing we had been working for. She was truly excited, and happily and excitedly embraced me. I responded, and only slight sexual overtones were present which I was about 90% able to disregard. After a moment, I pulled back, and gently put my hands on her face, one on each cheek, and thanked her for her help. However, there was no direct intelligent objective communication with her other than the above.* None was tried, as I was too excited at finally achieving the disassociation—and staying "local."

I then turned to the man, who was about her height, curly haired, some of which dropped over the side of his forehead. I tried to attract his attention, but was unable to do so. Again, reluctantly, I decided to pinch him gently, which I did. It did not evoke any response that I noticed. Feeling something calling for a return to the physical, I swung around and went through the door, and slipped easily back into the physical. Reason for discomfort: dry throat and throbbing ear.

After checking to see that the integration was complete, that I

---

*Mr. X reports that he has frequently experienced "intelligent responses" from physically embodied persons during his OBEs; but since the people almost never remembered it when he checked later, he did not believe that the technician had actually gone through the physical movements of an embrace.

"felt" normal in all parts of the body, I opened my eyes, sat up, and called to the technician. She came in, and I told her that I had made it finally, and that I had seen her, however, with a man. She replied that it was her husband. I asked if he was outside, and she replied that he was, that he came to stay with her during these late hours. I asked why I hadn't seen him before, and she replied that it was "policy" for no outsiders to see subjects or patients. I expressed the desire to meet him, to which she acceded.

The technician removed the electrodes, and I went outside with her and met her husband. He was about her height, curly haired, and after several conversational amenities, I left. I did not query the technician or her husband as to anything they saw, noticed, or felt. However, my impression was that he definitely was the man I had observed with her during the nonphysical activity. My second impression was that she was not in the control console room when I visited them, but was in another room, standing up, with him. This may be hard to determine, if there is a firm rule that the technician is supposed to always stay at the console. If she can be convinced that the truth is more important in this case, perhaps this second aspect can be validated. The only supporting evidence other than what might have appeared on the EEG lies in the presence of the husband, of which I was unaware prior to the experiment. This latter fact can be verified by the technician, I am sure.

Since Mr. X recalls rousing himself as soon as the second OBE was ended and reports a "normal" state (in which we would presumably expect a waking EEG pattern) shortly before that, as he "checked in" on his physical body, it should be possible to correlate the EEG pattern fairly closely with the experiences.

The following parallel between EEG patterns and reported experiences emerges. As he tried to produce an OBE, after the cigarette break, his EEG shows almost continuous alpha rhythm for a period of eight minutes (as much as 64 percent of the record would be filled with well-developed alpha)—which probably corresponded to his attempts to numb his painful ear. Then there was a four-minute period when the alpha was interrupted by short bursts of Stage 1 drowsiness;

then a ten-minute period of predominant Stage 1 drowsiness —interrupted, however, by bursts of alpha rhythm. This period probably corresponds to the fractional relaxation technique; whether it corresponds to the feeling of "warmth" and "roll-out" is unknown. There then followed a seven-minute period of Stage 2 sleep, which included the unusually high-voltage theta waves often seen in his recordings. It is possible that the "warmth" and "roll-out" could have occurred in this time rather than earlier. Then there were three minutes of Stage 1 dreaming sleep with REMs, a body movement and awakening that lasted about forty seconds; three more minutes of Stage 1 sleep with REMs; and a final awakening, at which point Mr. X called out to the technician and described his two OBEs. The EEG pattern during these two periods was clearly Stage 1 EEG, without the ambiguity of many of the other classifications. It seems probable that the first OBE occurred during the three minutes of the first stage-1 REM period, that the forty seconds of wakefulness corresponded to the "checking in, opening eyes, swallowing," and that the second three-minute Stage 1 REM period corresponded to the second OBE. The "warmth" and "roll-out" could also have occurred at the beginning of the first Stage 1 REM period.

The main difficulty in being certain of this parallelism between the EEG findings and the reported OOBE sequence was that Mr. X later reported to me that the OOBEs seemed to last for only about thirty seconds each, while the Stage 1 REM periods lasted three minutes each. Within the Stage 1 patterns of shorter duration, there could have been fine EEG changes that were not obvious to visual analysis, but this is conjectural.

Heart rate was 70 beats/min. during the first Stage 1 dream period and 65 beats/min. during the second, rates which were not at all unusual for Mr. X.

With respect to the question of whether there is an ESP component to Mr. X's OBEs, the evidence from this study is fairly positive but inconclusive. Mr. X did not claim to have seen the target number, which would have provided very strong evidence for the operation of ESP. However, he did provide information about the technician's activities that is mildly evidential.

The technician made the following notes on the EEG record at the conclusion of the experimental session:

Patient feels he succeeded in the experiment; in the first sleep he saw two men and one woman seated somewhere in the hospital—he pinched them. In the second sleep the patient saw me (the tech) and he said I had a visitor, which I did. However, it is possible that Mr. X may have heard the visitor cough during his [cigarette] break between sleeps. Mr. X states that he patted the visitor on the cheeks and tried to take his hand but that the visitor avoided. Mr. X recalls that he left the cot, went under it and out the door into the recording room and then into the hallway. . . . The patient did not see the number."

Thus, there is some indication that ESP may have been involved with respect to the technician's activities, but it is not at all conclusive. The material about the two men and the woman in the first OBE could not be checked.

DISCUSSION

In discussing the findings, some limitations of the present study should be kept in mind. The first is the great variability in Mr. X's EEG patterns during his attempts to produce OBEs—a variability whose significance is unknown because of a lack of published, normative data. The second is the tentativeness of sleep-pattern classification in many instances because of this variability. The third is the fact that only two brief OBEs occurred in the course of this study (and these two were really one OBE broken by a very brief arousal), so that is only a very small sample of Mr. X's OBEs. Further work with Mr. X is needed, and in the future I hope to continue this sort of study with better physiological recording techniques and computerized analysis of the EEG recordings. Thus, the conclusions below are tentative.

Two major findings warrant further discussion:

The first is that Mr. X can spend a good deal of time on the borderline of sleep; to what extent the liability of his EEG patterns is a factor in this is unknown. A number of traditional occult techniques (Carrington, 1958; Fox, 1962; Muldoon and Carrington, 1956; Ophiel, 1961; Yram, 1965) involve gaining control over thought processes in borderline states in order to make constructive use of the potentialities of these states, particularly the enhanced imagery that occurs. Modern scientific research on the borderline state is just beginning (Bertini, Lewis, and Witkin, 1964; Foulkes and Vogel, 1965; Vogel, Foulkes, and Trosman, 1966; Witkin and Lewis, 1965), and we know little more about the psychological potentials of the hypnagogic state than we knew decades ago (Leaning, 1925; Woolley, 1914); the concentration in the last decade has been on the later Stage 1 periods associated with REMs and dreaming. What has been done so far indicates that the initial Stage 1, borderline state is like later Stage 1 dreams in some respects and differs in others, both psychologically and physiologically. Little more can be said definitely about the borderline state at this time, although a number of research projects in various laboratories should provide us with far more knowledge in the next few years.

The fact that Mr. X spends considerable time in borderline states is also of interest in view of my earlier finding with the other gifted subject, Miss Z (Tart, 1968). This woman had several OBEs in the laboratory, and in her case they seemed associated with a borderline state. This borderline state was dominated by alphoid rhythms in the EEG. Mr. X showed such rhythms at times, although not as persistently as the previous subject. Future research should pay considerable attention to borderline sleep states.

The second major finding is that Mr. X's two OBEs seem to have occurred in conjunction with a Stage 1 dream state. Yet Mr. X sharply distinguishes his OBEs from dreams. This raises a number of problems of interpretation. To say that his OBEs are "just" dreams would be a gross oversimplification;* the two in the laboratory occurred in temporal conjunction with an EEG pattern usually associated with dreaming in normal subjects; yet Mr. X had several Stage 1 dreams, in the all-night session, that he did *not* awaken from and describe as OBEs. Are his OBEs dreams or something else?

The answer to this question centers around the term "dream." The term is commonly used as if there were only one kind of experience occurring during sleep, but a reading of many dream accounts will indicate that there are probably several psychologically distinct modes of mental functioning during sleep, all of which become lumped together confusingly under the term "dream." The distinction already found in many laboratories between the "slowed thinking" of Nonstage 1 sleep and the vivid, hallucinatory activity of Stage 1 sleep is a start toward more adequate classification and understanding. I believe future work will find several distinct types of experience occurring in the Stage 1 state also—such as the "lucid dream" of van Eeden (1913) and Arnold-Forster (1921). I have indicated elsewhere some of the varieties of unusual behavior that can occur in "dreaming" (Tart, 1965), and the OBE may be another type of behavior in which an ordinary Stage 1 dream becomes converted into "something else," the mysterious OBE.

Thus, the question of whether Mr. X's OBEs are "just" dreams cannot be answered definitively at present. I would tentatively hypothesize, however, that at least some of his OBEs (such as the two in the laboratory) may be a *mixture* of dreaming and "something else." That they are part dream may be concluded from their apparent conjunction with a Stage 1 EEG pattern. In the same experience, on the other hand, there is fair evidence of contact with reality, of ESP,

---

*Because dreams are scientifically acceptable while OBEs are not, the skeptic is tempted to say they are "just" dreams. It is of interest to consider the converse of this position—held by many occultists (Carrington, 1919; Fox, 1962; Muldoon and Carrington, 1956; Ophiel, 1961; Yram, 1965)—that dreams are "just" OBEs in which consciousness is poorly developed!

in his correct perception of the technician's absence from the equipment room and of her husband's presence. This is the "something else" that is mixed in with the dream. Many of the OBEs Mr. X reports in his book seem to fit a similar pattern, a mixture of dream and something else. Only further investigation will indicate whether there are differing physiological concomitants of the dream portions and other portions of the OBEs.

In conclusion, I would like to point out that the most important aspect of the present investigation, or of my earlier one, is not the tentative findings about Mr. X's and Miss Z's OBEs; rather, it is the demonstration that OBEs and similar "exotic" phenomena are not mysterious happenings beyond the pale of scientific investigation. With a proper respect for the phenomena and the persons who experience the phenomena, the advantages of scientific investigation can be gained, adding a valuable facet to our quest for understanding of the nature of man. If these studies should encourage other investigators to work with people who have such experiences rather than to automatically dismiss their experiences as "weird," they will make a lasting contribution.

REFERENCES

Arnold-Forster, M. *Studies in Dreams.* New York: Macmillan, 1921.

Aserinsky, E., and N. Kleitman. "Regularly Occurring Periods of Eye Motility and Concomitant Phenomena During Sleep." *Science* 118 (1953): 273–74.

Baldridge, B.; R. Whitman; M. Kramer. "Dream Development and Recall." Paper, Midwest. Psychol. Ass., Chicago, 1965.

Bertini, M.; H. Lewis; H. Witkin. "Some Preliminary Observations with an Experimental Procedure for the Study of Hypnagogic and Similar Phenomena." *Arch. d. Psicologia, Neurologia e Psichiatria* 25 (1964): 493–534.

Carrington, H. *Modern Psychical Phenomena.* New York: Dodd, Mead & Co., 1919.

_____. *Your Psychic Powers and How to Develop Them.* New York: Templestar Publishers, 1958.

Crookall, R.: *More Astral Projections: Analyses of Case Histories.* London: Aquarian Press, 1964a.

_____. *The Study and Practice of Astral Projection.* London: Aquarian Press, 1961.

_____. *The Techniques of Astral Projection.* London: Aquarian Press, 1964b.

Dement, W. "Dreaming: A Biologic State." *Modern Medicine,* July 5, 1965, 184–206.

Durville, H. *Le Fantôme des Vivants.* Paris: Librairie du Magnétisme, 1909.

Fiss, H., Klein, G. and Bokert, E.. "Waking Fantasies Following Interruption of Two Types of Sleep." *Arch. Gen. Psychiat.* 14 (1966): 543–51.

Foulkes, D. "Dream Reports from Different Stages of Sleep." *J. Abnorm. Soc. Psychol.* 65 (1962):14–25.

_____. *The Psychology of Sleep.* New York: Charles Scribner's Sons, 1966.

_____. "Theories of Dream Formation and the Recent Studies of Sleep Consciousness." *Psychol. Bull.* 62 (1964): 236–47.

Foulkes, D., and Vogel, G. "Mental Activity at Sleep Onset." *J. Abnorm. Psychol.* 70 (1965): 231–43.

Fox, O. *Astral Projection: A Record of Out-of-the-body Experiences.* New Hyde Park, N.Y.: University Books, 1962.

Goodenough, D., Lewis, H., Shapiro, A., Jaret, L., and Sleser, I. "Dream Reporting Following Abrupt and Gradual Awakening from Different Types of Sleep." *J. Pers. Soc. Psychol.* 2 (1965): 170–79.

Hart, H. "Hypnosis as an Aid in Experimental ESP Projection." Paper, *First International Conf. Parapsychological Studies,* Utrecht, 1953.

_____. "Six Theories about Apparitions." *Proc. Soc. Psych. Res.* 50 (1956): 153–239.

Hill, D., and G. Parr (eds.). *Electroencephalography: A Symposium on Its Various Aspects.* New York: Macmillan, 1963.

Kleitman, N. "Patterns of Dreaming." *Scientific American* 203 (1960): 81–88.

———. *Sleep and Wakefulness.* Chicago: University of Chicago Press, 1963.

Leaning, F. "An Introductory Study of Hypnagogic Phenomena." *Proc. Soc. Psych. Res.* 35 (1925): 289–412.

Monroe, L., Rechtschaffen, A., Foulkes, D., and Jensen, J. "Discriminability of REM and NREM Reports." *J. Pers. Soc. Psychol.* 2 (1965): 456–60.

Monroe, R. *Journeys Out of the Body.* Garden City, N.Y.: Doubleday, 1971.

Muldoon, S., and Carrington, H. *The Phenomena of Astral Projection.* London: Rider & Co., 1951.

———. *The Projection of the Astral Body.* London: Rider & Co., 1929.

Ophiel. *The Art and Practice of Astral Projection.* San Francisco: Peach Publishing Co., 1961.

Oswald, I. *Sleeping and Waking: Physiology and Psychology.* New York: Elsevier, 1962.

Rechtschaffen, A., Verdone, P., and Wheaton, Joy. "Reports of Mental Activity During Sleep." *Canad. J. Psychiat.* 8 (1963): 409–14.

Snyder, F. "The New Biology of Dreaming." *Arch. Gen. Psychiat.* 8 (1963): 381–91.

———. "Progress in the New Biology of Dreaming." *Amer. J. Psychiat.* 122 (1965): 377–91.

Tart, C.: "A Psychophysiological Study of Out-of-the-body Experiences in a Selected Subject." *Journal of the American Soc. Psych. Res.* 62 (1968): 3–27.

———. "Toward the Experimental Control of Dreaming." *Psychol. Bull.* 64 (1965): 81–91.

van Eeden, F. "A Study of Dreams." *Proc. Soc. Psych. Res.* 26 (1913): 431–61.

Vogel, G., Foulkes, D., and Trosman, H. "Ego Functions and Dreaming During Sleep Onset." *Arch. Gen. Psychiat.* 14 (1966): 238–48.

Witkin, H., and Lewis, H. "The Relation of Experimentally Induced Pre-sleep Experiences to Dreams: A Report on

Method and Preliminary Findings." *J. Amer. Psychoanal. Ass.* 13 (1965): 819–49.

Woolley, V. "Some Auto-suggested Visions as Illustrating Dream Formation." *Proc. Soc. Psych. Res.* 27 (1914): 390–99.

Yram, *Practical Astral Projection.* New York: Samuel Weiser, 1965.

6 | Out-of-the-Body Vision

JANET MITCHELL

In the fall of 1971 Dr. Karlis Osis, Director of Research at the American Society for Psychical Research (A.S.P.R.), conceived a plan to attempt to investigate the out-of-body experience. Celia Green describes the out-of-body experience as one in which "the observer seems to himself to be observing (phenomena) from a point of view which is not coincident with his physical body."

The present research is only one aspect of a larger A.S.P.R. project which is studying the possibility that the soul survives bodily death. Out-of-body experiences have been recorded in the parapsychological and medical literature for many years. If there is some conscious part of an individual that can operate independently from the physical body while one is alive, then it is highly suggestive that this "part" might be something that can survive after the body dies.

Dr. Charles Tart now at the University of California, Davis, published two papers on psychophysiological studies of people who claimed to have out-of-body experiences. His method was to look for correlations of physiological patterns occurring when a subject reports that he is out of his body and is attempting to view a hidden target or scene.

As it is my duty to monitor physiological response patterns in psi experiments at the A.S.P.R. Research Department, I decided to take a similar approach if we could find suitable subjects who could go out of their body at will.

The A.S.P.R. invited anyone who might be able to report on such an experience to communicate with us for purposes of possible research. With minimum publicity from us, people from all walks of life started calling and writing from all over the country. Case after case was examined, but since most were spontaneous in character and could not be repeated at will, they did not yield well to laboratory conditions.

Then one day Ingo Swann, an artist and writer in his thirties, came to our laboratory to tell me he could "exteriorize" from his body anywhere, anytime, although he couldn't always "see" perfectly.

Swann said that his first out-of-body experience happened at the age of three. During a tonsillectomy, while under anesthesia, he says he watched the doctor perform the operation and was able afterward to report accurately to the doctor some of the smallest details of the operation. After this event, his out-of-body experiences seem to have occurred spontaneously. When he was eight years old, he witnessed a childhood friend being killed in a high fall. This traumatic event brought about for the first time an awareness of the destructibility of the physical body, and seemed to suppress his abilities for many years.

As a young adult in 1957, however, while serving in the Armed Forces in Korea, he was pondering what direction his life should take. He concluded that "a man, if he is to live at all, must do only what is deepest in his heart." "This metaphysical conclusion," he says, "brought about an intense uplifting of awareness and a seemingly mature out-of-body experience."

Before coming to the A.S.P.R., Swann trained himself in his ability to leave his body at will. On occasion he has olfactory and auditory perception while out of his body, but the senses of taste and touch have not been operative as yet. He reports that he has the ability to speak through his body while being exterior to it. In our experiments, however, only visual reports of distant targets were elicited. His experience is under conscious control and he is fully awake during all experimentation. He describes his out-of-body experience as having a conscious point of view in space. This conscious control is extremely helpful in research because Swann can let us know the precise second when he feels he has just returned to his body.

Mr. Swann regularly came into the laboratory two or three days a week. Experiments were purely exploratory in nature and the object was to see if he could identify targets which were out of his visual range. These first experiments do not rule out the possibility that he was obtaining target information through clairvoyance, telepathy, or precognition but, because of this early work, methodology is now being developed to rule out these other possibilities.

Another aspect of this pilot work was to measure bodily functions when he reported being outside his body. Electrodes were placed on his scalp and regular recordings were

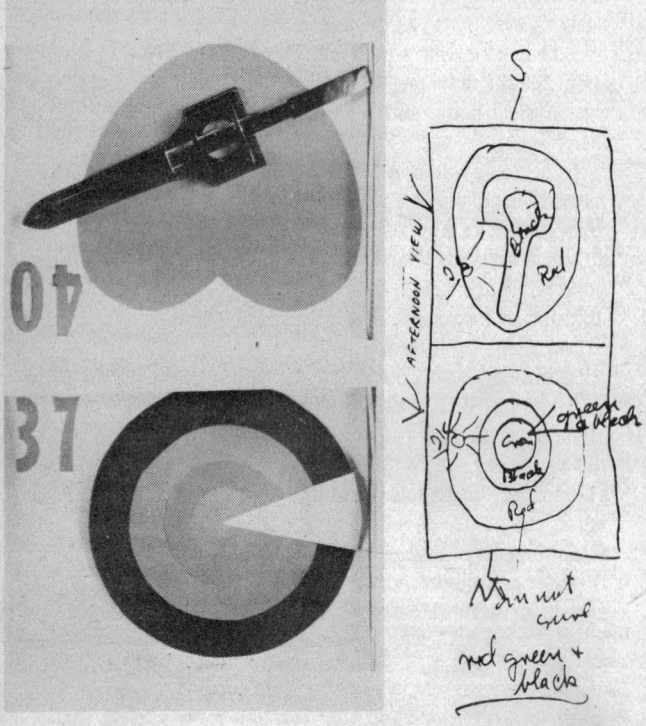

FIG. 3. These targets were used to test Ingo Swann's OB vision during controlled experiments at the American Society for Psychical Research. Swann's drawn responses are shown alongside the targets. *(Photos and drawings courtesy of Janet Mitchell.)*

taken of the left and right occipital lobes of his brain (the back of the head where vision is organized). Other recordings varied on different days.

The immediate target area was located at least ten feet off the floor in the room where Swann sat. Each day before he arrived, Vera Feldman, secretary to the director of research, prepared and placed targets on a platform suspended from the ceiling. Then she would lock the door to the room. Swann and I would enter the room only when we were ready to begin the experiment. At that time I would plug the leads from the electrodes on his scalp into a junction box which led to a polygraph machine in the adjoining room. Therefore, his movements were controlled all the time he was in the room (since any movement from the chair would disconnect the equipment). He would then "view" the targets, and make a drawing of his sighting.

There was a large partition in the middle of the platform, with one target placed on each side of it. The reason for this was to determine to some extent the point from which Swann viewed the targets in the out-of-body state.

For instance, if he claimed his point of view to be from the north side and he reported the target on the south side of the partition, it would seem clairvoyance may be in operation. On the other hand, if he described his position as being from the north and then drew an almost exact replica of what was on the north side of the partition, it would seem as though he was really somehow sighting the correct target.

At times Swann reported that certain lighting setups were glaring or reflecting off glossy surfaces and that this reflection obscured part of the target. Several adjustments had to be made on lighting arrangements, as well as in the selection of target material. A soft, diffused overhead light and simple construction paper which absorbed light seemed to work best. Primary colors seemed to come through more clearly than pastels. Strong familiar forms seemed to be more readily perceived than unfamiliar objects and shapes. Materials such as leather, fabrics, and clay seemed to work better than plastic, glossy pictures, or glass.

Another factor that would indicate more of a similarity to physical perception than to ESP is that Swann filled out questionnaires as to how good or bad his out-of-body vision was on a specific day (before seeing the targets, of course) and these questionnaires were correlated with his actual score on a given day as to whether he reproduced the target or not in his response. The data seem to show that he does know whether he is doing well or not.

From the subjective reports I have received from many who have experienced an out-of-body condition, exterior perception seems to be different from physical perception in several ways. One experient reported that it was like looking through a fish-eye lens. A circular visual capacity is often reported and distortions are usually mentioned.

In Swann's case, it appears that his exterior vision is capable of perceiving more than his normal vision. He says he perceives, for instance, the forms of certain light rays, ionization of the air around changing light sources and reflections off shiny surfaces.

Numbers and letters have been included in many of the targets and different subjects tell me that shapes and colors are perceived, but that the concept of number or letter is often beyond this type of perception. So far the subjects we have tested could not identify a number or letter in any other way than as a form.

The target and drawn response shown in the illustration are typical of those used in our early experiments. The south target is a black leather holder for a letter opener and scissors on a red heart cut out of construction paper. The other side is a bull's-eye cut out of construction paper. There are two numbers on each target and they are made out of a glossy-surfaced cardboard, which had been painted over to dull it. (See illustration.)

Swann's drawn response is clearly the black shape on the red. He did not identify the metal scissors and letter opener. On the other side, his first response was a red, green, and black bull's-eye. When he was asked to fill in the colors on the sketch in their right places, he reversed them. As he drew the slice you see in his response, he added, "I'm not sure if this center is green or black." This could be considered an unconscious response to the slice in the target. He did not respond to the numbers.

Eight sets of these targets and responses were randomized and given to Boneita Perskari, a psychologist who knew nothing about our experiment. We simply asked her to try to match up the pictures of the targets with the drawn response that seems to go with it. She correctly matched all eight sets. The expectation of this happening by chance is about one in forty thousand.

Excitement ran high from this fine result. New ideas for exploration poured in from various experts, such as perceptual psychologists, optical physicists, and engineers. Dr. Osis added these ideas to his own and began work on methodology for experiments to examine the central hypothesis of out-of-body experiences—that there is "something" of the human being capable of detaching itself from the physical organism and operating or perceiving outside the body.

We feel that a correct methodology should be able to establish certain validities of this type of experience and draw distinctions between it and other theories: for example, the hypothesis that out-of-body experience is a sort of traveling fantasy coupled with ESP. We now plan to test the properties of spatial organization of out-of-body perception in several different ways.

The physiological correlates of Swann's experience show that his brain-wave activity, as measured by an electroencephalograph (EEG), changes during the time he is reportedly out of his body. The procedure used to obtain this information was as follows: Swann was attached to the electroencephalograph and then left alone in a semi-darkened room to take his own time and attempt to "view" the targets. He was conscious at all times and could report any feelings, experiences, or make suggestions over an intercom system. He also had in his possession an electronic marker button which was connected to the EEG machine. He could push the button when he felt he

had just returned to his body, and record a mark on the
EEG record at that precise time. We went back to these
marks on the record, studied what was occurring just before the marks and also took some random points in the
record for standard resting-type activity. This is how the
physiological data were separated as to when he was out
of his body and when he was resting.

After working together some months, Swann told me that
he could go out of his body upon command and so we conducted several sessions in which I would give him an audio
signal to go exterior and then a signal to come back. I wondered immediately if these particular command data would
match up with his retrospectively reported data, and upon
checking, found that they did.

EEG records of both the right and left hemispheres of
Swann's brain were studied. Overall statistics revealed that
during the out-of-body condition, whether he reported it or
I directed it, there was a 19 percent decrease of mean amplitude in the right side. The left side showed a 16 percent
decrease in mean amplitude. This indicates that there was a
loss of electrical activity during those times Swann was reportedly out of his body. Overall frequency data showed a
decrease in alpha activity during the out-of-body state. This
decrease was more marked in the left than the right hemisphere. The statistical probability of the mean amplitude decreases occurring by chance was calculated at 1000 to 1 on
the right side and 200 to 1 on the left side.

Therefore, when he said he was out of his body, there was
a loss of electrical activity and a speed-up of the brain waves
in the visual, occipital region of his brain. His heart rate and
other functions of the autonomic nervous system remained
normal.

Our data concur with Dr. Tart's previous work on the
out-of-body experience to the extent that he indicated a flattened EEG as characteristic of the out-of-body state. He also
found that functions of the autonomic nervous system remained unchanged. Whereas Dr. Tart found a slowing of the
alpha frequency mixed with a Stage 1 dreaming pattern (alph-

oid waves) in the out-of-body state, our data show decreased alpha activity. It should be noted that his experiments were run at night and both his subjects found it necessary to go to sleep to achieve the out-of-body experience and our experiments were conducted in the daytime with the subject sitting up, fully awake, and conscious.

Interpretation of an amplitude decrease in an EEG is extremely difficult. So little is known about the EEG itself, that it is difficult to make firm conclusions at this time. It is enough to try to discover patterns and attempt to verify that something might be happening in an orderly fashion. In time, we may be able to interpret these patterns in a larger framework. We are working conscientiously to understand the parameters of this experience, and detect from our observations its meaning and implications concerning the nature of man.

Writing about cosmic consciousness in 1900, Dr. Maurice Bucke said, "Only a personal experience of it, or a prolonged study of men who have passed into the new life, will enable us to realize what this actually is. . . ." We are now at the same point with out-of-body experiences. Fortunately, today scientific and technological advancements can provide rapid progress in the serious study of men such as Ingo Swann.

7 | Out-of-Body Research at the American Society for Psychical Research

KARLIS OSIS

For the past two years, the American Society for Psychical Research (A.S.P.R.) Research Department has been fully engaged in exploring the question: Does the human personality survive after bodily death? Working within the scope of the Kidd legacy (see p. 88), we have been following up our central hypothesis: that a human being has an "ecsomatic" aspect, capable of operating independently of and away from his physical body—an aspect that might leave the body at death and continue to exist. Can one, we asked, really leave one's body temporarily (as in out-of-body experiences, or OBE) or permanently (as at death)?

"FLY-IN" PHASE OF THE OBE RESEARCH

After the pilot study with Ingo Swann (see chapter 6), we made a nationwide appeal for subjects, searching for people who felt they could induce an OB state at will, go to a definite place and bring back information that could be verified. Of the many gifted people who responded to this "fly-in" appeal, we tested more than one hundred. Before each testing session, one of several arrays of target objects was randomly selected and placed on a table in my office. The gifted persons were asked to induce an out-of-body experience at the appointed hour, fly in from their homes to my office, stand in front of the fireplace, and look at the targets. They then reported their experiences to us, on an elaborate questionnaire. Promising subjects in this test were later invited for laboratory testing. Success in the fly-in was evaluated by blind judging.

The overall results were not significant: that is, only some

of the OB-ers seemed to "see" things clearly enough for definite identification. However, we learned a lot from the data. For example, success was the same whether the OB-er was sitting up or lying down and whether he experienced having an "astral" body or felt he had none.

Good sessions, when "seeing" was clear, had on the whole the following characteristics: the person was not conscious throughout the time when he was making his exit from his body; he arrived at the destination suddenly, landed on the right spot in the office, and reported that his OB vision was as clear as it normally was for his OB trips. Conversely, the session was usually unsuccessful when the subject said that he left his body slowly and with difficulty, was conscious throughout his exit, experienced prolonged "flying through space" or seemed to be using a vehicle; when he did not land on the prescribed spot or could not find it. Very few persons succeeded who felt that their consciousness was located simultaneously in both the physical body and my office. Success seemed to depend on characteristics typical of OB experience rather than on general conditions known to be favorable to ESP performance, such as relaxation.

RECENT WORK WITH INSTRUMENTATION

Our methodology and instrumentation have now been developed much further, with the advice and consultation of several physicists and psychologists. Two instruments have been designed to help us try to distinguish between OB perception, on one hand, and telepathy or clairvoyance, on the other. These devices work on optical principles: each has a small viewing window through which, and *only* through which, the target can be seen in full. The idea is that a subject who does not "get out" and who relies on using clairvoyance is presumably making a perceptual sweep of the whole apparatus, and will therefore see the target as it actually is—whereas the OB-er, who claims to perceive from a particular point in space, should be able to see the target as it appears *through the viewing window,* at which point it has been transformed by optical devices. The subject himself sits or lies in a room separated from the apparatus—either in the adjoining laboratory or in the soundproof room at the far end of the building—and attempts to project precisely to the viewing window and look in.

1. *Optical Image Device:* This is a structure about 2 by 2 by 3 feet, inside which is a rotatable disc divided into four quadrants, each of a different color. On one of these quadrants a small picture (e.g., an image of a chalice) appears. Each time the switch is thrown, one out of five possible target images is randomly selected and becomes visible on one quadrant of the disc; the quadrant and its color are also randomly selected. The equipment is designed so that no one, including the experimenter, knows what the final combination of quadrant, color, and image is during the experiment. And the only way to see the target as a whole is by looking specifically through the small window at the front of the Optical Image Device. After the session the experimenter decodes information from an automatic recording machine to find out what the targets were.

2. *Color Wheel.* This device is based on a different optical principle to distinguish between various modes of perception. It is a sort of enclosed roulette wheel about fourteen inches in diameter. In this case the target is a colored image on a black background. Again the only way to see the target correctly is to look precisely through a small window, on the top of the box. The OB subject thus has to project to an exact spot in front of a window to score well with either of the apparatuses.

Our research with these optical devices is unfinished, but we have analyzed the first crop of data and can gain some preliminary insights: Are the scores consistent with the OBE hypothesis (subject sees picture through the window), or with the hypothesis of general ESP (a clairvoyant sweep of the box, or a kind of "mental x-ray")? Well, it seems that we have both. Some subjects score according to the general-ESP hypothesis, and appear to be totally unable to score on the OB aspects. Nevertheless, they *experience* going out-of-body, coming to the window of the apparatus, and looking through it—but the score says that they have not in fact been there.

But we also have subjects whose scoring patterns do support the OBE hypothesis. However, even among these individuals none has been able to "see" the targets the OBE way every time. It appears that even the most gifted persons achieve true OB vision at will only on some tries, not all, and are using general ESP on others—although subjectively they experience "being out" on all trials.

LEARNING

One subject, Alex Tanous, tried doggedly to learn to separate the wheat (OB vision) from the chaff. After each session was over, and before he was told his score, he would indicate which trials he thought had been the best. For weeks and weeks he stumbled and failed miserably in this effort, but he did not give up. Finally one day he hit upon certain criteria which do seem to work. Now he is able to state with some reliability which trials were in fact better than others. He told us his criteria for sifting out the chaff: he experiences himself to be without a body, something like a spot of consciousness, he says; it feels like light. This light first appears to him as rather large and amorphous. Then it becomes more and more concentrated. When it seems to be about the size of a dime he feels that he will start scoring. When the light appears concentrated to a point, he feels that he can do really well. The other criterion he uses is a feeling of oneness, or unity with existence, which he expresses in biblical terms, as an "I am" (that I am) feeling. His scoring patterns are consistent with the OBE hypothesis.

Other subjects did not develop such workable criteria for the "good" trials, but they, too, seem to have their exceptional days when their perception goes the OBE way. For example, a subject who scored very well in our preliminary fly-in experiment failed to show any results with our optical devices. She tried very hard—to no avail. Then at the final session she emerged radiant from the soundproof room and told us: "This time I got the results you wanted. The colors were luminous, brilliant, and I was more fully out than I ever was before." And indeed her scores agreed: the OBE scoring pattern was there, and the session was significant by itself; the probability of the results' being due to chance was 1 in 200.

As far as we can tell from still incomplete results, it looks as though our best subjects have in some sense really been *at* the viewing window at times when their physical bodies were somewhere else.

Is OBE vision really ESP, but ESP localized at a point in space in which the subject feels his consciousness to be? Or is it a kind of perception totally different from ESP? As far as our observations go, it seems to be a localized mode of ESP rather than something distinct from it. It seems, for instance, to possess ESP's established characteristics such as psi-missing* under unfavorable or nonpreferred conditions.

DIVING POOL

Another aspect of the OBE work involves a possible physical influence on the spot to which the OBE traveler has projected. We have built a device we call a "diving pool," an enclosed, electrically isolated space inside which an object is delicately suspended on a string; a very sensitive electronic instrument registers its slightest movement. Careful preexperimental monitoring ensures the stability of this suspended object. Then the OB projectionist, sitting forty feet away in a soundproof, metal-shielded room, is given the task of causing his ecsomatic self to "dive" into the diving pool and move the object, for example, swing it.

We have tested many subjects with this device and observed very little—maybe an occasional "bump" in the strip chart record, which can usually be explained by known physical causes. Our staff physicist, Jim Mereweather, was beginning to lose hope until Pat Price, another psychic, came from

*We use the term "psi-missing" to indicate when a subject performs statistically significantly *worse* or *below* normal chance expectation.—ED.

Add to Detcohear'
chapter

California. In Price's very first session the recording pen of the polygraph went wild—and Jim was all smiles. Careful measurements showed eight times as much variation in that session as in the ensuing control period. The differences are extremely significant. There is also much more to the results, which cannot be discussed here. Not all the sessions were so dramatic, but it looks as though we may have found a promising means of obtaining evidence of the ecsomatic existence of OB projections. Of course, these are just the first results, on which no final conclusions can be based, but it looks to us though this might develop into a real breakthrough.

PHOTOGRAPHY

James Kidd, whose legacy in part supported this research, thought that one might be able to photograph the soul. We tried various types of photography and television recording aimed at the OB projection areas (at both subject and target) but got nothing of interest. Did we ourselves ever see the OB projections as apparitions are seen? I personally did not see a thing, but during a fly-in experiment one of my assistants, Boneita Perskari, saw a ball of light and a blue mist; and a psychic who was there as an observer saw the same thing independently and from a different angle. At another OBE session we were preparing to videotape and photograph an OB visitor who was due a little later, when I saw my assistant get up and snap some shots with a camera. Shortly thereafter the phone rang and it was the current "visitor" complaining about our bad manners: flashing the camera right under her nose, she said! Was the "visitor" in the snapshot? It looks as though the gods guard their secrets well—the camera with the film in it was stolen!

Fortunately the story does not end here. Dr. Erlendur Haraldsson and I visited in India with yogis, swamis, and what the Indians call "god-men" (avatars). We made a long search, visiting ashram after ashram, and heard many striking stories that were not verifiable or did not withstand our probing. Finally we met two very exceptional persons who are said to be visible when they are on OB trips—not visible to one person only (which could be easily explained away as a hallucination) but to several observers and for a prolonged time. Apparitions as a rule are of short duration, a matter of seconds. They never last as long as in *Hamlet* or in television shows! In India, however, we were able to interview witnesses who had actually been with the swami in body at the same time that his apparition was seen by other witnesses (whom we also interviewed) on the other side of the Indian subcontinent. These apparitions interacted with the environment, talked, taught songs, handled objects. In the New Testament the apparition of Jesus is said to have appeared to his disciples and asked for fish, which he then ate. The apparitions of Indian god-men appear to have done the same—they drink tea, eat, even smoke and give away presents! Dr. Haraldsson and I had read with a critical eye a lot of writers' reports of these Indian miracles, feeling that "it's just a professional magician's tricks—too good to be true." Well, after our firsthand encounters with the god-men and their witnesses we were shaken up and changed our minds considerably. I have been in psychical research more than twenty years but have never run into anything comparable. Of course, we do not claim that these cases have already decided the issue. Much further, very careful, interviewing must be done. But we did bring back from India the conviction that, if extensively verified, these cases would lend testimony to the strong observation of the soul acting apart from the body. For now, this might constitute the best available approximation of the "proof" James Kidd asked for in his will: proof that the soul leaves the body at death. However, we were in for one more shock when we came home to the United States: our reports were met by colleagues with the same skepticism as we ourselves had had before the firsthand encounters in India. We must be careful not to reject these Indian cases out of hand as being merely "anecdotal and inconsequential." The extraordinary claims of yogis' psychic phenomena have as yet had little or no impact on parapsychology—but there are enough published observations to justify a careful study.

In Summary: The OBE research proved to be a difficult task, mainly because the full phenomenon is rarely reproduced at will. Our results thus far are consistent with the OBE hypothesis. After fully exploiting the research possibilities described above, we may indeed hope to have evidence for the ecsomatic existence of human personality.

8 | Experiments with Blue Harary

D. SCOTT ROGO

Everyone in parapsychology eagerly listens to the grapevine for news of the latest star subjects, and in 1973 ear-stretching reports began coming out of Durham, North Carolina, about a subject, Stuart Blue Harary, who could "project his mind" away from his body and perceive distant scenes and report correctly on them. With some help from a Parapsychology Foundation grant and the promise of a consultantship at the Psychical Research Foundation I was able to spend six weeks working with Blue Harary.

During the summer of 1973 I worked with Blue consistently, literally living with him for several weeks, experimented with him, socialized with him, philosophized with him, and explored every aspect of his OB talents that I could. The OBE has always fascinated me and is rather a specialty of mine. Several years ago I experienced a number of OBEs myself, which increased my interest in this phase of parapsychology. When I went to Durham I went not only as a scholar of the history and literature on the OBE, but also as one with some personal experience with the phenomenon. Despite these two assets, working with Blue proved to be an eye-opener.

Just who is Blue Harary? Blue is in his early twenties and recently graduated from college with an A.B. in psychology. He has had OBEs all his life, but at first didn't know what to make of them. In fact, he felt alienated from other people because of them. In 1972 the American Society for Psychical Research was getting interested in investigating the OBE. Since Blue was living in New York City; he volunteered as a subject in the A.S.P.R.'s first experiments. The head of the project was Dr. Karlis Osis, director of research, and Blue was tested by Osis's hardworking assistant, Janet Mitchell, who carried out several experiments with him. These pilot tests with Blue have not been published, but they consisted of his entering into the OB state and trying to float above his body to report on target objects placed on a shelf suspended from the ceiling or report on pictures seen through a hole in a box while out-of-body. The shelf was in such a position as to be accessible only by ESP or through viewing it in the OB state. During the entire test period Blue was monitored by psychophysiological devices such as the electroencephalograph, a brain-wave recording apparatus, and the polygraph. By the use of the EEG, and so forth, a psychologist or technician can determine what state of consciousness (waking, sleeping, dreaming, and so forth) the subject is in, since each of these states has indicative rhythms. When I flew to Durham I stopped over in New York and talked with Dr. Osis and Janet Mitchell specifically about Blue. Janet told me that Blue had been sporadically successful on the target studies and had been able to report, although distortedly, on the shelf targets. Osis showed less enthusiasm about the target studies, even though the first test had been strikingly successful, but admitted that the psychophysiological readings offered curious results.

Because of his college work, Blue decided his best bet would be to go to Durham and enroll at Duke University so he could both further his education and take part in parapsychological research. He first approached the Institute for Parapsychology of the Foundation for Research on the Nature of Man (FRNM), but his talents were not particularly suited for the types of ESP projects carried out there, so ultimately he became established at the Psychical Research Foundation (PRF), also based in Durham. PRF is especially endowed to carry out research into those psychic phenomena that indicate survival of death. His entry through PRF's door was the beginning of the most amazing and fruitful OB experiments ever undertaken.

The task of organizing and designing the experiments fell to PRF's research coordinator, Dr. Robert Morris, a veteran parapsychologist and animal behaviorist. (His doctoral dissertation in biological psychology was on the mating habits of ringed-necked doves.) The first experiments were designed to substantiate that Blue could induce some sort of mind-beyond-the-body state. To reach this goal, the first series of tests were on target studies. In OB research, this simply means the ability of the subject to travel in the OB state and report on what he sees in an isolated, sealed-off room. Since the PRF consisted of two adjacent buildings, Blue merely induced the OB state in one building and then traveled over to the next building and tried to see the target. Later, Blue OBed from various Duke University buildings about half a mile away. In these experiments the targets were large posters of colored alphabet letters hung on a wall or door of the experimental area.

The first trial was on February 13, 1973, at 7:30 P.M. Blue lay down in one PRF building, hooked up to several psycho-physiological recording devices, and while still conscious began to sink into the ultrarelaxed state during which he leaves his body. This entire "cool down" period, as it was dubbed, lasts anywhere up to fifteen minutes. Blue reported that while out of the body he saw a circle as the target, slightly elliptical in shape, and a flowerpot. When Blue returned to his body and merged back to full consciousness, he was shown a series of potential target drawings from which he had to choose what he thought to be the correct one. Among these targets were drawings of a flowerpot and a circle. Blue chose the flowerpot. This was a disappointment since the target had been a circle. This first experiment provoked the touchy question that Blue might be using ESP during his OBEs, which would be a complicating factor in trying to demonstrate experimentally the validity of the OBE on the basis of target studies. Another complication to the experiment was that one of the experimenters, Joseph Janis, a PRF staff member in the target room, had a subjective impression when Blue was "present" in the room with him which was borne out when the timings of the OBE were worked out.

During the second experiment Blue began to focus in on the target better and, as in the first experiment, Joseph Janis was monitoring the target room. As Blue records in his diary of these experiments, he was able to induce the OB state quickly and travel to the target room:

The room was very cold and uncomfortable. I felt pressure but put it and everything else that was on my mind aside. Finally got to Joe and stayed there. Only saw the target briefly and then my "back" was to it. What I saw looked like a "V." Color was hard to see since perhaps the lighting was poor. Stood in front of Joe and looked at his face. Tried to signal him and got excited over finding that I actually could touch him! So I flew right back to the ol' body.

Blue signaled Dr. Morris and wrote down his impressions. The target was a *W*. Blue was getting closer.

After a saddening failure on the third try, the fourth experiment improved. Blue wrote:

Left body and went to Joe (did not pass "go"—did not collect two hundred bucks). Actually, I had gone to Joe for a brief second. . . . I was behind Joe's left side in the air. He seemed to get up out of his body when I came in, turned and found me and then continued turning and reentered his body. I didn't see anything on the door at all at first. Concentrated harder and thought I saw a vague image of a circle—an even vaguer Z. It was very difficult to see anything and I wondered if I was actually seeing what I thought I had been seeing (for a moment). Saw a person to Joe's right side and focused back in on Joe to maintain the experience.* Got tired and came back into body. . . .

After returning to the body Blue induced a second OBE, focused on Joseph Janis, and saw a vague *K*. The actual target was an R, so Blue's perception seemed to be a distorted version of the target set for him. However, what was even more fascinating was that on his first visit he had reported a second person in the target area with Joe. After the experiment had ended, it was revealed that a second person *had* been introduced into the target area unknown to Blue, a PRF volunteer, Jerry Posner. What's more, during the test Jerry

---

*Blue likes to project to a person he knows well when attempting an OBE. It helps him reach the target area and maintain the OB state while there.

Posner reported to Joe that he had "seen" Blue's apparition. Joe Janis made a recording of the time and this directly correlated with when Blue was actually OBing, a time unknown to either Joe or Jerry. (When I questioned Jerry about the experiment months later, he described how he was startled to see a clear apparitional representation of Blue's face hovering in the air.) Indeed, at this point, the Harary experiments were entering into a new phase.

The March 18 experiment was a clear success and Blue was able to report the target precisely:

The experiment was from one PRF building to the other. I had some difficulty relaxing at first but put personal problems out of my mind and focused in on being a whole human being and was able to relax. I signaled Bob [Morris] when ready and went to the center of the room (OBE) to look at the target. It was a little dim at first but I got used to the light and saw it after a while. It was a blue arrow pointing up.

The entire series gave a good number of approximate and precise "hits" but did not seem totally suited to Blue's OB abilities, since he often had trouble "seeing" and often perceived objects distortedly. However, he had been a bit more successful at identifying the correct color of the letters than the letters themselves.

The experiences of Joe Janis and Jerry Posner alerted Dr. Morris and other PRF researchers to the fact that Blue might be better able to make his presence known to people or animals than reporting on targets. Further, if Blue could be detected habitually by humans, this would be stronger evidence than the target studies that he was somehow physically or ultraphysically present in the target area. Merely describing target objects could be ESP. So, for the next phase, "detectors" were used, usually PRF staff members or volunteers. For these experiments Blue would travel to one of the PRF buildings where he was to report on whom he saw in the experimental area and their relative positions. At the same time it was hoped that the detectors could "sense" when Blue was present. Usually three people would be randomly selected and positioned in the area. At first Blue was successful at reporting their positions, but even though his accuracy soon tapered off, some of the detectors did have visual or subjective sensations of his presence during the time Blue visited the target area while in an OB state. The detectors knew only that, in a given period of time (thirty to forty minutes, for example), Blue would OB over for a minute or so. They were, of course, kept in the dark as to the precise time. Again, at first, some detectors were highly successful, sensing Blue, seeing sparkling lights, or even an apparition. Jerry Posner was the most successful. But as might be expected, the detectors began to get self-conscious about their task and wound up "guessing" when they thought Blue was present, eventually losing the ability to relax and remain preoccupied or inattentive to the experiment, all of which seem to facilitate any ESP function. However, although the detectors themselves often became too attentive, the people running the experiments, although not detectors, began having fairly strong detection experiences themselves. This type of peripheral detection became common in all the Harary work. For example, when Dr. Morris began using animals as detectors, he went through a detection period himself. As Dr. Morris told me, "During one of these periods I experienced the feeling that Blue was in some sense there. It was not a strong impression, but it did impel me to make note of it at the time. My experience was totally internal—no sensations, visual or otherwise, involved. I thought of Blue, thought about the possibility that Blue might be having an OBE at the time. I felt very comfortably warm inside, a good feeling, as I would if I knew I were being visited by a friend. The feeling lasted no more than twenty to thirty seconds. I realized that I knew the odds were fifty-fifty that Blue was in fact experiencing an OBE at the time and that my description's main value was therefore the comparability of its details with other descriptions obtained under more impressive circumstances."

The use of human detectors had stagnated, so the next phase of the research was to use animals, and at first gerbils and hamsters were enlisted. For the experiments the rodent would be placed inside a 6- by 6- by 6-inch wire cage on top of a "jiggle platform." This consisted of a triangularly shaped metal base delicately balanced on ball bearings. When an animal moved about in this cage, the amount of motion could be recorded on a polygraph to which it can be hooked. In this way, one could judge those times when the animal speeded up or slowed down its movements significantly. Morris had previously found that small animals were able to show ESP by significantly slowing or speeding up their activity rates during more conventional animal-ESP (an-psi) research. It was hoped that when Blue projected, the rodents would interrupt their normal behavior. For the experiment a forty-minute detection period was agreed upon. About four feet away from the detection area an assistant would continuously record the animals' overt behavior. Blue was situated at Duke University, half a mile away, and at a randomly determined time would try to influence the animals' behavior while in the OB state. Unfortunately, the gerbils did not respond at all, although Blue told me that once one of the rodents did perk up and stare directly at him during the test.

The failure of the gerbils and hamsters to respond might have been foreseen, though, for the creatures are very gentle and tame animals that habituate easily to human beings around them. Perhaps they merely found nothing unusual about Blue's sudden OB appearances. Perhaps, too, it would have been better to use animals more readily influenced by Blue—a pet that would react more openly. And it was the use of Blue's own pets that offered the most striking experimental results.

To facilitate these tests, Blue adopted two kittens. When he first approached the litter, one kitten unhesitatingly and inquisitively ventured forward. Another soon followed the first, and these two were chosen, since Blue felt the first kitten's strong initial response to him would carry over more favorably into the formal experiments. The second kitten was kept on as a playmate for the first. The kittens were appropriately named Spirit and Soul. It was Spirit, the first, inquisitive fur-ball that became PRF's star OB detector.

For the experiments Dr. Morris used an animal activity board, an oblong shuffle-board-like apparatus (30 × 80 inches) marked off into twenty-four numbered, ten-inch squares. As with the gerbil experiments, the cats could be observed as they ran about the board. A reporter could keep track over how many squares the kittens ventured during a given period and the number of *meows* evoked. This would give a base-line figure of the kittens' normal activity rate. The tests were comprised of four experimental periods, and during two of them (determined randomly) Blue would try to project from Duke Hospital to PRF and visit the kittens. The results were amazing. During the first test, Spirit, usually an energy-charged kitten, suddenly calmed down, immediately stopped meowing, and ceased dashing over the activity board. It was determined that at this very time Blue had projected to it.

Because of the strong response to Blue, a series was run just with Spirit. As usual, four time periods were used, with only two comprising the OB attempts, and the observers were kept ignorant of these times. During the experimental periods, Spirit would dart about, try to escape from the apparatus, and vocalize regularly. However, in Blue's OB presence, the cat would cease all activity, calmly sit, and remain perfectly quiet. For example, during the total control periods, Spirit meowed thirty-seven times; during the OB periods, none. Figured statistically the results were astoundingly above what one would have expected by chance.

During these experiments some of the observers also detected Blue. It was Jerry Levin's duty to monitor some of the physical devices (thermistors and the like) to see if Blue would influence them during the animal experiments. Jerry was a talented young PRF worker and an undergraduate student in psychology who took part in several of the OB experiments. On one occasion he had a vivid detection of Blue during one of the animal studies. His report reads:

On the night of July 5 our experiment involved human, animal and physical detectors. A kitten was placed in an "open field" situation, its behavior observed by D.E. [Debbi Ewers] and R.M. [Robert Morris]. On a table next to the open field apparatus was placed a thermistor, insulated from air currents by Styrofoam and being monitored in the next room on a polygraph. I was operating the polygraph, seated in front of it, with no one else present in the room. All the people involved were instructed to note the time and character of any possible detection of the OBer that they might have.

The experimental design was such that there were four, two minute detection periods. . . . He [Blue] would actually have an OBE two out of the four detection periods. None of the detectors knew which period, as they were determined by a flip of a coin in the other building. In addition to the detection periods a warning period of varying length was used to obtain control data just before the detection period. I was just at the end of the first warning period when I saw a black streak in the periphery of my vision. Phenomenologically, the sensation appeared to be a thin black line about a foot away, between me and the polygraph. It was as if it were a fast moving black point leaving an after image behind. The streak was about the length of a pencil and lasted no more than a second. It was a very well-defined sensation which faded quickly. My impression was that the streak was an after image of some metallic part of the polygraph—there was a dim light in the room. I noted briefly the time and character of the sensation and went back to monitoring the polygraph. After the experiment was over we learned that the OBE had just started at the time of my detection response. That was my only detection response during that session.

Blue's OBE had been unusually vivid that night and he described how he easily induced an OBE lasting about five minutes. His vision was clear and he experienced himself as "a large, glowing ball of greenish tinted light which appeared to be about the size of a standard beach ball." He traveled to the experimental area, saw Spirit sitting calmly, and then returned to his body. Later he learned of the strong response by the kitten, corresponding to what he had observed, and of Jerry Levin's visual detection.

It was with all this material in mind that I went to Durham. I had heard quite a bit about Blue from Bob Morris over the phone and from Janet Mitchell at the A.S.P.R. I landed in Durham and was met by Bob and Blue. One usually expects a certain aura of theatrics when meeting a gifted psychic. Many of them talk incessantly, always about themselves, boast, and offer long recitations and credits. But there was none of this in Blue. He was quiet, almost reticent about his experiences; thoughtful; and very concerned with making me at home. He was living at the PRF building and I was billeted in the meditation center behind the PRF offices and separated from them by a grass quad. During the next six weeks Blue was my constant companion. We spent much of our time together, ate together, rambled about Durham together, and most important, experimented together. But it was not a case of a researcher and a subject. It was instead a collaboration based on mutual trust and friendship, each of us taking joy in the adventure of discovery.

My own introduction to the experiments was that same night. It was not part of a formal series, but was to see if Jerry Posner's dog would react to Blue's presence. The dog slept blissfully throughout the entire period, which nullified any hopes of getting a strong reaction, but half a mile away I was able to watch Blue in action. He entered an isolation booth at the psychophysiological laboratory in the engineering building at Duke. He doesn't like to be watched during the OB trial, so his voice is monitored through an intercom. As Blue relaxes he often gives little sighs and finally he whispers over the intercom a word such as "Soon"—and then silence. Blue is "out." Several minutes later he'll whisper again, tell his account, and then emerge from the lab. It takes him a few minutes to get back to normal and he sometimes feels pain in his chest, ranging from slight aches to recurrent jabbing pain.

My own work with Blue was carried out in conjunction with Bob Morris, and again an animal was used. I had discussed various ideas with Bob about animal experimentation. My own view was this: perhaps the use of kittens or any domesticated animal was really moving in the wrong direction. These animals are used to humans and might not react to an OB presence. Instead I felt that an animal that was distrustful or vigilant in the presence of people might be the best bet. Such an animal might react more violently to an intruder than a pet or an experimental animal such as a gerbil or hamster. My theory was in keeping with Bob's plans, since a member of Durham's parapsychological elite, Graham Watkins, was an animal behaviorist with a penchant for snakes. Graham had one exceptional snake that he had offered to lend to us. Graham had found the snake lying by the roadside and had merely picked it up to add to his collection. But the reptile's initial calm demeanor was atypical. No sooner had it been placed in captivity than it showed the orneriest, most vigilant disposition imaginable. It never accustomed itself to humans, and was alert at the slightest provocation. If held with a rubber glove, it would constantly attack and bite the gloved hand, whereas most snakes give up when they find their attack fruitless. The snake would strike at the glass terrarium in which it was housed if a hand came too close to the glass. The snake was ideal for our purposes.

For the first experiment, Blue, Bob, and Graham went to the Duke Hospital. I remained at PRF as chief observer, with Jerry Posner and, of course, the snake. The PRF building has a small isolation booth in which the snake was placed in its wood-shaving-filled terrarium. The booth has a large window through which I could watch the snake. Bright lights were focused on the snake from my position in the room so it could not possibly be alerted or influenced by my actions. As usual, there were four experimental periods. A phone signal cued us when a period was to begin, and Jerry signaled to me the completion of every ten-second time period of the three-minute session. Of course neither of us knew in which of the periods Blue would make his attempts.

During the entire duration of the experiment, the snake made only one odd response, which was noted by me at that time. Before the experiment I had observed the snake as it calmly explored its cage. During the first three-minute experimental period, the snake made no overt or unusual response. Although unknown to me at the time, no OBE had taken place during the first period. However, shortly after the beginning of the second experimental period, the snake began to speed up its activity rate and, stretching out completely, burrowed under the shavings at the bottom of the cage. The snake had done this during the preexperimental observation period while it explored its new home, but not with such violence or speed. After quickly burrowing, the snake started upward at the top of the cage, resting its head, throat forward, on the glass side. There it remained motionless for a moment, then quickly slid up the side of the cage (the side closest to me) until it was halfway up the glass. It then gnawed and bit wildly at the glass as though attacking something, or trying to "eat through" the glass. This lasted for about twenty to thirty seconds. The snake then suddenly became calm again. This reaction occurred in the middle of a three-minute experimental session. Prior to the experiment the snake had on two occasions opened its mouth and placed it against the glass. However, in both cases these reactions lasted for only a few seconds at most with no concomitant speedup of activity rate. After the violent reaction, the snake opened its mouth on only one other occasion.

When Blue, Rob, and Graham returned to the PRF we correlated times. It was perfect. During the second period Blue had projected and reported that he had visited the snake immediately after the beginning of the period. Before visiting the reptile he had floated about the room occupied by Jerry and me, hoping to get our attention. After using up several seconds in this attempt, he focused attention on the snake but did not record any specific action by it. By comparing Bob's timing to my own we found an almost exact correspondence. (During the fourth experimental period Blue reported a brief OBE to our area.) We were all very excited about the success and were eager to replicate the test.

Graham also had carried out an impromptu test that had shown some unusual results. He had left two electrodes from the polygraph open to pick up white noise in the room. During the two OB periods the noise level in the room housing Blue recorded a significant alteration. This would indicate that Blue's OB manifestation caused an alteration in the atmosphere of the room (such as a change in the ozone level). That is, if no other cause could be found. When Graham mentioned ozone to me I became excited, for during experiments with physical mediums, carried out in France in the 1920s and 1930s, it was often reported that the odor of ozone pervaded the room, heralding any phenomena. Could there be an important parallel here? Unfortunately, Graham's recordings were too vague to provide even a cursory attempt at isolating the variable that Blue was affecting, and this was never followed up. But it remains a tantalizing pointer to something about the energy source of Blue's OBE. Could he be taking power from the atmosphere in order to manifest outside his body? If Blue needed an energy source to manifest his consciousness apart from the body, there would be the requisite free-floating energy in the atmosphere. If Blue does utilize this energy about him when he travels out-of-the-body, one should expect a slight change in temperature in his general area, since as energy is extracted from the air it automatically cools. Another OB traveler, Ingo Swann, Karlis Osis's prize subject, had already carried out PK tasks trying to raise the temperature of pieces of Bakelite and graphite. When he succeeded, thermistors hooked to outlying and nontarget pieces of material dropped in temperature. This indicated that somehow, through PK, Swann had used energy in the air, transformed it, and redirected it by PK which, while raising the temperature in the target area, decreased the temperature in the outlying area. Does Blue use the same type of energy to manifest beyond his body? There is some tantalizing evidence that he does. Jerry Levin hooked up delicate thermistors in the experimental area during the animal tests. On one occasion (and one occasion only, alas) the thermistor did record dips in temperature when Blue approached it. One might also add that during hauntings these temperature drops have been recorded. And with the famous medium Stella C., Harry Price, the British psychical investigator, photographed thermometers systematically dropping in temperature during her séances and as telekinetic movements erupted in the séance room. Blue's freak actuation of the termistor is consistent with a whole range of findings in parapsychology and leads me to think that he manifests himself by the use of physical energy, using it to become semiphysical during this OB state. (Like most experiencers, Blue sees himself as traveling in the OB state alternately as an apparitional body, as an orb or shaft of light, or just as pure consciousness.)

A few days later we replicated the snake experiment, using the same procedure as before. But during the preexperimental period the snake burrowed into the shavings and never stirred for the rest of the test. It apparently slept, ruining the entire experiment.

Unfortunately, summer is always a hectic time in parapsychology, for the end of summer brings with it the annual convention of the Parapsychological Association. Because the convention serves as the meeting ground for the exchange of ideas and the presentation of new research, summer is often a mad rush to finish up research, get it analyzed and written up in time for the convention. The PRF was preparing to present two research briefs on Blue. This forestalled concentration on long experimental series, so we never ran a replication of the snake test. Further experiments with Blue had to be almost informal and the following researches were nearly one-shot affairs.

I must admit that I have a fondness for target studies. To be sure, animal detection experiments are much more suggestive that the subject is really leaving the body and traveling than are target studies. But somehow there seems to be an element of uncertainty with animal studies. Animals are unpredictable. Can we really judge their behavior objectively? Are we really only inferring that they are being affected by the OB-er? If I were to design an experimental project with Blue, I would use animal detectors as Bob Morris did. There is no doubt that, evaluated scientifically, this design gets to the heart of the OBE better than target studies. But if Blue were to go to a target area and describe accurately what was there, there could be no room for error in ascertaining that he had accomplished something extraordinary. To the experimenter the evidence from a well-designed target study can be more stunning and concrete than watching meditative cats or uptight snakes.

Blue has no special love for target studies. He feels they put him on a spot and place him in a position where he has, to "prove" himself. Nonetheless, during my Durham stay I constantly urged Blue to take part in some target studies with me. Since the formal detection experiments were in abeyance while the technical details on their findings were being written up, Blue acquiesced to my request and we were able to carry out two target studies with the assistance of Bob.

For the first test, on August 14, I remained at PRF while Bob and Blue were at Duke Hospital. The experiment was twofold; first, to permit me to carry out a target test while allowing Blue to become accustomed to a new apparatus Graham had developed. This odd-looking contraption consisted of a rotund cage with a bottom of depressible, pie-shaped planks. When an animal runs about the cage, it depresses the planks and an exact record of the animal's movements is punched out. We hoped to use this with the animal experiments. The top was screened over. After Blue left I randomly picked out several objects to decorate the top of the unit. I could have used anything in the PRF buildings. At the left rear of the unit I placed a large bottle sandwiched between two Frisbees lying flat. Being a musician, I had brought an instrument with me, an oboe. Blue had been interested in the long black wooden instrument, and I felt he might easily focus in on it. The oboe was assembled, placed on its open black rectangular case, and put *inside* the apparatus, but not obstructed by the bottle and Frisbees. And then I waited.

Bob called me from Duke Hospital at 9:46 P.M. to synchronize our clocks. At 10:11 Blue induced a three-minute OBE and at 10:14 reported the following impressions, which were written down at the time by Bob. Italicized portions represent correct responses by Blue or descriptions remarkably similar to the objects I had chosen for the test:

Got down deep, flip over there, real deep when there, T.V. looked on. Looked around room, above and around apparatus. Hard to see. *Round flat object like plate to front right in apparatus.* * Maybe glass. Hard to remember. *Something black and square diagonally.* Unclear. *Saw two things: both might have been same thing. Something tall standing in middle.* Might have created a kitten. *Long pencil on top. Something round.* Not the piece of wood, *maybe a Frisbee on top.*

After a few comments about his internal experiences Blue reported:

Maybe saw bottle. Shoe on top, to the right.

As the reader can see, Blue's impressions and language are confused. This is to be expected, since he is in a very dazed condition when he returns to the body and has to report on his experiences. But, sorting through the impressions it is remarkable how most of them are on dead center. Blue's reporting of a "round flat object like plate" and then "saw two things: both might have been same thing" are obvious and direct references to the two Frisbees. Eventually Blue was able to name the objects correctly. He initially reported seeing "maybe glass" and again described seeing the bottle. For one not familiar with musical instruments, his attempt at describing my oboe was successful. The case is jet black and rectangular. "Something tall standing in middle" could easily relate to the long thin shape of the oboe, which Blue probably perceived in the wrong perspective. This comment is augmented by his description of a "long pencil on top." It appears that Blue was "seeing" the target objects, but did not perceive them as we do with our normal vision. Instead he seems to be seeing one-dimensionally as though he did not have stereoscopic vision, as we all do in our physical bodies.

When Blue returned with Bob to the PRF, I had set up a

---

*Blue often has a reversal of sight or mirror vision during his OBEs, which would account for his correct description but incorrect placement of the object.

collection of objects from which Blue was to choose the target objects. Although his layout was different from mine, he chose six out of nine objects as the likely targets, of which five were ones I actually used. (Blue chose an additional object, a pair of black gloves, which he placed with the oboe case because of their color.) He correctly ascertained that the oboe was *within* the cage not atop it accompanying the other objects, although he thought it was standing upright not laid flat. (And the TV had not been turned on.)*

The test also gave me a chance to find out if suggestion played a part in Blue's OBEs. Could suggestion prompt him to see certain objects during his often opaque OB vision? When Blue, Bob, and I had designed the test and when Bob suggested that I choose PRF objects, I intentionally glanced over to a large globe in Bob's office. I made sure that Blue caught my eye and saw me glance at the globe. I wanted to see if somehow this "cue" would influence him to report seeing a globe. Such an impression might easily lodge and distort the impressions of someone using ESP. As can be seen, Blue rejected this cue totally, which impressed me very much.

The next target study was carried out using the same design. Unfortunately, there was a storm brewing and Blue is reluctant about OBing during electrical storms. Although he did project to the apparatus again, he reported to Bob only a very vague vision and specifically stated that he felt he had not been able to perceive the targets and the test was a failure from an evidential standpoint, although it is highly significant that Blue successfully predicted that he had done poorly. My target studies followed the same hex that plagued all my work with Blue—a fascinating initial test but circumstances circumventing the opportunity for a follow-up. Since Blue had no love for target studies, we discontinued the tests even though he had astounded me with his first target descriptions.

Up to this point my experiences with Blue had verified two

---

*It should be noted that when Blue made his decision about which objects I had used for the test, I had *already left* the room. In this respect he could not have chosen the objects by watching me for unconscious visual cues.

facets of his abilities: effecting animal detectors and seeing at a distance. There was one other prime facet of the abilities that was fascinating: the visual detection of the OB form by human witnesses. Although Blue often tried to make his presence known, it was only on occasion that people actually were able to detect his form, and this was usually only peripherally, as in Jerry Levin's case. Friends of Blue—Jerry Posner for one—recorded more vivid experiences. Blue records often traveling as a shaft or ball of light and reports that he can take apparitional form at will. Several close friends of his have reported, anecdotally, visual sightings in keeping with Blue's self-perception.

On my first day in Durham, Blue introduced me to Debbi Ewers, whom he saw quite often, and she recounted to me a particularly vivid experience that she associated with Blue.

It was 4:30 in the morning and I was literally exhausted. But the feeling of exhaustion was a rather pleasant one because I had just spent 10 very happy and peaceful hours with Blue. I had been in bed for only 10 minutes—when I saw a light up in the corner of the room near the ceiling. It was *not* a light that was flat on the wall, but one that was soft white and spherical, that was dim and then grew brighter. It grew dim again and then very bright when I mentally "spoke" to it. I assumed it was Blue. The light never changed its position in the room, only its intensity. When I began to get frightened (because this kind of thing hadn't happened before), I mentally "said" so, and it gradually faded away and I felt very peaceful again. This experience lasted at least twenty seconds. The light, at its peak intensity, appeared maybe two feet in diameter.

Miss Ewers was one of PRF's most successful detectors although she functioned not only as a detector but as an experimenter. Her job was to announce to the formal human detectors the beginning and end of a forty-minute experimental period during which Blue was to OB in twice at randomly chosen times. While engaging in unrelated activities when running the test, she twice felt the presence of someone invisible in the room. "It was an indescribable feeling of the room being 'full' as opposed to 'empty,' " and she even saw a blue circular light hovering for a second. Miss Ewers made a note of the times and both correlated precisely with Blue's OB visits.

The day before I left Durham for Los Angeles I finally was able to have one of these visual detections myself. Blue's farewell gift to me couldn't have been more apropos or welcomed. I had been with him that evening, and at 11:30 P.M. decided to retire for the night at the meditation center. Blue usually stays up until 4:00 or 5:00 in the morning and then sleeps well into the afternoon. I went to bed but sleep wasn't easy that night and I found myself still half-awake, tossing and turning at 3:15 A.M. (I have a habit of checking my wristwatch, which I wear even when sleeping, as soon as I wake at any time. So this timing is very precise.) I couldn't get comfortable, and tossed, turned, and rolled all over the bed, still drowsy, but awake. I was shifting from my right side to my left when out of the corner of my eye I saw a hovering red light. It was not reflected on the wall and my brief glimpse indicated it to be between my bed and the door of the bedroom diagonally across the room, which leads to a hallway. The ball was red and may even have been two orbs joined together. It was uncanny and it darted or streaked across the room and disappeared in the same manner that Jerry Levin's "shadow" had. Though still groggy, I literally catapulted out of bed and rushed to my desk to make a note of the time. It was an almost automatic reaction. I didn't decide to get out of bed, I just found myself rushing to the desk almost as if I had started from the bed before becoming sufficiently awake. It can best be compared to suddenly finding yourself out of bed running to answer a ringing telephone in the middle of the night with no real recollection of getting out of bed. I merely wrote down "thought I saw a red light in my peripheral vision" and noted the time: 3:22 A.M. Then I went back to bed.

The next morning I had a meeting to attend, and when I returned to the PRF buildings that afternoon, Blue was standing on the porch watching me with his usual implike grin. He had just got up and didn't say anything at all to me.

I was hoping, praying, that he would report his OBE to me, but he didn't. Finally I asked him if he had had an OBE after he had gone to bed. Blue, still dazed from sleep, said he had, so again I waited in anticipation, hoping he would say something that would independently validate what I saw. But he didn't and so I finally had to ask him point-blank if he recalled projecting to my room. Blue thought for a minute, as though trying to grasp a fleeting memory. Yes, he said, he did remember going to sleep telling himself he would try to visit me, vaguely remembered journeying to the meditation center, and then "flew off" to Virginia to see where he would be lodged during the Parapsychological Association convention to be held shortly in Charlottesville. He couldn't remember anything more. Because I had been forced to hint to Blue that I had had a detection, the evidence for the correspondence between my experience and Blue's was weakened. However, when I told him of the experience, but not the time, I asked him to try to determine the approximate time of his OB visit. He thought for a few moments and then said that since the OBE had taken place shortly after he had retired, and since he thought he had visited me first, he was able to isolate the time between 3:00 and 3:30 A.M. The timing was the key evidential factor, since it corresponded roughly to my 3:22 A.M. sighting. In addition it is a bit unusual for Blue to retire so early (for him!).

Although my experience was ephemeral at best, it tallied with many other detections by PRF workers. Like Jerry Levin, I perceived Blue only out of the corner of my eye as something unusual streaking past. Like Jerry's, my experience carried with it an inner compulsion to make a specific and exact note of the time. And like Jerry, Debbi, and many others, I was not making any attempt to detect Blue when the experience took place.

In each of the out-of-body trials Blue's psychophysiology was carefully recorded, both during the cool-down periods and during the OBEs. To get a firm idea of his bodily state during the experience, electroencephalograms were taken of the left and right hemispheres of his brain; skin potential, respiration, blood pulse volume, heart rate, eye movements, and muscle movements (EOG) were all monitored.

These readings are vastly complex, since to find correlations each recording must be compared to each of the same readings for every OBE. Then various recordings must be correlated with other types of psychophysiological records to see if there are significant patterns between them, and which might be direct links. Briefly, though, respiration, heart rate, and blood pulse increased significantly during the OBE while the EOG and skin potential decreased.

Dr. Charles Tart of the University of California, Davis, has reported that with his two subjects the EEGs showed odd patterns when they induced the OBE from the sleep state. A comparison of Blue's EEG between the cool-down and OB phases indicated little initial differences. However, when a more sensitive and exacting measurement was employed, the electrical activity of the left hemisphere of the brain showed a gradual decrease. This is in keeping with EEG monitoring and findings with Ingo Swann, who also induces the experience from the waking state, although his shifts are more marked than Blue's.

Significantly, the patterns of Blue's OBE psychophysiology were notably different from normal sleep and dreaming. His EEG tracings were those of a normal waking but relaxed state. Eye movements decreased during the OBE, while a proliferation of rapid eye movements is a prime dream trait. Blue's muscle tones was notably relaxed, different from both sleep and the effects of deep anesthesia. So we can be sure that, if anything, Blue is certainly not merely sleeping and dreaming with ESP during his out-of-body excursions.

All of these results will have to be closely analyzed before any meaningful correlates with the OBE can be isolated. However, it might be significant to note that the increase in respiration and heartbeat and the decrease in mental activity are similar to yogic breathing exercises, which, if mastered, allegedly can induce the OBE. It should also be mentioned that during the research analysis Blue was kept completely uninformed about his own responses so that he would not, unconsciously or automatically, use some form of biofeedback to regulate his psychophysiology to conform to his own precedents.

Although I had to leave Durham and my work with Blue, I have not lost my fascination with the experimentation done there with him. With Bob Morris gradually withdrawing from the PRF to carry out independent research, Graham Watkins, John Hartwell (a psychophysiologist), and Joseph Janis, all of whom had previously worked with Blue, took over the experimentation. Graham's work was to use the animal monitoring unit described in my target study to see if the animals would orient themselves in the direction of Blue. If he were to position his out-of-the-body self northward, would the cat do likewise? The first results looked promising, but the star cat, Spirit, quickly became accustomed to the apparatus and merely sat passively, and would not move at all once placed in the cage. In order to readapt the experiments, a large room was used, monitored by closed-circuit TV, into which a cat was placed. Blue was to OB over and stand randomly in one of the corners of the room. Again Blue's pets were used, and although no results were forthcoming—the cats roamed about totally oblivious to Blue's presence—one of the technicians began to have strong detection experiences. At first he recorded his impressions as to which corner Blue was in, and in the four trials in which he placed his impressions on record, he was 100 percent correct. During the last test the technician recorded actually seeing Blue's face over the monitor, and again his report of the OB presence was on target.

How can I sum up Blue parapsychologically and personally? Having had the experience myself during the years 1965–1967, I felt I had a good idea of what the OBE was. To me it seemed plain that when one is projecting out of the body, he is releasing some sort of ultraphysical "body" or apparition, semiphysical in nature. Blue's OB talents radically altered my conception. My first change in position was to revise this rigid, confining view of the OBE. To be sure, many persons undergoing this experience find themselves in a replica of the human body and, in fact, they are often seen as apparitions by observers. But Blue's experiences signaled to me a realization that the OBE is not one experience, but a continuum of experiences. In this respect, as I mentioned earlier, Blue can travel as an "apparition," as a ball or shaft of light, or merely as a point of consciousness dangling in space. These are all OBEs, but of different natures. There is no one prototype out-of-body experience; rather, there are varieties of out-of-body functioning.

Blue is neither theatrical nor boastful of his abilities. He is intrigued with them, yet he purposely avoids reading the reports of others in order to keep from being influenced by them. He views himself as an experimenter, not as a subject, and he takes an active role in designing and evaluating the research carried out with him. In my view, Blue is shy, retiring, sensitive, intelligent, and compassionate. His writings are literary, his poetry delicate.

Blue's personal shyness is manifested several ways. He rarely talks about his experiences unless asked and will not discuss certain aspects of them that he feels are too personal. He is quite the opposite of the usual psychic. He looks you straight in the eye, and in dead seriousness and with awe narrates an encounter or view about his experiences.

And that is the manner I try to adopt when discussing the enigma of Blue Harary.

9 | ESP and Out-of-Body Experiences: An Experimental Approach

JOHN PALMER

One advantage of an anthology of this type is that it gives the reader an opportunity to sample different approaches to the topic of study. I have approached the topic of out-of-body experiences (OBEs) from the standpoint of an experimental psychologist and parapsychologist. Because of this fact, I have adopted certain assumptions about OBEs, some of which will differ from those of persons who come from different backgrounds. Before describing my research and the conclusions I have drawn from it about the nature of OBEs, I would like to share with you some of the more important of these assumptions and briefly to defend their plausibility. I hope that by so doing I will help you better to understand and evaluate my research in relation to the contributions of other writers.

Assumption 1. The OBE is a common experience. The sensational treatment that "astral projection" has received in some occult literature and in the media is likely to create the impression that the OBE is a rare bird, and that people who have such experiences are special or "weird" because of this fact. However, survey data indicate that quite the opposite is the case. For example, a colleague and I conducted a random mail survey of seven hundred adult residents of Charlottesville, Virginia, and three hundred University of Virginia students, asking them about psychic and other related experiences (Palmer and Dennis, 1974). Included in the questionnaire was the following item: "Have you ever had an experience in which you felt that 'you' were located 'outside' or 'away from' your physical body; that is, the feeling that your consciousness, mind, or center of awareness was at a different place than your physical body? (If in doubt, please answer 'no.')" Of the 341 townspeople (49 percent) who returned the questionnaire and answered the item, 48 (or 14 percent) answered it affirmatively. Among the students, 266 (or 89 percent) answered the item, and 66 of these (25 percent) responded affirmatively. In the combined samples, 83 percent of those who reported an OBE reported having the experience more than once, and 34 percent reported having it eight or more times. Other surveys have produced comparable results, at least so far as the percentage of the sample reporting at least one OBE is concerned (e.g., Green, 1967; Hart, 1954). Thus, while the OBE is by no means as common as the ordinary dream, neither is it a rare event restricted to only a handful of special people (although there are certain people who stand out as having unusually frequent, vivid, or bizarre OBEs).

Assumption 2. An experience should not be denied classification as an OBE simply because it is undramatic or unimpressive to the experient. The literature on OBEs consists largely of personal accounts by people whose experiences were sufficiently dramatic or impressive that they were prompted to share them with scientists or submit them to occult magazines. Given the large number of people who say they have had OBEs, this literature obviously represents only the tip of an iceberg. While it would be naïve to assume that everyone who has a dramatic OBE reports it, it is equally unlikely that all OBEs are as dramatic as those described in most published anthologies.

But should the dramatic and undramatic experiences be classified together? I think they should. Consider dreams as an analogy. Some dreams are very dramatic: long, colorful, cohesive, bizarre, rich in symbolism and meaning to the dreamer. Most dreams, however, are short, fragmentary, and rather mundane. Nevertheless, we classify both types of experience as dreams, because they are related *qualitatively* in meaningful ways—for examples, they occur during sleep, they are visual, they do not accurately reflect "reality," and they involve common physiological mechanisms. From a scientific point of view, it would be absurd to decide whether or not a person had a dream or not on the basis of how dramatic was the experience. It would be equally absurd to classify OBEs on this basis, and for the same reasons.

Assumption 3. The OBE should be defined as any experience during which the experient felt that he was outside his (physical) body. This is potentially the most controversial of my assumptions, but it implies a very important distinction that must be made if the OBE is to be dealt with scientifically: the distinction between the content and/or quality of an experience, on the one hand, and the interpretation of that content or quality, on the other. In the case of an OBE, the person might experience, for example, a floating sensation in conjunction with a visual image of his body as it would appear were he three feet above it looking down. From this complex of proprioceptive and visual images, he then might *infer* that he was outside his body. Whether upon later reflection he decides to accept at an intellectual level that he was outside his body is not the issue; this decision will depend upon factors (e.g., philosophical predispositions) unrelated to the experience itself. The point is that I would say a person had an OBE if his immediate impulse, prior to critical reflection, was to interpret what was happening to him at the time as being outside his body.

In short, my thesis is that an OBE should be defined (at least at this stage of our knowledge) not in terms of the content or quality of the experience itself, but in terms of how the experient interprets it. There are two reasons for adopting such a definition. First, it is the only way to distinguish clearly an OBE from an ordinary dream, fantasy, or hallucinatory experience. Second, OBEs are of interest to parapsychologists as a distinctive entity because they are of such a nature as to convince some persons that they were outside their bodies. It is from this attribute of the OBE that its relevance to the question of survival after death and "seeing at a distance" derives. If this is the case, doesn't it stand to reason that this attribute be the cornerstone of our definition of the OBE?

Not all who would concede that the interpretation is a *necessary* criterion for classifying an experience as an OBE, however, would consider it to be *sufficient* for such classification. I often have heard people suggest, for example, that an experience is not an OBE unless the person has a visual image of his physical body or unless the quality of the experience is similar to waking consciousness. I find such restrictions arbitrary and unnecessary. I have heard many accounts of experiences that seemed like clear-cut OBEs except that they lacked one of these attributes, and I would be most reluctant to discount these experiences because of one such "deficiency." It has been my experience that most persons, including those with considerable psychological sophistication, are unable to describe adequately what it was about their experience that led them to conclude it was an OBE as opposed to a dream, fantasy, or hallucination. By adopting my definition, the decision of whether a particular experience is an OBE is left to the person best qualified to make it—the experient himself.

Later, it can be determined from empirical research what particular kinds of images, etc., are associated with strong conviction of separation from the body. Such research may lead to the designation of subclasses of OBEs defined by certain clusters of attributes, and this would be all to the good.

Assumption 4. It is desirable to study the OBE under experimentally controlled conditions. The advantages of studying the OBE under controlled conditions are the same as the advantages of studying any phenomenon of nature under such conditions—greater knowledge of and control over extraneous factors that might affect the object of study. Such control is especially important when the OBE is examined in relation to psychic phenomena such as ESP, where elimination of possible sensory cues and the capacity to define precisely the level of performance expected by chance are necessary if valid conclusions are to be drawn.

Even with respect to the OBE itself, a controlled environment is helpful. It allows one to vary systematically the conditions or "induction techniques" leading up to the OBE and to obtain an immediate, detailed report of the experience from the subject. It also allows monitoring of the subject's physiology, if suitable equipment is available.

Assumption 5. There are advantages to using unselected volunteer subjects in experimental research on OBEs. Virtually all OBE experiments have been conducted with highly selected individuals who claim the ability to induce OBEs in themselves more or less at will (e.g., Tart, 1967, 1968). This approach has the advantage of yielding a high probability that the subject will be able to have an OBE of good quality at the time the experimenter desires. Research with selected subjects already has contributed useful data about OBEs and should continue to do so.

The greatest advantage of studying groups of more or less randomly selected individuals is that the results of such research can be generalized to the population at large with greater confidence than can data from "gifted" subjects. Such selected subjects are often atypical in respects other than just having OBEs. Getting a large enough group of them together so that they *might* adequately represent a larger population would be extremely difficult and costly. If we assume that OBEs and ESP are widely distributed in the population, we want to draw conclusions that will be valid for this wider population.

Second, studying people with varying predispositions toward OBEs allows us to study systematically individual differences: for example, what personality types are most likely to have OBEs, and what induction techniques work best with which types of people?

I am *not* favoring one approach over the other. What I am saying is that research with both selected and unselected subjects is needed, and the latter approach so far has been underrepresented in the scientific literature.

Assumption 6. Mild OBEs can be induced in a controlled setting without drugs. This assumption could not be defended when my research began, but the results have clearly supported its validity. In deciding upon a method for inducing OBEs in the laboratory, I was influenced by the writings of persons who claimed success in inducing OBEs in themselves and who published their techniques. In particular, I was influenced by the writings of Fox (1962), Monroe (1971), and Muldoon (Muldoon and Carrington, 1929). I was impressed that their techniques generally contained two common elements. First, the subject gets himself into a very relaxed state, just on the verge of sleep. This state struck me as very similar to the "hypnagogic" state during which OBEs seem most likely to occur spontaneously. Second, while maintaining himself in this state, the subject imagines himself leaving his body, using some kind of fantasy technique (e.g., reaching for a point of light on the ceiling, imagining himself rising in an elevator) to represent this process to himself. Although I did not copy any specific technique suggested by someone else, I did adopt these two general principles.

Since hypersuggestibility often characterizes the hypnagogic state, once subjects were presumably in this state I gave them the suggestion that they would experience a floating sensation. Although I did not directly suggest an OBE, nor did I label the suggestion as hypnosis, I suspect that this and related statements functioned as hypnotic suggestions to have an OBE.* I did not use overt hypnosis for fear of encouraging fabricated reports of OBEs, and also because I thought it might be counterproductive with subjects who consciously or unconsciously resist attempts to hypnotize them.

Assumption 7. The OBE as such is not a psychic phenomenon. One often hears the OBE referred to as a psychic phenomenon. This usage is based on a confusion between the *experience* of being outside one's body and the *fact* of such transcendence.† The latter, if real, could be called a psychic

---

*One finding from my own research was a significant tendency for subjects reporting OBEs in my experiments to score higher on a measure of hypnotic susceptibility than subjects who did not (Palmer and Lieberman, 1976).

†What, precisely, it might mean to be outside one's body is a complicated metaphysical issue that I will not be able to deal with

phenomenon because the existence of a "soul" or some aspect of one's being spatially separated from the physical body does not follow from the laws of physics and biology as we know them. Indeed, conclusions about literal separation from the body have in the past depended heavily upon inferences from other psychic phenomena, such as ESP on the part of the experient at the time of his experience. However, the *experience* of being outside the body is just that—an experience. It may or may not reflect literal separation from the body or any other psychic phenomena. Moreover, it is valid as an experience regardless of whether anything paranormal is associated with it. What relationship, if any, exists between OBEs and psi is a question that must be answered by research. We learn nothing by declaring ex post facto that any OBE not associated with something paranormal is not a "real" OBE. What we must do is define the OBE independently of psi, and then see if certain types of psychic phenomena occur more frequently during OBEs than we would expect by chance, or more frequently than they occur at other times.

Assumption 8. With unselected subjects, ESP is the best psychic phenomenon to study in relation to OBEs. This assumption merely reflects the fact that ESP is the most common psychic ability manifested by ordinary people, both inside and outside the laboratory. Although testing the ability of a person during an OBE to appear to someone else as an apparition might be a more interesting experiment, it is doubtful that the typical unselected subject could succeed at this task. This is the type of experiment one might try with "gifted" subjects.

The foregoing list does not include all the explicit and

---

adequately in this paper. As a minimal definition, what I mean is that some nonphysical component of the organism (whether it be a "vehicle" such as an "astral body" or simply the mind or consciousness) is located at a point in physical space different from that of the physical body. The claim of some experients that they move to a different reality where physical space does not exist, while possibly true in principle, is outside the domain of the scientific paradigm within which I am working.

implicit assumptions that guided my research, but I hope it covers the most important ones. Next I will show how these assumptions were translated into actual experimentation.

THE EXPERIMENTS: WHAT WE DID

The project I am going to describe consisted of four formal experiments primarily undertaken to determine whether there was any relationship between reports of OBEs during the experimental sessions and scores on a concurrent ESP test. When the project began, I had no idea how many experiments would be conducted. However, each of the first three experiments raised questions that I wanted an additional experiment to resolve. Fortunately, funds and facilities were available to carry out these additional experiments.* By the end of the fourth experiment, I finally was beginning to feel a sense of closure. Furthermore, at this time I was leaving my post in the Division of Parapsychology at the University of Virginia School of Medicine to assume new duties at the University of California, Davis. This seemed like a good point to terminate the project.

Sometime during the third experiment, it became apparent to me that the individual experiments in the project could be treated as a single, larger experiment. By so doing, I would be increasing my sample size fourfold, allowing the application of more sensitive and powerful statistical tests. The experiments had a great deal in common, which made it natural to treat them cumulatively. Each involved three basic steps: a technique for inducing an OBE, a rating scale on which the subject described his experiences during the session (including whether he had an OBE), and an ESP test which involved the subject attempting to identify a picture while "outside his body."

Three of the individual experiments have been described in

*I am indebted to Dr. Ian Stevenson, director of the Division of Parapsychology, University of Virginia School of Medicine, and to the Parapsychology Foundation, Inc., for providing me with the resources and funds to carry out this research.

technical reports (Palmer and Lieberman, 1975, 1976; Palmer and Vassar, 1974) and I plan to publish such a report on the fourth experiment in the near future. What I will do here is give you an overview of the basic procedure and the more important variations.

1. *Subjects.* Most of our subjects were undergraduate students at the University of Virginia who expressed interest in participating in an experiment on ESP and altered states of consciousness. All were unpaid volunteers. We tested a total of 180 subjects in the formal experiments, 78 men and 102 women. We made no effort to select people with a previous history of OBEs or psychic experiences.

Subjects were tested one at a time. Immediately before each session, I met with the subject in my office. The main purpose of this meeting was to become acquainted with the subject and to give him a detailed description of the procedure and rationale of the experiment. Although the majority of our subjects were told that the purpose of the induction procedure was to induce an OBE, twenty simply were told that the purpose was to induce an ASC (altered state of consciousness) that would allow them to receive impressions of the target picture passively. We wanted to see if some of these latter subjects might have OBEs spontaneously during the session without having been given a mental "set" to have an OBE. All subjects were given an opportunity to "back out" at this time, but none chose to do so.

2. *ESP Targets.* The target pool consisted of fifty colored or black-and-white pictures mounted on legal sized white paper. The pictures, which were taken from photography magazines, covered a wide variety of themes, and many were abstract or "artistic." They were divided into ten sets of five pictures each, the sets being assembled so that the pictures in each set would be maximally different from each other. Before each experiment, a target picture was designated for each subject individually, based on a sequence of random numbers.

3. *Preparing for the Session.* As soon as the meeting in my office was over, I took the subject to our laboratory, which consisted of two adjacent rooms. I first asked him to examine

the outer room, in which the target picture would be located. I then led him to the inner room and seated him in a comfortable reclining chair or bed facing the outer room. After giving him a pair of headphones to place over his ears, I returned to my office to ascertain the identity of the target picture. I then went back to the outer room, withdrew the target picture from its pocket, and placed it face upward on a table in the center of the room. The door between the inner and outer rooms was always closed at this time, so there was no way the subject could see the picture. I then reentered the inner room and immediately took my seat behind the subject. After checking to see that the tape recorder was functioning properly, I turned off the lights and the session began.

4. *Progressive Relaxation.* The entire induction procedure was recorded on tape and played to the subject over the headphones. The first phase of the induction for all subjects was a fifteen-minute progressive relaxation exercise adapted from Braud and Braud (1973). Based on the Jacobson technique (Jacobson, 1938), the instructions ask the subject alternately to tense and relax specific muscle groups and to notice the contrast between the tension and the relaxation. These instructions are followed by suggestions to still and quiet the mind. The purpose of these exercises was to promote feelings of deep physical and mental relaxation, or to facilitate the hypnagogic state that I referred to earlier.

5. *Review of Instructions.* Following the relaxation exercises, the tape reviewed the subject's task for the upcoming reception period. Unless he was among the twenty subjects not given the OBE set, he was told that sometime during the reception period he would feel a sense of detachment or floating. At that time, he should imagine leaving his body and traveling through the wall to the outer room to "look at" the target picture. He was told that he could make as many "trips" as necessary to identify the picture. The other twenty subjects were given the suggestion that target-related imagery would spontaneously come to consciousness during the reception period, and they should simply be passive and open to it.

6. *Reception Period.* The second stage of the induction took place during the reception period, which lasted anywhere from ten to twenty minutes. Two basic types of induction techniques were used, both of which were designed to maintain and enhance the hypnagogic-like state induced by the relaxation exercise. The first set of techniques, employed exclusively in our first experiment, involved having the subject look straight into a rotating spiral disk illuminated by a strobe light passed through a black-light filter. The illusion created was of the disk collapsing into its center, like a vortex. The subject first was exposed to the disk for a ten-minute period sandwiched between the relaxation exercises and reception period, during which time he was to imagine being drawn into its center. During the reception period itself, he was to imagine going all the way through the disk and into the outer room. For some subjects the disk was illuminated during the reception period, while other subjects simply were asked to imagine it. During both the prereception and reception periods, a monotonous, pulsating 350 cps. tone was played through the headphones. In addition to blocking out extraneous sounds from the environment, we felt that this particular tone had a kind of "numbing" effect, which deepened the altered state. For a more detailed description see Palmer and Vassar (1974)

The second set of techniques, used in the remaining three experiments, were not quite so elaborate. The pulsating tone continued to be used in the second experiment, but it was replaced in the last two experiments by a complex series of tones developed by Robert Monroe, who has frequent OBEs himself and has written a book about them (Monroe, 1971). This sound tape retained the same monotonous quality of the earlier tape, and results with the two tapes seemed to be about the same. Half of the subjects experiencing this second set of techniques simply were asked to close their eyes during the reception period. The rest were asked to keep their eyes open and look through a pair of acetate hemispheres into a white light. The acetate hemispheres were really halves of Ping-Pong balls taped over the subject's eyes before the session.

This technique, called the "Ganzfeld," creates a uniform white visual field for the subject and is frequently used in sensory deprivation experiments. Finally, twenty subjects in the "eyes-closed" condition experienced a vibrator or "bed massage" during part of the reception period. This was an admittedly crude attempt to facilitate the "vibrational state" often reported as preceding OBEs (e.g., Monroe, 1971). The vibrator was abruptly cut off part way into the reception period, a procedure that we found produces a brief but intense floating sensation that we thought might trigger an OBE.

7. *Winding Up the Session.* The reception period ended with instructions for the subject to sit quietly for a few moments and review his imagery or "perceptions" of the target picture. In the meanwhile, I went to the outer room (closing the door behind me) and replaced the target picture in the packet containing the four other pictures in the set. In so doing, I was careful to put the target picture back in its original location in the sequence and to be sure that its edges were flush with the edges of the other pictures. I placed the packet on the table along with copies of the rating scales and questionnaires the subject was to fill out. I then left the laboratory and summoned my assistant, who supervised the remainder of the experiment.

8. *Rating Scale of Experiences.* The assistant disengaged the subject from the headphones and other paraphernalia and brought him to the outer room. The subject's first task was to complete a rating scale describing his experiences during the session. The most important item was the question about whether the subject felt he had an OBE during the session. This question, which was asked of all but the first ten subjects in the first experiment, was worded as follows: "Did you at any time during the experiment have the feeling that you were *literally* outside of your physical body?" The response alternatives were a simple "yes" or "no." Although other questions included in the later versions of the rating scale allowed for a more refined discrimination, we found that the simple "yes-no" format gave us our most meaningful and significant results.

Other questions on the rating scale dealt with such things as how relaxed the subject was, the vividness and quality of his imagery, and his expectancy of success at various stages of the experiment, in terms of both having an OBE and correctly identifying the target picture. Subjects who indicated they did have an OBE were asked to answer other questions about it (e.g., did they see their physical body, could they control the experience) and to describe it in their own words.

9. *ESP Judging.* After the subject completed the rating scale, the assistant (who did not know the identity of the target picture) removed the pictures from the packet and placed them in order in a row on the floor. The subject then read a two-page sheet of judging instructions. He was to give each picture a rating of 0 to 30 according to its degree of correspondence to his imagery or "perceptions" during the session. The instructions encouraged him to give some weight to partial, indirect, and symbolic correspondences, although the most weight, of course, was to be assigned to direct or literal correspondences.

Each subject's ratings were transformed into an ESP score. The score was based on the difference between the rating the subject gave the target picture and the average of the ratings he gave to all five pictures. If the target picture got a higher-than-average rating, his ESP score was positive. If this rating was lower than average, the ESP score was negative. If only chance factors were operating, we would expect these ESP scores to average out to zero.

10. *Post-Experimental Interview.* As soon as the ESP judging was over, the assistant summoned me back to the laboratory. I revealed the identity of the target picture and tried to give the subject an idea of how well he had done. I made it clear to the subject that we were going to base our conclusions on group data, and there was no way we could be sure whether ESP was operating in his particular case, and I urged him not to put too much weight on his results, whether positive or negative. As time allowed, I discussed his experience with him, and I offered to answer any questions he had

about the experiment. Almost all subjects said they enjoyed the experiment and found their experience pleasant. Only two of our 180 subjects had what might be called a "bad trip," and no one to my knowledge has ever been harmed by participating in our experiments.

RESULTS: DESCRIPTION OF OBES

When the data from all four experiments were tabulated, we found that exactly half of our subjects had responded affirmatively to the OBE question. That is, 50 percent had experiences during the session which they interpreted as OBEs.

What kinds of experiences were they? We have two kinds of data on this point: subjects' answers to specific questions about their OBEs, and their written descriptions. The questions were introduced at different stages of the project, so the number of subjects who answered each question varies somewhat. However, all of the questions but one were included in at least two experiments, and I will identify the exception. None of the questions was included in the spiral disk experiment.

Subjects reporting OBEs said they had anywhere from one to five per session, the average number being 2.26. They lasted anywhere from three seconds to five minutes. Sixty-one percent said they saw the outer room during at least one of their OBEs, but only 44 percent said they saw the target picture. Forty percent said they saw their physical bodies lying on the chair (or bed) during at least one OBE. Eighty-five percent reported that at some time during the session they had the experience of being both inside and outside their bodies simultaneously, but these occurrences did not necessarily correspond to their reported OBEs. On the other hand, 40 percent stated that their OBEs represented an abrupt change in their state of consciousness from the preceding moment.

A particularly intruging finding was that, despite our intention that subjects create their OBEs at will, 89 percent reported that at least one of their OBEs occurred spontaneously and when they weren't expecting it. Forty percent indicated that all of their OBEs were spontaneous. In general, subjects also felt they could not control their OBEs very well. On a four-point scale, the average rating of control was only 1.32.

In the last experiment, subjects reporting OBEs were asked to indicate whether they were most like dreams, waking fantasy, or waking vision. Sixty-one percent chose dreams, 27 percent waking fantasy, and 12 percent waking vision. However, several subjects told us that none of the alternatives came very close to describing their experiences.

How confident were our subjects that they really had an OBE? In the last two experiments we asked this question specifically. Out of 47 subjects who answered the two-choice OBE question affirmatively, 17 (36 percent) said they were "definitely" out of their bodies, 25 (53 percent) said they thought they had been out, but were not sure, and the remaining five (11 percent) said they might have been out, but doubted it.

Another way to get an idea of the kinds of experiences our subjects had is to look at how they described them in their own words. Subjects varied widely in their ability and/or willingness to articulate these private events in writing. I will share with you three articulate accounts that illustrate the range of OBEs our procedures induced. First, a simple one:

In [the] first experience I had a sense of sliding out of the back of the chair—I seemed to be still in my body but there was a definite sense of motion of two or three feet back.

In the second I just seemed to raise up a bit—a floating sense—like in a tank of water.

The following experience was more elaborate:

At first during the relaxation, etc., I felt like a rush of I guess excitement sort of and I felt completely detached from everything. Then when I was supposed to be trying to leave my body my mind became very alert and analytical and I felt in a box sort of inside a dead body. This continued the whole way through the experiment and when it was over I felt a big come down when the tape clicked off. I felt sort of the whole way through also like I could see my whole body down beneath me in the chair and once I felt like my mind was in a yellow glow right above my eyes close to my head and it was me but I could also see it and I tried to imagine the room with myself in it and I felt like I was very wide awake seeing the room. And there is an impression of a picture of blue-green and bright reddish brown but that could be a picture I just had in my mind.

Finally, here are excerpts from a report describing an experience in which the subject made it to the outer room.

. . . This one occurred spontaneously and was the most bizarre of the three. I entered the adjoining room to find it dark with a dim light on the table and the picture covered by a dish. This was the most dream-like because the dish made sense to me. I remembered [in the dream] that someone, a woman I think, didn't want me to see the picture for some reason. The tape ended as I was trying to comprehend this mess within my own mind. . . .

All of these experiences were reported by subjects in the "sensory deprivation" condition with eyes closed. It is my impression that this procedure yielded the "best" OBEs, but I can offer no numerical data to support this impression.

RESULTS: OBES AND ESP

The main purpose of my research project was to determine whether OBEs are associated with an improved level of performance on an ESP test conducted while the subject is in this state. More specifically, the experimental hypothesis was that the average (or mean) ESP score of persons reporting OBEs during the session will be significantly higher than expected by chance. Second, this mean score will be significantly higher than the mean of persons who do not report OBEs during the session.

Taking into account all 170 subjects who answered the OBE question, neither hypothesis was supported. However, closer inspection of the data revealed that the results depended upon the type of induction procedure used during the reception period. We found that both hypotheses were significantly confirmed when the induction was restricted to straightforward sensory deprivation procedures: the monotonous masking sound coupled either with the Ganzfeld or having the subject close his eyes in the darkened room—*and nothing else.* When the induction procedure included additional sources of stimulation, either the spiral disk or the bed vibrator, the relationship between OBE reports and ESP scores reversed. Under these conditions, subjects reporting OBEs tended to score below chance (i.e., they tended to give the target picture a lower rating than the other pictures), but their average score did not differ significantly from that of subjects not reporting OBEs. The positive OBE-ESP relationship in the "sensory deprivation" condition and the negative OBE-ESP relationship in the "sensory bombardment" condition differed from each other to a statistically significant degree.*

These findings would be more convincing had we been able to predict in advance that OBEs would facilitate ESP only when the "sensory deprivation" induction procedures were used. Among subjects who were told the experiment involved OBEs, a significantly greater proportion of those receiving this type of induction reported OBEs than of those who received the "bombardment" induction (63 percent vs. 44 percent).† Also, OBEs in the latter conditions may have been associated with specific responses to the spiral disk or the cessation of the vibrator, while the OBEs in the deprivation conditions were more natural. On the other hand, the rating scale responses gave us no concrete basis for inferring that the OBEs produced by the two types of induction procedures were substantially different.

We still have no evidence to help us explain the reversal. For some unknown reason, the additional stimulation may have guided subjects' ESP away from the target picture, per-

*From multiple regression analysis, $F = 6.56$, $df = 1/167$, $P < .05$. The mean ESP score of the "deprivation group" reporting OBEs was significantly above chance ($t = 2.66$, $df = 53$, $P < .02$).

†$X^2 = 4.28$, $df = 1$, $P < .05$.

haps causing some of them to pick up information from one or more of the four control pictures. Perhaps ESP was shut off entirely in these conditions. All we can do is speculate. If we are willing, nonetheless, to tentatively accept as genuine the confirmation of the OBE-ESP hypothesis under sensory deprivation conditions (and I think a reasonable statistical argument can be made for doing so), we are entitled to examine this relationship more closely to see if we can get some ideas about the reasons for its occurrence.

WHAT DOES IT MEAN?

If people having OBEs are able to acquire information about distant events, does this mean that some vehicle of consciousness leaves their physical bodies and travels to the distant location to "see" the event? Maybe so, but an equally plausible interpretation is that the OBE is simply a psi-conducive state of consciousness that predisposes one to receiving psi impressions.

The findings of our research seem most compatible with the second of these interpretations, for at least two reasons. First of all, if those of our subjects who reported OBEs obtained target-related information by literally going out and "seeing" the target, we would expect the ones who told us afterward that they actually saw the target during their OBEs to get better ESP scores than those who did not. However, no such difference turned up in our data; subjects who did not "see" the target during their OBEs scored as well as subjects who did. The former subjects apparently received their target-related impressions at other times during the session, or whatever it was they did experience during their OBEs had some connection with the target theme.

The second point has to do with the rating scale that subjects used to describe their experiences during the session. By means of a statistical technique called factor analysis, I transformed the major part of the scale into six new scales, each measuring a different aspect of subjects' reactions to the test situation. Each item contributed to each scale, but each contributed more to some scales than to others. Conversely, the major contributions to each scale were made by only a small percentage of the items, and these items formed the basis for determining what the scale measured.

For purposes of this discussion, I am only going to consider one of the six scales. The two items which made by far the strongest contributions to this scale were how relaxed the subject was during the reception period, and whether his imagery at that time was "intense, dreamlike, bizarre" as opposed to "structured, directed, rational." In other words, subjects who were very relaxed and had a great deal of what we might call "primary process" imagery in the Freudian sense got the highest scores on the scale. It immediately occurred to me that such subjects could be characterized as having been in a hypnagogic state during the reception period. Therefore, I decided to call the scale the "Hypnagogic Scale."

There are two interesting things about this scale. First, there was a statistically significant positive correlation between scores on this scale and ESP scores, but only in those conditions where the "sensory deprivation" induction procedure was used.* In other words, the Hypnagogic Scale was associated with ESP scores in precisely the same way as the OBE reports.

The second interesting thing about the Hypnagogic Scale helps to explain why this happened. In addition to relaxation and "primary process" imagery, a third item also made a strong and significant contribution to the scale, although not as strong as that made by the two just mentioned; as you probably have already guessed, this item was the OBE item. To make a long story short, what I found was that the OBE reports and the Hypnagogic Scale were confounded as predictors of ESP scores; OBE reports considered apart from the Hypnagogic Scale no longer were significantly related to ESP scores, and when the OBE item was removed from the Hyp-

*$\rho = +.27$, N = 80, P < .02. Hypnagogic scores were not computed for subjects not receiving the OBE set, because some of the items were not relevant to them.

nagogic Scale, the latter's correlation with ESP scores likewise was reduced to nonsignificance. It was the combination of being in a hypnagogic state and having an OBE that facilitated ESP in our experiments.

What does this fact tell us? There is a growing amount of evidence that techniques such as the Ganzfeld, which are intended to produce a hypnagogic state in experimental subjects, facilitate ESP scoring even under conditions where subjects do not report being outside their bodies (Braud, Wood, and Braud, 1975; Honorton, 1977).* We also know from the literature on spontaneous OBEs and from the techniques suggested by people like Muldoon and Monroe that the hypnagogic state provides an excellent background for OBEs. The deeper a hypnagogic state a subject is in, the more likely he is to report spontaneous OBEs, particularly in an experimental situation such as ours where he is led to expect and encourage such experiences. Thus we may infer that, generally speaking, those of our subjects who reported OBEs in addition to relaxation and primary process imagery were in the deepest hypnagogic state.

My conclusion is this. The reason why those of our subjects who reported OBEs under sensory deprivation conditions did so well on the ESP test was that they were in a deeper hypnagogic state than subjects who did not report OBEs. Spontaneous OBEs occurred as a byproduct of being in this state, but they had nothing directly to do with successful identification of the target.

SOME POSSIBLE COUNTER-EXPLANATIONS—AND THE BIGGER PICTURE

In concluding this article, I would like to anticipate and respond to certain objections that might be raised regarding the relevance of my research to the larger question of the metaphysical reality of OBEs. I have concluded that in my own research the association between OBEs and psychic

*For a dissenting view, see Rogo (1976).

phenomena can be explained without assuming that OBEs involve a separation of mind and body in any real sense. Does this conclusion have any bearing on those often more spectacular OBEs that occur out in the real world? I am going to argue that it does.

The first objection I see to this contention is that our subjects interpreted their experiences as only OBEs because of the bias introduced by our telling them that an OBE was the type of experience we intended to give them. Without such a set, they would not have interpreted their experiences as OBEs and thus, according to my own definition, the experiences would not have been OBEs. The only OBEs worth talking about are those that can be recognized as such without such a biasing set.

I would be the last person to deny that the psychological set had a great deal of influence on the OBE reports of our subjects. In fact, we systematically manipulated this factor in our second experiment (Palmer and Lieberman, 1975). We found that among subjects who were told that the purpose of the induction procedure was to induce an OBE, 65 percent answered the OBE question affirmatively. Among subjects who received essentially the same induction procedure but were told nothing about OBEs, only 20 percent answered the question affirmatively. Although the two induction procedures could not be completely similar (e.g., only the former group of subjects exerted any effort to get out of their bodies), the set quite likely contributed to the difference.

However, it is my opinion that psychological sets, far from being mere biasing artifacts, are an integral part of the formation of OBEs, including those that occur spontaneously in the real world. We know that OBEs occur relatively frequently in situations where there is a possibility of imminent death—accidents, surgery, high fever, and, of course, terminal illness. It is tempting to interpret OBEs in such situations as the soul beginning to separate from the body in anticipation of death —a kind of "dry run," or maybe even an actual but aborted death. However, another relevant factor is that these are situations where the person, at least at an unconscious level, is aware that death may be near. Because of our religious upbringing (whether we accept it intellectually or not), death means the possibility, or at least the hope, that our soul is real and will leave the body to carry on in another state. Therefore, a psychological set favoring an OBE is just as present in these "real life" situations as it is in the laboratory. Even in less crucial situations, changes in body image or awareness associated with the hypnagogic state may upon occasion be interpreted by the unconscious mind as a kind of death that could trigger an OBE. This latter point is highly speculative, but unconscious psychodynamic processes should not be ruled out as an explanation of any experience that can be as psychologically powerful as OBEs often are.

Furthermore, we should keep in mind that psychological set can influence not only the interpretation of the experience, but the experience itself. For example, the unconscious mind may present the conscious mind with imagery that it can readily interpret as an OBE precisely for the purpose of assuring such an interpretation. I plan to publish in the near future a theoretical paper that elaborates upon just such a possibility.

A second objection I can see to generalizing from my research also draws upon the fact that the OBEs achieved in my experiments generally were not as clear-cut as those one often finds reported in the popular and scientific literature of spontaneous cases. Perhaps if we had sampled more heavily from this subclass of experiences, a relationship between OBEs and ESP more clearly separated from the hypnagogic state could have been demonstrated. Still a third possibility is that ESP is so prevalent in the hypnagogic state because all hypnagogic states involve separation from the body. It is just that only rarely are we conscious of separations or do we interpret them as OBEs.

Either of these interpretations could be valid in theory. However, two facts still remain to be overcome: (1) OBEs, both in the laboratory and in the real world, are especially likely to occur in hypnagogic or similar states of consciousness, states which evidence strongly suggests are psi-conductive in their own right, independent of OBEs. There is no evidence that this is any less true of "strong" OBEs than of "marginal" OBEs. (2) The psi-conducive qualities of the hypnagogic state can be most easily and economically explained by well-known psychological principles that do not require the ad hoc assumption of separation from the physical body (see Honorton, 1974). Although the issue has yet to be ultimately resolved, the burden of proof falls on those who accept the separation theory of the OBE to demonstrate that their theory is scientifically preferable to the psychological theory I have chosen to apply to my own results. In fairness to the defenders of this position, it should be pointed out that the relationship between OBEs and apparitional phenomena offers stronger support for the separation theory than the OBE-ESP relationship. While I believe that a psychological theory can account for these findings as well, a discussion of this point is beyond the scope of this paper.

I have purposely adopted a polemical tone in this article because I want you to think critically about those literal interpretations of the OBE so confidently proclaimed in most popular literature, and even perhaps those interpretations suggested to you by your own experience. Although it is fashionable these days to assume that "direct experience" is the best route to knowledge, we must balance this philosophy with an awareness that our minds are quite capable of playing tricks on us. If I have done nothing more in this paper than make you stop and think about this, I will have accomplished my major objective.

REFERENCES

Braud, W. G., and Braud, L.W. "Preliminary Explorations of Psi-conducive States: Progressive Muscular Relaxation." *Journal of the American Society for Psychical Research* 67 (1973): 26–46.

Braud, W.G., Wood, R., and Braud, L.W. "Free-response GESP Performance during an Experimental Hypnagogic State Induced by Visual and Acoustic Ganzfeld Techniques: A Replication and Extension." *Journal of the American Society for Psychical Research* 69 (1975): 105–13.

Fox, O. *"Astral Projection: A Record of Out-of-the-Body Experiences."* Reprint. New Hyde Park, N.Y.: University Books, 1962.

Green, C. E. "Ecsomatic Experiences and Related Phenomena." *Journal of the Society for Psychical Research* 44 (1967): 111–31.

Hart, H. "ESP Projection: Spontaneous Cases and the Experimental Method." *Journal of the American Society for Psychical Research* 48 (1954): 121–46.

Honorton, C. "Psi-conducive States of Awareness." In E. Mitchell and J. White (eds.), *Psychic Exploration: A Challenge for Science.* New York: Putnam, 1974, pp. 616–38.

————. "Psi and Internal Attention States." In B. B. Wolman (ed.), *The Handbook of Parapsychology.* New York: Van Nostrand-Reinhold, 1977.

Jacobson, E. *Progressive Relaxation* (2nd ed.). Chicago: University of Chicago Press, 1938.

Monroe, R. A. *Journeys Out of the Body.* Garden City, N.Y.: Doubleday, 1971.

Muldoon, S., and H. Carrington. *The Projection of the Astral Body.* London: Rider, 1929.

Palmer, J., and Dennis, M. "A Community Mail Survey of Psychic Experiences." In J. D. Morris; W. G. Roll; R. L. Morris (eds.), *Research in Parapsychology 1974.* Metuchen, N.J.: Scarecrow Press, 1975, pp. 130–33.

Palmer, J., and Lieberman, R. "ESP and Out-of-Body Experiences: A Further Study." In W. G. Roll; R. L. Morris; J. D. Morris (eds.), *Research in Parapsychology 1975.* Metuchen, N.J.: Scarecrow Press, 1976, pp. 102–6.

————. "The Influence of Psychological Set on ESP and Out-of-Body Experiences." *Journal of the American Society for Psychical Research* 69 (1975): 193–213.

Palmer, J., and Vassar, C. "ESP and Out-of-the-Body Experiences: An Exploratory Study." *Journal of the American Society for Psychical Research* 68 (1974): 257–80.

Rogo, D. S. "Research on Psi-conducive States: Some Complicating Factors." *Journal of Parapsychology* 40 (1976): 34–45.

Tart, C. T. A Psychophysiological Study of Out-of-the-Body Experiences in a Selected Subject. *Journal of the American Society for Psychical Research* 62 (1968): 3–27.

———"A Second Psychophysiological Study of Out-of-the-Body Experiences in a Gifted Subject." *International Journal of Parapsychology* 9 (1967): 251–58.

10 | Remote Viewing of Natural Targets

RUSSELL TARG AND
HAROLD PUTHOFF

This paper presents a series of experiments in which a subject is asked to describe a remote site chosen by experimenters and unknown to the subject. This work was undertaken to test the idea that natural geographic places or manmade sites that have existed for a long time are more potent targets for paranormal perception experiments than are artificial targets prepared in the laboratory. This is based in part on the suggestions of two of our subjects, Messrs. Pat Price and Ingo Swann, who consider the use of artificial targets to be a "trivialization of the ability," as compared with natural preexisting targets.

In order to build a physical theory for the explanation of psychical phenomena, it is necessary to have a clear understanding of what constitutes the phenomena to be explained. In this paper we endeavor to present a series of coherent and repeatable experiments that represent a sufficiently stable data base against which to test various theories for psychical functioning.

In these experiments we have three principal findings. First, we have definitely established that it is possible to obtain significant amounts of descriptive information about remote locations. Second, the physical distance separating the subject from the scene to be perceived does not greatly affect the accuracy of perception. In our experiments the distance was varied from two miles to two thousand miles. Finally, the use of electromagnetic shielding does not in any apparent way degrade the quality or accuracy of the descriptions obtained. These facts taken together cast great doubt on theories for psychic perception based on a conventional use of electromagnetic radiation. Although it is possible for extremely low frequencies to penetrate our shielded room, we question whether signals of such low frequency have the necessary information-carrying capacity to account for the experiments described in this paper.

In our experience, a subject is more likely to describe accurately a remote site chosen at random from hundreds of nearby locations than he is to select correctly an integer from zero to nine chosen by a similar random process. In a later section we describe the protocol used to quantify the correspondence between the subject's description and the observables present at the target location. We consider that this difference in task difficulty lies in the fact that a subject can make a perfect mental picture of each numeral from one to ten from his own imagination, whereas he is more likely to try to make his mind a blank when attempting to perceive pictorial information from remote locations about which he has no mentally stored data.

In experiments carried out in our program to investigate the abilities of a New York artist, Ingo Swann, he expressed the opinion that the insights gained during experiments at Stanford Research Institute had strengthened his ability (researched before he joined the S.R.I. program)* to view remote locations.

To test Swann's assertion, a pilot study was set up in which a series of targets from around the globe were supplied to the experimenters by S.R.I. personnel on a double-blind basis. In our estimation, Swann's ability to describe correctly details of buildings, roads, bridges, and the like indicated that he could perceive remote locations, sometimes in great detail, given only their geographic latitude and longitude. Thus we considered the descriptions were sufficiently accurate to warrant our setting up a research program in remote viewing.

We present here the results of a remote viewing experiment, carried out with a second subject in the remote viewing

*K. Osis, *ASPR Newsletter*, no. 14, Summer 1972.

program (Pat Price). This experiment consisted of a series of double-blind, demonstration-of-ability tests involving local targets in the San Francisco Bay area which could be documented by several independent judges.

In each of nine experiments in which Price served as remote viewing subject and S.R.I. experimenters as a target demarcation team, a remote location was chosen in a double-blind protocol. Price, who remained at S.R.I., was asked to describe this remote location, as well as whatever activities might be going on there.

Data from the nine experiments are presented in the following paragraphs. Final judging indicated that several descriptions yielded significantly correct data pertaining to and descriptive of the target location.

In the nine double-blind remote viewing experiments, the following procedures were used. A set of twelve target locations clearly differentiated from each other and within thirty minutes' driving time from S.R.I., had been chosen from a target-rich environment (more than one hundred targets of the type used in the experimental series) prior to the experimental series by an individual in S.R.I. management, the director of the Information Science and Engineering Division, not otherwise associated with the experiment. Both the experimenters and the subject were kept blind as to the contents of the target pool, which were used without replacement.

To begin the experiment, an experimenter was closeted with Price at S.R.I. to wait thirty minutes to begin the narrative description of the remote location. The S.R.I. locations from which the subject viewed the remote locations consisted of an outdoor park (Experiments 1, 2) a double-walled copper-screen Faraday cage* (Experiments 3,4,6-9), and an office (Experiment 5). A second experimenter would then obtain a target location from the divi-

*The Faraday cage provides 120 dB attenuation for plane wave radio frequency radiation over a range of 15 KHz to 1 GHz. For magnetic fields the attenuation is 68 dB at 15 KHz and decreases to 3 dB at 60 Hz.

sion director from a set of traveling orders previously prepared and randomized by the director and kept under his control. The target demarcation team, consisting of two to four S.R.I. experimenters then proceeded directly to the target by automobile without communicating with the subject or experimenter remaining behind. Since the experimenter remaining with the subject at SRI was in ignorance both as to the particular target and also as to the target pool, he was free to question Price to clarify his descriptions. The demarcation team then remained at the target site for an agreed-upon thirty-minute period following the thirty minutes allotted for travel. During the observation period, the remote viewing subject would describe his impressions of the target site into a tape recorder. A comparison was then made when the demarcation team returned.

In general, Price's ability to describe correctly buildings, docks, roads, gardens, et cetera, including structural materials, color, ambience, and activity, sometimes in great detail, indicated the functioning of a remote perceptual ability. However, the descriptions contained inaccuracies as well as correct statements. To obtain a numerical evaluation of the accuracy of the remote viewing experiment, the experimental results were subjected to independent judging on a blind basis by five S.R.I. scientists who were not otherwise associated with the research. The judges were asked to match the nine locations, which they independently visited, against the typed manuscripts of the tape-recorded narratives of the remote viewer. The transcripts were unlabeled and presented in random order. The judges were asked to find a narrative which they would consider the best match for each of the places they visited. A given narrative could be assigned to more than one target location. A correct match requires that the transcript of a given date be associated with the target of that date. Table 1 shows the distribution of the judges' choices. For purposes of display we present the table so that the main diagonal corresponds to the correct choices. The number of correct matches by Judges A through E is 7, 6, 5, 3, and 3,

TABLE 1

DISTRIBUTION OF CORRECT SELECTIONS BY JUDGES A, B, C, D, AND E IN REMOTE VIEWING EXPERIMENTS

Of the 45 selections (5 judges, 9 choices), 24 were correct. Boxes heavily outlined indicate the description chosen most often for each place visited. Correct choices lie on the main diagonal.

Descriptions Chosen by Judges		Places Visited by Judges								
		1	2	3	4	5	6	7	8	9
Hoover Tower	1	ABC DE								
Baylands Nature Preserve	2		ABC	E		D		D	D	D
Radio Telescope	3		CD	ACD		BE				
Redwood City Marina	4				ABD E		E			
Bridge Toll Plaza	5						ABD		DCE	E
Drive-In Theater	6			B		A	C			
Arts and Crafts Garden Plaza	7							ABC E		
Church	8					C			AB	
Rinconada Park	9					CE				AB

respectively. The expected number of correct matches from the five judges was five; in the experiment twenty-four such matches were obtained.*

Among all possible analyses, none is more conservative than a permutation analysis of the plurality vote of the judges' selections assuming assignment without replacement, an approach independent of the number of judges. By plurality vote, six of the nine descriptions and locations were correctly matched. Under the null hypothesis (no remote viewing and a random selection of descriptions without replacement), this outcome has an a priori probability of $P = 5.6 \times 10^{-4}$, since, among all possible permutations of the integers one through nine, the probability of six or more being in their natural position in the list has that value. Therefore, although Price's descriptions contain inaccuracies, the descriptions are sufficiently accurate to permit the judges to differentiate among the various targets to the degree indicated.

REMOTE VIEWING WITH "ORDINARY" SUBJECTS

Based on the results of the Price experiments we decided to extend our investigations to include the two outstanding (ordinary) subjects who had been uncovered in a broad-based screening experiment including 147 volunteer subjects. The subjects for this experiment were an S.R.I. scientist, Mr. D.E., and a professional photographer, Ms. H.H.

Target Selection

The protocol for the experiments was as follows: one experimenter would remain at S.R.I. with the subject while the other experimenter went to the remote target location. The target was selected by the traveling experimenter after he left S.R.I. and while the subject was monitored by the other experimenter. The traveling experimenter, who had a list of six San Francisco Bay Area locations that could be reached

*The a priori probability of such an occurrence by chance, conservatively assuming assignment without replacement on the part of the judges, is $P = 8 \cdot 10^{-10}$

in no more than thirty minutes' driving, then cast a die to determine which place would actually be visited.

After a half hour's wait, the subject remaining at S.R.I. began to relate his impressions about the place where the other experimenter was located; these narrations were recorded on magnetic tape. The experimenter remaining behind with the subject had no information about the target location.

Four such experiments were performed with these two subjects, two with each. Locations were generated from a list that included such possible targets as a drive-in theater, Hoover Tower on the Stanford University campus, a toll plaza on the east side of the Dumbarton bridge across the San Francisco Bay, Palo Alto Methodist Church, Artificial Intelligence building in foothills west of S.R.I., Baylands Nature Preserve, Allied Arts crafts plaza, the Alpine Inn beer garden in the foothills, Rinconada Park swimming pools, and Redwood City Marina, among others.

The four target locations used in this series of experiments were a miniature golf course in Redwood City, the Bay Area Rapid Transit (BART) station in Fremont (across the bay), a shielded room at S.R.I., and (as a special long-distance task) a vacation resort in Costa Rica. For this last target, the subject was asked to supply a drawing and written description.

In the preexperiment orientation, the subjects were told that since they had demonstrated paranormal perceptual ability in previous tasks, we were confident that they could do this additional task, since we had already observed two other subjects performing such tasks successfully.

Summary of Experiments

The following gives a summary of the four experiments done with the two "ordinary" subjects from the screening study.

In the first experiment, Ms. H.H. described a "red, wooden building with a pointed roof." The building was further described as being made with "overlapping boards and has a white trim." Furthermore, she said, the "building is empty, as though nothing is going on inside. And the whole place seems artificial like a movie set." The building where the experimenter, Puthoff, stood was a 4.5-meter-high caricature of a schoolhouse on a miniature golf course—both empty and artificial. The shape, color, and construction were all accurate.

In a second experiment, the experimenter (Phyllis Cole) was led by a throw of the die to a shielded room on the second floor of S.R.I.'s Engineering building. D.E.'s description had her "sitting rather quietly alone on the corner of a rather large room. Not so much an office, but more like a classroom, a larger room. And as she was sitting there in the room she was writing, she was looking at perhaps something on the wall and writing something." (In fact, at about this time the experimenter was observing graffiti on the wall, and mentally composing her own for the collection.) A detailed description fits well with the row of a half-dozen large heavy black metal machines on a work bench to the right of the experimenter that she touched at approximately this time during the experiment: "I have some impressions that I can't understand—it's like some heavy black things that she could either be sitting on or that she's touching. Sort of an amorphous shape that I can't pick up, but it feels heavy and black and of a distinguishable shape, but its exact form is not angular—doesn't seem angular, and I can't interpret a shape from it." This description was substantially correct and would have fit no other target used in any experiments up to that time. The description was unique in the set of descriptions with which it was compared.

In a third trial, the experimenters (Russell Targ and Phyllis Cole) went to the Bay Area Rapid Transit (BART) station across the bay from S.R.I., again chosen at random from a prepared list. D.E.'s description closely matched the target: "a simple, heavy, solid building with a unique function" in "relatively natural surroundings" (all correct). In his further description, D.E. said (correctly), "They are standing at a metal railing looking out over a scene. They are up high enough that they can see some buildings down below." He sensed some ambiguity as to whether the experimenters were inside a building or not. "I have the sense they're outside, though, but they're near a building. There's a larger building-like structure. Feels like it has sort of one function. One primary function. And although they're outside, they're relating to the building and its function." In fact, the experimenters were on the open station platform waiting for a train. About 11:22 he said, "I have the impression that Russell is feeling a smooth metal surface. Sort of large plates, large metal plates. Somewhat rectangular." The timing and description are highly accurate. Targ was looking at the large metal BART route map, just before the train's arrival. At exactly 11:25, D.E. said "everything changed" and "I don't see them anymore." That is the precise time the target pair boarded the BART train and left the station.

In addition to the remote viewing of local targets, one subject (H.H.) participated in a long-distance experiment. In this experiment one of the experimenters (Puthoff) spent a week traveling through Central America on a combination business/pleasure trip. That is all that was known to the subject about the traveler's itinerary. The experiment called for Puthoff to keep a detailed record of his location and activities, including photographs, each day at 1330 PDT. Five daily responses were obtained from the subject. Two were in excellent agreement, two had elements in common but were not clear correspondences, and one was clearly a miss. In the first of the two matches, Puthoff was driving in rugged terrain at the base of a volcano, and the subject's response was "larger bare table mountain, jungle below, dark cool moist atmosphere," a match both with regard to topography and ambience. In the second match the subject submitted that all she got was a "picture of Dr. Puthoff sitting in a beach chair by a pool," which was entirely correct.

During the course of the Central America experiment, on one occasion when the test subject was unavailable, one of the authors (Targ) volunteered a drawing of an image he obtained at the beginning of one of the daily experiments. (The target for that day was an airport, an unexpected target associated with a side excursion at midpoint of the week's activity.) The match was good.

Conclusion

We have presented evidence for the existence of a biological information channel whose characteristics appear to fall outside the range of known perceptual modalities. The precise nature of the channel or channels is as yet undefined, but may involve either direct perception of hidden information content, perception of mental images of persons knowledgeable of target information, precognition, or some combination of these or other information channels.

We have worked with three individuals whose remote perceptual abilities were sufficiently developed that they were able to describe geographical material blocked from ordinary perception.

From these experiments we conclude that:

1. a channel exists whereby information about a remote location can be obtained by means of an as yet unidentified perceptual modality;

2. as with all biological systems, the information channel appears to be imperfect, containing noise along with the signal;

3. while a quantitative signal-to-noise ratio in the information-theoretical sense cannot as yet be determined, the results of our experiments indicate that the functioning is at the level of useful information transfer.

It may be that remote perceptual ability is widely distributed in the general population, but because the perception is generally below an individual's level of awareness, it is repressed or not noticed. For example, two of our subjects (H.H. and P.P.) had not considered themselves to have unusual perceptual ability before their participation in these experiments.

III. REPORTS FROM GIFTED SUBJECTS

Introduction:
Autobiographical Accounts

D. SCOTT ROGO

The American public of the 1920s knew very little about the OBE. In fact, anyone who even talked about having such experiences was usually whisked off to a psychiatrist. Even today, many people become frightened or concerned about their mental health when they begin having OBEs. Yet, since the turn of the century, a few gifted individuals have been publishing articles and books detailing their habitual and voluntary OBE encounters.

Why should we be interested in these firsthand testimonials? What can they tell us about the OBE that laboratory experiments cannot? If anything, the preceding papers have emphasized the fact that we know relatively little about the OBE. The phenomenon is a kaleidoscope of contradictions. Some OBE-ers leave the body in an apparitional form, others fly about as a pinpoint of light, and so on. Some OBE-ers are able to manipulate physical matter, while others are not. And we don't have the slightest understanding why. Any data that can shed light on these enigmas must be carefully considered.

Most people who have OBEs usually report only one or two experiences during their lifetimes. Dr. John Poynton of the University of Natal, South Africa, found that 56 percent of the people who reported OBEs to him in answer to a newspaper survey had recorded only one experience thus far in their lives (Poynton, 1975). Only 18 percent of his correspondents intimated that they could possibly induce another one. Celia Green found that 60.9 percent of her 302 correspondents claimed to have had only a single experience, and only 20 percent claimed more than six (Green, 1968).

The usual OBEs about which we read so often are also relatively brief encounters. Although many experiencers describe their OBEs as "timeless" or that they had "no idea of time," it is clear from their accounts that their experiences could have lasted only a few minutes at most. For example, an OBE-er will be listening to a piece of music on the radio when he has his experience. On returning to his body and "awakening" he will discover that the same piece of music is still being broadcast. So these anecdotal once-in-a-lifetime experiences may not be telling us very much about the potential of the OBE. This same criticism is valid for much of the laboratory work that has been carried out on the OBE. This research sheds little light on the range of OBE phenomena. Experimental approaches to the OBE are primarily designed to validate the phenomenon; little of it has explored the parameters of the experience in any depth.

So after collecting firsthand accounts and running experiment after experiment, what have we learned about the OBE? It may be that we are getting a very myopic picture of what it is really like. And this is where the autobiographical accounts of gifted OBE subjects become of the utmost importance to us. The person who has a typical brief, once-in-a-lifetime OBE has little time to investigate his experience. He is usually sleeping or relaxing or has just had an accident when his OBE occurs. Hardly has he had time to get over his surprise when—zoom!—he snaps back into his body.

However, there are a few people on record who apparently have frequent OBEs. Take Blue Harary, for instance. He has had, quite literally, thousands of them during his life. And Blue is only one in a long succession of people who can induce OBEs at will and who have recorded their experiences for posterity. A person who has undergone several OBEs and who can induce the experience at will might be in a far better position to describe and comment on the state and the world in which he travels than anyone else. For one thing, these subjects record experiences of longer duration than most people who have spontaneous experiences. Being accustomed to the state, these percipients are better able to make observations about the OBE world, examine it, and experiment with it. Because they are able to enter the OB state so readily, habitual OBE projectors also have greater opportunity to experiment with themselves. They can judge how long they can stay out of the body, what new vistas of consciousness they might explore, determine their relationship to the physical world, and so on. These are matters that the once-in-a-lifetime experiencer does not usually have time or inclination to concern himself with. Laboratory experiments have only just begun exploring these aspects of the OBE. However, these experiments have not yet enabled us to develop even an infant understanding of the OBE spectrum. Our research is still at a prenatal stage. People like Blue Harary have proved their OBE capabilities. So what they have to say *about* the experience should be considered with unquestioning seriousness. Many people have accidentally encountered the OB world. But people such as Harary and Ingo Swann have been able to *explore* it.

As I stated earlier, the general public of the 1920s knew very little about the OBE, a phenomenon more commonly called at the time "astral projection." However, the American public became a little more educated about this unusual phenomenon in 1919 and 1920 due to the efforts of Hereward Carrington, a psychical investigator who specialized in writing books on psychic phenomena for the general public. In his book *Modern Psychical Phenomena* (1919–1920; there were two almost simultaneous editions), Carrington devoted a chapter to the research of Dr. Charles Lancelin of France. He even reprinted H. Durville's alleged photograph of an OBE phantom that the French investigator had secured while experimenting with Mme Lambert, a French psychic. Carrington's chapter focused on the methods Lancelin developed to help people experience the OB state for themselves. As Carrington said of Lancelin's research, "This is the first time that this occult knowledge has ever been divulged, and it has caused no little stir and sensation in France."

The general public still took little interest in the OBE until 1929 when Carrington and Sylvan Muldoon, who had experienced a wide variety of OB phenomena, teamed up to write their now famous book, *The Projection of the Astral*

Body. This volume is perhaps the most famous book ever written on the subject.

Sylvan Muldoon was a frail, sickly, bed-ridden youth who lived in the midwest. Psychic phenomena were no strangers to the lad, whose mother was a Spiritualist of sorts. While hardly a teenager, Muldoon realized that a faculty was developing within him which compensated for the fact that he had to stay in bed for lengthy periods of time—he was developing the ability to leave the body. At first Muldoon was puzzled by his experiences and started reading books on psychic phenomena hoping to find some material that would shed light on his out-of-body adventures. In 1927 he came across Carrington's *Modern Psychical Phenomena* and, after reading it, boldly wrote to the senior investigator:

I have recently finished reading your volumes on the "Occult and Psychical Sciences." . . . I was much interested in your chapter on "Astral Projection," as I have been a "projector" for twelve years— long before I knew that anyone else in the world ever did such things. . . . What puzzles me most is that you make the remark that M. Lancelin has told practically all that is known on the subject. Why, Mr. Carrington, I have never read Lancelin's work, but if you have given the gist of it in your book, then I can write a book on the things that Lancelin does not know! . . . I have been wondering whether M. Lancelin is in fact a conscious projector. From what you have given, I have concluded either that Lancelin does not project at all, or that his subjects are not in the clear conscious state while exteriorized. Is this not reasonable? If M. Lancelin or his subjects were clearly conscious, could they not give every detail of the phenomenon? Of course they could! But they do not. . . . Now I have been all through this, and I know every emotion, every move, every lost detail that takes place from clear consciousness in the physical, out, into the astral with that same unchanged consciousness and back into "coincidence"* . . . But the thing I marvel at most is that so little is said

*"Coincidence" is a word Muldoon uses to describe the state when the apparitional body is loosened from the physical body but still occupies the same space before leaving or reentering completely.— ED.

about the astral cord—the very foundation of the whole phenomenon. Is it possible that none of Lancelin's subjects ever examined this cord, nor even saw it? . . . Nothing is told as to how this cord works, how it stabilizes the phantom, or throws it into instability. How large it is while the bodies are nearly in coincidence; how it decreases in size and resistance up to a certain distance (which I have measured exactly), and so forth. Lancelin says that the phantom appears as if rocked by the wind, but he does not say what causes this. . . . Lancelin does not tell how to control the astral cord, the mechanism which is the vital factor. He says that the astral body emerges from the solar plexus—which is anything but true. The bodies separate at all places simultaneously. The cord centres at a given plexus, and the ideal spot is the *medulla oblongata,* which has direct control over the organs of respiration in the oblivious physical body. Lancelin says nothing of suppressed desires and the condition of the heart-beat through the cord; nor how to stabilize the phantom after the exteriorization is accomplished. He says nothing of the form the phantom takes; how it moves in coming out; how a cataleptic state ensues while the phantom is under control of the subconscious mind, and is still conscious. . . . He has not told of the various degrees of sight and hearing in the phantom; nor how it travels, nor how it gets into a condition where it is helpless and unable to travel. . . . The Will Power part of the process is greatly over-stressed. There are other ways of accomplishing this besides will power. In fact, several other ways. And the Good Health idea is nothing short of a blunder. I say, and can prove it, that the nearer dead a person is, the easier it is to project.

. . . I could go on telling you many more things about astral projection; but I suppose that after all was said you would reply, "Prove it." But it cannot be so readily proved! It would require a treatise upon the subject. I once thought of writing a book upon this topic, but abandoned the idea when everyone told me that I was "crazy," and found that no one would pay any attention to it. . . . Just the same, I have exteriorized enough to know that if you have given the gist of what is now known, then indeed there is much darkness upon the subject. . . . I might add that I am a boy twenty-five years old, and that if you even read this letter and take it seriously, it will be an honour to me. . . .

Far from being offended by this brash letter, Carrington was tremendously excited. Here, he thought, was an opportunity to question a young man who seemed to possess the ability to leave the body at will. Carrington and Muldoon soon engaged in a lengthy correspondence, Carrington asking questions about the OBE and Muldoon answering in detail. Ultimately, Carrington even suggested experiments for Muldoon to try while out-of-body, and Muldoon would soon write back detailing the outcomes. The results of the correspondence and Muldoon's further explorations of the OBE became the subject upon which *The Projection of the Astral Body* was based. Muldoon kept Carrington abreast of all his discoveries as he began to explore the OBE in earnest. For instance, the following is typical of the records he sent to Carrington:

This morning I had an accidental projection while lying on my stomach and in complete light . . . and this is what I discovered. While lying on my stomach the sensations while moving through the air are reversed and vice-versa. The only way to tell the true direction of movement is my sense of sight. I would have sworn that I was moving downward, but on looking I saw that I was moving upward! . . .

However, the heart of Muldoon's writings is concerned with making detailed observations on the "silver cord" connection that so many OBErs have seen linking their apparitional and physical bodies. Lancelin had made no mention of the cord in his volume and it was this fact that prompted Muldoon to write to Carrington. Muldoon had spotted the cord during his first OBE when he was about twelve years old. He was accompanying his mother on a visit to a Spiritualist camp meeting. The Muldoons retired early the evening of their arrival. But for Sylvan it was the beginning of a great adventure.

Muldoon slept for several hours that evening and awoke early the next morning. Somehow he felt queer. He was awake, but he felt as though he had awakened from an unnatural type of sleep. His body was cataleptic and his sensory perceptions were dulled. He could see or hear practically nothing and he was quite uneasy about his predicament. The room was dark and Muldoon could not figure out what was happening to him.

"Eventually the feeling of adhesion relaxed," he reminisced, "but was replaced by another sensation equally unpleasant—that of floating. Occurring at the same time, my entire body—I thought it was my physical, but it was my astral—commenced vibrating at a great rate of speed, in an up-and-down direction, and I could feel a tremendous pressure being exerted on the back of my head, in the *medulla oblongata* region. This pressure was very impressive, and came in regular spurts, the force of which seemed to pulsate my whole body."

Eventually Muldoon's hearing and vision returned to him. As he continues:

No sooner had the sense of hearing come into being than that of sight followed. When able to see, I was more than astonished! No words could possibly explain my wonderment. I was floating! I was floating in the very air, rigidly horizontal, a few feet above the bed. The room, my exact location, was now comprehended. Things seemed hazy at first, but were becoming clearer. I knew well where I was, yet could not account for my strange behaviour. Slowly, still zigzagging with the strong pressure in the back of my head, I was moving toward the ceiling, all the while horizontal and powerless.

I believed naturally that this was my physical body, as I had always known it, but that it had mysteriously begun to defy gravity. It was too unnatural for me to understand, yet too real to deny—for, being conscious, being able to see, I could not question my sanity. Involuntarily, at about six feet above the bed, as if the movement had been conducted by an invisible force present in the very air, I was up-righted from the horizontal position to the perpendicular, and placed standing upon the floor of the room. There I stood for what seemed to me about two minutes, still powerless to move of my own accord, and staring stright [*sic*] ahead. I was still astrally cataleptic.

Then the controlling force relaxed. I felt free, noticing only the tension in the back of my head. I took a step, when the pressure increased for an interval and threw my body out at an acute angle. I managed to turn around. There were two of me! I was beginning to believe myself insane. There was another "me" lying quietly upon the bed! It was difficult to convince myself that this was real, but consciousness would not allow me to doubt what I saw.

My two identical bodies were joined by means of an elastic-like cable, one end of which was fastened to the *medulla oblongata* region of the astral counterpart, while the other end centred between the eyes of the physical counterpart. This cable extended across the space of probably six feet which separated us. All this time I was having difficulty in keeping my balance—swaying first to one side, then to the other.

After realizing that he was out-of-the-body, Muldoon began to explore the cabin which he, his mother, and his brother were sharing. However, ". . . I noticed a pronounced increase in the resistance of the cable. It was pulled with a stronger and stronger tug. I began to zig-zag again under this force, and found presently that I was being pulled backwards toward my physical body. Again I found myself powerless to move."

Muldoon found himself hovering over his own body once more, and he slowly dropped back down into it. "At this moment of coincidence," Muldoon reported, "every muscle in the physical jerked, and a penetrating pain, as if I had been split open from head to foot, shot through me."

This odd "repercussion effect" is often reported by people undergoing OBEs. Crookall (1964) discovered that 10.7 percent of his correspondents who reported "natural-type" OBEs experienced the phenomenon, and 5.4 percent of those reporting "enforced-type" OBEs reported it.

Muldoon's book contains such a wealth of data about the OBE that it is diffiuclt to do it justice in short summary. It is essential reading for anyone interested in studying the OBE. I can touch only briefly on several aspects of Muldoon's experiences and views here.

To begin with, Muldoon discovered that the process of leaving the body could take several different modes. He might be conscious of physically separating from the body, or might suddenly find himself out-of-the-body but in the same room with it, or on some occasions could instantaneously project to a location miles away. He also noted that the out-of-the-body phantom (he always perceived himself in an apparitional form while out-of-body) could move at different speeds. It could "walk," float quickly, or travel at an incredible velocity. Muldoon also learned that the OBE could occur instantaneously. He writes:

One night, a few years ago, I was coming down the stairs of my home. I had been sleeping, and was still quite drowsy. There were fifteen steps, and I had trodden up and down them hundreds of times, having lived in the house all my life. Just *why* I do not know, but, as I reached the bottom step I tried to take one step more (many of us have done this), and the impetus jarred me vigorously.

A breathtaking sensation shot through the pit of my stomach, and even before the physical dropped to the floor, I found myself projected from it, in a perfectly conscious state. . . . I both *saw* the physical mechanism fall to the floor and also *felt* it fall, while standing several feet from it.

Muldoon made copious notes on the sensations of leaving and reentering the body. He felt that the parasomatic body always projected from the body via the same route: first, it lifts upward from the physical body, vibrating as it rises, and advances inch by inch although often regressing back to near the body; but proceeds until it is finally about twelve inches above the physical body. The parasomatic form then zigzags as it travels higher and higher until it is three to six feet above the body. The "feet" of the phantom then draw toward the ground as though attracted by a magnet and the parasomatic body stands erect. (Muldoon does not state whether or not this process is adhered to during instantaneous projections.)

Muldoon was a bit dogmatic in claiming that the parasomatic form always travels via this route. Far from his belief that "the subconscious Will ejects the phantom in a specific route," OBE percipients have recorded a variety of ways in which they have left the body. Many report being "drawn through the head," while others talk of "spiraling" out of the body. Muldoon's experiences may have been unique to himself. I remember an OBE I once had during which I literally catapulted from the body into the air. On another occasion I simply lifted out of the physical body and then my parasomatic body reversed position, like a weathervane struck by a sudden gust of air. On yet another occasion I had the distinct and unpleasant feeling that I was being pulled out of my body through my head.

Muldoon was most fascinated by the "silver cord," as I mentioned earlier. Talk of the silver cord pervades his entire book and he apparently saw this connecting link hundreds of times as he explored the out-of-body state. As he comments, this cord "is a sort of side-show mystery, participating in the main event called 'projections.' "

According to Muldoon, the cord is elastic in nature. It becomes thinner as the projected phantom moves away from the physical body and its circumference ranges from that of a silver dollar to the thinness of a thread or a spider's web. Muldoon believes that when the parasomatic body is too close to the physical, the cord acts as a vital link communicating information and energy between the two forms. He called this sphere of influence "cord activity range." As for the cord itself, he states:

It is in appearance of a whitish grey color, and when greatly extended, is not unlike a long single strand of cobweb. From coincidence to the end of cord-activity range, there is always a double action taking place in the cord—that is, as far as one's eyes can determine. Yet I dare say that there are many activities present which are too subtle to be seen by the consciously projected individual, even if he observed the cable at close range.

Muldoon goes on to say:

When exteriorization occurs there is always a constant pushing and pulling sensation of the cable, which can be felt in a noticeable degree by the projector, when within cord activity range. If you can imagine a mighty giant holding you by the back of the head, with a steady grip, at arm's length, pushing you slowly away from him, drawing you back towards him, moving you from side to side, yet always maintaining a steady hold on your head, and in that very grip you could feel a regular pulsation, then you can imagine how it feels to the conscious projector within cord activity range.

Once the phantom moves about fifteen feet from the body, Muldoon contends, the parasomatic form becomes liberated from these pulsations.

Karlis Osis would probably be fascinated by another topic on which Muldoon made copious notes. Muldoon was well aware that visual and auditory perception while in the OBE state was eccentric and capricious, to say the least. As he says, "The senses, within cord activity range, function so capriciously that it would be difficult, if not impossible, to give an entirely satisfactory account of what might, and might not, happen in the 'sense field.'"

Muldoon commented on the fact that OB vision might initially be blurred and there might be a great deal of confusion between what the physical body's eyes are seeing and what the OB consciousness is perceiving. The OBE-er might even see scenes of the future. This comment is provocative, since Osis confronted just such a problem during his A.S.P.R. fly-in experiments (see introduction to Part II). Muldoon's main point of discussion on ODE perception was on the subject of dual sensory experience: the out-of-body experiencer might confuse OB sensations with physical sensory input being received and processed by the physical body.

Muldoon was a little more successful than Harary seemed to be (see chapter 8) when it came to producing telekinetic effects while out-of-body. Here is one of his accounts:

The experience which I shall now relate occurred on the night of February 26, 1928. For some time I had been suffering from a serious stomach complaint. I slept alone, on the lower floor of the house, my mother and small brother occupying a bedroom on the upper floor.

Between 11:30 and 12 o'clock that night, I was suddenly overcome by unusually severe pains in my stomach. Unable to help myself, I called several times for my mother; but, as she was sound asleep, she did not hear me. I continued to call in vain for several minutes, then I decided to get out of bed and crawl along the floor to the hall, which leads to the stairs, hoping that from that spot she could hear my voice.

I managed to get out of bed and started for the door, but the pain grew so intense that I could not reach it, and fell over in a faint. I soon recovered consciousness again, and, by exerting all my will power, managed to advance a few feet further; but, having been confined to my bed for almost a month, the exertion was too much for me, and I fainted again.

This time I awoke outside my body, and found myself moving up the stairs, under crypto-conscious control—that is, without direction or effort on my part. Here, if ever, the crypto-conscious Will was in a determined mood, for I never before remember being so completely under its deliberate influence. Naturally I wanted to look at my physical body—which is always the first thing one does—but my thought to that effect had no influence upon the controlling power this time.

Advancing up the stairs, I went through the wall of my mother's room and saw her, and my small brother, lying upon the bed, sound asleep. This impression was very distinct, but at this point a gap came in my consciousness. On again becoming conscious, I found myself standing near the foot of the bed. I cannot say exactly what my movements were during this gap in consciousness, but on awakening I saw both of them (my mother and brother) in confusion, the former standing on the floor near the bed and the latter almost off the bed; they were talking excitedly about the mattress having been lifted up and rolling them out of bed, while they were sleeping!

All this was very distinct. I was as conscious as ever I was in the flesh. Instantly I vanished from the room; I was drawn down to my physical body and pulled into it with a spiral motion—experiencing a conscious repercussion while coinciding.

I immediately called out to my mother again, and she hurried down the stairs, very excited—so excited in fact, that she forgot all about my being out of bed and lying on the floor, and began to tell me how "spirits" had lifted up the mattress and rolled her out of bed!

She said that they had lifted it not once but several times, and she confessed that she was terrified for a moment.

On other occasions Muldoon was able to set a metronome in motion and produce raps.

It is clear that Muldoon did not encounter a wide range of OB phenomena during his experiences. He *always* saw himself as an apparition; this body was *always* a duplicate of the physical body; and he *always* moved about familiar earthly locales while out-of-body. Nowhere in his records are there any hints that he projected in any form other than an apparitional body. Muldoon's OBEs seem restricted, as though he were chained to a discrete out-of-body world just as we are chained to the physical world. There are rarely any surprises as we read his accounts.

Nonetheless, this phantom form that Muldoon projected, whatever its nature, did have some peculiar properties. On rare occasions Muldoon, like Harary, could make his presence known to "detectors." The most dramatic instance of this sort occurred when Muldoon decided to prove his OBE talents to a skeptical girlfriend:

I had often told my friend about projection of the astral body and explained it to her; but although she would listen, she always had her doubts After I discovered this relatively easy method of projecting the astral body to her side, I hit upon a plan which I hoped would get results and convince her that I really could project my astral body. I wanted very much to convince her, and cared not whether anyone else believed me or not.

So we agreed upon this plan. Both of us were to awaken at two o'clock, and lie awake, conscious but drowsy. I was to think of projecting myself into her room. She was to visualize my doing so. I hoped, by this method, to use not only my own powers of projection, but also to utilize her psychic force to assist me. We were to allow our passive Wills to work upon our desires, in the dead of night, at the same time.

Several weeks passed, and during this time I succeeded in projecting myself into her room several times, and becoming conscious when there. But I had no recollection of having travelled the intervening distance; in other words, I remained unconscious until the time when I awakened. On one occasion when I awakened, she was awake too, but did not see me.

A queer thing did happen, however; I decided, on the next occasion, to do certain things, which I would not tell her, and see if she could describe to me what I did—provided she admitted seeing me.

I accordingly went over to her dresser, put my hand upon her hair-brush, walked over to her and put my hand upon her shoulder, stood there for a few moments, then went back and placed my hand upon the hair-brush, then back to her again, etc.—repeating this about a dozen times. All the time she was apparently sleeping.

The next day I enquired if she had seen me in her room. "No," was the reply, "but I dreamed that you were there."

"What did you dream?" I asked her.

"I dreamed that you were trying to brush my hair," she replied, "and that you kept running back and forth, trying to find the comb, and that I kept telling you it was on the dresser."

The young lady must have liked her astral romancer. I recently learned that after the publication of *The Projection of the Astral Body,* she and Muldoon married, but subsequently divorced.

This account brings to mind a curious experiment co-designed by Blue Harary and Dr. John Palmer, while the latter was still on the staff at the University of Virginia. Palmer tested to see whether Blue could OB himself to a sleeping friend and influence the content of her dreams. At the present time, though, this experiment and its results have not been published.

There is also another striking coincidence between Blue's and Muldoon's experiences. Blue likes to project himself to familiar places and to people he knows. He feels this helps him home-in on the location to which he is traveling. Muldoon shared this idiosyncrasy. He states firmly in his autobiography that it is easier to project to familiar rather than to unfamiliar locales and that the OBE-er, if he is not careful, will find himself automatically drawn to familiar locations.

Reading Muldoon's book today, almost fifty years after it

was written, provides a puzzling experience. It is a collection of detailed records, but these are mixed with metaphysics, antiquated views on psychology, and a healthy dash of unsophisticated occultism. Yet Muldoon's book remains a vastly important document, although it is obvious that Muldoon, for all his experience, actually confronted a rather limited range of OB phenomena. In fact, his experiences seem to conform quite neatly to the Spiritualist concept of "spirit projection," which was taught among the Spiritualists of his day. Muldoon's experiences should awaken us to the fact that the OBE may be a uniquely personal experience as well as an archetypal one. The content of the experience might be molded by the expectations of the percipient. This is a theme I will return to later.

One also gets the impression while reading *The Projection of the Astral Body* that Muldoon was a man of great wisdom and experience. He writes like a man seasoned by age and drawing upon a rich memory of experiences. It is hard to remember that he was hardly more than a teenager when he and Carrington began their joint project. Yet he does reveal one trait of youth throughout his book. He is dogmatic. He is quite explicit about what one can experience while out-of-body and what one cannot. One almost senses that Muldoon saw himself as an infallible source of information on the OBE; an authority not to be questioned. He often even snipes at other writers on the OBE with whom he disagrees.

The later years of Muldoon's life are not a matter of public record. He co-authored another book on the OBE with Carrington in 1951, entitled *The Phenomena of Astral Projection,* which merely reprinted several firsthand OBE accounts that they had collected from various sources. This book was a sequel to *The Case for Astral Projection* (1946), another casebook, which Muldoon had written himself.

Muldoon retired from public life after the 1950s. Over the years his health had improved, and as his physical body became stronger his ability to induce OBEs became more sporadic. In fact, he had hardly any OBEs after reaching middle age. He lived in a small town, Darlington, Wisconsin, during those years, where he was the proprietor of two beauty salons. The people of Darlington had little inkling that their neighbor was actually a famous psychic. During the last years of his life, Muldoon neither wrote nor said anything about the OBE. He usually refused to answer any letters on the subject.

In 1968 I was able to elicit a few brief comments from Muldoon through correspondence. Had he told us about everything he had encountered while out-of-body? Or did he, like Harary, experience things that he could never bring himself to write down? The answer came on June 30, 1968, in a note that said simply: "I did not go into everything because I thought I would be asking them [the public] to swallow too big a pill!!! I have plenty which I have not said."

I was never able to get Muldoon to fill me in on any details. These words were probably the last he wrote on the subject of OBEs. He died in 1971, and his secrets died with him.

At about the same time that Muldoon was chronicling his out-of-body adventures, an English occultist name Oliver Fox was actively exploring the OB world. Even Hereward Carrington considered Fox's narratives "the only detailed, scientific, and first-hand accounts of a series of conscious and voluntarily controlled astral projections which I have ever come across" (Muldoon and Carrington, 1929).

Everyone who writes on the OBE quotes Fox. (I once submitted an article on the subject to a magazine, which included a short account of Fox's experiences. The editor wrote on the manuscript, "Not Fox again!") Unfortunately, though, nobody has ever sat down to analyze his experiences systematically. While writers have been quoting Fox for years, no one has examined what he was revealing about the nature of the OBE.

We know very little about Fox personally. His real name was Hugh Callaway, he belonged to many occult circles in England, and he recorded his out-of-body adventures for many years, from the 1910s to the 1930s. He originally published his narratives in the now defunct *Occult Review* (1920) and later expanded them into book form (Fox, 1939, 1961).

At first Fox's OBEs conformed to the stereotype. He usually found himself projected in his own room after he had gone to sleep and, like some first-timers, had difficulty distinguishing his OBEs from dreams. But he quickly came to realize that the world he had contacted through the OBE was an imitation world. He made this discovery one day when he projected himself outside his house:

I dreamed that I was standing on the pavement outside my home. The sun was rising behind the Roman wall, and the waters of Bletchingden Bay were sparkling in the morning light. I could see the tall trees at the corner of the road and the top of the old grey tower beyond the Forty Steps. . . . Now the pavement was not of the ordinary type, but consisted of small bluish-grey rectangular stones, with their long sides at right angles to the white kerb. I was about to enter the house when on glancing at these stones, my attention became riveted to a passing strange phenomenon, so extraordinary that I could not believe my eyes—they had seemingly all changed position in the night, and the long sides were now parallel to the kerb!

It finally dawned on Fox that he was not dreaming an ordinary dream, and he later concluded that he had had an OBE:

. . . Never had I felt so absolutely well, so clear brained, so distinctly powerful, so inexpressibly *free*. The sensation was exquisite beyond words; but it lasted only a few moments and I awoke. As I was to learn later, my mental control had been overwhelmed by my emotions, so the tiresome body asserted its claim and pulled me back. For though I did not realize it at the time, I think the first experience was a true projection and that I was actually functioning outside my physical vehicle.

Fox dates this experience Spring 1902, and over the years the OB world he encountered would change drastically. His last recorded OBE was on March 1, 1938. Fox's exploration of the OB state began in earnest in 1912, and at first the world to which he found himself projected seemed to imitate the "real" world. This stage of his OBEs lasted for several years.

In July 1914 Fox had one of these "typical" experiences. He had lain down quietly and soon dozed off only to find himself across the room from his bed. He could feel both his physical body in bed and his parasomatic self standing apart from it. He walked through the hall of his house, then opened his front door and closed it behind him. (As Fox notes, ". . . but of course it was not the real door that I opened.") As he walked down the street a "force" overtook him and he was borne away at a tremendous speed only to be set down in a strange town where he walked about for a time before feeling a tugging at the back of his head. "I shot backwards at an amazing speed, entering my body so violently that the trance was instantly broken . . . ," he reports.

Even in 1914, though, Fox realized that the OB world he was experiencing was partially an imaginary one, and he gradually began to comprehend that he could use the OBE to explore all sorts of worlds and environments. (This was a possibility that Sylvan Muldoon emphatically denied in his book. However, Crookall discovered that many OBE-ers find themselves in a richly beautiful environment while others find themselves enveloped in a mist-filled world [Crookall, 1964].) Fox even claimed that he met "beings" in these OB worlds. This tallies well with Blue Harary's experiences; he, too, believes that he has made contact with other world beings while out-of-body. In fact, this phenomenon is not rare, although it plays only a small role in Muldoon's book. Crookall, for example, discovered that people having spontaneous OBEs often feel as if someone is accompanying them during the OBE or is helping or trying to prevent them from having an OBE at the onset of the experience. For instance, the following cases are typical of this phenomenon and are reported in Crookall's *More Astral Projections*.

(1)

A few years ago I experienced astral projection not knowing what it was, I was much afraid each time. I was always in my bed. I felt a weight holding me down, especially my head. The next thing I knew I was out of my body. I walked around my bedroom and looked down the stairs into the kitchen. I thought I would look at myself in the glass, but could not see anything. On one occasion I thought when coming back, "I'll look at myself on the bed." As I looked I saw my mother instead of myself. She had been passed over quite a long time. . . . Now I always feel that the real Me is apart from and working through, my physical body. I now know for sure that we have two bodies. I think my mother is with me when I am projected: I hear her voice and once saw the back of her (in a robe). She said, "Come along" and took me through doors without opening them.

(2)

I had a bad fit of depression. I rested on my bed and, as I lay there, someone, or some being, came and sat on the side of my bed, as a doctor might. He took my hands and floated with me through the window and into the garden. I glanced back and saw myself on the bed.

Then I was back, healed, and saying, "How glorious! It will be like that when I die!" All my troubles had dropped from me like a cloak.

So Fox's experiences should not strike us as odd or unbelievable.

As Fox began to explore the OBE world more and more he also began experiencing odd things during his adventures. He was transported to strange environments and met bizarre creatures. He did not have any such encounters until about four years after he started systematically to practice OBE travel.

This new phase began on February 6, 1916, when Fox projected himself out-of-body with the intent of visiting a lady of his acquaintance who lived several miles away. He lay down as usual and soon a numbness overcame him. He became cataleptic and gradually slipped into the OBE state. Almost as soon as he had induced the separation he saw "a vague white, filmy, formless thing, spreading out in queer patches and snake-like protuberances." He noted that the room was illuminated even though there was no accountable light source and he began to realize that his environment was departing from normal reality. He saw glowing masses of vibrating circular objects and heard imaginary voices.

Fox had another strange OBE encounter only two months later, on April 10. This experience was a little different from his previous OBEs for, although he now was an expert at projection, he was overcome by fear. He imagined hearing the voice of his wife—who was in bed next to him—pleading with him not to go any further, but he ignored the warnings, walked through the walls of his bedroom, and into the next room. ". . . I moved off at great speed and came to rest in a modern brilliantly lighted room," recorded Fox. "Here a man and a woman were seated at a table, having a meal. They did not seem to see me."

Fox suggested to himself that he be projected to India, and then:

It seemed to me there was a sort of hole or break forward into the continuity of the astral matter, and through this, in the distance—as though viewed through a very long tunnel—I could see something indistinct which might have been an entrance to a temple. . . . I then moved forward again, but to my disappointment came to rest almost immediately in another room, where three women were seated. . . . Apparently none of them could see me.

The tunnel arrangement was coming into view again, then something must have occurred which broke my trance—though what, I do not know. Instantly I rushed back to my body and awoke.

It did not take Fox long to exploit this breakthrough, and he found himself in bizarre, inhabited environments. These worlds would "crumble" and new ones would be constructed in a kaleidoscope of universes. By 1928 Fox was freely traversing these new dimensions and during one experience found himself in a beautiful garden where robed people were assembled. They saw him but one inhabitant told him he did not belong there, so he returned to his body.

Gradually, though, Fox lost the ability to have these surrealistic OBEs and, as the years rolled by, he usually found himself projected to mundane, earthly scenes.

The OBEs recorded by Muldoon and Fox are very different. *Why* should their experiences be so radically dissimilar?

I have already given a partial answer to this question. The out-of-body experience, like a psychedelic drug experience, may be personal and unique to each individual undergoing it. The key may be "expectancy." People who, for instance, take

LSD, thinking that they will have a deeply religious experience, usually do. People who think that the LSD experience will be a terrifying ordeal usually have "bad trips." A more scientific term for expectancy is "psychological set." We may be up against a similar phenomenon when confronting the OBE. Although there can be little doubt that many people have remarkably similar experiences as they go through the OBE, there does seem to be a vast range of OBE phenomena one might encounter. Fox was an occultist and his experiences were bizarre, unworldly, surrealistic. Since he was a student of occult lore, his experiences were consistent with what he might have expected the OB world to be like. Muldoon was a simpler man, a country boy with little knowledge of involved occult doctrines. He subscribed to a simple Spiritualist faith, which had little use for such concepts as "higher worlds" and "astral beings." So, his OBEs did *not* encompass the types of experiences that played such a dramatic role in Fox's records. Perhaps Muldoon and Fox had different types of OBEs simply because they were psychologically set for different types of phenomenology while out-of-body. We might self-limit what we experience in the OB state because of our own psychological reaction to it.

Interestingly enough, another occultist, who wrote under the name "Yram," had several OBEs that closely matched the unworldliness of Fox's experiences (Yram, n.d.).

For years, Yram has been a man of mystery to writers on the OBE. Until just recently no one had any idea who he was or anything about his life. It was only in 1969 that Leslie Shephard, an authority on the history of the occult, was able to identify him as Marcel Louis Forhan, a French mystic who authored several books on metaphysics. He was born in 1884 and died at an early age in China, in 1917.

Forhan's initial experiences with out-of-body travel closely parallel those of Fox. They were undramatic and he usually found himself projected to mundane locations after he left the body.

Forhan was especially intrigued, though, by the process of separation and return to the body. Thus he spends much time

in his autobiography discussing the sensations of exteriorization. His comments concerning leaving and entering the body
rank second only to Muldoon's. Unlike Fox, who left his
body easily by slipping out of it or projecting from sleep,
Forhan escaped the body in a variety of rather startling ways.
Sometimes he would literally catapult out. As he records:
"During one of these experiences I had the unpleasant sensation of being hurled head first into space. There is naturally
at first a moment of surprise which we must do our best to
reduce as soon as possible."

Just as Fox was often whisked away at violent speeds by
a vortex, Forhan would be taken from his body by similar
means:

The sensation of being sucked up violently by a sort of huge vortex
is felt, and there is an immediate and conscious contact with other
worlds. This extraction from the body is never painful. But, as we are
generally unaware of the spot on which the whirlwind is going to
drop us, it is wiser to stay on the defensive.

In order to keep better control, I made it a habit to project myself
into my room before soaring to other dimensions.

As Forhan suggests in the passage above, it did not take
him long to realize that he was not trapped within the physical world while out-of-body. At first he projected himself over
Europe, watching the ravages of the First World War, but he
soon lost interest in our world and began to explore what he
called a "fourth dimension." He, too, began having surrealistic experiences similar to those Fox recorded.

Unfortunately, Forhan's book, *Practical Astral Projection*
(translated from the French) is devoted just as much to metaphysics as to the OBE. Nonetheless, his experiences seem to
be an extension of the type of OBEs most people experience
spontaneously.

These autobiographical accounts written by experienced
OB travelers present us with several puzzles. As I questioned
earlier, why should their experiences be so much more involved and intricate than those recorded by people who have
had fleeting, spontaneous OBEs? There are two possible ex-

planations. Either Fox, Forhan, and the others were simply fabricating when they wrote up their experiences, or these gifted OB travelers had greater opportunity to explore and make observations on the OB realm. The latter explanation strikes me as more logical, and I shall return to it in the conclusion of this book. This theory is partly substantiated by the fact that sometimes two people undergo an OBE together, and each reports having had similar surrealistic experiences during the adventure.

Joint OBEs are not recorded often in the literature on the subject. But a few cases have been reported that are impressive enough to warrant our attention. Forhan, for instance, often had OBEs during which he was accompanied by his wife. Blue Harary has reported one experience that is an example *par excellence* of this phenomenon:

I found myself floating out of my body which lay below me on the bed. I had this experience many times in the past and so was not suprised. I now could travel to find my old friend. I decided to bring my close friend George, who was living elsewhere in New York, with me. I concentrated on George and soon was floating above him where he lay asleep on his bed. I awoke George's out of the body self and grasped his hands and pulled him up out of his body. George readily decided to accompany me. None of this seemed the least bit unusual to either of us. We passed a barrier and then had only a short distance to travel. On the way to Maine, George and I walked through wooded areas, and up and down green, rolling hills. At one point when we stopped to rest on a hillside, George began to wander too close to a pool of pink, hot, bubbling liquid. I warned George not to wander too close because it was dangerous, even in an OBE state.

We reached an area near where we thought the woman would be, and were surprised to find that the woman had been waiting for us. I recognized her reddish blond hair and high cheekbones. We sat for a long while and discussed many of the things that had been disturbing all of us in our Earth lives. We seemed to find calm and reassurance in existence in that other-worldly level and in each other's warm company.

We said our goodbyes and George and I went back, and I helped him into his body which still lay asleep on his bed. I went back and found my own body safe and sound where I had left it. I floated in the air for a moment and then climbed back into my body. The next morning I awoke with complete recollection of the experience.

I didn't see George again until later the next day. He said that when he awoke in the morning, he had the strangest sensation of having forgotten something.

Later in the evening when George and I were discussing dreams a sudden strange look came across his face. He held his hands over his eyes and then pointed a finger at me and looking up with a shocked expression said, "Last night!" He then proceeded to ask me if we had been out of our bodies together and if what seemed so real to him at the time actually was a real experience. I told him very little at first and asked him to tell me all of the details that he could remember. "A lady," he said; "there was this fantastic lady." "Was she an elderly lady?" I asked him. "Yes, but not with gray hair like most old ladies," he answered, "but with reddish blond hair and with high cheekbones." He also remembered that there had been a danger and "something about a pool."

In some mysterious way, Blue and George had experienced the same world during their mutual experience. So these OB dimensions, even if they are only mental constructs, do possess some quality of consensus reality for those undergoing them.

Of course, Fox, Muldoon, and Forhan are not the only gifted subjects who wrote books on their OB adventures. They are just the most famous. One might also refer to Vincent Turvey's *The Beginnings of Seership,* Cora Richmond's *My Experiments Out of the Body,* Caroline Larsen's *My Travels in the Spiritual World,* Gifford Shine's *Little Journeys into the Invisible,* and to portions of Ingo Swann's recently published *To Kiss Earth Good-Bye.* (Some of these books were published around the turn of the century and are now difficult to locate.)

There has been only one full autobiographical account by a gifted OB traveler published in recent years. In 1971 Robert

Monroe, the Mr. X of Charles Tart's experiments, finally published his *Journeys Out of the Body*. The book received mixed reviews. Some reviewers lauded it as a worthy successor to the richly introspective writings of Fox and Muldoon. Monroe certainly had a considerable amount of credibility on his side. He had partially demonstrated his OB ability for Dr. Tart, so he could point to these experiments if anyone questioned his veracity when he spoke about his OBEs. However, some reviewers were very cautious toward the book, which at times reads like science fiction. Monroe's out-of-body adventures often seem to out-Fox Fox! His constant allusions to everything from astral gnomes to astral sex certainly stand in sharp contrast to the almost Victorian purity that marked the writings of his predecessors.

However, other aspects of Monroe's book look suspiciously as if the author were altering his accounts. In 1962 Dr. Andrija Puharich published a nearly incomprehensible book entitled *Beyond Telepathy,* in which he recounted the out-of-body experiences of one Bob Rame. According to Puharich, Rame was a "forty-four year old highly successful New York radio producer, writer and business executive." This description fits Monroe perfectly, and Puharich admitted that "Bob Rame" was a pseudonym. Let's take a look at the experiences described by Monroe in his book and compare them to the "Bob Rame" accounts.

According to his *Journeys Out of the Body,* Monroe first began having OBEs after suffering from an illness that initially resembled food poisoning. No doctor could diagnose the problem, and Monroe considered the illness as an integral step to his eventual discovery of the OBE (see pages 21 ff. of his book). The illness eventually subsided, but a new symptom began to plague Monroe. Periodically, he would feel odd vibrations over his body. Then:

Several months passed, and the vibration condition continued to occur. It almost became boring, until late one night when I was lying in bed just before sleep. The vibrations came and I wearily and patiently waited for them to pass away so I could go to sleep. As I lay there, my arm was draped over the right side of the bed, fingers just brushing the rug.

Idly, I tried to move my fingers and found I could scratch the rug. Without thinking or realizing that I *could* move my fingers during the vibration, I pushed with the tips of my fingers against the rug. After a moment's resistance, my fingers seemed to penetrate the rug and touch the floor underneath. With mild curiosity, I pushed my hand down farther. My fingers went through the floor and there was the rough upper surface of the ceiling of the room below. I felt around, and there was a small triangular chip of wood, a bent nail, and some sawdust. Only mildly interested in this daydream sensation, I pushed my hand still deeper. It went through the first-floor ceiling and I felt as if my whole arm was through the floor. My hand touched water. Without excitement, I splashed the water with my fingers.

After this experience, Monroe removed his hand from the floor and began to realize that these "vibrations" were heralding partial OBEs. He had been in that state when he projected his "hand" to the floor.

Now let us take a look at the Rame account. Rame mentions nothing about an illness. His OBEs were deliberately prompted by glue-sniffing. In fact, Rame credits just about all his OBEs to chronic glue-sniffing. Compare the following from Rame with the Monroe extract quoted above:

Later I went into a similar condition when lying in bed. I curiously reached over the side of the bed and felt the floor. Using my sense of "power" I pushed on the floor, and suddenly my hand slipped right through it to the sub-floor. I felt around on the sub-floor and there was a nail, a chip of wood, and some sawdust. I pushed deeper, and my hand went through the sub-floor and went into a small stream of running water. I moved my hand around in the water for some time, and didn't go deeper because my arm was extended as far as I could make it go. I then carefully withdrew my hand, looked at it, but it was dry, then my sense of power faded after which I felt my hand with the other to be sure it wasn't wet. I have often wondered what would have happened if I had let go of the power when my hand was stuck elbow deep in the floor?

There can be no doubt that Monroe and Rame are the same person. And there can be just as little doubt that Monroe, when writing his book, was not completely honest about his experiences. Why is there no mention of his glue-sniffing habit, which plays such an important role in the Rame account? In the Monroe account, this hand-through-the-floor experience initiated the OBEs. But, according to the Rame account, the author had OBEs before this particular incident occurred. Monroe writes as though he were surprised at what was happening to him. Rame tells us a different story.

I could go on and on comparing the Rame and Monroe accounts point by point, But these two extracts alone support my contention that one must read Monroe's book guardedly. Discrepancies as severe and serious as these simply cannot be overlooked.

Another strike against Monroe's credibility comes from New York writer David Black. When Black was collecting material for his book *Ekstasy: Out-of-the-Body Experiences* (1975), he was unable to locate, or substantiate the existence of, people and places mentioned by Monroe in his book. Black suggests that there are "hints of invention in Monroe's stories." When he confronted Monroe with the evidence, "Monroe shrugged off inaccuracies in his book as easily as he avoided specific dates and names in conversation."

The experiences that Monroe recorded in his *Journeys Out of the Body* were certainly interesting, but a book must be judged on the basis of its author's credibility. So each reader will have to evaluate the reliability of Monroe's book for himself.

I have touched on only a few OB experiencers in this introduction. One can readily see that the OBE domain is often perceived quite differently by those who travel it. Although the reports of people like Muldoon and Fox rest solely on their own work and testimony, their autobiographical accounts are still very important to us as we evaluate the OBE. Laboratory experiments, by their very nature, can explore only certain aspects of the OBE, aspects that may be only superficial. To understand the OBE's vast complexity and depth, we have to delve further into the phenomenon than experimental science can take us. People such as Muldoon, Blue Harary, Forhan, and talented out-of-body travelers of future years will serve as our guides.

Part III includes three papers, each devoted to a different aspect of the OBE as viewed introspectively. The first, by Blue Harary, was specially written for this volume. In his report, Harary describes not only what it feels like to explore the OBE, but also discusses the impact it has made on his life and the range of emotions his experiences trigger in him. The second report is by Professor J. H. M. Whiteman, probably one of the most unusual OBE experiencers alive today. He is professor emeritus of mathematics at Capetown University, author of papers on topics ranging from music to quantum physics, and a first-rate philosopher as well. Many students of parapsychology are familiar with his theoretical writings in the field, but few are aware that he has himself undergone hundreds of OBEs. In his paper, "The Process of Separation and Return during Experiences Fully 'Out of the Body,'" Whiteman discusses the sensations of exteriorizing and rejoining the physical body. Using his own experiences as the cornerstone of his discussion, he also cites the experiences of others and makes a comparative analysis. The final, brief report, by Lucien Landau, discusses one of the rarest forms of OB encounters. He himself saw an OBE phantom and his observations matched the experiences of his wife, who was undergoing the phenomenon.

REFERENCES

Black, David. *Ekstasy: Out-of-the-Body Experiences.* Indianapolis: Bobbs-Merrill, 1975.

Carrington, H. *Modern Psychical Phenomena.* New York: Dodd, Mead, 1919.

Crookall, R. *More Astral Projections.* London: Aquarian Press, 1964.

Fox, O. *Astral Projection.* New Hyde Park: University Books, 1961 (reprint; original, *c.* 1939).

Green, Celia. *Out-of-the-Body Experiences.* Oxford: Institute of Psychophysical Research, 1968.

Monroe, R. *Journeys Out of the Body.* Garden City, N.Y.: Doubleday, 1971.

Muldoon, S. *The Case for Astral Projection.* Chicago: Aries Press, 1946.

Muldoon, S., and Carrington, H. *The Phenomenon of Astral Projection.* London: Rider, 1951.

———. *The Projection of the Astral Body.* London: Rider, 1929.

Poynton, J. "Results of an Out-of-the-Body Survey." In J. D. Poynton (ed.), *Parapsychology in South Africa.* Johannesburg: South Africa Society for Psychical Research, 1975.

Puharich, A. *Beyond Telepathy.* Garden City, N.Y.:Doubleday, 1962.

Shephard, Leslie. "Introduction," in H. F. Battersby, *Man Outside Himself.* New Hyde Park: University Books, 1969 (reprint).

Yram. *Practical Astral Projection.* London: Rider, n.d.

11 | A Personal Perspective on Out-of-Body Experiences

STUART BLUE HARARY

The term "out-of-body experience" does not signify a single "standard" experience, but rather, refers to a general category of experiences that vary along a series of continuums. My out-of-body experiences vary in vividness and in the degree to which a clear distinction may be made between "subjective" and "objective" input. What we deem as "reality" may be characterized as seeming to have the properties that most individuals would agree are a part of our usual waking experience (consensus reality), or may appear to be totally unlike common waking experiences (nonconsensus reality). In an out-of-body state, reality may appear to be at any point along a continuum between these two extremes.

During one experiment in which my OBE contained strong elements of consensus reality, I experienced visiting a target location a quarter-mile away and later described the object that had been randomly chosen and placed in a designated area there for me to "see" and report to my fellow experimenters. The target object in this experiment was a gas mask. My report of my OBE following the experience seemed to describe several elements of the gas mask, such as the glass of its goggles. A picture that I drew in order to convey more accurately my impressions also resembled the base of the gas mask. After my descriptive data were recorded, I was driven the quarter-mile distance to the target area by a fellow experimenter, Graham Watkins, who also had not yet been informed of the nature of the target object. The experimenters stationed in the target area had randomly selected four additional objects and placed these, in a randomized order, along with the actual target. This created a "pool" from which I was to select the object actually used during the experiment. To avoid any possibility of sensory-cuing, all those who knew that the gas mask had been the target object for this experiment left the area prior to my arrival and were not permitted to return until after I had made my selection from among the pool of five objects. Basing my choice upon what I had "seen" during the OBE, I correctly selected the gas mask as having been the target.

In an OBE my perception of my personal form and self-awareness varies independently of the particular OBE reality of a given moment. Regardless of the consensus or nonconsensus qualities of the OBE reality during a specific experience, I may feel myself to be a ball of light floating in space, a body-shaped form, or simply a point of awareness that either focuses upon a particular area or merges, to varying degrees, with the surrounding environment. There are times when I am intensely aware of being at more than one location, in more than one form, simultaneously within a given experience.

The ball-of-light form is generally experienced as a sensation of glowing with variations in intensity, size, color, and depth of hue. The degree of similarity between my actual body and the body-shaped OBE form also varies from a very general similarity of shape to a similarity that is so highly detailed that I may not immediately recognize that an OBE is occurring. For example:

Late one evening, while relaxing in bed, I gradually noticed the sound of a television in the next room along with the sound of water forcefully rushing in the bathroom down the hall. Intrigued and mystified by the sounds (my roommate was vacationing out of town and I had not left the television on or the water running), I decided to investigate. When I noticed my body still lying on the bed behind me after having felt myself get up, it became obvious to me that an OBE was occurring. My form seemed to be almost identical to that of my actual body, but the reality which I experienced appeared to have been "rearranged."

During the experience, the atmosphere felt strangely "charged" while the lighting in my apartment was not as I would have expected it to be. Furniture was moved about in odd positions. The portable television set, turned to its loudest volume, was resting on the floor immediately in front of my bedroom door. Down the hall, rusty-orange water gushed from brand new pipes into the bathtub. The front door of the apartment was partially opened. After I had turned off and moved the television set, and shut off the water faucet in the bathtub, I stood in the living room and considered reorienting the furniture. I decided that it would be too much trouble. Instead, I closed the front door and quietly concentrated upon my body which was lying back in the bedroom. Upon doing so, I immediately found myself lying in bed awake, with full recollection of the experience. A quick check of the lighting signalled to me that reality was back to consensus. The feeling was as if I had been directly transported from one point to another, not as if I were awakening from a dream.

This experience, like others of my OBEs, was subjectively distinguishable from dreaming in much the same way that waking consciousness is distinguishable from dreaming or imagination. An experience such as this one is personally meaningful and may be useful in portraying the subjective nature of OBEs. Out-of-body experiences may be subjectively "real" whether or not they produce objectively verifiable information or measurable effects. Either type of OBE may produce information that is interesting and instrumental in helping us move toward a clearer understanding of the phenomenon.

As illustrated in the OBE just described, the experience of becoming separated from the body is sometimes a discrete sensation of floating or stepping out of the body. At other times, achieving this "separation" is experienced as a gradually deepening awareness of already being out-of-body. There are times when, for a brief instant, conscious awareness is lost, followed immediately by becoming aware of being in an OB state. Similar sensations, in a reversed direction, accompany the experience of returning to the body.*

Many of my OBEs are characterized by "traveling" from

*This ties in with the findings of Dr. Robert Crookall who found, upon analyzing hundreds of cases, that many OBE-ers experienced a "black-out effect" upon leaving and reentering the body—ED.

one location to another. I achieve this "traveling" by passively focusing my attention on an area that I wish to "visit." This is followed by my either feeling myself "fading into" the area of focus, while feeling myself "fading out" of the original location, or I may feel as if I were floating through the air or walking from one place to another. When there is no particular area that I wish to experience visiting during an OBE, I simply allow myself to feel comfortable with "flowing freely," rather than passively focusing my attention on a certain place. "Letting go" in this manner, and discovering where and in what state I find myself "traveling," is both exciting and intriguing! Very often, this appears to bear some relationship to my psychological state of the moment, which makes "letting go" something of a personal learning experience.

I "travel" to places that I am not at all familiar with during some OBEs. Later, I may actually find myself in these places in my normal waking state and have feelings of déjà vu, and may recognize various specific details of the previously unfamiliar environment. I also "visit" familiar areas in my OBEs. Many times I have had experiences during which I feel myself seemingly traveling through time. In these instances, time appears to take on the dimensional qualities of space. By "moving" through this dimension, I feel as if time were transcended during the experience. Déjà vu is also experienced when events later occur that I recognize from these seeming time-transcendent OBEs.

Specific details of an OBE are not always immediately recalled following an experience. Recollections may occur at a later time (especially if triggered by some event) or possibly not at all. Regardless of whether or not I can remember specific details of a particular experience, I do recognize when an OBE has occurred by the unique sensations that accompany its onset and termination and by general impressions of the nature of the particular OBE that I do recall. For example:

At a few minutes past 4:30 one morning several years ago, I drifted into a comfortable state of near-sleep and sensed the onset of an out-of-body experience. The welcomed sensation quietly flowed through me as I passively focused my thoughts upon a close friend, Debbi Ewers, and decided to attempt to "visit" her in the OBE state. Within moments, I began to feel myself "separating" from the body and being drawn toward my friend. I then apparently lost conscious awareness. Later that morning, around 10:30, an insistently ringing telephone awakened me from a deep sleep. Though I remembered having had a number of OBEs over the past six hours, I did not remember the specific details of all those experiences. My only recollection of the initial OBE was of the powerful sensation of being drawn toward my friend just before blacking out.

Still feeling slightly disoriented, I answered the telephone and was greeted by Debbi's cheerful voice. Her call was in response to an experience she had had and wanted me to verify. At about 4:35 that morning, Debbi had seen a three-dimensional luminous sphere floating in the corner of her room near the ceiling. She related that the sphere grew tremendously brighter upon her mentally asking the light if it were myself. Mental expressions of affection also created such an effect. When she added that this experience (which was a novel one for her) was scaring her to death, she saw the sphere of light slowly disappear. At this point she checked her windows to see if there were any possibility of a strange reflection but found none. She wondered if I might remember having had an OBE in which I attempted to "visit" her at that time! During the months ahead, in the course of her participation in controlled OBE experimentation at the Psychical Research Foundation, Debbi had many similar responses in which she accurately detected the randomly selected times of my laboratory out-of-body experiences.*

Laboratory OBE research and spontaneous detection experiences have not yet established any clear relationship between the OBE form in which I may experience myself and the forms reported visually by witnesses. Detection responses

---

*Miss Ewers's personal account of this experience is recounted in my report on Harary in chapter 8. The following material, which covers detection experiences in general, is based mostly on research carried out with Harary at the Psychical Research Foundation in 1972 and is also reported in full in chapter 8.—ED.

that include visual or other sensory imagery conceivably could involve direct sensory responses to tangible stimuli associated with OBEs. Equally conceivable is that these visual detections could be translations of input on a psi level (i.e., a psychic awareness of my "visit"), or on some other level, into a form of imagery that is acceptable to the conscious mind of the detector.

Spontaneous and laboratory detection responses have involved many different types of reported sensory imagery, as well as nonsensory feelings. No specific relationship has been found between the nature of detection responses* and their accuracy. In the laboratory, however, we found during our research that humans are more likely to respond with accurate detections of my OB "visits" when they are not put under pressure to do so (for instance, they may be told that their primary task is only to monitor equipment). A large proportion of human detection responses to OBEs seem to be visual in nature. This may be due to the fact that human beings are primarily visually oriented animals.

My OBEs are almost always in full color. The colors can appear as they usually do, or they may seem to be more intense or otherwise quite different from usual. My "visual perspective" may seem similar to my waking visual perspective, or it may seem to encompass a 360-degree field of vision. At times, both types of visual perspective appear to provide information simultaneously and *independently* of one another. OB "vision" can also appear to take on an x-ray quality. During one OB experiment carried out at the American Society for Psychical Research in 1972, my OB "vision" was totally black and white. This experiment was also characterized by an unusually high degree of discomfort on the part of my fellow experimenter, Janet Mitchell, and myself. My sensations during and following the OBE were of feeling more strained than usual, although I did not feel myself to be in any particular danger. Later, a radio news report brought to our

*For example, refer to Dr. Robert Morris's experience related in my report on Harary (chapter 8).—ED.

attention the fact that unusually intense sunspot activity had been occurring at the time of the experiment. Whether or not the sunspot activity actually had any influence on my OBE, or upon the state of mind of those who participated in the experiment, is unclear. This was, however, the only time that I recall having had a black-and-white visual experience during an OBE. Also of interest is that one of the targets used in this experiment was primarily black and white.

During this same experiment, I also reported to Janet my feeling that something terrible was happening or was about to happen. Toward the end of the experiment, I had a premonition and reported feeling that the President, or a presidential candidate, was in danger of being killed and that this feeling was somehow associated with Central Park. (The American Society for Psychical Research is located directly off of Central Park West in New York City.) Janet thought that the premonition was an indication of my boredom and discomfort with the experimental situation that evening, so she decided that we should end the experiment. A few days later, headlines were made in New York City when a man who had tried to hire a Secret Service agent in Central Park to murder the President was arrested. Quite often such premonitions or possibly precognitive feelings follow an OBE, although there is not always an opportunity to check their accuracy.

Auditory, tactile, gustatory, and olfactory experiences in the OB state also vary in intensity and in the degree to which they are similar to my usual sensory perceptions. Occasionally, there are feelings of seeming to "know" something directly about my environment without actually seeming to perceive it and without having encountered it previously. These nonvisual aspects of my OBEs possibly may be capable of providing objective information. However, most studies in the past that have attempted to explore the veridical aspects of OBE impressions have focused solely on the visual components of the experience.

Experiments that focus on how accurately an experient may "perceive" his OBE environment may help us to understand certain aspects of the experience. Such experiments, however, can neither prove nor disprove the veridical nature of the OBE phenomenon as anything more than a psi-conducive state coupled with a vivid imagination and imagery. Even those experiments in which the experient is asked to "perceive" target objects from a certain perspective do not settle this problem.* It should not be assumed that OB "perception" always has the experiential dimensions of bodily senses or that psi is incapable of conforming to the demand characteristics of an experimental situation. Detection responses (especially those that have been spatially discrete) that have sometimes been accurate when the experient's description of the environment was not accurate must be taken into consideration. Personal or environmental circumstances may affect the experient's "perception" or his recollection of an experience without noticeably influencing the strength of possible detections of that experience by outside witnesses. An experient may also accurately "perceive" his environment without being noticeably detected. Nonetheless, OBEs in which accurate descriptions of the environment are coupled with accurate detection responses may offer the strongest evidence for the veridical nature of out-of-body experiences and may help us better to understand the actual basis of the phenomenon.

When an OBE contains elements of "nonconsensus reality," the origin of these elements is uncertain. Nonconsensus elements could, conceivably, originate from personal projections on the part of the experient, or could reflect actual aspects of the environment that we are unaware of while not in an OB state.

Occasionally, sensations of dreaming seem to occur at the same time that I am having an OBE. The sensation, in this kind of experience, is as if I were simultaneously receiving separate input from both the OBE and the dream. Perhaps this sensation is due to a very rapid change between ex-

---

*See, for example, the Osis experiments reported in chapter 7. —ED.

periencing the OBE and the dream state. It is also conceivable that awareness is capable of occupying more than one state simultaneously. The nature of conscious experience in a particular moment could possibly reflect the states of awareness upon which attention is focused, in addition to other factors.

When "viewed" from an OBE state, my body often appears as a silhouette or a dark shadow rather than as a pattern of easily observable specific characteristics. Other persons (such as detectors) usually appear to me as they would when observed from a waking state, although they occasionally appear to take on a transparent or semitransparent appearance.

My body basically remains inactive during my OBEs and sometimes feels moderately to intensely paralyzed just prior to, during, and immediately following them. I usually maintain some passive focus ("in the back of my awareness") upon my body and activities surrounding it during OBEs, although the intensity of my bodily awareness varies. Disturbances in or near my body may lead me to terminate an OBE, or to focus more intensely upon my body while maintaining the OBE voluntarily.

I occasionally experience vibrational waves, which vary in intensity and which flow through my body while in an out-of-body state. Sometimes my experiences are followed by feelings of disorientation, especially when they are initiated at will in the laboratory. Chest pains are not uncommon following some experiences both in and out of the laboratory.

Some theorists have suggested that OBEs may be illusions resulting from a sudden decrease in general bodily awareness at a particular moment. Bodily sensations may in fact provide some input into OBEs, but it is probably inappropriate to suggest that OBEs are entirely due to the bodily sensations of the experient. Experientially, bodily awareness and sensations seem to vary independently of other aspects of out-of-body experiences. Physiological measurements of muscular electrical activity (EMG) have not uncovered significant correlations between muscular activities and my out-of-body experiences. There does, however, appear to be a significant relationship between a reduction in eye movements and my

OBEs. (These physiological measurements were taken during the course of our experimentation at the Psychical Research Foundation.)

Expectancy, early experiences, and psychological need may affect the "self-awareness" of the experient and may play a significant role in defining other aspects of the reality of particular OBEs. Out-of-body experiences may also be influenced by other psychological and environmental factors—such as volition or the presence of other persons who are themselves experiencing various states of awareness—in ways that are not fully understood at present.

The question of whether or not the OBE represents a literal externalization of the self into the environment may be independent of the question of whether or not the experience involves the operation of psi at some level. If the OBE involves a literal externalization of some aspect of the self, the mechanism through which this self interacts with its environment might well involve the use of psi. The OBE could be simply a psi-conducive state that involves a particularly vivid brand of imagery. This imagery, which creates the sensation of seemingly being separated from the limitations of the body, might help the experient to organize scattered psi impressions into a meaningful pattern. Both the OBE and more general psi-mediated phenomena may, however, reflect some third relationship between the self and the environment. Apparent separations between self and environment, and the apparent localization of self within the confines of a body, may be illusions that are created by a focusing of attention toward the body, rather than toward some transpersonal "greater self." Just as the experience of leaving the body may be affected by expectancy and past experiences, so may the experience of being confined to the body be created by, and based upon, cultural or other expectations. Perhaps the OBE may represent a focusing of attention toward other "locations" within the self, just as psi may be a process of noticing what one already knows at some transpersonal level of awareness.

12 | The Process of Separation and Return during Experiences Fully "Out-of-the Body"

J. H. M. WHITEMAN

The easiest kind of out-of-the-body experience to discuss is that in which the physical body and its sense organs appear to be asleep or entranced while the subject himself is singly-conscious in another space and body, or multiply-conscious in spaces other than the physical. I shall describe it as *full separation.* In some cases the space revealed may appear to resemble physical space in character and content. But even then the sense organs by which the phenomena are observed are not located in the physical body, nor are they visible to other people normally conscious in the physical world. So in all cases one is justified in regarding the conscious self as functioning, at those times, in a nonphysical space.

This kind of experience is comparatively easy to discuss, because dream, in spite of its unreality and the fantastic nature of its content, provides an obvious analogy. Everyone who has had a dream knows, at least vaguely, what it is to be "in another world" and to have nonphysical senses. There are other kinds of out-of-the-body experience, distantly analogous to thought and intuition, in which the physical body appears to be awake, so that there is a degree of doubly-conscious awareness of both physical and psychical (or mystical) spaces at once or in quick alternation. These will also be called *separation,* if the primary consciousness is unmistakably in a nonphysical body. But our field of inquiry must be drastically limited if we are to avoid losing ourselves in a maze of unresolved difficulties, aside from our main line of attack. Those other kinds of out-of-the-body experience, accordingly, cannot come in for more than passing reference.

The method of investigation adopted here will be by

brief commentary on firsthand descriptions of experience, some recorded by other people and accessible in print, but most taken from my own records and not yet published. In selecting descriptions two further limitations have been imposed: (1) experiences involving detailed knowledge, by the subject, of his separated human form have been altogether ignored (but precise observations of a more general kind have been occasionally admitted); (2) experiences involving knowledge of the existence and character of other people in the separated, nonphysical state have been excluded, except for a very few cases the ignoring of which would seriously impoverish the inquiry into the process of separation and return.

As far as my own records are concerned, the experiences classified as *full separation* number about 550. The first consideration above reduces the number quotable to about 250. The second reduces the number further to perhaps 150. These limitations also result in all the most mystical experiences being ignored or receiving only passing mention, while the mystical aspects of the experiences quoted are for the most part rudimentary. This means that the experiences judged to possess the greatest a priori value and the most permanent reality have nearly all had to be passed over.

As regards content, therefore, the descriptions chosen form a very unrepresentative sample. But I do not think that a distorted view is presented of the process of separation and return or of the general conditions out-of-the-body, as these appear in my experience, whether the separation is psychical or mystical in character—provided it is of the kind described as *full*. And I do not think that there is any cause to regard the experiences that have been selected as lacking reality compared with physical ones. The impression, at the time and after, was quite the reverse. . . .

DESCRIPTIONS SPECIALLY RELATING TO THE PROCESS OF SEPARATION

(A). Initiated by Shock, Physical Weakness, Drugs, or Other Physical Influence

Among descriptions already published (of other people's experience), this is by far the commonest method of initiation. Approximately a third of the M. and C. cases,* for instance (46 out of 140?), fall into this category. The following is the only reasonably clear case, presumably in this category, in my own experience:

[2] (Probably 1919, at the age of 12). In the course of an experiment with yellow phosphorus in a small laboratory at the top of the house, a piece caught alight and stuck to one of my fingers for a moment. I felt no pain, but walked downstairs in order to have the burn dressed. In the kitchen my mother hastened to get a piece of cloth, while I stood watching her at the other end of the room.

Presently I noticed the light in the room taking on a glowing, dream-like quality, and almost immediately the ears appeared to go deaf. The objects in the room then appeared to become more distant, without, however, shifting their positions. Next, the sense of sight was removed, so that I stood with only the senses of touch, bodily feeling, and spatial position. After another few seconds the feeling in the feet disappeared. It was not that the feet went numb, but simply that I appeared to have no feet. Space was either empty or annihilated there. The emptiness rose gradually higher in the legs, until I appeared likewise to have no lower part of the body.

Then came a sudden change. All feeling in the body disappeared, but at almost the same instant I realized that I was still standing, aware, in a curiously interested but detached way, of the sound of some heavy object falling down about eight feet away, behind and slightly to the right. Before having time to reflect, I became conscious in the usual way, to find myself lying on the floor, having fallen down

*Sylvan Muldoon and Hereward Carrington, *The Phenomena of Astral Projection* (London: Rider, 1951).

in a faint. I arose at once, feeling perfectly normal, and very ashamed at having apparently fainted when nothing whatever was wrong.

The strangeness of hearing the sound of the fall from outside, without feeling anything, was very puzzling, but having no knowledge of the possibility of separation from the body I did not consciously think of the experience in those terms.

A similar description of gradual process is given in the "Annenkof Case":*

. . . I felt myself become more and more weak, physically and morally. My first impression was that my legs and arms had no more weight, then my stomach, then my breast. Soon I found myself beside my body. . . .

In nearly all cases of this class, however, the subject becomes suddenly aware of being out of the body, without knowing how it happened.

B. Emergence of the Separated Consciousness from a Dream-state through the Revival of Recollection in the Course of the Dream†

This is the commonest method of initiation with me. The experience following, numbered [3] is described very fully considering the smallness of its content, for the reason that it was the first separation in my experience definitely exceeding the physical state in impression of reality. The other description, [117], is also given at length, in order to provide a clear example of stable, objective conditions during the longer separations, and also to show, by contrast, the advance made possible through the discovery of the Transcendent Unity toward the end of 1929, and a seven-month period of intensive rebirth following.

*Muldoon and Carrington, p. 199. The passage is translated from the French.

†Whiteman defines *recollection* as a perceptual mode typified by "a developing of detachment and a freeing of all imaginal powers until time can, as it were, be stopped or put aside."—ED.

[3] (1927). This was an awakening to a level very close to that of the physical world, so that the change was as little abrupt as it well could be. The immediate cause lay in the power of Recollection becoming active, from habit and associations, during dream (I had practised Recollection for about two years before this date). But I think that what occasioned this specific experience was the fact that the previous evening I had been able to maintain a continuous recollected state during a concert by a celebrated string quartet, with such effect that at one time I appeared to be rapt out of space by the extreme beauty of the music, and held for a few moments in a new state a steady contemplation and joy.

After this I remember going to bed with mind peacefully composed and full of a quiet joy. The dream, during the night that followed, was at the beginning quite irrational, though perhaps more keenly followed than usual. I seemed to move smoothly through a region of space where, presently, a vivid sense of cold flowed in on me and held my attention with a strange interest. I believe that at that moment the dream had become lucid. Then suddenly, the dormant faculty of Recollection having become stirred, all that up to now had been wrapped in confusion instantly passed away and a new space burst forth in vivid presence and utter reality, with perception free and pinpointed as never before; the darkness itself seemed alive. The thought that was then borne in upon me with inescapable conviction was this: "I have never been awake before."

At that time, in spite of two previous incipient awakenings, I had no knowledge of the possibility of separation, not to mention the manner of its occurrence; and this ignorance was no doubt responsible for my inability to remain in that state longer and recognize more. I believed that I had in some way seen the bedroom from another space in which one could be really alive, but was scarcely ready to recognize the duplication of the bodily faculties (in spite of the fact that my consciousness seemed to be strangely orientated in the room, being as if upright and nearer the centre). These relations of space and form, being metaphysical, are extraordinarily elusive, and confuse one's understanding greatly at first. Consequently, after a few moments, I returned to the physical state, with nothing more to record than what has been said, but with an abiding impression for future inspiration and guidance.

[117] (October 1932). In dream I heard a voice of unpleasant quality asserting of a certain place that it was "where Tiberius planned one of his murders." Immediately there was a fairly clear view of an ornamental tower or gateway resembling the "Gate of Honour" at Caius College, Cambridge. On reflecting that the voice was malicious and untruthful, I became aware of being in a separated state (the habit of detachment from fixed ideas established recollection). Everything that now proceeded was rationally observed. The light was at first like that of a dark night in the physical world, but intellectually dark, because corresponding with mental or spiritual limitations. The appearance was as if I was carried slightly left, in a smooth motion, along the raised bank of a river, which lay at my right hand. The water was not seen, the river and its position being indicated by intellectual idea only.

On the bank, a little to the left and in front, as the ground rose slightly, there then appeared three men garbed as labourers, looking across the river. A persuasion to think less of them on account of their appearance was defeated; and with that, another and smaller human form, in which I also seemed to be (one space within another), in an inverted position with the head downwards, reversed itself and became upright. Forthwith I was directed to turn to the right, still as if on the bank and to look across the river.

Now, as I faced due forward, what had been represented as the river appeared as a rather low-lying level expanse, significative of water because it divided one kind of manifestation from another. Beyond, perhaps 200 yards away, a wonderful sight met my eyes. A palace or temple of superb beauty and vast proportions, but entirely unostentatious, flashed out, completely vivid in a light that shone glowingly against a background of holy darkness as of the night sky, a darkness not deadening to the perceptions, but showing the power of goodness through it.

In front, rather below the level of the place where I appeared to stand, was seen a broadly arched entrance, about 50 yards wide, and a long flight of hundreds of steps mounting within. At the top, deep within the building, there came a glow of light from a huge stained glass window, curved above like the arch of the entrance, and having designed upon it the forms of majestic human figures like those painted by Michelangelo on the ceiling of the Sistine Chapel. The small forms of living people seemed to proceed up and down the steps.

Having observed this scene in admiration for perhaps half a minute, I turned slightly to contemplate the rest of the building. As I did this, I was gently raised a little and carried by a smooth motion, perfectly controlled from within by obedience, further along the bank towards the left, thus being enabled to survey the palace from various angles. It appeared to be on a vast site, and stretched away to the left without any break or separation in the building. While the contour was beautifully varied, it formed nevertheless one single building, extending to the left for at least the four or five hundred yards that I could see.

But presently intellectual wondering took me within the seeing, to ask of interior causes. And for a few moments, in a more purely intellectual state, it was imparted to me (or so I understood it) that this entire manifestation sprang from a perfect kind of memory—not in any way my own memory, but the joint memory of many human beings, worked out and fulfilled over a very great period of time, so as to be part of the basis of their joint life. During this new contemplation I seemed to be in a brighter light, no longer night, but day.

But these impressions were too abstract to be maintained; and by a gentle process I was brought back to the physical world, refreshed in spirit and body.

That the moral side of life cannot be divorced from the intellectual side is shown, in such experiences as this, by the fact that the raising and liberating of our state is brought about by the successive rejecting of fixed ideas, uncontrolled reaction to persuasive influences, inclinations to superiority, judging from appearances, respect for persons—in short, of fixation of every kind. And every fixation is at once anti-intellectual (in blinding our perceptions) and antimoral (in acting contrary to the Good).

It is also evident, from such an experience as this, that everything in a separated state, including positions and movements in space, is representative of deeper mental conditions having an objective basis but perceived according to subjective capabilities or tendencies. The palace itself, for instance, was objective, on the right, and in glowing light; but I could see it only from a darker state, to the left, and as at night-time.

C. Initiation from a State of "Opening"

The mode of vision in which bright interior scenes are observed through a more or less circular opening made in the physical field of view is common with many people. Crystal gazing is vision of this kind induced in certain familiar ways; it most often runs into fantasy merely, but is sometimes veridical.* Visions described as *hypnagogic* in the literature of psychical research† may also be classified as Openings. But they seldom show a clear boundary, and generally lack three-dimensional reality in an obvious way, so that they take on the character of imaginations. The Openings considered here were vividly three-dimensional, and free from fantasy.

While Openings in general may be regarded as common, the transition from a state of Opening to a state of Separation, illustrated here, is comparatively very rare with me, but also particularly instructive, I think.

[1923] (29 April 1950). While in bed and apparently awake, I perceived a visual opening with circular boundary, within which there was presented a scene in bright sunlight and vivid colours. It appeared to be a park, with many people walking peacefully about. At the same time I was aware of the physical body lying on its back in bed, but not altogether as if I were in that body. It was as if I were apart and watching the physical body watching. Again appearing to think in the physical body, I conceived a wish to transfer consciousness to a free personal form. Immediately I rose and walked forward towards the opening. The opening appeared to enlarge itself gradually, but before entering wholly within it I had to pass over a patch of sandy-coloured ground, as if bared for excavation. It seemed to represent a gulf between two spheres of existence. Passing through, however, I reach the park and mix with the people. There is difficulty in distinguishing details, as if the eyes are out of focus and cannot be brought under steady control; but a general brightness of the light

*See, for example, the experiences of Miss A. discussed by F. W. H. Myers in *Proc. S.P.R.* 8 (1892): 498 ff.

†"An Introductory Study of Hypnagogic Phenomena," by F.E. Leaning, *Proc. S.P.R.* 35 (1925): 289 ff. See particularly pp. 331–36.

around is very noticeable. My form is small, seeming from its size and manner of walking to be that of an infant aged about two years or less. There is a rather general though very definite sight and feeling of clothes below, such as a child of that age might wear. Looking up at the sky, I see a perfectly clear and beautiful pattern of clouds, of the cirrus type.

[476] (April 1935). I was in a state of relaxed watchfulness while lying in bed, when the visual field opened out so that a scene was presented in bright light, inside a circular boundary. In the centre was a large rock of some substance like granite on a sandy beach, near the water's edge. The thought occurred to me that I might get through the opening on to the beach, and almost at once I left the body and approached the rock. There was no particular sensation of passing through the opening, but I merely came quite near to the rock, till I could see its surface glistening with points of light, making an impression of greater vividness than in the physical world. No sooner had I arrived near the rock, however, than I became conscious of difficulty in breathing, which distracted me and brought me back in a few moments to the physical body.

In the next experience to be described the Opening was of the kind I call *spatial,* and the separation took place instantaneously, so that it almost comes under the category of "free separations"* (effected by relaxation and mental detachment alone):

[1493] (4 June 1945). This separation began with a "spatial opening" in which the surface of a whitewashed wall, two feet or so away, was studied, with a full clarity of perception and the usual impressions of precise spatial position and of seeing "through the eyelids" of the physical eyes, which remained consciously shut. The opening then changed to one in which heath-like country was seen in a wide panorama, with steep ground in front; and almost at once I was conscious for a few moments of being separated and amidst that scene.

---

*Whiteman defines *free separation* as an OBE in which consciousness is simultaneously retained within both the physical and mental bodies.

Spatial Openings, as described here, are rather common with me, about 160 having been recorded. Sometimes the whole bedroom is seen in this way, "through the eyelids." But usually something quite different is seen, in one case a bright sky with clouds, seen as if through a circular hole cut in the ceiling. The epithet *spatial* means that the spatial effect is exactly as if some physical object or scene were being observed from the physical body, but the light is not physical. The physical eyes are nearly always shut, and consciously so.

The concluding example under this head is an elaborate one in which the opening occurred not at the beginning, but in the middle, after a partial return:

[1861] (4 November 1949). This was a long separation, in five distinct stages, the last highly mystical. It began with a lucid dream or fantasy-separation, and when the improprieties were overcome I found myself in a strange wood-panelled room at the top of a building, through which I descended, finding a young woman "secretary" in a ground-floor room, conditions being extremely like physical ones. At that point I opened the eyes of a "duplicate" form, and saw the light of the physical world (as it fully appeared) coming into the bedroom through a window with burglar-guards. Being unwilling to remain in that state or to awaken in the physical world, I closed the duplicate eyes, and then saw (with more interior eyes) an opening into a state with the brighter and more beautiful light of a garden. The opening was small at first, but by the voluntary calling forth of courage, faith, or obedience, it enlarged itself, and I passed through into the garden . . . [the other two stages are omitted].

D. Similar or Related Experience-types
(cases already published)

The following dream-initiated projection of Muldoon* seems to be a fantasy-construction built upon the process just described:

*Quoted by R. Shirley in *The Mystery of the Human Double* (London: Rider, n.d.), p. 94.

I was dreaming that I had entered a massive hall . . . it was now a small room and there was but one small hole in the centre of the ceiling through which I could see light. . . . It seemed that I stood there for some time when suddenly I wondered if I could not fly through it. I began to rise in the air but as I was passing through the hole I became caught fast in it. . . . At this point I began to awaken and realize what was taking place . . . the position of the astral body corresponded with the position it held in the dream. I was just half-way through the ceiling of the room when I became conscious.

It would be quite possible, I think, for the sensation of being "stuck" in the ceiling to be what I call a fantasy-construct (determined largely by subjective prepossessions), and still to be quite as vivid and realistic as in the physical world.

An unnamed correspondent of the *Occult Review** claims a power of more or less voluntarily seeing people in distant parts by the following process:

I close my eyes and concentrate on the person. I seem to project my consciousness forward and in a few minutes I see the friend. It is as if I was looking through the reverse end of a telescope, something similar to Miss Okeden's "tunnel." At other times I seem to be actually in the room with the friend . . . (some veridical experiences are then mentioned).

These experiences might be classified as free separations, like [1943] above. "Miss Okeden" was a previous correspondent, who wrote as follows:

I close my eyes and have a feeling of going over backwards . . . and I find myself going down a long, dim tunnel. . . . At the far end is a tiny speck of light which grows as I approach into a large square. . . . In nearly every case I can describe the room my friends are in. . . .†

The tunnel would, in my view, be a fantasy-construct, but the scene and final projection (veridical in this case also) merit being called *real.* In one of my own experiences I

**Ibid.,* pp. 29–30.
†*Ibid.,* p. 29.

seemed to pass through a tunnel, in a dream-like state, and emerged through the opening at the end into a scene in bright sunlight.

Sometimes the opening through which the conscious "I" passes in order to achieve full separation is not a visual one, but is apparently located elsewhere in the body. A writer quoted by Shirley states that in his experiences he had "the extraordinary sensation of being drawn out horizontally through a small hole in the centre of the skull."* Similarly, in another M. and C. case, the subject states that she had on several occasions "been conscious of leaving her body from the top of the head.†

E. Other Illustrations of Separation Initiated from a Balanced State of Dissociation

The instances grouped under this head, all of which are in some sense voluntary, may be roughly grouped under four subheads: *(a)* not unexpected, and probably assisted by some kind of voluntary detachment; but the process itself spontaneous; *(b)* the wish to separate is easily and quickly fulfilled, as in getting out of bed in the physical world; *(c)* some calling-forth of a *decision from self,* or *exertion of self-will,* effects separation. The resulting state is then of poor quality, and sometimes very distressing; *(d)* some calling-forth of *Obedience* (poised denial of self-will) effects separation. The resulting state is then of better quality, and more refreshing than the physical state.

I first give an instance coming clearly under the first subhead:

[750] (December 1936). While awake in the body, lying on my back in bed, I found myself consciously dissociated and looking at a point on the ceiling (i.e., a "duplicate" ceiling). The wish to "pin-point" the attention so that the details might be steadily observed, without strain or fixation, led to an effect like the focusing of the eyes. After a few seconds there was a change, and I became fully conscious of floating in a separated form apparently a little above the physical body.

Ibid., p. 138.
†Muldoon and Carrington, p. 212.

The next instance is of *successive* separations, the first of which probably comes under subhead *(a)* and was strikingly real, while the second probably comes under subhead *(c)*, requiring some effort from self, and was accordingly subject to fantasy:

[1202] (23 November 1941). Aware of the balance of spaces in a quasi-physical state, I emerged in an inner form from the side of the bed, and almost at once appeared as if floating high up in the air, while looking down on a dark scene. A squarely-built house was almost due below, with bright lights shining from the windows. The sense of spatial reality, as in the physical world, was intense and vivid, but so unusual that a return was caused to the quasi-physical state, so that the body appeared again in bed, and I was again conscious of the balance of spaces. A second separation then occurred, also from the side, and while this took place I was objectively conscious of the physical body lying face downwards. But consciousness resided almost wholly in the separating form. The state now began to merge into fantasy. The separated form appeared to be on the floor, trying to rise from a position half under the bed, which, however, next appeared like a settee with hanging drapery. The separation forthwith became entirely dreamlike in character, uncontrollable, though the mind still reflected and tried to perceive clearly and understand.

The distinction between subheads *(b)* and *(c)* is very indefinite and artificially drawn. I regard the following experience as probably coming best under subhead *(b)*:

[463] (April 1935). Becoming aware of the disjunction of spaces which sometimes initiates separation, and being to all appearances in bed, I rose in the separated form, leaving the physical body still sleeping. The room in which the separated form was placed bore only a general resemblance to the physical bedroom, though there was a persuasion to think it the same. A mirror was at hand, but knowing from previous experience that curiosity to look at one's appearance sometimes leads to effects of fantasy, I refrained from looking, and proceeded to the door. This, however, had no handle; and again disinclined to make actions from self-will, I turned to the windows and opened them, partly to look

out or escape, and partly because the air in the room seemed stuffy, so that breathing was difficult. On trying to take deep breaths, a strange feeling, almost like a smell, was very realistically felt in the lungs. Passing somehow through the window, I floated to the ground in the silence of the night, everything being quite dark. Throughout this experience there was a lack of higher reflection and obedience. And instead of continuing, it quickly lapsed, and I returned to the physical body in an entirely normal way.

Not more than three or four of my experiences have been definitely initiated by effort from self—subhead *(c)*. The distaste for the resulting state and a peculiar form of anguish afterward, together with shame at having succumbed to a harmful temptation, in those few experiences, have been quite sufficient to inhibit future efforts that way entirely, unless very slight. The following is a curious example in which I was induced to make too strong an effort:

[1891] (14 January 1950). Becoming aware of the freedom to separate, I made a voluntary decision to move from the bed, in a separated form, out into the room. When out, however, the state of consciousness changed suddenly so that from the new point of view it appeared that I was still in the position of the physical body and that separation had not in fact taken place. A second movement of separation was then made, requiring a more appreciable effort. Returning almost at once, I was affected with some restlessness and distaste—the aftermath of self-determined effort without inner obedience.

In contrast to my experience, the author calling himself "Yram" seems to use the method of self-effort persistently, as a matter of confirmed experimental policy.* It does not seem to me surprising, therefore, that we find continual references in his book to unpleasant or painful effects, for instance:

"I received a terrific slap in the face" (p. 52); "a highly-strung nervous condition" (p. 53); "grinning shapes . . . a nameless fear" (p. 57); "nervous tension" (p. 64); "this painful situation" (p. 65); "an in-

* *Practical Astral Projection* (Philadelphia: McKay, n.d.).

stinctive fear" (p. 69); "furious with rage, my teeth clenched" (p. 101); "kicked twice on the head" (p. 101); "drenched with perspiration" (p. 108); "unreasonable fear . . . paralysis" (p. 110).

The distinction between subheads *(c)* and *(d)*—self-effort and Obedience—may seem very slight and unimportant. But it is, in my view, the difference between fixation and freedom, fantasy and reality, bad and good. Naturally, however, Obedience is a very difficult faculty to develop, and sometimes a certain degree of effort from self may be warranted, as being the only method of voluntary action known to us or within our power.

From the terms in which the following separation is described, one could not judge whether it comes under subhead *(b), (c),* or *(d).* The joy, and improvement over physical conditions, however, indicate that the prompting was chiefly by obedience:

[836] (August 1938). "Waking up" during the night, in a balanced state, I was aware of lying on my front in bed. Nevertheless I rose, in a separated form, and stood on the floor, feeling joyful at being in a form more properly corresponding to my mind or real nature than my physical form. . . .

When the condition that I call Obedience is properly maintained, the separations that result are normally *free separations* or *mystical form liberation,* and are accordingly beyond the scope of this inquiry.* But two simple cases of full separation may be given here, the first initiated by Obedience, and the second successively uplifted as a state of Obedience was voluntarily restored during the course of events. Since the second of these cases concluded in a state of Obedience, it seemed to end with a transition into *free separation.*

*Whiteman defines *obedience* as a mental state typified by "a conquest of the tendency to decide for oneself absentmindedly or presumptuously, instead of being continuously open to a higher wisdom." *Mystical form liberation* is defined as a state "in which the spiritual powers of our inmost being find a fulfillment in all essentials, so that we have, within our outerman, as it were, a continuous threefold knowledge, life, and security."—ED.

[843] (October 1938). Becoming aware, during the night, of being in a dissociated state, I denied the temptation to make an effort from self, knowing this to be contrary to Obedience, and substituted an attitude of surrender. I was then lifted up and entered a state of noticeable spiritual freedom; but this was only general and for a few moments, because I was unable to sustain it.

[841] (October 1938). Having risen from the bed voluntarily, in separation, I noticed a general lack of freedom. The wish for better freedom led to a change of state in which I appeared to be floating, in a rather indefinite form. The further wish to feel solid ground (actually and representatively), associated with the recalling of Obedience, then led to the clear sensation of walking and a brief sight of spiritual sunlight, expressive of intelligence and love. On returning to the physical state it was as if the physical body had been awake as well as the real self within, and did not have to be jolted into wakefulness.

A longer and entirely specific revelation initiated by Obedience has been published in my paper on *The Vision of Archetypal Light.**

It appears to me likely that the ruling faculty which I have called Obedience may, with some other people, be replaced by a similar faculty better called Faith (there being apparently two contrasted types of mystic).† In either case, however, a poised centering on the Transcendent Unity, as a greater Wisdom with us or in us but not of us, is implied.

F. Parallel Consciousness in Two or More Spaces: Mixture of Spaces

These are features often (perhaps always) found in the beginning of separations, or in transitions from one kind of separation to another. Following are four illustrations of varied types:

*The Review of Religion, March 1954, pp. 153–54.
†See, for example, Evelyn Underhill, *Mysticism* (London: Methuen, 1930), pp. 415 ff.

[1953] (10 August 1950). This long and elaborate separation was in two parts, the second following on the first after a short interval of apparent wakefulness. At the end of the second part I was raised rather high, as in the air, and the Divine Sun was shown me for about half a minute. The mental state of the soul was one of adoration at its glory, almost dissolving into tears from joy and loving humility. At intervals, however, while filled with this joy in the soul-life, I was also aware, by double-consciousness, of a lower manifestation according to which the body (or rather, another body) was gently rocking, in a horizontal position, face upwards. And around this lower state, or intermediate between it and the higher state, was a "divine blackness," out of which the inner Sun had emerged or risen. Thus a material light, a sublime darkness, and a supreme light, were simultaneously knowable, and two personal forms, one of them much more properly my own.

[1980] (4 November 1950). I became suddenly aware of a blaze of light, of spiritual quality, while apparently in a separated state. Because the effect was still indefinite, though vivid, I tried to increase the precision of perception by recalling the state of recollected "one-pointedness." This did not come spontaneously, however, and the effort was followed by awareness, in a lower state, as of the separated form on the floor beside the bed, while simultaneously the consciousness appeared in part to reside in another form in process of separating from the position in bed. Both these separated positions were surveyed (with disapproval) from a higher state.

[2285] (6 December 1953). In sleep I became suddenly aware of having been walking along a road through open country for some time. I proceeded to reflect (while still separated) whether I could be said to have been really separated in myself during that previous time, or whether perhaps it was an entity partly identified with me, whose memory had been carried over. A new accession of wakefulness then followed, which I described as being due to the Will becoming awake. But I was unable to see properly, the eyes being as if clouded over. The effort or wish to see more clearly resulted in a clearer but more material light, as of the physical world, displacing the other from the left. I considered carefully whether the new light should be described as more real or less real than the other, that is, whether the former light should be said to have any imaginative quality. But the new light was also beyond proper control, and since I seemed (while contemplating it) to be in bed (in a duplicate state), I began to weigh up whether or not to make a decision to leave the bed in voluntary separation . . . (a new separation, of lower type, then followed).

[534] (October 1935). I seemed to be awake in bed, the light being that of early morning, but was fully aware that the state was one of separation or incipient separation. On trying to rise, there was a definite hindering force as if I were being held back, so that muscular effort was needed. This, however, did not enable me to get free, and I then looked to the right and noticed, in a clear light, some strange objects which I could not bring into proper focus, close to the bed. Alongside I perceived, in a startling flash, a human head, turned away so that chiefly the back of it was seen, the person being instinctively named within me as "myself." Being unable to control an unreasoning reaction of fear, I reached out with a hand (in the separated state) in an endeavour to confirm or refute this presence. For a few moments I was conscious of the warm feel of the head and hair, being too startled, however, to see anything further. On [my] becoming able to see again, the person was no longer there, and my attention was turned to the objects mentioned. Two spaces were clearly superposed. In the one was a representation of the bed and the objects, as if out of focus (in a mental way); in the other, which was taken to be physical space (but which must have been a second duplicate space, since it was seen by interior eyes), the corner of the sheet and a handkerchief on a chair seemed to correspond with the out-of-focus objects (still visible) in position and outline. A strong persuasive influence tended to take hold of the mind, to make it believe that the strange objects were "really" the sheet and the handkerchiefs, seen in a physical state, so that I was "really awake after all." Only the knowledge that the state was really one of separation enabled me to counter this persuasion and prevent an abrupt return to physical wakefulness.

This last description (a half-separation) illustrates the rare effect that I shall call *mergence*, whereby the phenomena of one space seem to adapt themselves and merge into the phenomena of another space of similar character, when a transition from the one space to the other is about to occur. Mergence sometimes occurs in a surprising way, as in another experience [1809], when a human being seen in a separated state moved carefully into a certain position, and then appeared to merge into the outline of a wardrobe in the "duplicate" bedroom; and again a strong persuasion that it was "really" the wardrobe that was being seen caused an abrupt waking—when it became obvious that there was in fact no resemblance in outline between the person and the wardrobe. Sometimes it is the duplicate bedroom that is adjusted so as to make it correspond better with the phenomena proper to an interior sphere, as in the following half-separation.

[860] (February 1939). I appeared to wake in the night, hearing the sound of the house dog scratching at the mat outside the bedroom (which it had quite possibly been doing). On looking up, in full wakefulness, I was surprised to see the hall light on, as a bright light under the door showed. A noise then began again, but this time was obviously made by the clumsy steps of a person coming into the room and approaching the bed, though the door had not been opened. . . . The form stopped beside the bed, then stretched out a hand and touched my hands as I lay on the bed. At this point I was unable to maintain steadiness of control, and with a slight jolt the state changed to a normal physical one. I then observed, first, that the hall light was not on; then, that I could not see the crack under the door from the bed. And finally, my physical hands were under the bedclothes, and so could not have been touched from the outside.

Experiences such as this seem to indicate that *(i)* there is a purely intellectual "pattern" of the objects and scenes in this physical world (including bodies of living beings); but *(ii)* that pattern can be actualized only by the power of individual minds, whose influences are blended together so as to produce a more or less complete and rational synthesis in a duplicate state.

Such a hypothesis will also explain why the human form representative of the mind in a separated state may differ in locality and appearance from the physical body. For the intellectual pattern of the physical body is not necessarily very like

the intellectual pattern of the mind; and the two might therefore be actualized in quite different ways.

The hypothesis also explains the phenomenon of *doubles*
(as in experience [534] above). For the intellectual pattern of
the physical body might be actualized by any intelligent enti-
ties whose minds corresponded in some way with it, while we
ourselves were actualized according to the state of our mind
at the time.

Apart from the ordinary sense of bilocation that occurs
when the interior body is just separating from the physical
body, or just returning to it, published examples of simultaneous or mixed spaces are difficult to find. The following,
from the M. and C. collection, seems to be an example:

I seem to know that my body is lying on the bed when I am walking
through the apartment, or it is as though for a second I am going like
lightning to lie on the bed, and then am up again. . . . Or perhaps
I am in both places at once! (p. 166).

On the other hand, the following account suggests to me
strongly the state of *free* separation:

Usually when I leave the body it is in the semi-conscious state between waking and sleeping, and at times I seem to be living in two
worlds simultaneously. I can see my body lying upon the bed and I
can hear the voices in this world, and in the other state of existence
(p. 66).

A very curious instance of mixed influence is the following:

I had been reading. The hall clock struck *one*, so I said to myself,
"I had better go to bed." As I turned to the bed I saw *myself* lying
there, on my back. I wondered if I were dead, but the "corpse"
moved, and then the bed was empty (p. 213).

G. Apparent Participation in Another Individual's Personality and Memory

Two examples will make sufficiently clear what is meant by
this:

[1914] (8 April 1950). During the night, in a state between waking and sleeping, the inner and outer spaces were recognized as in a condition of balance, and a firm decision was made to step out of bed to the left, in a separated form, leaving all attachments. Whether the decision should be called mine or not remained doubtful, however, since on becoming separate I was aware of a division in consciousness, one part properly mine, the other part not properly mine, but lower, and observed by the higher part which was properly mine. As the separated form moved to the hall and into a room on the other side, the lower part found everything extremely familiar, a table in the centre of the room and an ash-tray upon it being particularly noted. But the higher part knew that these were not familiar at all, having no counterparts in my physical existence. The table and ash-tray were clearly and vividly seen, with a reality convincingly like that of the physical world, while the higher part was assessing the character of the state. Suddenly, but without abruptness, the room faded out both from view and spatially, as if the entity that was observing it became absorbed or withdrawn. For a moment there was an impression of blankness, and then gradually a more acceptable state, recognized as a character of space or unseen light, with the other entity no longer present, emerged into a definite perception. Physical wakefulness followed after two or three seconds.

[1756] (2 July 1948). I appeared, in separation, to be standing by a bed in a room where there were two other beds. Although the room was a strange one, from another point of view (as of another personality) it made a definitely familiar impression. The smoothness of the counterpane on the nearest bed was clearly discerned. From still another point of view I was conscious of the physical body in bed, as if separation had not occurred, while the tendency to separate was felt as a characteristic stress in the region of the solar-plexus. . . .

In the second of these experiences there were three personal consciousnesses, namely: *(i)* myself *A,* separated; *(ii)* the other entity and its memory, known as if myself *B,* except for the memory; *(iii)* myself *C,* still in bed.

I believe that what may be called "the real I" (individuality, soul) is found in its purity and perfection only in mystical states; that in lower states the personal life is still "me," but is composite through being fused with darkening and inwardly conflicting influences from which it cannot detach itself (and does not even appear to wish to do so, because of fixation). Hence a lower "me" has less ultimate validity than a higher or relatively pure one.

Tyrrell gives an interesting case that appears to offer clear support to a theory of this kind:

I was lying in bed cogitating about doing something extremely agreeable but entirely selfish. I was suddenly aware of being in two places at once. One "me" was still lying in bed looking as I normally do. The other "me" was standing at the foot of the bed, very still, very straight, dressed in white with a Madonna-like veil over the head. I was aware of the extreme whiteness of the clothes. We then had a spirited discussion. . . . I was definitely both "me's" and conscious in both places simultaneously. . . . Each me could see the other, with its expected exterior surroundings all the time. The white "me" felt sympathy, but contempt for the other "me." I may say that the white "me" won. . . .*

Consistently with the theory mentioned, and the illustrations just given of "blended consciousnesses," the following interpretation may be offered: the white "me" was a blend of a higher "me" and a more advanced "guardian" entity, participating in the same personal manifestation; and the other "me" was also a blend, in which foreign and selfish persuasions were appropriated (because of fixation) and so seemed to be thoughts and desires of "the real I." But the lack of harmony with "the real I" eventually resulted in those desires being rejected and the lower "me" disintegrated.

H. Inner Awakening through Recognition of "The Waters"

In transitional states between the physical state and a psychical one, or between a psychical state and a mystical

*G. N. M. Tyrrell, *The Personality of Man* (London: Penguin, 1946), p. 195.
There is a misprint here in the original Tyrrell text. "The white me 'felt' sympathy" should read, "The white 'me' felt *no* sympathy." —ED.

one, instead of the one space gradually or suddenly displacing the other, there is sometimes a kind of dissolution of the "world" into a condition of shapeless fluidity, when all we are conscious of is a substantial movement as of currents eddying and interweaving in space. Then, in due course, the new "world" and our new personal form are condensed out of "the waters." In these transitional states mental control is difficult, fantasy-influences sometimes take hold, and the separation may lapse into a dream of flying, floating, or swimming.

While the physical body is in a relaxed and partly dissociated state one may be able to discern a movement of currents eddying and interweaving within the form of the body. These seem to be almost material in character; they could easily be mistaken for physical sensations. But they have the evident effect of gradually releasing the body from fixation, and seem to be one of the means provided for bodily and spiritual refreshment during sleep. Then, when the currents have done their work of releasing us from fixation, one is ready to separate (or fall asleep). The following experience illustrates such a process, though communication of its psychological and spiritual nature through the medium of words is almost impossible:

[2049] (13 July 1951). In a vividly objective half-separation, the body was represented as lying down and caught in fixation. An operation proceeded from within to throw off the constraints. There was a vivid calling forth of spontaneous manipulative movements and purified will-activity against antagonistic forces. Presently the fixation appeared to be thrown off, so that a free form emerged.

After separation, the movement seems to continue, but by then the separated form has partly condensed, so that it may seem to be gently floating, in a more or less determinate form (as in many published experiences).*

If, during a floating or flying dream, recollection awakes

*For example, M. and C., p. 163: "a gentle rocking sensation"; p. 91: "I floated out of my body."

through memory or understanding of the condition, usually the next thing that happens (in my experience) is that one becomes aware of "the waters" as a fluctuating movement in inner space. The dream is then seen as fantasy, while "the waters" are objective. Recollection must then be enhanced so that further fixation (which might induce a fantasy-like separation) is removed, and the inner form condenses properly. Sometimes the separated form still seems to be flying; in which case it is usually best (in my opinion) to resolve to find the ground and walk normally. Then the state becomes more objective and rationally controllable. This is a common method of initiation, illustrated by the following four descriptions:

[2024] (18 March 1951). During a flying dream, reflection on the movement caused awareness of the inner currents and their gradual steadying. Upon the decision to adopt the motion of walking instead, my feet came to rest on the ground, the mental impression being definite and substantial. A dog like a setter was seen on the right, and I approached with a wish to fondle it. A return to the physical state quickly ensued, from some cause unknown.

[1021] (November 1940). In the course of a dream, while seeming to walk along a raised path, I became aware of flowing currents in space. Consciousness in separation followed, and objective perception of walking. The mind then became more recollected, so that there was a general view of sunlight, golden in quality. Buildings were around, and by a voluntary strengthening of recollection I gained some ability to bring these into clear perception, and see the bright sunlight on some of the walls. . . .

[1853] (1 October 1949). In a flying dream, reflection on the incongruous method of progress (by flapping the arms) caused wakefulness within, followed by a decision to cease that movement and observe things rationally. The separated form then appeared horizontal, on its back. Its relation to the physical body at that time was obscure, but it appeared to be at a higher level, above the bed, and in slight movement. It then lifted up gradually to a normal walking position. During that process stars in the night sky were distinctly seen above.

Proceeding to walk, I turned right, in at the gate of a house, the state now beginning to resemble dream, and the experience broke off.

[1268] (9 July 1942). I became aware of flying, in a state of separation. Studying the condition revealed a strange but vividly objective feeling of muscular action at the back of the shoulders, as if wings were being used. A beautiful panorama was seen below. . . .

DESCRIPTIONS SPECIALLY RELATING TO THE RETURN

After the foregoing full discussion of the process of separation, few of these descriptions will need further comment.

A. Gradual Approximation of Bodily Forms

[587] (8 January 1936). In a dream, after crossing a frozen rivulet, I proceeded to walk up rising ground covered with snow. As the path forked at a bush, I became conscious of the cool ease of the substance of the separated body. Then, by restraint of a temptation to become bodily excited, and by recollection of the familiar circumstances of separation, full inner wakefulness broke forth.

Instead of the snowy Winter, the scene was now glorious Spring. At the first sight of the sunlight and the fresh colours of the vegetation, being insecurely grounded, and swayed by the shock of surprise, I appeared to pass through the air, off the ground, with a kind of smooth bouncing motion; but by restraint of this tendency also, presently I began to walk steadily and to see more clearly.

The place resembled a small opening in a wood, or a corner of a park, not very much cultivated; for the grass was thick underfoot, and the colour a rich green. A few trees and bushes in flower were near at hand. There seemed to be small animals or birds on the grass a few yards in front, and these I understood to be embodiments of affection, from the feeling which entered the heart as I looked. But steadiness at the heart was not sufficiently developed in me, and as I looked, the animals changed to clumps of flowers, one being a small cluster of daffodils, clearly seen in their bright yellow colours. As this change occurred a bird flew up from the ground, rather like a dove, but with a lifeless appearance. Realization of my deficiency gave me a feeling of sorrow, with a touch of shame.

Continuing through the park, which now definitely took on the character of a wood, the way began to narrow, and the bushes and trees on either side began to close in. The trees around, and in front especially, then began to grow taller as I passed further on, and the light grew darker, with a quality of awe, as when evening approaches in a solitary wood (this darkening appearance always heralds a necessary return to the physical world).

Realizing that the physical world was exerting its call, I first made an unavailing (and foolish) attempt to pray for light to be continued, and then perforce yielded to Providence. Very smoothly and gently the inner form of consciousness became lifted off the ground, and equally gently inclined backwards until it appeared to rest horizontally about five or six feet above the ground. During this process, the inner space gradually melted away, at the same time as the space of a parallel world* began to appear, both spaces being recognizable at once. Next, as the parallel world became predominant, the (inward) body began to be lowered into coincidence with the physical body, whose position was now clearly discerned. At the same time, the light of the other world began to close in, a boundary having been formed between it and the apparent light of the physical world, visible from a duplicate state. Then, lastly, as the arms seemed to come into coincidence with their physical counterparts, there came a flooding of life-energy, with a powerful and bitter tingling, entering at the solar-plexus and spreading through the body. With this, the connection between the spaces was complete, and consciousness appeared again in the physical world.

[1387] (4 October 1944). At the end of a separation of moderate length, I was lifted up and smoothly carried backwards into gradual conjunction with the physical body. While moving into the horizontal position it was suggested to me that I should alter the orientation of the separated body, and see what happened. A partial turn, following the suggestion, was made to the right; but the separated body was compelled back again to the face-upwards position as it became more horizontal.

*By the "parallel world" I mean a space very close to, or like, physical space, but not necessarily a duplicate one.

One of the M. and C. cases (that of Dr. R. B. Hout) shows a return of rather similar kind:

. . . as the pull of the body became stronger and less easily governed, I suddenly stiffened in my astral form, assumed a position parallel to and immediately above the physical counterpart and dropped into it. The reassociation of the two vehicles occasioned a slight jolt . . . and I was back in the physical again (p. 120).

I have never myself observed any stiffening of the separated form, which is always perfectly relaxed.

By the "solar-plexus" I mean a centre of psychical sensation, often completely vivid and real, placed (so far as I can tell) about one or two inches above the navel, and perhaps two inches within the body.

B. Direct Fusion of Spaces

[422] (August 1934). At the conclusion of a short separation of fantasy type, not otherwise noted, I was resting on open ground in a rather bright light when the need for a return was recognized, the state being at that time relatively free from fantasy. I appeared to be brought back so that the conscious form came into coincidence with the physical form, but not so that physical space was finally confirmed. The bright light and open ground in the one space could be perceived, at the same time as the body appeared to be in bed in the other space. Moreover, by the exercise of a free choice and decision, the former space could be more and more confirmed, so that the latter faded away, and once again I appeared to lie on the open ground in a bright light. And again, by relaxing the intention, the space as of the bedroom could be gradually restored, while the other space faded away. In fact, the two spaces were held for a few seconds in perfect balance, both being as if present simultaneously, and twice the space of the open ground and bright light was voluntarily restored before a final confirmation of physical space was made.

[698] (25 April 1936). At the end of a varied separation during which I was walking on grassy ground I realised that a return was imminent. Kneeling down in resignation, I felt, at the same time (the two spaces being superposed or alternating spontaneously) the grassy

ground, and the feel of the sheets on the physical body. I compared carefully the two types of perception as regards vividness, reality and general spiritual quality, before the physical perceptions were allowed to supplant the inner ones.

Two experiences of this kind are described by Yram:

. . . without completely reincorporating myself, I found myself at the exact point of balance where the material sensitivity passes into the next body, or plane. By a mere act of will I found myself able to incline the balance towards one point or the other. As soon as I favoured the idea of projection . . . I began to feel lighter. . . . As soon as I brought my mind back to my physical body . . . I could feel the slight roughness of the sheets. . . . Taking my mind back towards the idea of projection. . . . I once more found myself in the state which I had just left, and began to enjoy the peace, the cool sweetness, and the inexpressible sense of well-being of this state (*Practical Astral Projection,* p. 49).

I hardly formed the idea that I wanted to return to my body when, immediately, I clearly felt the bed on which I was lying. . . . Did I wish to leave it? Like a flash all those feelings disappeared. I could see my body stretched out on the bed . . . (*op. cit.,* p. 74).

C. *"False Awakenings" of Two Kinds*

In the first kind of "false awakening" one believes one has made a proper return to the physical world, or has become properly awake in it after being asleep, only to discover after a few moments that it is really a duplicate state. In the second kind, one makes what appears to be a normal return to a dissociated state (which should duplicate the physical one), but finds the bedroom quite a strange one. One illustrative example of each kind is given:

[133] (December 1932). After a short separation in which difficulty in breathing was noticeable, I returned to the physical state (or so it appeared) and took deep breaths, glad to breathe again more freely. After a few moments, however, I noticed that the feeling as I breathed was not quite as in the physical world. In fact, coincidence of the spaces had not occurred, and I was still in a duplicate space.

On recognition of this, a proper coincidence followed.

[1131] (26 August 1940). Towards the end of a fantasy-separation I became aware of the necessity to return, and the state then became subject to a high degree of reflective control. The separated form began to rise in the air, and after an unavailing attempt had been made to prolong the separation, a view was presented of the ceiling above, seen as by looking up from a horizontal form. But there was a pattern on it, rather as if it were linoleum (unlike the ceiling in the physical bedroom). From that position the separated form was gradually let down into coincidence with the physical form, free watchfulness being maintained throughout. On looking round, as in physical space (but recognizably in a duplicate space), I noticed that the room was larger than the physical bedroom and quite different in the impression given by the furniture, windows, etc. I rose again from the bed by a voluntary movement, knowing the possibility of doing so in separation. My form was smaller and far lighter than the physical body; and full of a comforting joy in the freedom and acceptability of that form, expressive of the mind, I began spontaneously to dance, joying in the lightness and smooth beautiful movements of the limbs. A return followed without noticeable process.

A particularly striking "false awakening" is described in the "Manstead Case" (M. and C., p. 88):

Early in the afternoon I awoke to find myself walking through the hall which adjoined my bedroom. . . . I was half-way down the hall when I woke up. . . . "Of all things!" I said to myself, "I have been walking in my sleep! I surely will catch more cold." . . . I turned around and went back, and as I passed into my bedroom through the open door, I was shaken with amazement—there I was still lying in bed! . . . I was so real that I kept feeling myself to make sure that this was not a hallucination. . . . Then I remembered falling or gliding sideways, and struggling to get back into my body, which was like being put into a case. . . .

D. Lapse into Other Nonphysical Conditions

Besides lapsing into a state of simple dissociation preparatory to full coincidence of the bodies, a separation may lapse into *(a)* half-separation, *(b)* spatial-opening, *(c)* free separation, or *(d)* dream or fantasy-separation.

"False awakenings" come under category *(a),* and it is not necessary to give further examples. Only one case under category *(b)* is within my experience, and it is not necessary to quote this. An example of *(c)* is [841], already given, and of *(d),* [1202].

E. Return through Earth or Water

[800] (September 1937). In separation, I rose from the ground upon consciousness of the ability to do so, and floated past trees, the body remaining vertical. The comforting feeling of the warmth of the sun was felt in the limbs. Then the separated form was caused to sink back, descending into a darker state, so that there was a strange but vivid impression that it was sinking through the surface of the earth into a grave.

[900] (October 1939). After voluntarily descending to the ground in separation I felt clearly the touch of my feet on it, but almost at once seemed to descend further, so as to pass through the ground. As this happened, a stress of life-substance was felt in the breast, and I awoke in the physical world.

I do not regard these experiences as the result of fantasy. What I have called fantasy-constructs are the creation of subjective prepossessions, fixed ideas, or self-centered thinking, made habitual in this world and so sticking in the memory regardless of objective inner realities. Hence, in a separated state, they impose themselves on what is objective, as a kind of distortion. The experiences above, however, were recognized at the time as being a twofold manifestation—one, the "world" known in separation, the other, an objective and significant representation of the change, such as occurs in mystical states. Accordingly, there was no fear or distaste, only sorrow at one's state becoming lower and darker.

Such significant representations have been illustrated before, in the impression of a river [117], or of sandy ground [1923], between two spheres. The surface of the earth similarly represents a boundary between spheres of fixation and spheres of freedom, and human beings actually appear to sink or rise through it according as fixation takes hold or is gradually released. The apparent motion thus objectively represents the actual condition of the mind.

This being so, restoration of Obedience overcomes the sinking tendency, as in the following brief extract:

[1352] (5 March 1943). Towards the beginning of a long separation I began to sink downwards, so that I seemed to be half below the surface of the earth. On steadying the mind, through Obedience, I rose to the surface again (the separation then continued).

The following experience, illustrative of sinking through water, evidently involves a very considerable fantasy-element. It ends in an obvious mixture of (1) quasi-physical manifestations, (2) significant ideas, corresponding to the process, and (3) fantasy-constructs due to loss of self-command, and it illustrates the unfortunate results that may follow on a lapse from Obedience (which was hardly in evidence at all in this experience):

[2080] (24 November 1951). Towards the end of a vivid quasi-physical separation into a strange house, I tried to get out by ascending a small staircase. But the way up suddenly contracted, and realizing that fantasy-obstacles were being imposed I turned back again. The floor of the room towards the left began to take on the appearance of sloping away in darkness, and almost at once it was as if I were being drawn, or were gradually slipping, towards a rectangular pit or well of water placed there (the details were not discernible, but the significance of darkness, depth and water, was frighteningly strong). Involuntarily struck with fear at this situation, and having lost poise of mind, I called out for help, in an attitude of prayer. Suddenly there was the sound of someone hurrying down the stairs from above. A man like a coloured servant appeared, and with an anguished look on his face he tried to pull me back into the room. But by that time

I was far sunk down, my head almost level with the floor. There came the vivid sound of rushing water in my ears, and I awoke in the physical world. I had never forgotten that the experience was a separation. But understanding (from the head) is unable to save us from an unpleasant situation, without Obedience (from the heart).

F. Other Symbolic Returns

In this section I give brief references to a few published cases illustrating returns that may also be called symbolical, in a loose sense, but that are of types unfamiliar to me. These are all taken from the M. and C. collection.

(The Cole Case, p. 61). On my left there was a bright light, while on my right there was a dark tunnel of swirling shadows, into which, after I had said, "I will go back," I turned. There was a tiny light at the far end of this tunnel of shadows, and I struggled instinctively towards it, while shadows rushed past me. . . . It seemed a long time before I managed to reach the light at the end . . . then I was physically awake again.

(The Marks Case, p. 91). In a short time I floated over my physical body and sank down into it. I seemed to go in through the pores of the skin.

(The Sidney Case, p. 149). Immediately I found myself rushing back, down into my physical body . . . striking first the head, where I entered and went right through the full length of my physical body . . . with a violent shuddering sensation.

(The Rogers Case, p. 95). Then I felt something pulling me downward and when I hit my physical body I seemed to bounce. . . . Then to my amazement I turned around inside my body—revolved from head to foot.

(The Beth Case, p. 191). In each case . . . he approached and went back through a cleft in his head . . . exactly in the middle of the skull, and extending several centimetres forward from the back. . . . In his second interiorisation . . . instead of slipping in easily, he found he had to make three distinct pushes, before he could pass through the crevice into his physical body.

(The Manstead Case, p. 89). Then I remembered falling or gliding sideways, and struggling to get back into my body, which was like being put into a case.

(The Parker Case, p. 63). The strange sensation . . . as if a bag were being pulled down over my head and onward to my feet, came over me.

(The Annenkof Case, p. 200). I re-entered my body through my feet. [On another occasion.] I approached my body and tried to reenter it. . . . I· felt it absorbing me immediately, like a sheet of blotting paper, or as a sponge absorbs water.

(The Riggs Case, p. 79). I entered my body through my mouth.

These examples evidently illustrate effects of *mergence,* in some cases influenced by fantasy. For the separated form is in one space, and the physical body in another. It seems to me, however, that the mergence is not directly into physical space but into a duplicate or possibly more archetypal form of the physical body, convincingly felt to be the same. The actual physical body could not, in my view, be perceived by the nonphysical sense organs of the separated body.

After the mergence, a further slight jolt or abrupt change in the state of consciousness would as usual be required to convert the still dissociated state into the normal state of consciousness in the physical world. Light may be thrown on the underlying nature or causes of this "jolt" by experiences such as those coming under the next head, which is the last in this survey of methods of return.

G). Absorption of or in Other Personal Entities on Return

The two principal illustrations to be given under this head are taken from experiences of exceptional power and significance, not at all "symbolical," though difficult to describe in plain terms. It is as if one passes within the representation of the return, whatever it may be, to discover something of the subtle mechanism controlling it from a more "intelligible" level. The quotations must be brief and the discussion very cursory, lest the main issue be confused by the raising of perplexing questions concerning the projected body and the knowledge of other people in a nonphysical state.

In the one experience ([2421], 6 March 1954) I came face to face with an entity of "evil" tendency, but steadily objective control was maintained for fifteen seconds. A certain change occurring then, the influence was no longer kept entirely at bay, and

a momentary consciousness of a kind of paralysis because of that influence was followed almost at once by the remarkable effect as of a man-spirit entering into me and violently throwing my arms about in order to escape. I seemed to be hurled from that state back to the physical world, returning with a sharp jolt at the solar-plexus.

In this experience there were evidently four personal structures, each with its own kind of integration, and of thought, feeling and character-disposition: (1) that of the obsessing entity, studied for fifteen seconds, (2) that of my free consciousness, out of the body, fully recollected and in an acceptable form, (3) that of the "man-spirit," who was not really myself, and (4) that of the physical personality to which I returned, and which apparently included the entity (3) and perhaps others as well. When the "man-spirit" entered, there was an indubitable perception that it was other than myself, though intimately similar in some general way. Then, on the restoration of the physical personality, it was as if a blend of personal structures had occurred, thus making the physical personality composite and derivative (as, indeed, I always feel it to be, in relation to the purer recollected consciousness).

The other experience to be principally mentioned ([1224], 3 January 1942) was a long one in three distinct parts, the second part mystical, while the third was at a lower level but steadily objective. In the third part I approached a tall man, in a room where many people were about, and stood face to face with him for about five seconds. I became aware of an intention on his part to press closer, and this filled me with a certain amount of fear. Retaining control, I moved away to another part of the room; but presently, looking back, I saw the man approaching from behind. There then came the strange but very clear impression that he was part of myself (i.e., my outer or physical self), and that it was impossible for me, at that time, to keep myself (i.e., my true self) distinct. A deep sorrow at having to relinquish my purer nature afflicted me. For a moment or two, it seemed difficult to say who I was, since I had partly taken on the physical personality again, though still remaining to some extent in the purer recollected consciousness and form proper to me in that separated state. Then I awoke in the physical personality, with only an analytical or remembered knowledge of my purer self, like a free conscience within.

Some experiences showing a very similar phenomenon on return from *free separation* are described by Mrs. Willett.* Thus: "I can't remember who I am. I know I'm somebody and I'm all coming together, you know, and the bits don't fit" (p. 149). The state in which other *monads* are freely distinguished from the monad which is our true individual being, while nevertheless we remain mystically unified with them, is described by her in the following terms: "The room seemed full of unseen presences and of their blessing; it was as if barriers were swept away and I and they became one. I had no sense of personality in the unseen element—it was just there and utterly satisfying" (p. 181). *Personality,* it seems, is appropriate for the description of a constellation of monads, but not for the description of a single monad. This experience of Mrs. Willett's, incidentally, is one that I should classify as a *mystical liberation*—deeper than a *free separation,* but not sufficiently explicit to reveal the "intelligible" human form of the monad.

An experience of blending with another monad (or perhaps, rather, with a personality), so that the two are only just kept distinct, is testified to in Mrs. Willett's reference to "an intensely vivid impression of Fred's presence. I can only describe it (she says) by saying I felt myself so blending with him as almost to be becoming him" (p. 181).

All these types of experience, as well as (less clearly) most of the other cases of separation mentioned, thus point to a very great difference in structure between our free personal consciousness in a separated state, clear of fixation, and the normal state of our personality when we are immersed in this world. If the former be described as a *monad* which is the expression of our proper individuality, then these experiences (as Lord Balfour argued in the case of Mrs. Willett) exhibit the physical personality as a constellation or Platonic *Republic* of monads, of which only a certain "battle-array" is openly presented to the world.

Going into further details, it is evident that when that constellation is re-formed after separation, and we become conscious again in our physical personality, the other monads are no longer seen as separate. So the fluctuating thoughts, feelings, and intentions, in the midst of which we are, inevitably seem to be our own, obscure or vivid according to the closeness of the union between us and the monads in which these things are concentrated. But insofar as fixation is overcome, and the constellation begins to be freely analysed, we see the particular thoughts, feelings, and intentions as separate. And the monad which is properly our own then takes on the character of a conscience in command of the whole situation—like the philosopher-guardians in Plato's *Republic.*

The puzzling experiences, mentioned above, of simultaneous spaces and consciousnesses, now obtain an easy explanation on the ground that they are simultaneous *monadic* consciousnesses with which we, and probably others too, have blended temporarily, the release of fixation in the separated state having permitted a partial analysis.

From the point of view developed in this section—a view to which the evidence taken as a whole seems to lead strongly—the process of separation is essentially a simplification of the physical personality, by the sloughing-off of some or all of the improperly harmonized monads in it. Hence we arrive also at a reasonable explanation of the fact that those who have experienced separation almost invariably state or imply that their conscious life has thereby become *purer,* better harmonized, and more truly their own, even sometimes to the extent of really finding themselves alive at last after a physical life that in comparison seems like a dream or prison:

I must come back, you know. It's just like waking up in prison.*

For the first time I knew what it means to LIVE.†

*Balfour, *op. cit.,* p. 218.
†Muldoon and Carrington, p. 81.

13 | An Unusual
Out-of-the-Body Experience

LUCIAN LANDAU

I knew my wife, Eileen, for quite a number of years before we were married, and she frequently used to talk to me about her out-of-the-body experiences. These were of the usual kind, and on some occasions I was able to verify that something paranormal had, in fact, occurred. For example, she went to bed one afternoon, saying that she would see what our friend, who was on a holiday in Cornwall, was doing. When she woke up, she was able to give an accurate description of a rock plant, which our friend was photographing, the details of the surroundings, also of a gentleman who was with him. All this was subsequently confirmed, and, what was interesting, our friend was under the impression that a shadowy figure passed near him at the time.

At the beginning of September 1955, I was not very well. Much fuss was made about it, but a thorough medical examination failed to show any real trouble. Eileen, who was then living with her mother in Kent, spent several nights in my house, occupying the spare bedroom, which was opposite mine, across the landing, on the southwestern corner of the house. One morning she told me that she had come into my bedroom during the night (minus her physical body!) to check my pulse and respiration. I asked her to do this again the following night, this time trying to bring some object with her; I gave her my small diary, weighing thirty-eight grams.

That night we left the doors of both bedrooms open, as I could hardly expect a physical object to pass through solid wood. Before falling asleep, I asked myself to awake, should anything unusual occur in my room.

I woke up suddenly: it was dawn, and there was just about enough light coming in through the partly drawn curtains to enable one to read. At the point marked *A* (see Fig. 4) stood

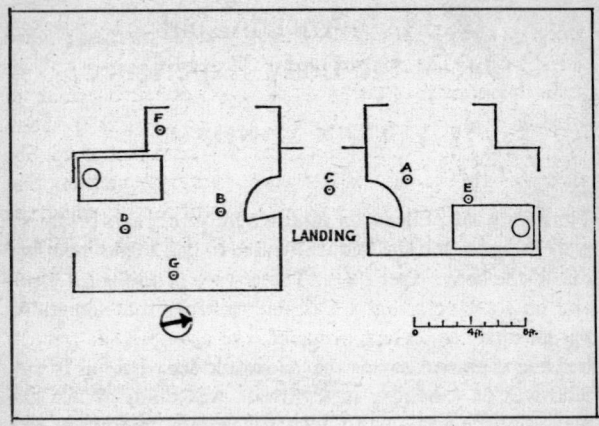

FIG. 4

the figure of Eileen, facing northwest, and looking straight
ahead toward the window. The figure was wearing a night-
dress, its face was extremely pale, almost white. The figure
was moving slowly backward toward the door, but it was
otherwise quite motionless; it was not walking. When the
figure, progressing at the rate of about one foot per five seconds, reached the position C, I got out of bed and followed.
I could then clearly see the moving figure, which was quite
opaque and looking like a living person, but for the extreme
pallor of the face, and at the same time the head of Eileen,
asleep in her bed, the bedclothes rising and falling as she
breathed. I followed the figure, which moved all the time
backward, looking straight ahead, but apparently not seeing
me. I kept my distance and ultimately stood in the door of
the spare bedroom, when the figure, now having reached the
position D, suddenly vanished. There was no visible effect on
Eileen, who did not stir, and whose rhythm of breathing
remained unchanged.

I moved quietly back to my room, and at E, on the floor,
found a rubber toy dog, which belonged to Eileen, and which

stood on a small chest of drawers in position marked *F* when I last saw it. The dog weighed 107.5 grams.

In the morning, after breakfast, I questioned Eileen about the diary. She said that she first went to the desk (position *G*) on which it was, and somehow could not pick it up. She then thought that it would be easier to carry something that belonged to her, and she decided on the rubber toy, which she managed to take with her to my room. It was a pity that I woke up some thirty seconds too late.

NOTE BY MRS. LANDAU

I remember getting out of bed (but do not recall exactly how), going over to my desk, and seeing the diary. As a child, I had been told never to handle other people's letters or diaries, so probably for this reason I did not want to touch this one. Instead, I lifted my rubber toy dog, and I remember taking it through the door, across the landing, to the other room, but do not remember actually *walking*. I did not find the dog heavy, or difficult to hold. I have no recollection of what I finally did with it. I remember seeing Lucian asleep and breathing normally. I felt very tired and wanted to go back to bed. Up to this moment my consciousness appeared to me normal, and so did my ability to see my surroundings, which also appeared normal to me. I do not remember anything about going backward to my room, or entering my bed.

(signed) EILEEN LANDAU

IV. CAN WE EXPLAIN THE OUT-OF-BODY EXPERIENCE?

Introduction:
Conceptual Models

D. SCOTT ROGO

Trying to find an explanation for the OBE is, in many respects, like trying to solve a crime. We have clues, but we don't know how complete they are. We have leads, but there is no telling how many may be false. We have more than enough witnesses, but we don't know how accurate their observations are, since their stories don't always match.

The OBE seems to be a composite phenomenon incorporating a large number of both psychological and parapsychological attributes. On one hand, the state is clearly psi-conducive, since ESP and PK (albeit less frequently) are commonly reported by-products of the experience. So the OBE, at face value, would appear to be a paranormal state. That is, the experience is itself a psychic phenomenon. But the OBE also resembles certain aberrant psychological phenomena such as autoscopy, depersonalization, ego-splitting, and so forth. One can only wonder whether the OBE is a blood relation to these purely psychological cognitive disorders.

This dual aspect of the OBE reminds me of a statement once made by the well-known author Arthur Koestler, when talking about his adventures with gurus in India. Koestler kept asking the Indians, "Is so-and-so a genuine or fraudulent wonder-worker?" After a great deal of experience, he realized that he was asking the wrong question. He shouldn't have been asking if a particular guru were genuine *or* fraudulent, he should have been asking, "How *much* genuine and how *much* fraudulent?" (Koestler, 1973). In the field of parapsychology, things usually aren't black and white. This is especially true of the OBE. Maybe we shouldn't be asking whether the phenomenon is parapsychological or psychological. Perhaps we should be asking, to paraphrase Koestler, "How *much* parapsychological and how *much* psychological?" The OBE might represent an interface between both disciplines.

There are three self-evident conceptual schemes by which we can explain (or explain away) the OBE. The first is what I call the "naïve psychological model." According to this theory, the OBE is a purely hallucinatory phenomenon, either psychological or neurophysiological in nature, which should be studied by psychiatrists rather than by parapsychologists. Freud, Rank, and Reed have all advanced such theories. Unfortunately, these models cannot explain the psi factors that we run into so often as we explore the OBE.

The second scheme is the "naïve parapsychological approach." This theory supposes that the OBE is the literal separation of the soul (or consciousness) from the body, which thereupon clothes itself in an apparitional body. Apparently we all possess this vehicle. This theory can explain a great deal of OBE phenomenology, but not all. For example, many people see no apparitional body while OBEing. Even Blue Harary does not usually see any parasomatic double while out-of-body, although he can conjure one up at will! Harary also oftentimes "sees" the physical world incorrectly with his alleged "astral" eyes. If an astral body (or whatever) were projected from his body into physical space during his OBEs, why should this type of confusion arise? So, accepting the naïve parapsychological model would be like claiming to have solved a crime, but for the simple fact that the prime suspect has a watertight alibi.

A third approach to the OBE would be to view the experience as a hybrid. In other words, we can view the OBE as an outcome of a series of psychological *and* parapsychological processes at work. We can call this approach the "psychopsychic model." These types of theories deserve a more concentrated appraisal than most writers on the OBE have usually given them.

One interesting approach to the OBE along these very lines comes to us from Dr. Jan Ehrenwald, a Czech-born, New York–based psychiatrist who has written several papers and two books on the interrelationship between parapsychology and abnormal psychology. Ehrenwald turned his eyes to the OBE in 1974 when he presented an essay, "Out-of-the-Body Experiences and the Denial of Death," in the *Journal of Nervous and Mental Disease* (Ehrenwald, 1974).

Ehrenwald is well aware of the fact that the OBE is a psi-conducive state, but he still feels that the experience is primarily a psychological manifestation which, for some as yet unknown reason, helps the experiencer use ESP and PK. (In other words, Ehrenwald does not believe that the OBE represents the physical release of the consciousness from the body, but argues that this aspect of the OBE is really only a hallucination.) To Ehrenwald, the OBE represents a means by which the experiencer proves immortality to himself by symbolically defying death (i.e., via a delusion of releasing the soul from the body). He begins his argument by pointing out that, stripped of its psi and esoteric overtones, the OBE is suspiciously similar to such disorders as depersonalization and distortion of body-image, which are often reported by people under stress and by psychotics. Thus, argues the psychiatrist, the OB journey is itself merely hallucinatory.

But why do so many normal people have OB hallucinations? As Ehrenwald explains, "OB experience . . . can be described as an attempt to dissociate one's self from the debilitated, mangled, perishable body, and in doing so, *denying* the reality or possibility of death." In support of this view, he points out that the "magical flight" to the "higher worlds" reported by shamans in primitive cultures are, so to speak, OB-type experiences in which the shaman demonstrates his mastery and defiance over death to himself and to his culture. Similarly, he continues, the mystical ecstasies reported by Christian ascetics (who often talk of being "taken out of themselves") serve a similar psychological function for these gifted individuals. The OBE reported by the average person is a like experience to that of the shaman and the mystic and therefore serves the same purpose.

Ehrenwald further supports his theory by pointing out that many habitual OBE-ers had their initial experiences when confronting death. Ingo Swann (1974), for example, had his first OBE while a small boy undergoing the trauma of a tonsillectomy. John Lilly (1972) had several OBE-like experiences after he had accidentally poisoned himself. In each case, Ehrenwald believes, the OBE was a psychological vehicle used to defy the threat of death. However, he does not deny that the subject may use ESP and PK to help substantiate the reality of his experiences. As he concludes:

On reviewing the whole spectrum of pertinent observations, ranging from frankly pathological cases of depersonalization in organic conditions, in neurotic patients, and in individuals subject to classical OB experiences, we see that they all have one thing in common: they exhibit a variegated set of defenses and rationalizations aimed at warding off anxiety originating from the breakdown of the body image, from the threatening split or disorganization of the ego, and, in the last analysis, from the fear of death. Viewed in this light, OB experiences, stripped of the stigma attached to their pathological variants, are expressions of man's perennial quest for immortality; they are faltering attempts to assert the reality and autonomous existence of the "soul"—a deliberate challenge to the threat of extinction, sometimes amounting to near suicidal experiments with the process of dying itself. Man may be unable to ward off his final encounter with Death, the Reaper. But he takes it upon himself to challenge his power and to score at least ephemeral victories over him. It is such short-lived victories which seem to carry with them sufficient rewards to make up for the self-imposed ordeals attending the ecstatic flight of the Siberian shaman, the Christian saint, or the OB exploits of a western subject. By the same token, such experiences may serve as rehearsals for or defenses against the threat of ego destruction or the terror of organic dissolution in cases of gross psychiatric pathology.

Ehrenwald's views are interesting but I think he makes an important error in logic. He seems to be arguing that: (1) since we can find a psychological reason or meaning for the OBE, then (2) this proves that the experience is itself of a purely psychological nature. This conclusion does not necessarily follow. For example, there are many psychological reasons why mankind believes in a life after death. But just the fact that man has a psychological need to believe in an afterlife does not automatically mean that we do not survive death. There are also many psychological reasons why we believe in ESP. All infants go through a stage in their young lives when they believe that their thoughts can directly affect the physical world. But, once again, just because these psychological factors exist does not mean that ESP does not. Likewise, just because the OBE may be a method of defying death does not mean that it is a purely symbolic and/or hallucinatory experience. One could easily accept Ehrenwald's model but still argue that the OBE actually is the physical detachment of the mind from the body. His model might readily explain the psychodynamics or meaning of the OBE, while not explaining its actual mechanics. In fact, I find the idea that the OBE is a "rehearsal" for death a very attractive theory. Yet I also believe that during the OBE something does "leave the body" and exists spacially apart from it. So Ehrenwald's scheme, while helping to make psychological sense of the OBE, does not necessarily explain the paranormal nature of the state. Nor does his model necessarily rule out the possibility that the OBE is a genuine projection of the mind away from the body.

Ehrenwald clearly sees the OBE as a symbolic journey. Let's proceed with this idea. If the OBE is a basically symbolic experience, we might expect to find that people having introspective mental journeys (such as reliving their births while under hypnosis, or fantasizing about death while under the influence of a psychoactive drug) would report experiences similar to the OBE.

This possibility was brought to my attention in 1975 when Dr. Stanislav Grof, a psychiatrist doing research on LSD at the Maryland Psychiatric Center, published his first book, *Realms of the Human Unconscious: Observations from LSD Research.* Grof is one of the world's leading authorities on LSD, and he reports in his book on several subjects who symbolically traveled back in time, relived their births, psychologically merged with other people, or had other transpersonal experiences while under LSD. Grof labels one class of phenomena he has often observed as "rebirth experiences"—experiences during which the LSD-intoxicated subject seems to relive his coming into the world. Such experiences, he points out, can manifest in either physical or symbolic modes.

Interestingly enough, some of Grof's subjects report experiences suspiciously similar to typical OB phenomenology. People having rebirth fantasies describe seeing golden lights, hearing roaring sounds about them, and traveling down narrow canals. These are all types of phenomena that people undergoing OBEs report quite regularly. Very often the OB experiencer will feel as though he is traveling through a tunnel or canal during his exit from the body (Crookall, 1964). Several of Dr. Crookall's correspondents reported seeing golden or silvery lights toward which they moved during their separation from the body. And many OBE-ers describe hearing roaring noises as they projected. These coincidences between the experiences reported by people having OBEs and by those undergoing rebirth experiences under LSD are striking. Could the OBE itself be a rebirth fantasy of sorts?

This idea is tantalizing, but it can be criticized on the same grounds as can Ehrenwald. Although the OBE may be a symbolic rebirth journey, this factor still does not necessarily mean that the experience is a hallucination. It could well be that the person undergoing the OBE uses memories of his physical birth as a *model* on which to base the phenomenology of his OBE.* After all, liberating the mind from the body is a "birth" in one sense. The "silver cord" might, if we accept this analogy, be a representation of the umbilical cord. So we might argue that the mind-body separation during the OBE is objectively real, but merely models itself after a psychological experience we all have had. This

---

*Grof has uncovered considerable evidence that people do retain memories of their births and can relive them during the LSD session. Several psychologists, notably Otto Rank (1929) and his followers, maintain that the birth experience drastically affects our psychological development. This would imply some sort of memory of the experience. Nandor Fodor (1949), a psychoanalyst, uncovered evidence that we retain some memory of our immediate prenatal lives.

might be similar to the way in which ESP vision sometimes models itself after physical sight, as Dr. Bender's research revealed. The birth fantasy would be a vehicle or prototype for the OBE, not an explanation for it. Of course, all this is purely speculation, but it does suggest why different people have different experiences while out-of-body. Each individual might base his experience on a different physical model, since no two births are exactly alike. We may each perceive our own births quite differently. (I am offering these theories as possibilities and do not wish to imply that I necessarily endorse them.)

The fact remains, though, that even if the OBE is a symbolic rebirth or death experience, it is also subjectively real to the person undergoing it. And—even more importantly—it seems to be an objectively real experience as well as illustrated by Mrs. Landau's experience recounted in chapter 13. So, as I suggested above, the OBE may have a psychological meaning behind it, but still be a psychic phenomenon. I should add, though, that I don't think we can afford to dismiss purely psychological explanations for the OBE out-of-hand. These theories might offer us clues about why the OBE occurs, who will experience it, and why different experiencers undergo dissimilar phenomenology. But purely psychological explanations should be viewed only as clues to solving the OB mystery, not as solutions in themselves.

Overly simplistic parapsychological explanations for the OBE also meet with certain difficulties. Take the views long promoted by Dr. Robert Crookall, for example (Crookall, 1969, 1970). He believes that we each possess an ultraphysical body that is enveloped in a "vehicle of vitality," a plasmic shell connecting the physical and parasomatic bodies. This vehicle of vitality is both a force and a substance and is the power which, when projected from the body, produces psychokinesis. Crookall argues that if the parasomatic body is dense (that is, carries the vehicle of vitality with it when it leaves the body), then the OBE-er will be able to affect the physical world by producing telekinetic effects and might be observed as an apparition. If, on the other hand, the parasomatic body projects without the vehicle of vitality (which would remain within the physical body), the projector would be invisible and would not be able to affect the physical world in any way.

In support of his model, Crookall has pointed out that people who undergo OBEs often describe a two-stage release. First, they find themselves out-of-the-body but enveloped by mist and fog, which clouds both vision and hearing. This mist then clears, leaving the OB percipient in full command of his sense modalities. (Sylvan Muldoon's first OBE, which was recounted in the introduction to Part III, is a perfect case in point.) Crookall has found this pattern reported in many unrelated cases (Crookall, 1970). Obviously this pattern is consistent with the notion that some sort of "density factor," which is subsequently shed, leaves the body with the parasomatic form. The basic reason for the OBE, suggests Crookall, is as a rehearsal for death. The British geologist believes that we survive death, and maintains that the OBE and the OBE body will be the vehicle by which we will survive.

Crookall's theories do help us understand a great many features of the OBE. But his model cannot explain many other aspects of the experience. It cannot explain why many people OB about as orbs or streaks of light, or as other vehicles that do not resemble bodies at all. Crookall's whole argument is based on the premise that we all possess a parasomatic body, which is projected during the OBE. This view is not backed up by the data we have accumulated. Also, one must ask, if the person undergoing the OBE is leaving his body and projecting into physical space, why should experienced projectors such as Oliver Fox and Blue Harary make faulty observations about what they "see?" Fox once saw all his living-room furniture rearranged. Yet this rearrangement did not physically exist. Crookall's schematics do not account for these paradoxes. So his views must be accepted as only a partial explanation for the OBE, not as a comprehensive one.

The following papers more fully discuss the various models

that have been proposed to account for the OBE. As you will see, none of these models offers more than a procrustean fit when it comes to explaining all aspects of the OBE. Thus the following papers present only the beginning of our journey to understand one of mankind's strangest experiences.

Part IV consists of two essays. The first is by David Black, who reviews several purely psychological explanations for the OBE. Although these explanations do not generally take into account the psychic aspects of the OBE, they are not without value. Black himself understands this, but also clearly understands that any theory which ignores these factors can never be a comprehensive one. His essay ends on a note of uncertainty about the ultimate cogency of much psychological thinking about the OBE. Dr. Charles Tart's paper, which follows, is a natural complement to Black's contribution. Just as Black objectively overviews psychological explanations for the OBE, Tart summarizes the most commonly promoted parapsychological explanations for the experience. And just as Black ends by pointing out the shortcomings of simplistic psychological thinking, Tart ultimately questions the legitimacy of most parapsychological approaches to the phenomenon as well. However, he does make a valiant attempt to find a more coherent explanation for the experience.

REFERENCES

Crookall, R. *The Mechanisms of Astral Projection.* Moradabad: Darshana International, 1969.

———. *More Astral Projections.* London: Aquarian Press, 1964.

———. *Out-of-the-Body Experiences: A Fourth Analysis.* New Hyde Park: University Books, 1970.

Ehrenwald, J. "Out-of-the-Body Experience and the Denial of Death." *Journal of Nervous and Mental Disease,* 159 (1974): 227–33.

Fodor, N. *The Search for the Beloved.* New York: Heritage, 1949.

Grof. S. *The Realms of the Human Unconscious.* New York: Viking, 1975.

Koestler, Arthur. "The Perversity of Physics." In A. Angoff, and B. Shapin (eds.), *Parapsychology and the Sciences.* New York: Parapsychology Foundation, 1974.

Lilly, John. *The Center of the Cyclone.* New York: Julian Press, 1972.

Rank, Otto. *The Trauma of Birth.* New York: Harcourt, Brace, 1929.

Swann, Ingo. *To Kiss Earth Good-bye.* New York: Hawthorn, 1975.

14 | Psychoanalytic and Psychophysiological Theories about the Out-of-Body Experience

DAVID BLACK

The first significant psychoanalytic study of the experience of encountering the self was written by Otto Rank, an Austrian psychologist who studied with Freud and who, for a short time, was considered heir to Freud's kingdom of mind, until he broke with Freud in the early 1920s. Rank focused on the individual and creative aspects of personality, preferring to emphasize the differences rather than the similarities among people, and developing what came to be considered a functional, as opposed to a diagnostic, approach to therapy.

In 1914 Rank published the first version of his study of the phenomenon, "Der Doppelgänger," an essay that he expanded into a book-length investigation and republished in 1925 as *Der Doppelgänger: Fine Psychoanalytische Studie.*

Rank regarded all forms of the double as related, and he included in his examination such diverse phenomena as the sensation of seeing the physical self from a point of view outside the body, *doppelgängers,* symbolic representations of the self, split personalities, and mythic twins—all of which he described as aspects of the same complex psychic dodge. Nevertheless, his general theory can be tentatively applied to the specific event defined as an out-of-the-body experience.

In his book, he explained: "The most prominent symptom of the forms which the double takes is a powerful consciousness of guilt which forces the hero no longer to accept the responsibility for certain actions of his ego, but to place it upon another ego, a double. . . ."

This self-created double, which has become responsible "for certain actions of [the] ego," is an ambivalent creature, a target for either narcissistic longings or self-hatred, depending upon the circumstances under which it is encountered. As examples of both the benign and malevolent forms this double can take, Rank quoted two accounts of a self's interaction with its mirrored image. The first was taken from a newspaper item describing a contemporary trial:

A young lord had locked up his beautiful, unfaithful sweetheart for eight days' punishment in a room whose walls consisted of panes of plate glass. . . . In the course of the days and nights which the young girl spent partly awake, she felt such a horror of the ever-recurrent image of her own face that her reason began to be confused. She continually attempted to avoid the reflection; yet from all sides her own image grinned and smiled at her. One morning, the old serving-woman was called in by a terrible rumpus: Miss R. was striking the reflecting walls with both fists: fragments were flying around and into her face. . . . She kept on smashing, with only the purpose of no longer seeing the image of which she had conceived such a horror.

The second account, quoted from a historian, Edward Fuchs, describes how mirrors in "places of amorous activity" have been used to heighten eroticism:

She was surprised by the marvel of seeing, without moving, her charming person in a thousand different ways. Her likeness was multiplied by the mirrors—thanks to an ingenious arrangement of the candles—and offered her a new spectacle, from which she was unable to avert her gaze.

These same reactions to the self's mirrored double are occasionally reported in accounts of out-of-the-body experiences, although self-love is more often described than self-loathing. In Yram's occult classic, *Practical Astral Projection*, a do-it-yourself handbook in which out-of-the-body experiences are interpreted as flights of an "astral" self from the flesh, the author struck a balance between the autoerotic and the autophobic:

During another exercise . . . I became aware of myself by a definite slowing down of the breath, followed by the sensation of trying to squeeze through a narrow space. Then I felt more free and was no longer cramped. This time the room seemed rather dark. I contemplated without enthusiasm my physical body, whose shape showed through the bedcovers. I touched it; it seemed soft. I kissed myself and came away with the feeling of having kissed someone who had only been dead a short time.

Yram's reaction to himself, a flirtation that trembled on the edge of an autoerotic necrophilia, betrayed a fascination with the self and with death which is not uncommon to those who meet themselves or their doubles. Referring to Oscar Wilde's novel, *The Picture of Dorian Gray,* Rank linked these two fascinations: "One motif which reveals a certain connection between the fear of death and the narcissistic attitude is the wish to remain forever young."

And the wish to remain forever young generates an idealized image of the self, a soul which in most cultures is conceived of as being eternally youthful, uncorrupted by time. "The thought of death is rendered supportable by assuring oneself of a second life, after this one, as a double."

According to Rank, then, the out-of-the-body self, like a personalized secular Christ, is both a scapegoat, created to take responsibility for actions which the individual can no longer accept, and a soul-double, which assures the individual of a continuation of being after death. When the two theories are fused, Rank's argument forms a benign circle: the "powerful consciousness of guilt which forces the hero no longer to accept the responsibility for certain actions of his ego" becomes a universal guilt born of the realization that the self will someday die; and the specific action of the ego, which the self attempts to avoid responsibility for, is the ultimate action, the collaboration of each of us in our own inevitable death.

Half a decade after Rank published the first version of "Der Doppelgänger," Sigmund Freud touched on the experience of seeing the self, in his essay "The 'Uncanny.' " He began by describing an experience he had while traveling in a sleeping car on a train. The train jolted, and Freud mistook his own reflection in the mirror on the swinging door to the small washroom for a stranger gliding into his own compartment, a stranger whose looks he did not like at all.

Like Rank, Freud classified all the different experiences of encountering the self together, assuming that the experiences (all subjective) had a common root. And he presented the phenomena as examples of the uncanny, which occurs "either when repressed infantile complexes have been revived by some impression, or when the primitive beliefs we have surmounted seem once more to be confirmed."

When coincidence appears meaningful, for instance, it seems uncanny because it hints at the efficacy of sympathetic magic:

As soon as something actually happens in our lives which seems to support the old, discarded beliefs, we get a feeling of the uncanny; it is as though we were making a judgment something like this: "So, after all, it is true that one can kill a person by merely desiring his death!" or, "Then the dead do continue to live and appear before our eyes on the scene of their former activities!", and so on.

If an out-of-the-body experience seems uncanny, it is because the conviction that one can separate his consciousness from his body may be a "primitive belief"—either true or false—which "we have surmounted" and which seems "once more to be confirmed."

The uncanny, however, is only the feeling—both familiar and unfamiliar at the same time—which surrounds an experience, not the experience itself. When analyzing the sensation of meeting the self, stripped of its uncanny aura, Freud first tipped his hat to Rank, describing the creation of the double as a ploy to frustrate the annihilation of the ego that comes with death, an act prompted by "primary narcissism."

But Freud followed this thought further, witnessing the transformation the double undergoes in the developing personality:

The idea of the "double" does not necessarily disappear with the passing of the primary narcissism, for it can receive fresh meaning from the later stages of development of the ego. A special faculty is slowly formed there, able to oppose the rest of the ego, with the function of observing and criticising the self and exercising a censorship within the mind, and this we become aware of as our "conscience". . . .

The fact that a faculty of this kind exists, which is able to treat the rest of the ego like an object . . . renders it possible to invest the old idea of a "double" with a new meaning and to ascribe many things to it . . . all those unfulfilled but possible futures to which we still like to cling in phantasy, all those strivings of the ego which adverse external circumstances have crushed. . . .

The out-of-the-body self, then, under Freudian analysis, becomes a sensible projection of the conscience, which is both a self-censor who demands autonomy in order to accomplish its work and a focus for "all those unfulfilled but possible futures to which we still like to cling in phantasy. . . ." The out-of-the-body adept is only someone who is compensating for the unfulfilled aspects of his life in reality by creating a second life in a fantasy which he can control: Blue Harary, a withdrawn, friendless child, inhabits an out-of-the-body universe that he shares with phantom friends; Tart's Mr. X, a worldly businessman, takes refuge in an out-of-the-body universe in which he engages in extravagantly spiritual exercises.

If evidence of paranormal abilities were ignored, Freud's theory could rationalize some out-of-the-body episodes. Even if that evidence were not ignored, the theory could form a basis for understanding the type of narcissistic or frustrated personality most open to this particular kind of psychic phenomenon.

Unlike Rank and Freud, C. G. Jung dealt with the out-of-the-body experience directly, accepting it as a unique phenomenon in which consciousness appears to separate from the physical body. His responsiveness to the concept was partly a result of a personal episode.

In his autobiography, *Memories, Dreams, Reflections,* Jung described an experience he had early in 1944, when he broke his foot and, while in "a dream or an ecstasy," felt as though his consciousness had extended itself outside of his body into space, where he looked down at the blue earth. As he turned his attention away from the planet, he perceived in space "a short distance away . . . a tremendous dark block of stone, like a meteorite," which had an entrance that led into its hollow interior.

To the right of the entrance, a black Hindu sat silently in lotus posture upon a stone bench. . . . Innumerable tiny niches, each with a saucer-shaped concavity filled with coconut oil and small burning wicks, surrounded the door. . . .

As I approached the steps leading up to the entrance . . . I had the feeling that everything was being sloughed away . . . the whole phantasmagoria of earthly existence . . . fell away or was stripped from me. . . . I had the certainty that I was about to meet the people who knew the answer . . . about what had been before and what would come after. . . .

But, like a scene in a serialized adventure movie, the episode ended with a cliff-hanger. Jung's doctor called him back to earth, and Jung "profoundly disappointed . . . thought, Now, I must return to the 'box system' again."

While Jung was unconscious, or in an altered state of consciousness, his nurse noticed that he was "surrounded by a bright glow," "which was a phenomenon she had sometimes observed in the dying."

His near-death experience was similar to both the deathbed visions that Karlis Osis had studied* and to the out-of-the-body states reported by Blue Harary and Ingo Swann: he perceived as though his out-of-the-body consciousness were a disembodied ego; he encountered intelligent presences in his out-of-the-body world; and he floated, if not to the constellation Sagittarius, at least into earth orbit.

Although the event was fantastic, Jung was convinced it

---

*Dr. Osis has studied the visions and elations sometimes reported by people on the verge of death. See his monograph, *Deathbed Observations by Physicians and Nurses* (New York: Parapsychology Foundation, 1961).—ED.

was not a fantasy. In talking about both his out-of-the-body experience and certain subsequent visions, he categorized them as being "utterly real" and explained them as moments when the self is fulfilled, when a person completes a process of psychic growth, when one accidentally stumbles into the eternal.

"The objectivity which I experienced . . . in the visions is part of a completed individuation," Jung said. "It signifies detachment from valuations and from what we call emotional ties."

Everything that ties a person to an earthbound ego, especially affects, are in part products of our projections, and "it is essential to withdraw these projections in order to attain to oneself and to objectivity." The process of becoming more and more oneself is, Jung suggests, in some way equal to the process of perceiving the world with complete objectivity, unhampered by emotional ties. "Objective cognition lies hidden behind the attraction of the emotional relationship; it seems to be the central secret."

Since the world is colored by the way we feel about it, to experience "objective cognition" would be equivalent to seeing reality without any illusions, from the point of view of a disinterested god. To achieve such a passionless perspective, one must continually "withdraw projections." But as old illusions and misconceptions about the world are destroyed, new illusions and misconceptions may take their place. The meteorite temple, the Hindu, the eternal company which Jung expected to meet in the belly of the huge dark block may have been a new phantasmagoria, created from Jung's imagination to replace the old "phantasmagoria of earthly existence"—an illusory reality as much a product of projections as the world Jung left on earth.

Jung's out-of-the-body experience could have been real, but all the stage sets, all the props that furnished the experience could have been illusions. Had Jung pushed further and further toward "the central secret," destroying one set of illusions after another, he may have found that, to some extent, all reality is a product of our projections, and objective cognition, if it were possible to attain, would be an awful void, an absence, a world without form.

Jung described this state outside space and time as "transpsychic reality," and he identified it as the condition in which paranormal events occurred. In a letter written in May of 1960, which Aniela Jaffé quoted in her book, *From the Life and Work of C. G. Jung,* Jung explained:

The comparative rarity of such phenomena suggests at all events that the forms of existence inside and outside time are so sharply divided that crossing this boundary presents the greatest difficulties. But this does not exclude the possibility that there is an existence outside time which runs parallel with existence inside time. Yes, we ourselves may simultaneously exist in both worlds, and occasionally we do have intimations of a twofold existence. But what is outside time is, according to our understanding, outside change. It possesses relative eternity.

Jung's model leads to a theory that during an out-of-the-body experience one perceives both this reality and "transpsychic reality" from the viewpoint of the second component of our "twofold existence." But the "relatively" eternal is outside the scope of scientific analysis, so any investigation of the paranormal must limit itself to observations from this side of the boundary separating "existence inside and outside time." In his essay "Synchronicity: An Acausal Connecting Principle," which was published in 1952 and revised and translated into English in 1955, Jung attempted to explain the out-of-the-body phenomenon from the standpoint of an observer inside time, using a theory that would not violate any of the laws of a time-bound universe.

He described a near-death experience in which a woman, unconscious and bleeding extensively as a result of a difficult birth, accurately perceived herself, the hospital room she was in, the doctor, the nurse, and her relatives, as though her consciousness had fixed itself at a point in the ceiling and was looking down at the activity around her bed.

Jung dismissed the idea that she was actually semiconscious and hysterically fantasizing a dissociated awareness.

Accepting the phenomenon as a real event, Jung suggested that "during a coma the sympathetic [nervous] system is not paralyzed and could therefore be considered as a possible carrier of psychic functions."

This theory, while attractively rationalistic, fails to explain why the sympathetic nervous system would seem to organize sensory information from a point outside the body as though the "eyes were in the ceiling."

A year after Jung first published his essay on synchronicity, Caro W. Lippman published "Hallucinations of Physical Duality in Migraine" in the *Journal of Nervous and Mental Diseases* (volume 117). In this article, Lippman indicated that the "sensation of physical duality, during which such mental qualities as observation, judgment, perception, etc., are transferred to 'the other,' or 'second body' . . . usually lasts for a few seconds, coming and going before, during, or after" the migraine. Sometimes, he said, it can occur days before the attack; other times the hallucination can appear among those he called *migrainoids,* "the sons and daughters of parents who suffer from classic migraine headaches."

Although Lippman drew no conclusions, by merely offering evidence of a relationship between migraines and out-of-the-body sensations, he hinted that both phenomena had related organic causes.

In "The Double: Its Psychopathology and Psychophysiology," an article written by John Todd and Kenneth Dewhurst and published in the *Journal of Nervous and Mental Diseases* (1955, volume 122), the authors offered a stew of theories, drawn from Rank, Freud, Jung, and neurology. They suggested that autoscopy could be a result of narcissism; extraordinary powers of visualization; archetypal thinking (conceptualizing in symbols drawn not from the personal, but from the collective unconscious); and "irritative lesions in the somatognostic areas of the brain," those sections of the brain which govern everything from the primary sensations like pain, heat, and pressure to self-image, general body-sense, and specific awareness of the body in relationship to the rest of the world—an assumption that would not necessarily contradict Lippman's conception of the connection between autoscopy and migraine.

N. Lukianowicz (in "Autoscopic Phenomena," an article published in the August 1958, issue of the *A.M.A. Archives of Neurology and Psychiatry,* volume 80, number 2), noted that autoscopy appeared related not only to migraines but also to epilepsy. He made a distinction between symptomatic (organically caused) and idiopathic (psychogenically caused) autoscopy, interpreting the first type as a result of "a known organic causation," possibly "some irritating process in the temporoparietal lobes," and the second type as a result of "a compensatory or a wish-fulfilling mechanism." He also related autoscopy to

such parahallucinatory phenomena as imaginary companions, eidetic [vivid and unreal] images, self-appearances, clairvoyance, hypnagogic imagery, and some "anatomically incomplete" body image disturbances, such as phantom limb and the group of delusional reduplication of parts of the body.

In his article on autoscopy in *Tōhoku Psychologica Folia* (1960), Serio Kitamura judged the phenomenon to be a hallucination during which the body is usually imagined as shorter than it really is if the subject has his eyes open and as larger than it really is if the subject is blind.

Although the connection between autoscopy and migraine was supported by my research—many of the people I talked with who experienced out-of-the-body sensations also suffered from migraine—neither that observation nor any of the other psychophysiological observations or theories explained away the evidence of paranormal powers that are often manifest in out-of-the-body episodes; and since in each of these discussions the phenomenon was assumed to be something other than what it was experienced to be, these traditional interpretations are best accepted as metaphors, useful fictions. They can help us understand the psychophysiological conditions that are likely to produce out-of-the-body experiences, just as the theories of Rank, Freud, and Jung can help us understand the psychological conditions under which the phenomenon can occur.

One of the more common psychological and psychophysiological conditions that can trigger the out-of-the-body experience is the near-death state, brought on either by an accident, as in the case of Jung, or in the normal course of a fatal illness. In 1970 Dr. Russell Noyes, Jr., a University of Iowa psychiatrist, started collecting descriptions of near-death episodes with the intention of putting together a map of the moment of dying. While gathering material, he kept coming across accounts in which people reported the feeling that their consciousness had left their physical body, descriptions that greatly interested him.

"I'm a pretty straight sort of fellow as you can see," Noyes said. "I'd never really ventured off into the parapsychological, and this particular thing with the mystical dying experience is a kind of far-out thing for me."

Dwelling on death can have the same effect on a nervous system as learning not to blink while sticking a contact lens into an eye, and Noyes displayed that fixed openness which invited trust and discouraged familiarity. He spoke hesitantly about his work, aware that he had intruded on a field in which it is impossible to gather altogether trustworthy data because it is hard for people to discuss near-death experiences without skidding into speculation on death. Death can only be perceived by its reflection in life, as though it were a curled hair which, floating invisibly on the brightly lit surface of tub water, casts a shadow on the enameled tub bottom.

Ever since he was a boy in Bloomington, Indiana, Noyes had been curious about death from a nonmystical point of view. He cultivated this detached passion at DePauw University, at Indiana University Medical School, and at Philadelphia General Hospital, where he interned.

"There was a young man who had a small tumor in his chest," Noyes said. "We did surgery and found that it was inoperable cancer. I felt that when he awoke I should inform him of what we had found, but I discovered myself feeling quite fearful in confronting him. In fact, I told him nothing. Surprisingly enough, he asked me nothing. We never spoke about what was the most obvious thing."

That experience focused his interest in death and dying. He began digging into the literature on the subject and discovered that dying was often reported as a subjectively pleasant experience during which the conscious mind seemed dissociated from the failing body.

"I also began looking for cases among the people who came to me here at the University," said Noyes.

One twenty-five-year-old racing-car driver, who was involved in two potentially fatal accidents in the late spring and early summer of 1971, described for Noyes a collision on a racetrack in Knoxville, Iowa, which flipped his super-modified sprint car thirty feet in the air:

Everything was in slow motion, and it seemed to me like I was a player on a stage. I could see myself tumbling over and over in the car. It was as though I sat in the stands and saw it all happen. . . . I saw flashes of colors. I distinctly remember blues, greens, and yellows. Everything was so strange. . . . I remember being upside down and looking backwards. And I saw the man who won the race pass under me. The guy looked up, and I remember that he had an amazed look on his face.

After reading of Noyes's work, a seventy-nine-year-old woman contacted him about a near-drowning experience she'd had when she was thirteen during a vacation at an artificial lake in Paris, Illinois. She wrote:

The area skirting the shore was shallow, but dropped quickly into a deep channel. I didn't know how to swim. . . . Suddenly one of the group slipped into the channel. As I reached for her, I slipped into the channel myself. My head was under water. Feeling her long hair, I caught ahold of it and pulled. I knew the shallow water was only a step or two away, but I could not find it immediately. At that moment I felt no fear. I had no appreciation of the urgent crisis. It was all so instantaneous. I knew death was imminent. At that point a series of clear pictures appeared before me. I recognized them as the complete replaying of the events in my life in proper sequence. They appeared in a flash. Each was framed and distinct.

In this account, as in many others that Noyes gathered, it is hard to separate the sensation of actually being outside the body and perceiving a life-review from the sensation of having the life-review flash through one's imagination. This discrepancy could be due to differing interpretations of a single experience: someone who is open to paranormal belief may feel he has actually left his body even if he hasn't; someone who is closed to paranormal belief may feel out-of-the-body sensations are merely subjective fantasies even if they aren't. Or there may be two distinct experiences: one normal and subjective, in which someone has the sensation of reliving past experiences; the other paranormal and objective, in which someone, ripped from his physical body and existing temporarily outside of our traditional concepts of time and space, actually perceives his past spread out for him as though "on a stage."

Noyes did not differentiate between the two interpretations. Any feeling of a consciousness dissociated from the physical body, according to him, was a result of an altered state of awareness, which could be triggered by drugs, sensory deprivation, or exhaustion as well as near-death episodes.

"I think they're experiencing a different level of consciousness," Noyes said about people who report out-of-the-body sensations. "Now what interpretation to place on that is something I can't say. One day I went to see a patient. She had a serious physical illness. She was delirious. I asked her what date it was and where she was. She said, 'I'm half in heaven and half on earth.' There was a lustrous look in her eyes, and she had a rapturous smile. She looked far off as though she was having grand visions and was in ecstasy. I asked her what it was like up there, naturally. And I was disappointed. She said, 'There's a lot of people, and there's a lot of work to do.' I said I thought it sounded just like it was down here.

"I like to look at this kind of experience as regression.

When a person regresses, there is a reversion to more child-like ways of behaving, and there's a conservation of energy involved. Anyone who gets sick regresses. His sphere of interest shrinks. He takes less responsibility for things about him. He depends more on others. He's less autonomous. His energy is conserved. Now, if this process were to move rapidly to some kind of completion, one might think that there would be some sort of discharge of energy. It seems to me that most of us have quite an involvement in our future, and if you deprive a person of that, there'd be really a tremendous redirection of that energy."

Noyes stopped short of explaining precisely how or why this redirection of energy would elicit the sensations of being outside-the-body, but he implied that it would be through perfectly normal means. One didn't have to abandon Western culture's generally accepted version of the world to account for it. Because Noyes avoided any consideration of evidence for paranormal phenomena associated with the dissociation of consciousness from the physical body, his theory—like other traditional psychoanalytic and psychophysiological speculation—was incomplete.

If the out-of-the-body phenomenon is real, and if it is a paranormal event, any analysis limited to this side of the boundary separating what Jung called "existence inside and outside time" can only be wanting. It may be impossible to formulate what Rosalind Heywood called "the right questions" within our familiar sciences. To track down the phenomenon it may be necessary to deal with the world outside time and to entertain, at least temporarily, more esoteric theories than those to be found in everyday reality.

REFERENCES

Freud, Sigmund. *Studies in Parapsychology.* New York: Collier Books, 1963

Heywood, Rosalind. "Attitudes to Death in the Light of Dreams and Other 'Out-of-the-Body' Experiences." In

A. Toynbee (ed.), *Man's Concern with Death.* New York: McGraw-Hill, 1968.

Jaffé, Aniela. *From the Life and Work of C. G. Jung.* New York: Harper Colophon Book, 1971.

Jung, C. G. *Memories, Dreams, Reflections.* New York: Vintage, 1963.

Lippman, Caro. "Hallucinations of Physical Duality in Migraine." *Journal of Nervous and Mental Diseases* 117 (1953).

Lukianowicz, N. "Autoscopic Phenomena." *American Medical Assoc. Arch. of Neurology and Psychology,* 80 (1958).

Noyes, Russell. "The Art of Dying." *Perspectives in Biology and Medicine,* Spring 1971.

———. "Dying and Mystical Consciousness." *Journal of Thantology* (Jan./Feb. 1971).

———. "The Experience of Dying." *Psychiatry* 35 (1972).

Rank, Otto. *The Double: A Psychoanalytic Study.* Chapel Hill: University of North Carolina Press, 1971.

Yram. *Practical Astral Projection.* London: Rider, n.d.

15 | Paranormal Theories about the Out-of-Body Experience

CHARLES T. TART

Many investigators have attempted to find a theory that would account for OBEs. Such theorizing is in its infancy, since we have very little solid, factual information about the experience, but I will sketch the three major theories that have been proposed so far, suggest a new approach to OBEs, and add one theory of my own that complements the other theories.

THE INDEPENDENT-SOUL EXPLANATION

The "natural" explanation that almost all people who have the experience subscribe to and that has been formally proposed by some investigators is, in effect, that there is no need to explain it: it is just what it seems to be. Man has a nonphysical soul of some sort that is capable, under certain conditions, of leaving the physical body. This soul, as manifested in what we call the second body, is the seat of consciousness. While it is like an ordinary physical body in some ways, it is not subject to most of the physical laws of space and time and so is able to travel about at will.

The main objection that has been raised to this theory hinges on the observation that in many cases the OB experiencer finds not only that he has a second body but that it is fully clothed in familiar clothing, such as the pajamas that he wore to bed. Many people are willing to believe that a human being has a soul—but his pajamas? To account for clothing and various nonphysical objects encountered in OBEs by ascribing a soul to essentially everything makes the idea of a soul so diluted in general that it does not really "explain" anything.

There is another major disadvantage of the independent-soul explanation: *soul* is not simply a descriptive term but one that has all sorts of explicit and implicit connotations for us because of our culture's religious beliefs. Even though a person may have had no formal religious training or may have consciously rejected his early training, such an emotionally potent concept as soul can have strong effects on us at a subconscious level. Since a prime requirement of scientific investigation is precise description and clear communication, a word like *soul* is difficult to deal with scientifically because of the deep, hidden reactions it may evoke in the human practitioners of science.

THE HALLUCINATION-PLUS-PSI EXPLANATION

Those who find the idea of a nonmaterial soul unproved or unacceptable explain OBEs as hallucinatory experiences of some sort—for example, a lucid dream, the kind in which one knows that one is dreaming (Stewart, 1972; van Eeden, 1913). That is, it is a (lucid) *dream* in the sense that no *thing* leaves the physical body and goes to another location. For those cases of OBEs in which veridical information about distant events is obtained, it is postulated that ESP, which is well proved, works on a nonconscious level, and this information is used by the subconscious mind to arrange the hallucinatory or dream scene so that it corresponds to the reality scene.

The problem with this kind of explanation is that it is too general. Since we do not have any idea about what the limits of ESP are, we can use this type of explanation to explain anything in those terms. For instance, it may not be true that you are *actually* reading this book at the moment: you may be having a hallucination in an altered state of consciousness that, by the operation of subconscious clairvoyance, corresponds perfectly to the experience you would have from actually reading this book, so you will never be able to tell the difference.

Until we know some actual limits of ESP, it is difficult to know how far to extend this theory. It does have the advantage, however, of accounting for the pajamas of the second body very well. They are just as "real" or just as "unreal" as the second body itself.

THE MENTALLY-MANIPULATABLE-STATE EXPLANATION

The problem of where the pajamas come from has led to a third class of theory, which postulates that there is indeed a second body in some real, albeit nonphysical, sense. However, the realm or space of the universe in which this second body operates is conceived of as being easily changeable or manipulatable by the conscious and nonconscious thoughts and desires of the person whose second body is in that space. Since we ordinarily think of ourselves as clothed, and this is a totally automatic and deeply ingrained habit, when having an OBE, the stuff (sometimes called the *psychic ether*) of that space is molded into the clothing we normally picture ourselves as having. Thus, this theory can account for clothing and other nonphysical objects without attributing some kind of souls to them.

The major problem with the manipulatable-state explanation is that we have little independent evidence for the psychic ether or something similar, so we are explaining one unknown by invoking another unknown.

Note that the independent-soul explanation and the manipulatable-state explanation of OBEs can both include the fact that other kinds of ESP, such as telepathy, clairvoyance, or precognition, can also occur in conjunction with OBEs.

We may not have to decide which of these theories is right in some ultimate sense but, rather, which theory applies to which particular case. I have emphasized what we might call "classical" OBEs in this chapter, where the experiencer feels totally at a distant spatial location, while feeling fully conscious and totally disconnected from his or her physical body. This is the sort of case that fits the independent-soul theory well. But there are cases that have been called OBEs in which the experiencer vividly images (or hallucinates) what it would feel like to be at the distant location but retains some awareness of his or her physical body and surroundings. This fits the hallucination-plus-psi theory much better. These latter kinds of cases might be better called *mental projections,* to use an old term, or *visualized* OBEs. Ingo Swann's OBEs have some qualities of the latter type of mental projection, while Miss Z's and Monroe's are classical OBEs.

Future research will have to begin making these and similar distinctions in order to refine our understanding of OBE phenomena; at present we do not know enough scientifically to make good distinctions.

THE ALTERED-STATES-OF-CONSCIOUSNESS APPROACH

In thinking about these explanations, we approach the problem from our normal state of consciousness; that is, our biological computer, our brain or mind, is programmed with all sorts of commonplace assumptions that make the problem of explaining OBEs take the particular form that it does. Elsewhere (Tart, 1972), I have argued that we need to develop what I have called *state-specific sciences;* that is, certain kinds of phenomena occurring in altered states of consciousness should be investigated *in* those states of consciousness, and explanations and theories developed in those states and tested there. This would involve an unusual extension of scientific method but still be in accord with the basic principles of science. I have not developed this idea in any detail with respect to OBEs, but I offer it here in this very brief form just to remind us of the many hidden assumptions characteristic of our ordinary state of consciousness that bias us in even attempting to explain OBEs. I have recently examined some of these assumptions elsewhere. (Tart, 1974).

THE INTERACTION EXPLANATION

From my general knowledge of parapsychological phenomena I have no doubt that basic extrasensory phenomena (telepathy, clairvoyance, precognition) do exist, as does PK. Since these phenomena are completely inexplicable with our current knowledge of the physical universe, they indicate that our current physical picture of the universe is quite incomplete. The area that our physical, scientific world-view leaves out is the whole area we might call "mind." From my psychological, as well as parapsychological, knowledge—and particularly the developing science of transpersonal psychology, which deals with man's spiritual potentials—I suspect that mind does indeed constitute some kind of space or energy that exists, in some sense, independently of physical matter.

Applying this to classical OBEs, the picture I have developed of man is the following: A man is composed to two sections, a physical, biological unit, and a certain quantity of mind. While each of these two domains has laws and properties of its own, we do not have a *direct* personal experience of either one alone. What we experience is mind and body forming a complete, closely linked gestalt, the whole that arises from this. This is our everyday experience of ourselves: mind intermeshes so firmly with body and body so firmly intermeshes with mind that we cannot tell the two apart. By virtue of *inter*acting, mind alters the nature of body, and body of mind.

In an OBE, I theorize that we have a partial-to-complete separation of body and mind. Thus, we have a chance to get a temporary look at body without mind influencing it as strongly as usual and, from the person's experiences, at mind without its being as strongly influenced by body.

Both body and mind are very dynamic, active, self-regulating mechanisms to a high degree—that is, each contains feedback stabilization systems to hold bodily and mental functioning within certain "normal" limits. Even though mind is part of the regulatory system for body and vice versa, we could expect each system to function in the same overall pattern for a while after the removal of the other (controlling) system because of the strength of conditional habits.

So in the usually brief OBE, we see consciousness functioning just as it does when ordinarily associated with the person's body, our ordinary state of consciousness. This goes to the point of continuing to treat the mental image of the body as still real. Thus, one has a second body that performs like one's ordinary physical body. The physical body, insofar as we have observed it from outside in these laboratory studies, shows no marked changes from its usual pattern of functioning. The patterns of body functioning are still highly conditioned to the imprint of mind-in-body, and the patterns of mental functioning are still highly conditioned to the imprint of body-in-mind.

In prolonged OBEs, on the other hand, where the interactive control of one system over the other is greatly reduced, I would expect that the characteristics of mind-in-itself and body-in-itself might begin to manifest themselves, and the scant evidence we have, primarily from case reports and the occult literature, supports this idea. Monroe, for example, found that prolonged (thirty minutes or more) OBEs resulted in his body feeling cold and stiff when he "returned," and so, fear of serious malfunctioning has made him avoid prolonged OBEs. It is as if the body by itself, without the interacting mind pattern, cannot completely regulate itself to maintain the pattern we call a living body, and small errors in control start to accumulate until the danger level is reached. I would predict that really prolonged OBEs would lead to serious illness or death, an idea frequently met with in the occult literature.

Looking at the person's experience in prolonged OBEs, we find that the pattern of mental functioning may indeed change away from that of ordinary consciousness in a variety of ways. The second body may change in shape or function from its physical form or disappear altogether. Mystical experiences may occur. Repeated OBEs for a given person may have a similar effect of allowing a quite different pattern of mind functioning to emerge. Thus, our understanding of OBEs will not progress much faster than our understanding of altered states of consciousness in this area.

The second case in this chapter, an OBE resulting from imminent death, illustrates the kind of mental changes that can occur with prolonged OBE or a grossly malfunctioning physical body.* If the separation of mind and body is never fully complete in an OBE, then gross malfunctions of the physical body should make alterations of consciousness more likely also, as if a regulatory connection from the physical body still exists but now, transmitting highly unusual information, it cannot hold conscious functioning within its usual limits.

The interaction theory is similar to the independent-soul theory. It differs primarily in attempting *not* to start with a

---

*This case was reported by the well-known physician Sir Aukland Geddes. Although Geddes reported that this incident had occurred to a patient of his, it is probable that he was recounting a personal experience:

On Saturday 9th November, a few minutes after midnight, I began to feel very ill, and by two o'clock was definitely suffering from acute gastroenteritis, which kept me vomiting and purging until about eight o'clock. . . . By ten o'clock I had developed all the symptoms of acute poisoning: intense gastro-intestinal pain, diarrhoea; pulse and respirations became quite impossible to count. I wanted to ring for assistance, but found I could not, and so quite placidly gave up the attempt. I realised I was very ill and very quickly reviewed my whole financial position. Thereafter at no time did my consciousness appear to me to be in any way dimmed, but I suddenly realised that *my* consciousness was separating from another consciousness which was also me. These, for purposes of description, we could call the A- and B-consciousnesses, and throughout what follows, the ego attached itself to the A-consciousness. The B-personality I recognized as belonging to the body, and as my physical condition grew worse and the heart was fibrillating rather than beating, I realised that the B-consciousness belonging to the body was beginning to show signs of being composite—that is, built up of "consciousness" from the head, the heart, and the viscera. These components became more individual and the B-consciousness began to disintegrate, while the A-consciousness, which was now me, seemed to be altogether outside my body, which it could see. Gradually I realised that I could see not only my body and the bed in which it was, but everything in the whole house and garden, and then realised that I was seeing not only "things" at home, but in London and in Scotland, in fact wherever my attention was directed, it seemed to me; and the explanation which I received from what source I do not know, but which I found myself calling to myself my *mentor,* was that I was free in a time-dimension of space wherein "now" was in some way equivalent to "here" in the ordinary three-dimensional space of everyday life. —ED.

philosophical or religious concept of soul, with all the cultural connotations of that term, but to be descriptive of the classical OBE phenomenon, as we know it currently, and provide a theoretical framework that can be worked with scientifically. Classical explicit ideas about the soul, such as immateriality, immortality, and special relationships to the Creator, are too abstract to deal with by current scientific procedures. The theory of mind being capable of existing independently of the body fits well with current data, but its primary function is to stimulate us to collect more data, refine one's ways of investigating this phenomenon, and try to make predictions that can be tested. This is the function of any workable scientific theory.

The interaction theory can be seen as a supplement to the altered-states-of-consciousness approach and the other theories.

REFERENCES

Stewart, K. "Dream Theory in Malaya." In C. Tart (ed.), *Altered States of Consciousness.* New York: Wiley & Sons, 1969.

Tart, C. "The Assumptions of Orthodox Western Science." In C. Tart (ed.), *The Transpersonal Psychologies.* New York: Harper & Row, 1975.

———. "States of Consciousness and State-Specific Sciences." *Science,* July 1972, 1203–10.

van Eeden, F. "A Study of Dreams." *Proceedings of the Society for Psychical Research* 26 (1913): 431–61.

CONCLUSION

The Out-of-Body Experience:
Some Personal Views and Reflections

D. SCOTT ROGO

Throughout this anthology I have been reticent about voicing my own beliefs, theories, and conceptions concerning the OBE. Instead, I have tried to offer a representative overview of the many different ways by which this fascinating experience may be approached. Now, however, before concluding this volume, I would like to explain my own ideas about the OBE. I am not claiming that my theories necessarily represent the final solution to the OBE mystery. Rather, I hope to explore some tentative thoughts about the out-of-body experience as I have come to see it over the last few years. What follows is a personal conceptualization, which I have found helpful in trying to make sense of the oftentimes contradictory information we have about the OBE. In this respect, these concluding remarks should be viewed separately from the rest of the papers that comprise this volume.

My paper, "Experiential Aspects of Out-of-Body Experiences" (see chapter 2), provides the key to my own concepts about the OBE. Many theorists have tried to conceptualize the OBE as either simply the projection of a parasomatic body, or as a psi-mediated hallucination. The problem is not so simple, for the OBE probably represents a hierarchy of different types of experiences, as is so well pointed out by Dr. Michael Grosso in chapter 3. It seems substantiated that only on some occasions is an apparitional form released or seen during the OBE. Although the Landau case (see chapter 13) indicates that this "body" has some physical attributes (i.e., that it is a spacial entity in its own right distinct from the physical body) or powers, the evidence we have accumulated about the OBE would suggest that Mrs. Landau's experience was only one type of OBE and not necessarily a prototype indicative of all OBEs.

Since the OBE may or may not include the release of a "body," one can only wonder whether or not the phenomenon is "physical." That is, does some element of consciousness, or a self-aware apparitional body, physically leave the body during the OBE and occupy physical space apart from the body? Or is the OBE only an illusion, which adopts a complex drama (including astral bodies and silver cords) as a mediating vehicle for psi? According to this theory, consciousness *functions* independently of the body and senses as an entity but does not invade any space independent of the body. There are arguments for both concepts.

First of all, there are certain experiential features of the OBE which suggest that this so-often-seen parasomatic body is actually a distinct and space-occupying organism. Dr. Robert Crookall has outlined several characteristics of the OBE that would seem to indicate that this body is more than just an illusion. As I pointed out earlier, Crookall breaks down these characteristics into several categories: the double is observed to leave through the head; a blackout occurs on release; the released double is horizontal at first; becomes horizontal before reentry into the physical body; a blackout again occurs; and rapid reentry causes physical shock or repercussion; a silver cord is seen connecting the physical and apparitional bodies (Crookall, 1964). It is hard to explain away these characteristics on the theory that the OBE body is merely a mentally created image. For example, people experiencing distortions of body-image hallucinations while subject to abnormal pathological states do not describe these types of experiences. In fact, Crookall devoted an entire book, *Mechanisms of Astral Projection* (1969), to comparing the characteristics of distortion of body image to those of the OBE and demonstrated crucial distinctions between them.

The cases that I collected while at the Psychical Research Foundation support Crookall's contentions rather well. Nine out of twenty-eight of our case reporters described how their parasomatic bodies became horizontal upon release. Three correspondents reported blackout effects. In three cases the parasomatic body resumed this horizontal position at the terminal point of the experience. In two cases a "cord connection" was seen and in one case it was felt, but not actually seen. (Of course, some correspondents reported seeing no body at all.)

This peculiar "cord connection" phenomenon also indicates that some entity is actually leaving the body during the OBE. Some theoreticians have argued that these "silver cords" are cultural artifacts. We see them, they argue, because in our culture we expect to see something connecting our "souls" to our bodies. This can hardly be the case, though, since these cords have been recorded by OB percipients in different eras and cultures. For example, "silver cords" were even recorded by the early French researchers who coerced OBEs through hypnotic induction (Durville, 1909); by contemporary housewives and American Indians (Crookall, 1961); deathbed observers (Crookall, 1967); and by habitual projectors (Muldoon and Carrington, 1929). There is even an old Chinese print depicting an OBE which shows the cord connection (reprinted in Muldoon and Carrington, 1929) and allusions to a silver cord can be found in Polynesian folklore. If the OBE were a hallucination, even a psi-mediated one, why would a cord be seen so often? Furthermore, the psychological literature on body-image distortion makes no mention, to my knowledge, of such an appendage. It is true, however, that Celia Green in her study (1968) found practically no evidence for, or cases mentioning, such a cord. It has therefore been suggested that this "cord" might have been only a tradition about the OBE that has now died out.* Our case reporters, on the other hand, do talk about this cord in no uncertain terms:

---

*This is a commonly suggested theory. For example, the eminent British parapsychologist John Beloff wrote in a letter to me that the silver cord might be "a typical piece of modern mythology . . . that was popular when astral travelling was a novelty." Later, Beloff suggested that the cord might be a Jungian-type archetype signifying in a symbolic sense the connection between the soul and the body.

Late one night, having retired some 3 or 4 hours before (I would estimate) I had the sensation of being awake and looking down upon which I can only describe as my physical form or "being." As it was night, I saw only as much as a person would see after his eyes became adjusted to the darkness; however, I distinctly remember the presence of a silver cord, perhaps finger width or less, attached to both my spiritual form and the physical.

Also among our cases were some in which the percipient had typical and characteristic physical sensations of leaving and reentering the body. This would indicate some sort of physical process involved in the OBE:

In late 1966 and prior to the arrival of our first child I began having very vivid experiences. . . . I would be lying in bed, just before going to sleep, and a strange feeling would overcome me, my eyes would go to tunnel vision and I would feel like some huge suction was pulling on me. Then suddenly I would be plastered against the ceiling and could see my body lying in bed. I wanted back in that body more than anything else, but something pulled on me and would take me into the hallway. I would struggle with every ounce of energy I could muster against this. Then when the fear would reach its peak I would be "lowered" back into my body.

If the OBE is only illusory, why do people undergoing it so often report gross physiological sensations?

Of course, the key evidence supporting the idea that the OBE and the OBE "body" are physically real experiences rests with those cases in which the OBE-er is seen as an apparition, ball of light, etc. In some cases, this apparition has been known to move physical objects during the OB apparitional experience (Landau, 1963). Further cases of OBE-PK effects have been recorded in the literature as well (Durville, 1909; Green, 1968; Muldoon and Carrington, 1929).

We could easily conclude from these data that although the OBE may represent only a release of *consciousness* on some

---

Beloff seems to be suggesting in part that when the public first learned about "astral projection" and "silver cords," they began seeing them when they had OBEs because they *expected* to see them.

occasions and an actual parasomatic body on other occasions, this does not indicate that the parasomatic body—when it is perceived—is only illusory.

Nonetheless, there are many quasi-illusory aspects of the OBE as well. So let's take a detailed look at them in turn.

Although there is strong evidence supporting the existence of some type of parasomatic body being projected during the OBE, there is also evidence that this vehicle is only vaguely like the physical body. In other words, sometimes this body seems to function as though it *were* illusory. For example, some people who have undergone OBEs describe being caught up in a dream-like world. The bodies in which they perceive themselves seem almost the same as the bodies in which we perceive ourselves in dreams. It is also sometimes more complete than the physical body (one percipient noted that the teeth missing in his physical body were quite present in his etheric one), and at times much more attractive! (One percipient noted how much more lovely she was while out-of-body as she viewed her astral self in a mirror.) This seems to be a psychological factor, since our mental images of ourselves (how we see ourselves in our minds' eye) are usually more glamorous and attractive than reality would warrant. While the parasomatic body may be real, so is it also true that it seems to have attributes common to our subjective mental self-images. Now, however, let us go on to another enigma about the OBE.

According to both Crookall and Hornell Hart, the OBE is typified by the physical separation of a "soul body" from the physical body, which projects spatially into the physical body's very physical world. In other words, the OBE-er is projecting into physical space. There is some evidence that this is either incorrect or an oversimplification. The OBE may be vastly more complex, having subjective as well as objective characteristics.

If the OBE is caused by the projection of an "etheric" duplicate of the physical body, then we might expect that this body would perceive or employ sensory functions similar to the way the physical body does. It is logical to assume that its organs of perception would be based on similar principles which govern physical sensory perception and processing. Some evidence for this view has been accumulated by Dr. Karlis Osis and his co-workers during their experiments with Ingo Swann (see chapter 6, by Janet Mitchell). Nevertheless, there seem to be subtle differences. Certain spontaneous OBE-ers describe perceptual problems that are inconsistent with the simplistic Hart-Crookall model. For example, one OB experiencer wrote to us:

The moment the mask (anaesthetic) was administered and the gas began to penetrate it I was aware of a whirring motion inside my head. . . . At first everything was pitch black . . . like a void . . . and I was looking for someone to show me the way out of it. I seemed to be in the air above my body and I could see the operating table, myself on it, the doctor bending over me. There were other people there around him, but they were blurry. I felt so free, and I sailed around with no effort. Something seemed to tell me that I had to go back but I didn't want to give up this freedom. I felt great disappointment when I realized I had no choice. The next thing I knew, I awakened in my hospital room.

The percipient's remarks that the people she saw seemed "blurry" is interesting in view of the fact that she could see the doctor clearly.* This type of "focusing effect" vision during the OBE is common and suggests that OB vision is very unlike physical perception and does not necessarily follow the normal laws of optics. In fact, OB vision seems to be a mixture of a physical type of perception mixed and polluted or filtered by an X-factor that drastically affects it. Janet Mitchell, in a recent overview of OB vision, uncovered similar data. She found that OBE-ers often reported that their vision was like "looking through a fisheye-lens" or they complained about circular vision (see chapter 6).

Another interesting feature of the OBE is that while the subject may *seem* to be projected into the "real" world, he

*This may tie in with Blue Harary's experiences. Harary prefers to have someone he knows at the target site, where he is to project during experimental OB sessions, whom he can "home in" on.

does not necessarily see things that correspond to it, and is often incapable of distinguishing this fact except through analytical reasoning. The most famous case of this type is recorded by Oliver Fox (1962) whose OBEs were, in fact, prompted by one such experience that the projector at first thought to be a dream. I cited this report in my discussion introducing Part III, but it has such an important bearing on the nature of the OBE that I would like to repeat it here. As Fox records:

I dreamed that I was standing on the pavement outside my home. The sun was rising behind the Roman wall, and the waters of Bletchingden Bay were sparkling in the morning light. I could see the tall trees at the corner of the road and the top of the old grey tower beyond the Forty Steps. . . . Now the pavement was not of the ordinary type, but consisted of small bluish-grey rectangular stones, with their long sides at right-angles to the white kerb. I was about to enter the house when on glancing at these stones, my attention became riveted to a passing strange phenomenon, so extraordinary that I could not believe my eyes—they had seemingly all changed their position in the night, and the long sides were now parallel to the kerb!

At first, Fox thought that he was dreaming, but later came to the conclusion that he had had an OBE:

Never had I felt so absolutely well, so clear brained, so distinctly powerful, so inexpressibly *free*. The sensation was exquisite beyond words; but it lasted only a few moments and I awoke. As I was to learn later, my mental control had been overwhelmed by my emotions; so the tiresome body asserted its claim and pulled me back. For though I did not realize it at the time, I think this first experience was a true projection and that I was actually functioning outside my physical vehicle.

This same enigmatic feature can be found in some of the spontaneous cases we collected as well. The following is a similar type of case:

At one time when I was living in Oxford, England, I had an apparent out-of-the-body experience during the night. As in most of my other experiences I only moved around in the room in which I was sleeping. The case was somewhat unusual in that the windows had a different set of curtains in my experience than the curtains which were in fact in the room and which I knew to be there. I do not know whether the room ever had the curtains which I "saw" in my out-of-the-body experience.

An even stranger "illusory" characteristic of the OBE is that actions may be carried out during the experience that *seem* to affect the physical world but, in fact, do not. (This is certainly not a general rule though. Sylvan Muldoon, for example, records overturning a mattress during an OBE, which was perceived as a case of telekinesis by two witnesses [Muldoon and Carrington, 1929].) There are, of course, reports of PK occurring during OBEs, which would indicate the physical, or at least semiphysical, nature of the experience. But one must also take into consideration cases in which OBE-ers attempted to affect the physical world and even thought or perceived that they had, only to discover later that their "physical acts" had in no way affected the "real world." In such cases the percipients seem incapable of discriminating whether or not they really have affected the "real" world. As one disconcerted percipient wrote to us:

Late in 1971 I was having a lot of these [OBEs] so decided to try for proof. One time while out I got a pencil, which I could barely grasp and wrote on the wall. Nothing was there when I came out of it.

Blue Harary has also had this same type of experience. The following is typical of this enigmatic characteristic of the OBE:

One night I awoke in an out-of-body state floating just above my physical body which lay below me on the bed. A candle had been left burning on the other end of the room during the evening. I dove for the candle head first from a sitting position and gently floated down toward it with the intention of blowing out the flame to conserve wax. I put my "face" up close to the candle and had some difficulty in putting out the flame. I had to blow on it several times before it finally seemed to extinguish. I turned around, saw my body lying on the bed and gently floated back and back into it. Once in the physical [body] I immediately turned over and went back to sleep. The next morning I awoke and found that the candle had completely burned down. It seemed as if my out-of-the-body efforts had affected only a non-physical candle.

In these cases then, the OBE would seem to be nothing more than a hallucination. So one can see that the OBE is both an objective *and* an illusory experience at the same time. This is no mean paradox!

How can we explain this contradictory evidence about the physical yet nonphysical nature of the OBE? One conceptual model that can explain these irregularities has been propounded by J. H. M. Whiteman (1961, 1967) and John Poynton (1973), and is one that I have incorporated into my own thinking about the OBE. Whiteman's theories start from the premise that a physical object is not merely what we *perceive* it to be in our physical world, but might also be part of a "substructure or potential universe transcending the physical universe." In other words, a physical object might have nonphysical properties perceivable to a person in a nonphysical state. When a person undergoes an OBE he is thus thrust into a world of relationships corresponding to his normal concept of what "reality" is like. In other words, he is projected into a mimic sort of reality, closely resembling the physical environment in which his physical body rests. This reality may not be a physical one, but in fact a distinctly nonphysical one, which either duplicates (mimics) the physical world or is only that aspect of the physical world that is extending into "psychical space." This is an old concept in parapsychology and is analogous to Raynor Johnson's concept of "etheric duplication" (1953) and Hart's theory of "astral matter" (1964), both of which postulate nonphysical extensions of physical objects (or vice versa).

To go on with the Whiteman-Poynton concept: when an individual undergoes an OBE he is not perceiving the physical universe, but only a replica of it coordinated to some extent by his expectations and his mode of selective perception. But this world or a specific object, while replicating the physical world or object, might well have subtle differences. (Remember how one of our correspondents saw the curtains in his room as different from the ones that normally hung there?)

Poynton (1973) has summed up the theory this way while commenting on his own studies of the OBE and on Whiteman's concepts:

It follows that if the object enters into some OBE "occasion of observation," differences between physical manifestations are bound to occur since different (entirely non-physical) "processes of selection" and "integration" are taking place. Therefore it would be naïve to insist that what is observed in an OB experience must be an exact copy of the physical world if the experience is to be considered veridical.

Poynton goes on to argue that at the onset of a *series* of OBEs, the percipient is able to perceive only a close relationship between the physical and nonphysical worlds. In fact, oftentimes he might not even be able to tell them apart. The percipient automatically employs this selective observation (seeing only those aspects of the nonphysical that correspond to normal reality) to reassure himself of the "realness" of his experience. And he can only evaluate that he is undergoing a real experience (as apart from a hallucination) by how his OB state conforms to the real world. In other words, expectancy and process of selection condition the percipient as to how he will view the OBE world. This in turn leads the percipient to mistake this world as his securely physical one. However, I should emphasize that this does not mean that this nonphysical world is illusory. It might be just as "real" to the OB experiencer as our world is to us. (Remember that Blue Harary and his friend George had a joint OBE and shared mutually corroborative observations about the world in which they had found themselves projected.) The correspondence between the OBE world and our world would be so close, in fact, that actual separation would be impossible, leading to cases where the OB experiencer could on some occasions manipulate "our" world by manipulating his.* This would result in those rare instances where telekinesis occurs during the OBE. All these factors only lead the percipient to mistake his world (the nonphysical) for the physical one. As Poynton goes on to explain:

> The results of my survey induce me to follow Whiteman in believing that this is a mistaken view. The physical environment including the actual physical body, cannot be perceived by the non-physical sense organs. It is not the physical body and other physical objects that are being perceived (or actualized) but rather non-physical copies of them extending in the actualized spacial field of the observer while in the OBE.

The only crucial objection to this theory rests in the fact that a large number of percipients do see their own bodies during the OBE. This, in fact, is a major characteristic of the experience. If one were in a nonphysical body viewing only other nonphysical (etheric) copies of objects, one would expect that the physical body would be imperceptible, since the only body that could be perceived would be its nonphysical duplicate. But this would be the body *from* which the percipient is observing! How does one get around this seeming paradox? First, it should be noted that Oliver Fox specifically noted in his memoirs that he was *continually unable to see* his own physical body. This is a point in support of Poynton's hypothesis. However, this does not explain all the anecdotal evidence that the OB subject really does see his own physical body. The reason for this paradox is that Poynton has made the mistake of construing that *all* perceived objects during the OBE must necessarily be nonphysical duplicates. This is, in fact, the same error in reverse that percipients make when interpreting objects seen during the OBE as necessarily being physical. This need not be so. Let's make a slight revision of the Whiteman-Poynton model. We might suggest that there

*This theory is partially my own, and is not developed by Poynton and Whiteman.

is no permanent distinction between the physical and non-physical, but that the correspondences between physical space and psychical space represent an active interaction. At times these two worlds might interface. These worlds are really not separate ones, they actively interact with, and influence, one another. Any manipulation of one world might affect the other, and vice versa. The OB percipient might be seeing a mixture of physical objects and etheric duplicates and be unable to distinguish which is which.

The Whiteman-Poynton viewpoint can also be reconciled with Crookall's theories about the existence of a discrete "soul-body," since the projection of some sort of "vehicle" during the OBE (which Whiteman certainly does not deny) might, in fact, spatially exist at some levels of both physical and psychical space. "Mind" might be a type of energy. When the mind leaves the body it might be able to mold a vehicle for itself from this energy. Different types of OBE states might have corresponding vehicles, which might change structure when the psychical environment changes or as the percipient becomes less and less dependent upon it. The "parasomatic body" might exist, but be malleable and change form and function for the OBE-er. This would account for various "types" of OBEs and OBE vehicles. This amalgamation of the views of Crookall and Whiteman initiates a first step in reconciling opposing concepts about the OBE, both of which seem supported by good empirical evidence.

In conclusion, then, I think we may be able to predict what sort of experiences one might have during the OBE. In perusing OBE literature it is obvious that persons having had one or two OBEs are more prone to describe their experiences in terms of physical reality, while the experiences reported by habitual projectors such as Fox, Blue Harary, and others are more bizarre and surrealistic. I pointed this out in my introduction to Part III. So it might be interesting to evaluate the experiential content of a series of OBEs reported by a single subject and see how his or her OBEs evolved.

I was able to do just this with Oliver Fox's experiences when I decided to analyze them in depth in 1973. I graphed all his experiences in chronological order (since he dated all of them in his book), noting how surrealistic his experiences became in time. I noted each time that Fox contacted a "new dimension" or saw objects having no physical counterpart in the physical environment from which he projected. My charts totally confirmed the Whiteman-Poynton model. As time went on, Fox had more and more OBEs during which he left physical reality and contacted new dimensions, and so forth. These types of experiences and encounters became more common as he became a more proficient projector. However, toward the end of his life the process reversed and Fox became chained once again to an OB state that mimicked normal reality. It would seem that as he became more accustomed to the OB state, the range of his experiences and observations increased accordingly.

In light of these comments and theories, just what kind of OBE research should we design for the future? To me, it is clear that the conventional type of ESP-PK tasks that we have been asking our OBE subjects to perform gives us a faulty view of the OBE. Instead, we should be thinking about how to test, explore, and learn about the OB state itself, not just how it relates to ESP and PK. Perhaps one fruitful approach would be to have two or more proficient OBE subjects jointly project to the same place or environment. Afterward we could analyze where their reports agree and where their observations differ. This approach might help us to understand the relationship between the OB state and physical reality.* This type of approach might eventually experimentally confirm the Whiteman-Poynton model and help us learn when the OB percipient might be able to employ ESP and PK and when he would be incapable of employing these faculties. We may also begin to learn what the OBE world is really like. Then and only then will the OBE make any sense to us.

*See Dr. Charles Tart's paper "States of Consciousness and State Specific Sciences" (1972) for a discussion of the value of training observers to independently view nonphysical reality within an experimental framework.

REFERENCES

Crookall, R. *Events on the Threshold of the Afterlife.* Moradabad: Darshana International, 1967.

———. *Mechanisms of Astral Projection.* Moradabad: Darshana International, 1969.

———. *More Astral Projections.* London: Aquarian Press,
1964.

———. *The Study and Practice of Astral Projection.* London:
Aquarian Press, 1961.

Durville, H. *Le Fantôme des Vivants.* Paris: Librairie du
Magnetisme, 1909.

Fox, Oliver. *Astral Projection.* New Hyde Park: University
Books, 1962 (reprint).

Green, Celia. *Out-of-the-Body Experiences.* Oxford: Institute
of Psychophysical Research, 1968.

Hart, H. *Toward a New Philosophical Basis for Parapsychological Phenomena.* New York: Parapsychology Foundation, 1964.

Johnson, R. *The Imprisoned Splendour.* New York: Harper
& Row, 1953.

Landau, Lucien. "An Unusual Out-of-the-Body Experience."
Journal of the Society for Psychical Research 42 (1963):
126–28.

Muldoon, S., and Carrington, H. *The Projection of the Astral
Body.* London: Rider, 1929.

Poynton, John. "Parapsychology in South Africa." In *Parapsychology Today: A Geographical View* (proceedings of an
international conference). New York: Parapsychology
Foundation, 1973.

Tart, C. "States of Consciousness and State Specific
Sciences." *Science,* June 16, 1972: 1203–10.

Whiteman, J. H. M. *The Mystical Life.* London: Faber and
Faber, 1961.

———. *The Philosophy of Space and Time.* London: George
Allen and Unwin, 1967.

About the Contributors

DAVID BLACK, a New York-based free-lance writer, is the author of *Ekstasy: Out-of-the-Body Experiences,* an investigative report on out-of-body research.

MICHAEL GROSSO first studied classics but eventually turned to philosophy and took his Ph.D. at Columbia University in 1971. He currently teaches philosophy at Jersey City State College. He is author of articles and reviews on theoretical topics in parapsychology and has concentrated on the study of the out-of-body experience.

STUART BLUE HARARY recently received his A.B. in experimental psychology from Duke University. During that time (1972–1975) he was a research assistant at the Psychical Research Foundation, where he was both an experimenter and the primary subject for an intensive exploration of the out-of-body experience. He is currently a research associate at Maimonides Medical Center's Division of Parapsychology and Psychophysics in Brooklyn, New York.

LUCIAN LANDAU is an industrial consultant and inventor whose interest in parapsychology has led him to lecture on the subject before the Cambridge University Society for the Study of Parapsychology and the College of Psychic Science. He has been a frequent contributor to the *Journal of the British Society of Dowsers; Light;* and other publications.

JANET MITCHELL was a research assistant at the American Society for Psychical Research before enrolling as a doctoral student in psychology at the City College of the City University of New York. She is now a research assistant in the psychology department of City College.

KARLIS OSIS received a Ph.D. in psychology from the University of Munich in 1950. After coming to the United States he became a research associate at the Duke University Parapsychology Laboratory from 1951–1957. From 1957–1962 he was director of research for the Parapsychology Foundation in New York and subsequently became director of research for the American Society for Psychical Research. He is currently the Chester F. Carlson Research Fellow at the A.S.P.R. His publications range from reports on experiments on long-distance ESP, to animal ESP research, to the study of deathbed visions. He is the author of the monograph *Deathbed Observations by Physicians and Nurses.*

JOHN PALMER received his Ph.D. in psychology from the University of Texas (Austin). He spent two years as an associate professor of psychology at McGill University before becoming a research associate in the division of parapsychology at the University of Virginia School of Medicine. He has been an associate research psychologist at the University of California, Davis, where he was engaged in research on ESP and learning. He now serves on the faculty of John F. Kennedy University in Orinda, California.

HAROLD PUTHOFF received a Ph.D. in electrical engineering from Stanford University in 1967. From 1969 to 1970 he was a lecturer at Stanford. For eight years he worked in the Microwave Laboratory at Stanford and is now a senior research engineer at Stanford Research Institute. He is coauthor of a text, *Fundamentals of Quantum Electronics,* and of *Mind-Reach,* a book on remote viewing.

D. SCOTT ROGO has been a visiting research consultant at the Psychical Research Foundation in Durham, North Carolina (1973), a visiting researcher at Maimonides Medical Center's Division of Parapsychology and Psychophysics (1975), and director of research for the Southern California Society for Psychical Research (1974–1975). He is the author of over ten books on parapsychology, including *Parapsychology: A Century of Inquiry; An Experience of Phantoms; In Search of the Unknown;* and a monograph, *Methods and Models for Education in Parapsychology.* He has been book-review editor of *Psychic* magazine and has also published some thirty papers in leading parapsychological and psychological journals. He is a long-time resident of Los Angeles, California.

RUSSELL TARG is a senior research physicist at Stanford Research Institute and joined their electronics and bioengineering laboratory in 1972. Previously he was a physicist specializing in laser and plasma research at Sylvania Corporation. He carried out graduate work in physics at Columbia University, where he also taught as a research assistant. In 1959 he was a research associate at the Polytechnic Institute of Brooklyn. He is the author of several papers on various aspects of physics and has a number of inventions to his credit, including the high-power gas-transport laser. He is co-author of *Mind-Reach*.

CHARLES T. TART received a Ph.D. in psychology from the University of North Carolina and subsequently held a postdoctoral research fellowship at Stanford University. From 1965–1966 he was an instructor at the University of Virginia School of Medicine. He is currently a professor of psychology at the University of California, Davis. He is the author of *On Being Stoned: A Psychological Study of Marijuana Intoxication* and of the monograph *The Application of Learning Theory to ESP Performance*. He has also written over sixty papers on subjects relating to hypnosis, consciousness, and parapsychology, and has edited two anthologies, *Altered States of Consciousness* and *The Transpersonal Psychologies*.

J. II. M. WHITEMAN is associate professor emeritus of applied mathematics at the University of Cape Town. He has also served as a lecturer on music, a subject in which he has a graduate degree. He has authored numerous papers on parapsychology and its relationship to physics and is the author of two books, *The Mystical Life* and *Philosophy of Space and Time*.

A selection of books published by Penguin is listed on the following page.

For a complete list of books available from Penguin in the United States, write to Dept. DG, Penguin Books, 299 Murray Hill Parkway, East Rutherford, New Jersey 07073.

For a complete list of books available from Penguin in Canada, write to Penguin Books Canada Limited, 2801 John Street, Markham, Ontario L3R 1B4.

If you live in the British Isles, write to Dept. EP, Penguin Books Ltd, Harmondsworth, Middlesex.

Selected nonfiction titles from the Penguin list

A DICTIONARY OF PSYCHOLOGY
James Drever

CHECK YOUR OWN I.Q.
H. J. Eysenck

KNOW YOUR OWN PERSONALITY
H. J. Eysenck and Glenn Wilson

AN INTRODUCTION TO JUNG'S PSYCHOLOGY
Frieda Fordham

ALCOHOLISM
Neil Kessel and Henry Walton

THE DIVIDED SELF
R. D. Laing

SELF AND OTHERS
R. D. Laing

SANITY, MADNESS AND THE FAMILY
R. D. Laing and A. Esterson

THE PSYCHOLOGY OF CONSCIOUSNESS
Robert E. Ornstein

PENGUIN BOOKS

MIND BEYOND THE BODY

D. Scott Rogo has had a long association with parapsychology and is currently working in this field full time. He was educated at the University of Cincinnati and California State University, Northridge, where in graduate school he concentrated on the psychology of music before turning to parapsychology. In 1973 he was a visiting research consultant at the Psychical Research Foundation in Durham, North Carolina, during the foundation's two-year experimental exploration into the out-of-body experience. In 1975 he was simultaneously a visiting researcher at Maimonides Medical Center's Division of Parapsychology and Psychophysics and director of research for the Southern California Society for Psychical Research. Active in education as well as research, Mr. Rogo coordinated and taught an experimental course in parapsychology at the University of California, Los Angeles, for the academic year 1968–1969 and subsequently received a grant from the New York–based Parapsychology Foundation to study education in parapsychology further. He has written a monograph on education in parapsychology as well as a textbook for undergraduate courses. Among his other publications in the area of paranormal phenomena are *In Search of the Unknown* and *Exploring Psychic Phenomena*. He lives in Los Angeles, California.

MIND
BEYOND
THE
BODY

The Mystery
of ESP Projection

Edited and with Commentaries by

D. SCOTT ROGO

PENGUIN BOOKS

Penguin Books Ltd, Harmondsworth,
Middlesex, England
Penguin Books, 625 Madison Avenue,
New York, New York 10022, U.S.A.
Penguin Books Australia Ltd, Ringwood,
Victoria, Australia
Penguin Books Canada Limited, 2801 John Street,
Markham, Ontario, Canada L3R 1B4
Penguin Books (N.Z.) Ltd, 182–190 Wairau Road,
Auckland 10, New Zealand

First published 1978

LIBRARY OF CONGRESS CATALOGING IN PUBLICATION DATA
Main entry under title:
Mind beyond the body.
Includes bibliographies.
1. Astral projection—Addresses, essays, lectures.
I. Rogo, D. Scott.
BF1389.A7M53   133.9′2   77–26770
ISBN 0 14 00.4690 9

Printed in the United States of America by
Offset Paperback Mfrs., Inc., Dallas, Pennsylvania
Set in Times Roman